A battle between past and present love!
An irresistible single dad!
The city girl and the rancher!
And a marriage foiled by the best-man!

Stolen Moments

Four short stories perfect for those
stolen moments on lazy summer days.

About the authors:

Barbara Stewart says that one of her first memories is of being taken to the library by her father and bringing home stacks of books as tall as she was. She's been reading—and writing—ever since. But she didn't begin writing professionally until she'd been teaching it for ten years, when she decided that actually *doing* it had to be easier! Her decision to concentrate on romance was a natural one—she says she loves happy endings.

Merline Lovelace was, until recently, a career air force officer who served tours of duty in Vietnam, at the Pentagon and at bases all over the world. During her years in uniform, she met and married her own handsome colonel—and stored up enough exciting adventures to keep her fingers flying over the keyboard for years to come.

Alina Roberts is a native of Washington, D.C., but after having lived in Colorado for eighteen years, she now considers it her home—although she does admit that the winters there are a bit too long! Stories by Alina have appeared in many magazines, and *Prairie Summer* is her second published novel. The incidents described in the book are based on actual events.

Anne Marie Duquette has travelled extensively throughout the United States, first as an air force 'brat' and then as a member of the military herself. She started her writing career as a young girl, with lengthy letters to relatives and friends describing her impressions of countless new duty locations. Now married to a career naval officer and the mother of two young children, she still likes to travel—though with a family and a successful writing career, she finds less time for it!

Stolen Moments

LOVE ME NOT
Barbara Stewart

MAGGIE AND HER COLONEL
Merline Lovelace

PRAIRIE SUMMER
Alina Roberts

ANNIVERSARY WALTZ
Anne Marie Duquette

MILLS & BOON

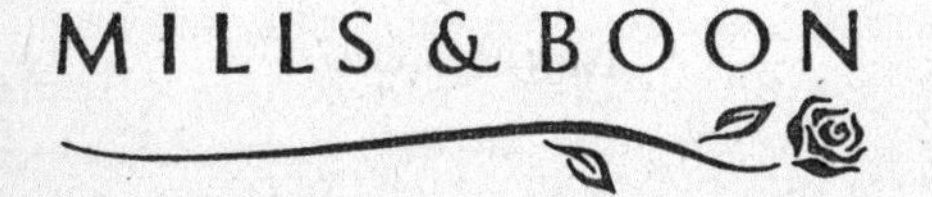

Harlequin Mills & Boon Limited,
Eton House, 18-24 Paradise Road, Richmond, Surrey, TW9 1SR

LOVE ME NOT—
Special thanks and acknowledgement to Barbara Rae Robinson
MAGGIE AND HER COLONEL—
Special thanks and acknowledgement to Merline Lovelace
PRAIRIE SUMMER—
Special thanks and acknowledgement to Jane Choate
ANNIVERSARY WALTZ—
Special thanks and acknowledgement to Anne Marie Duquette

ISBN 0 263 79806 2

49-9605

Printed in Great Britain by
BPC Paperbacks Ltd

LOVE ME NOT
Barbara Stewart

This book is dedicated to the memory
of Daryl Stewart Robinson

One

"Lynn Frazer!"

She ignored the intrusive voice coming from somewhere behind her and tightened her grip on the wooden railing of the weathered pier as she stared at the shrouded horizon in the distance. *Oh, Nick, where are you?* she silently repeated.

"Hey! What are you trying to do, kill yourself?"

The crashing waves rolling toward shore muffled the deep voice in the distance. A stiff breeze pelted her with raindrops from the dark dense clouds overhead and whipped strands of hair into her face. She brushed at the strands, her eyes focusing on the roiling sea and a solitary mast in the distance. Someone was still out there among the tossing waves. Trying to catch a few more fish. Just like Nick had been doing that day when his boat was caught in a sudden spring squall.

Footsteps echoed on the planks behind her.

Lynn heaved a sigh. Those who knew her left her alone when she was on the pier. They understood.

As she reluctantly turned, a strong hand grabbed her arm and yanked her several feet away from the railing. "You'll get washed out to sea!" A stranger's voice boomed.

A breaking wave surged over the end of the pier, soaking her shoes and the bottom of her jeans. She shivered, as much from resentment at having her solitary vigil interrupted as from the cold water.

"I'm all right," she said, brushing off the grasp. "Don't get so excited. This is only a mild October storm." She pulled her jacket more tightly around her.

Then she shifted her gaze to the man towering over her. And stared.

Rugged, powerful, masculine. Those were the words that came to her. She stepped back. In the waning light of dusk, his eyes were dark and penetrating, almost as if he could see right into her soul.

She trembled, her apprehension growing. "How... how'd you know my name and where to find me?"

"Pete Duncan told me."

At the mention of Pete's name, she exhaled the breath she realized she was holding. Pete was too good a friend to send someone to her he didn't trust.

The stranger reached for her again. "Let's get off this rickety pier," he said. "I need to talk to you." His voice was gruff and hard.

"What about?" She sidestepped, avoiding his grasp. The water in her shoes chilled her feet. A hot bath would feel good right now.

"Let's talk about it on shore." He strode away from her, obviously expecting her to follow.

"This pier can take a stronger storm than this," she muttered as another wave broke over the weathered boards and swept toward her. Conceding defeat, she reluctantly headed for shore.

The man was waiting for her at the street end of the pier.

"Who are you and why did Pete tell you where to find me?" she asked, studying the rugged contours of his face in the pale glow from the lone streetlight.

"The name's Vince Coulter."

"So you're that friend of his from Long Island—the one who was supposed to be here a week ago."

"Yeah. Had a bit of car trouble along the way—actually a lot of car trouble." He laughed, a deep rumble with no joy in it.

They crossed the narrow street and stepped up on the boardwalk in front of the only grocery store in Garrett Cove.

"What do you want from me?" she asked.

"I need to sell some pottery I brought along. I used practically all the money I had just to get here. I need some cash."

"Didn't Pete tell you I only take pottery on consignment?" The words came out more petulant-sounding than she'd intended.

He frowned. "Will you look at what I have before you make that kind of decision?"

She faced him, unsure where her peevishness was coming from. Maybe it was her wet feet. Or being interrupted out on the pier. She tried to make her tone matter-of-fact. "I've only bought three pieces outright in the past year. They were unique. None of the other potters who sell through my shop have made anything like them."

"Mine are unique."

"I've heard that before." She started down the wooden boardwalk fronting the row of businesses that made up the commercial district of the tiny town on the central California coast.

"Well, let me at least show you what I have."

She stopped under the awning of the store and turned back to him. "I'd like to change my wet clothes. Can't it wait until tomorrow?"

"I don't believe in wasting time," he replied. "I have lots to do tomorrow if I'm going to get settled in here."

The encroaching darkness shadowed his features, making him appear almost sinister. But Pete *had* talked of Vince Coulter in glowing terms. He said they'd grown up in the same New York neighborhood and had remained friends, despite the distance that had separated them the past few years.

"All right," she said reluctantly. "Get your work and meet me at my shop." She pointed to the next building. "The one in the middle. I'll be back in a few minutes."

She left him standing and walked around the end of the building and up a slight incline toward her house on the top of the closest knoll.

Ten minutes later she returned to the boardwalk in dry shoes and jeans, curious to see what Vince Coulter had with him. Pete only sent artists to her whose work met her standards.

Vince was standing by the door to her shop, a cardboard box cradled in his arms. She unlocked the door and flipped on the interior lights. "Come on in," she said, staring into dark eyes as cold as the sea and wondering what had happened to the man to make him so harsh and bitter. Then she remembered Pete had mentioned an accident.

"Thanks," Vince replied. "I appreciate your taking the time to look at what I have."

Something in that low somber voice told her he was sincere. A slight spark of interest kindled inside her. She tried to ignore the feeling and walked to the counter in the middle of the room.

Display cases and shelves lined the walls of the shop and were filled with all manner of pottery, glassware and other gift items. The scent of candles and potpourri mingled and permeated the entire room.

Vince followed her into the store and set the box on the counter next to the cash register. She sidled around to the rear of the counter, letting the wooden structure serve as a barrier between them. Something about this man unsettled her.

Because her curiosity had gotten the better of her, she took another good look at him, trying not to be too obvious. Faded jeans hugged narrow hips, and a flannel shirt and jacket encased broad shoulders. He was too rough around the edges to be called handsome. Compelling—yes, that was a better word to describe him. Then she added the word "brazen" to her assessment as she realized he was boldly looking her over in return. "Let's see what you have," she said in her best professional tone, while wondering if this was a man she wanted to do business with at all.

"Here's the first box. I have three more of the same kind of stuff in my van," he said as he opened the lid and carefully, almost reverently, unwrapped the packing material from around a teapot and six matching cups and set the pieces carefully on the counter. Then he brought out a delicate bowl in the same intricate pale blue pattern, handling it with the same meticulous care.

Lynn recognized the superb artistry of the work even before she picked up the bowl to examine it more closely. A strange excitement grew inside her as she slowly turned the piece of pottery in her hand, inspecting the exquisite hand-painted detail—a blue-petal design interwoven with seemingly fragile greenery. She smiled. Vince was right. His work was unique.

"Can't you give me something for these?" he asked, stepping back.

She set the bowl on the counter and turned her smile to the man towering over her. "You have a rare talent, Vince. I'll have to make an exception for you." Mentally she calculated the value of the pieces in front of her and multiplied by four. "Only one problem," she said, her brow wrinkling in a frown. "I'm not sure

I can afford to buy all you have right now if the other three boxes are filled with things as good as these."

Distress flared briefly in his eyes before they resumed their cold dark stare. "You're the only show in town," he said. "I'm at your mercy."

She ran a finger over the intricate pattern on the delicate teapot, impressed with the smoothness of the surface. "I can give you part of the money to start with," she said, and named a figure. "I'm sure these will sell." Her eyes met his. "You have to understand. This is a slow time of year for beach crowds and the businesses that cater to them."

He started replacing the pieces in the box. "I need to find a place to live, a place where I can set up a studio."

"As I get more cash from sales, I can give you more. That's the best I can do right now."

"Then I'll have to take it. I'll go get the other three boxes."

"Just a minute," she said, and went to her tiny office in back of the shop, closing the door behind her. She extracted her checkbook from the floor safe and wrote out a check. Returning to the outer shop, she handed it to him. "You can bring the other three boxes tomorrow. I trust you," she said, looking up at him as she realized she did.

"Thanks," he said, stuffing the check into his pocket without looking at it.

When the door of the shop had closed behind them, she turned to him. "Well, good night, Vince."

"Uh...I'll walk you up to your house. Awfully dark now, what with the clouds and rain."

"That isn't necessary." A certain wariness crept into her voice.

"But I want to." His voice was quiet, the harshness gone.

She shrugged. "Suit yourself," she said, and stepped off the boardwalk onto the muddy path leading up the hill to her driveway. The light rain continued to fall.

Halfway up the driveway he stopped. "That your garage?" he asked, looking at the wooden structure not ten feet from the house. The raised overhead door revealed her little blue Honda off to one side.

"Yes," she said hesitantly, her brow furrowing. "Why?"

"Pete said you had a nice big garage," he replied, "with a good, solid concrete slab for a floor. May I take a look?" At her nod he strode to the weather-beaten wooden structure and stopped at the door. She followed closely behind.

"What's so interesting about a garage?" she asked. She flicked on the light switch by the door.

He kicked at the concrete floor. "I know Pete was joking when he said it, but he told me you had a garage big and sturdy enough for a studio." He turned to her. "I need a place to set up a temporary studio. I'd like to rent your garage—until I have enough money to get the kind of place I need."

"Sorry, it's not for rent." The words came out in a rush, automatically. She couldn't even consider such a request.

He ignored her and stepped into the middle of the garage. She put her hands on her hips and watched him as he spun around, taking in all the details of piled furniture, boxes, dirt and grime. His shoulders straightened and he seemed infused with a new energy. When he turned back to her, his mouth had curved into a genuine grin and his dark forbidding eyes now blazed with a sudden fervor. He took several steps toward her.

"Please think about it," he said. "I have to have a place to work."

"You aren't listening to me. I said it's not for rent," she repeated, turning away to hide her rising panic. She didn't want anyone so close, especially not a man like Vince Coulter. If Nick truly *was* dead, she intended to build herself a life so independent she'd never need anyone else again. That way she'd never be hurt again.

He spun around once more, his eyes glowing with an inner fire. "I can almost feel the wet clay in my hands," he said, "spinning on the wheel.... It's been a long time."

"No!" she said, then realized with a pang of guilt that he'd have the money to rent something if she'd been able to give him what four boxes of his pottery were really worth.

"I could get Pete to help me put in another door, so I wouldn't have to use the overhead door all the time," he said, excitement permeating his voice. "I can move the rest of this stuff to one corner. Properly stacked, it'd give me enough room to work."

She felt the warmth of Vince's hand close around her arm, and a tingle of awareness flitted through her body.

"Please, Lynn. At least consider it. I need a place to work so I can make a new start out here on the Coast. It's very important to me."

She glanced down at the strong hand on her arm. How long had it been since a man had touched her... made her feel like a woman? He pulled her around to face him, a wide smile on his face. A beguiling smile. He did have a certain charm when he chose to use it—too much charm to be so near.

She pulled out of his grasp. "I can't," she said, with no attempt to keep the desperation out of her voice. "I can't let you use it."

"I don't see why not. You'd benefit, too." His voice had completely lost its hard edge and had a certain buoyancy. "I'd be turning out pottery for you to sell in your shop."

He looked deep into her eyes and she felt her resistance slowly eroding. Something about this man spoke to some inner need in her, a need she didn't quite understand.

But she'd be unfaithful to Nick even to consider such an arrangement, wouldn't she? A strange man working in the garage? Another thought filtered into her consciousness. *Had* Pete been joking when he'd told Vince about her garage? Or had he really thought it was a good idea for Vince to work here? She wished Pete was here now so she could ask his advice.

"I hope your hesitation means you're reconsidering," Vince said, his eyes still holding hers.

She stalled a little longer, trying to think of other excuses. But all she could think of were reasons why she *could* do it. Added income from the rent. More lovely things to sell in the shop. Helping a friend of Pete's. Helping a talented artist in need. Besides, she'd be down at her shop most of the time and wouldn't have to see him every day....

"All right," she said, her voice almost a whisper.

Two

Vince sighed with relief. He'd been so sure she'd stick with her refusal, despite all that hesitation. ''Thanks,'' he said. ''You don't know what this means to me.''

Her lips drew into a soft smile. ''Let's just say I'm doing it because you're a friend of Pete's.''

He cocked a brow. ''Pete's going to be surprised when I tell him.''

She tilted her chin and her smile widened, but he saw a certain sadness in her light blue eyes. ''I owe Pete—and Maria—more than I can ever repay. They helped me through some really rough times.''

Vince nodded but didn't say anything. Pete had told him about her husband's fishing boat capsizing with four of them aboard. Two survived and two hadn't. Pete felt guilty because he was one of the lucky ones.

Vince gazed at her and felt the stirrings of interest. Pete said he'd like her. And, despite their rather stormy—in more ways than one—introduction out on the pier, she seemed to be thawing toward him.

He liked her small pert mouth. And her tiny tipped-up nose. She reminded him of that petite blonde he'd met at the gallery in Manhattan last year. Lynn had a certain genuineness. A completely natural woman. Not even a hint of makeup on her face. And her long blond hair hung about her shoulders unrestrained. He liked that, too.

Only one more thing to do. He wouldn't be able to sleep tonight if he didn't tell her the truth. He thought of the tea set and bowl he'd left in the shop. And the three boxes of similar ware in his van.

"Lynn . . . there's something I haven't told you yet. Something you should know." He frowned. He didn't like admitting his weaknesses. "Those pieces I just gave you—I won't be making any more like that." His words came out in a rush. Afraid to look at her face, afraid he might see disgust there, he stared at the concrete floor.

"An auto accident—two years ago," he continued. "A deep cut on my right wrist that damaged the nerves. I can't do the intricate painting anymore, and I'm not even sure I can do the delicate shapes of the pieces."

"Oh, dear." She said the words softly.

He felt her hand on his arm and turned to her. "I'm so sorry," she said, a tear glistening in the corner of her eye.

"I don't want your pity," he snapped, and brushed her hand away. "I have to learn some new techniques for throwing pots, since my right arm no longer functions the way it used to. That's what I'll be working on in your garage. What I need is a chance, a new start."

He hadn't meant to react so fiercely. She looked stricken and afraid. From somewhere deep inside, he felt the sudden urge to gather her in his arms and reassure her. But he resisted the impulse. That was something he might have done before the accident. Now he had too much work to do. No time for a woman, especially one with problems of her own. Besides, he didn't have anything to offer a woman, any woman. He'd be lucky if he could still support himself as a potter. But he had to try.

"See you tomorrow," he said, leaving her standing in the garage.

"Lynn! I can't believe you've done this," Carol Snyder said in her usual big-sister tone. "You rented your garage to a man you don't even know?"

"He's a friend of Pete's." Lynn picked up a wool duster and swished it over the shelves and the pottery pieces.

"And any friend of Pete's is a friend of yours...." Carol shook her head, but a smile played on her lips.

Lynn smiled back at her sister, a diminutive brunette with laughing blue eyes. "Don't worry about it. Believe me, the garage is as close as the man's getting."

Carol quirked an eyebrow. "Why do you say that?"

Her tone implied more than casual interest. Lynn realized she'd revealed too much already but couldn't take back the words. "No man gets inside my house except family or Pete." She said the words in as even a tone as she could manage. She couldn't admit, especially to Carol, that Vince Coulter intrigued her.

Carol leaned against the counter in the middle of the shop. "Are you going to pine away for Nick forever? He's dead, Lynn. He won't be back."

Lynn sighed. "You don't know that he's dead any more than I do. I still can't help hoping that some foreign fishing boat picked him up and he has amnesia and is wandering around the world not knowing where he belongs. . . ."

"And his memory will be miraculously restored and he'll come sailing back to you," Carol finished for her. "You know that's not logical. We've looked at all the possibilities, time and time again. Nick is dead." She enunciated the words carefully. "Pete saw him roll off the deck as the boat turned over."

Lynn lifted her chin stubbornly. "Tim's body was found right away. Pete and Dave were rescued by the coast guard. Someone else could have found Nick floating on some debris and carried him far away from here."

Carol threw up her hands and shook her head. "You can't really believe that."

"I want to," Lynn replied. "That way I at least have hope."

"But you have that Late Death Registration issued by the court," Carol said. "Nick is dead," she repeated. "When are you going to come to your senses and accept it?"

Lynn looked directly at her. "That death registration is just a piece of paper. It proves nothing. It means nothing. Larry should have left things as they were."

"We all thought you'd accept the court's ruling," Carol said. "That's why Larry went ahead and gathered the evidence and petitioned the court. If you'd only look at all the evidence and the transcripts, you'd realize Nick couldn't possibly be alive. Larry has said he'll bring the entire file home from the office any time you want to see it."

"Just because your husband's a lawyer doesn't mean he had to interfere," Lynn said.

"It's been a year and a half," Carol replied. "Plenty of time for you to accept that Nick's gone and not coming back. Do you really want to be alone for the rest of your life?"

"Yes," Lynn answered automatically. Then an image of the dark stranger—of Vince—crept into her consciousness. Could she ever love again? No. No, absolutely not.

Carol started for the door. "You're impossible. Just as stubborn as you've always been."

"I can take care of myself," Lynn said. "I have my business. I'm self-supporting. I don't have to depend on a man, and I never will again."

Carol stopped just short of the door. "Look, I didn't come here to argue with you." A smile softened her features. "Can you get away for a couple of hours on Sunday for Dad's birthday dinner?"

"Make it after five and there's no problem. That's when I close the shop."

"All right. Six o'clock, at our house." Carol reached for the doorknob just as the door flew open. She stepped back, wide-eyed.

Vince strode in, a box in his hands. "I have the other three boxes. Where do you want them?"

"Set them down anywhere," Lynn said. "I'll unpack them when I decide where I'm going to display all the new pieces." She smiled at the look of surprise on Carol's face and introduced the two of them. Curiosity kept Carol from leaving, for which Lynn was glad. She'd just as soon not be alone with Vince.

As for Vince, he seemed ill at ease with an audience. He brought in the other two boxes, then approached her. "Pete will be here in a couple of hours with a door he found, and we'll start working on the garage. Uh...could I use your keys to back your car out of the garage? I'll start cleaning while I wait for Pete."

"Sure." Lynn retrieved the keys from her purse in the office and handed them to him. He took them with a half smile and left hurriedly.

Carol grinned broadly, a look of mischief in her eyes. "On second thought, maybe you're not as crazy as you seem. See you later."

"What's that supposed to mean?" Lynn asked as Carol closed the door behind her. She let out an exasperated sigh and turned to her task, unpacking the pottery in the three boxes and making a list of the contents. Then she rearranged the items displayed on the shelves along one side of the shop to accommodate the new ones. With each piece she placed on the shelves, her excitement grew. The work was exquisite. Vince Coulter was an artist.

She sighed. What a shame to lose the ability to exercise such talent. How she wished he could still do this kind of intricate painting.

She picked up a vase. There she was—wishing again. Wishing things were different from the way they were. Just like with Nick. She was always wishing his body had been found. Then she'd know for sure in her heart that he was dead.

Cradling the delicate vase in her hands, she studied the design. Lavender blossoms—iris with green spiky leaves. Soft, ethereal lavender blossoms, looking as if they were floating on a breeze.

She set the slender vase aside. This one she'd buy for herself and put it on the little buffet against the wall in the living room. She couldn't bring herself to sell all the pieces, though she knew without a doubt she'd be able to.

At noon Lynn closed the shop, put her Be Back Soon sign in the window and headed up the hill for a quick lunch. Pete's green truck, loaded with lumber and tools, and a maroon van sat in the driveway. Her Honda had been moved around to the back. The left wall of the garage sported a gaping hole where Pete was fitting a new door, one with a window in the top of it.

The overhead garage door was up and she could see Vince pounding nails in what looked like shelves. Pete saw her first and met her in the driveway. "Lynn, I want to thank you for the way you're helping Vince. You won't be sorry."

She smiled at the sandy-haired man in front of her and realized he was at least a couple of inches shorter than Vince, then wondered why she'd even thought of it.

"I hope I won't be sorry," she said. "I don't even know the man. But he's your friend. Let's just say I'm doing this for you." She looked up and saw Vince watching her from inside the garage. She waved to him, then turned back to Pete.

Pete grinned. "Whatever your reasons, I appreciate it. And so does Vince. I've known him for years. He's a great guy."

"I believe you."

He tilted his head. "Come on now, fess up. Aren't you just a little bit interested in him?"

She glared at Pete. "Don't you even dare *think* of playing matchmaker," she said in a low but forceful tone. "I'm not interested in any man, and you of all people should know that."

He chucked her under the chin. "Someday, my sweet little friend, you'll change your tune. I just hope you don't wait too long. You're missing out on a lot in life."

She frowned. "Nick was your best friend. How can you say that?"

"Nick's gone," Pete replied. "You're still here—a living breathing woman who needs someone to love."

"I have lots of family and friends around here. That's enough for me."

"It won't always be." Pete shrugged. "I have a great-aunt who lost her husband at an early age and never remarried. She's the most crotchety old biddy I've ever known. I don't want to see you end up like her."

Lynn laughed. "Pete, you worry too much. I'm not your responsibility."

"Yes, you are," he said, his voice suddenly serious. "Whether you want to be or not."

Her brow wrinkled into a frown. "I can take care of myself. I prefer to be alone."

He looked her straight in the eye, his face solemn. "About a year before Nick died, we made a pact," he said. "He was to take care of Maria and the kids if anything ever happened to me. I agreed to look after you if something happened to him. And I know Nick wouldn't want you to be alone for the rest of your life."

"You've been a good friend, and I appreciate everything you've done for me. Just don't overstep the bounds of friendship by trying to find me another husband. I don't want one."

Vince ambled out of the garage. "My ears are burning. Everything all right?"

"No problem, old buddy," Pete said. "Just a friendly discussion," he added, with emphasis on the "friendly."

Vince seemed a bit nervous as he turned to Lynn. "One more favor to ask of you," he said. "I hope you don't mind if I park my van next to the garage. I'm going to have to sleep in it for a while. All the places for rent around here cost more than I have right now."

"Where'd you sleep last night?" she asked, a mild panic returning at the thought of his being right outside.

"Pete's couch." He grinned. "And I had three little rug rats piling on me about seven this morning."

Pete laughed. "No wonder you won't stay with us."

"Oh, it's not the kids," Vince said. "They're no problem. I just don't want to impose on you and Maria."

"You wouldn't be imposing," Pete said.

"I don't know how long it will be before I can rent a place," Vince said. "I slept in the van all the way across the country. A little while longer won't hurt me. There'll be plenty of room after I get all my tools and equipment out of it and into the garage."

"That doesn't look like a completely, uh, outfitted van," Lynn said with a grimace.

"No problem. I'll use that rest room down on the beach." Vince gestured toward the gray building to the right of the pier. "And Maria's offered to let me shower at their house. Everything's taken care of." He grinned broadly.

Lynn simply stared at him. She'd be able to look out her bedroom window and see the van, with him in it, every night. Too close.

Her comfortable complacent life-style was suddenly being eroded and she seemed powerless to do anything about it. All she wanted was for Vince Coulter to go away! But how could she back out now?

Three

"Aren't you the least bit curious to see what I've done to your garage this past week?" Vince asked. He stood in the center of the driveway, blocking Lynn's path as she headed home for the evening.

She stopped a good six feet away from him. "I've peeked in the window a time or two," she admitted. In fact, she'd tried her best to ignore the activity going on so close to her house, just as she'd tried to ignore the man himself. She let her eyes roam over his sturdy male physique and wondered what it was about him she perceived as dangerous. That's when she felt the pounding in her chest. She turned away, intending to walk around him and retreat to the safety of her house.

He reached for her arm. "Come here. Just for a minute." He gestured with a nod of his head. "It's finished—my studio." The expression on his face indicated a need for her approval.

She pulled away from his grip and took a deep breath. "All right, I'll come look—just for a minute."

He led her to the door of the garage and opened it with a flourish. She could see the pride and the joy in his dark eyes. And when she gazed inside what had once been a dusty cluttered garage, she saw a remarkable transformation. But it all looked so permanent. She couldn't ignore the sinking feeling in the pit of her stomach.

Everything was there—everything needed for a potter's studio. Cabinets, shelves, an electric kiln in one corner, vented to the outside. The potter's wheel in the middle of the floor. And various potter's tools sitting on surfaces or attached to a Peg-Board hanging on the wall. Even the odor of wet clay coming from a damp closet.

"I'm now a studio production potter," he announced.

She heard the hint of resignation in his tone and thought of the hand-painted pieces on display in her shop. She'd already sold several this week. "You could still be an artist," she said. "You don't have to do intricate hand-painting for your work to be of artistic quality. Why don't you learn some new glazing techniques, or try for distinctive shapes?"

He glared at her, all pleasure gone from his gaze. "I'll be turning out the kind of ware that always sells—the mugs, the bowls, the teapots, the vases. They'll pay the rent and buy the groceries."

She ignored the cold harshness in his eyes and the anger she sensed underlying his restrained tone. "But you have so much talent—too much to waste on becoming just a production potter."

"I can't do the kind of work I used to do," he said. "I told you that."

This time the hard edge to his voice was unmistakable, but she didn't relent. "Then learn a new artistic technique," she countered. "Expand the limits of what you already know."

"I can throw pots and glaze them," he said. "That's what I'm going to do now."

"That's a defeatist attitude. So you've had a little setback. Get up and brush yourself off."

"The accident was more than a little setback. You don't know what you're talking about."

The flare of anger in his dark eyes told her more than his words that something else had happened because of that accident. "Do you want to talk about it?" she asked, softening her voice.

"No! Just drop it."

Instead of intimidating her and sending her scurrying away, his harsh words held her fast. Realizing she'd hit a nerve, she scanned the interior of the garage, groping for a topic of conversation to ease the tension between them.

"You've put a lot of time and money into all this," she said at last, waving her hand toward the shelves and cabinets.

"Just for some of the lumber and fittings," Vince said, his tone still gruff and unyielding, as if he felt he had to defend himself. "Pete and his uncle contributed quite a bit. Pete had already bought the hardware—it was for projects he hadn't gotten to yet. His uncle ran the two-twenty line for the kiln and gave me most of the lumber we used, leftovers from some of his building projects.''

''Very impressive,'' she said, hazarding a glance at his face. His dark eyes no longer sparked with anger.

''Pete's uncle had the saws and other equipment we needed, including the brick-laying stuff. Did you see the kiln outside? He even had the old fire bricks that we used, from a chimney he'd torn down.''

''Another kiln?'' she asked, remembering the sacks of cement and the bricks she'd seen in Pete's truck several days ago when she'd gone home for lunch. Her sense of unease returned.

''For gas-firing,'' he said. ''I can't do everything with one little electric kiln. Come look at this one.'' He led her around to the back of the garage, to a lean-to on a new slab.

''We put it back here,'' he said, ''facing away from the ocean. It had to be outside, because of its size and because of its need for ventilation.''

She stared at the impressive yellow-brick structure. It, too, appeared rather permanent. Her apprehension was increasing by the minute.

''None of this looks at all temporary,'' she said. ''When you asked to rent my garage as a studio, you said you needed a temporary place to work.''

''Uh...I'll have to dismantle everything to move it,'' he said. ''But it can be moved. Pete'll help—when I can afford a place of my own.'' He shrugged. ''Until then, I'll have to work here.''

''Are you ready to start throwing pots?'' she asked. ''Is everything in place?''

"Glad you mentioned it." He looked directly at her. "There's only one more thing I need. A source of hot water."

She sighed. "I guess you can't just run a pipe?"

"It'd be a little more complicated than that. I have an easier solution," he said with uplifted brows. "I don't suppose you'd let me carry water from the laundry tub on your back porch?"

She started to tell him to get his water from the rest room down on the beach, then remembered with a slight feeling of panic that there was only cold water down there.

"Please, Lynn," he added. "I won't disturb you any more than I absolutely have to."

She took a deep breath and expelled it while she pondered this latest attack on her citadel of privacy. "Since I'm gone most of the day," she said, "you'd have to have a key to the back door."

"That shouldn't be a problem." He stared into her eyes. "Or is it?"

The intensity of his gaze pierced her defenses. "All right. I'll get you the spare key."

He followed her to the house and waited on the back porch while she rummaged through a drawer in the kitchen until she found the key.

She held it out to him, then dropped it into the palm of his outstretched hand, without touching him. "But the porch is as far as you go," she said, avoiding his eyes. "I'm locking this door into the kitchen." *Tomorrow,* she added to herself. *As soon as the hardware store opens and I can get a lock.*

He laughed. "Won't that be inconvenient for you, since your bathroom's out here?"

"I'll manage," she said.

He stepped forward, impelled by some force he was only vaguely aware of, and lifted her chin with his fingertips until he was gazing directly into her soft blue eyes. "I don't understand you at all, Lynn Frazer. One minute you're haranguing me, delving for the dark secrets of my past. The next you're erecting a wall to keep me out." He continued to gaze into her eyes, surprised she hadn't turned away or brushed off his hand. And surprised at himself for even daring to touch her.

"Can't we just be friends?" he asked. "Meet on some kind of neutral ground?"

"I was doing just fine until you came along," she murmured, staring back at him.

"And now I'm invading your house, encroaching on your territory and making you uncomfortable." He dropped his hand but maintained the contact with her eyes a moment longer. "What are you afraid of? Me—or yourself?"

Without waiting for her response, he strode from the house, closing the door behind him. He glanced back. Why was he baiting her like that? He didn't need the entanglement any more than she did. But something about her...

He walked straight down the hill, toward the one café in Garrett Cove.

Lynn watched him from the window. She had to admit he'd summed up the situation and the questions in her own mind admirably. Was it him she was afraid of? Or her reaction to him? One thing she did know. He was not the type of man she could ever have simply as a friend.

He disappeared into the café, where he seemed to be eating most of his meals when he wasn't at Pete's. She realized she knew more about his daily activities than she cared to know.

Why couldn't she get him out of her mind? She changed from Loafers into sneakers, grabbed her hooded jacket and headed for the pier.

Once out on the wooden structure, the stiff salty breeze whipped at her hair until she adjusted and tied the hood of her jacket, confining the errant strands. Clouds obscured the horizon and any remaining sunlight as dusk approached. She took a deep breath of the bracing air and strolled resolutely to the railing at the end of the pier, to the one place where she felt closest to Nick. They'd shared many sunset hours, standing right there, during the two years they were married.

Grasping the weathered railing, she stared at the undulating waves. The sea was frothy, but not tumultuous. No waves threatened to engulf the pier this evening. The only threats were in her mind as her thoughts strayed from Nick to Vince. She tried to analyze what there was about Vince that bothered her, and decided that "bother" was too tame a word to use to describe the disquieting effects he had on her.

He stirred her interest in a way no man had since she'd first met Nick. She'd even been dreaming of

Vince—sleeping outside in that van of his, so close yet so far. But they were definitely wrong for each other. They were two people each battling their own demons. And both losing. He couldn't accept the loss of his artistic ability, and she couldn't accept that Nick was truly gone. There was nothing either of them could do for the other.

Darkness closed in, dropping down around her like a cloak, when she realized with a guilty awareness that she'd been thinking far more of Vince than of Nick. She turned around, took three steps and ran into a solid muscular wall.

Vince's arms closed around her, drawing her to him. "Hey, you're going to fall barging around like that."

Her next breath drew in the heady scent of masculinity as he held her tightly against his chest to steady her. She had the overpowering urge to bury her face in his sweatshirt and cling to his strength. Instead, she pushed away from him as if he were fire and she was afraid of being burned.

"Let me go. What are you doing out here?" she demanded, her voice breaking.

"Are you claiming this pier as your private domain?" he asked with a note of irony in his tone.

"I...I..."

"Let me inside that wall you've erected," he said gently. "Maybe I can help you. Your husband is dead, whether you want to admit it or not."

She stared at the dark outlines of his face, barely visible on the cloudy night. How dare he talk to her about something so personal? "I don't need your help.

It's none of your business. Even if it was, there's nothing you can do." She turned away and faced the stiff breeze that stung her cheeks.

"I can offer you comfort," he said behind her, softly. "A shoulder to lean on, someone to talk to."

"No," she said, more loudly than she'd intended. "I have friends, family—if I need them."

"I'd like to be your friend, too." He grasped her arm and pulled her around to face him again. "You offered me a chance to talk a while ago. Now I'm offering you the same chance. Maybe it's what we both need."

"We're complete strangers," she said, twisting away from him again. "It wouldn't work. I've changed my mind."

"You're shutting me out. I've had experience with grief. I. . . I lost a brother a while ago. There were just the two of us."

"You can't help me," she said, glaring at the dark eyes she could barely see. "It would be like the blind leading the blind. You haven't solved your own problems. You're still grieving for the loss of the use of that hand. You've given up art to become nothing but a craftsman."

"I know my physical limits."

She put her hands on her hips and faced him squarely. "And I'll grieve in my own way. Please, leave me alone. Go away. I don't want you here." She stomped her foot, a muffled sound against the roar of the waves.

"All right. If that's what you want. Live with your ghost." He stalked away down the pier.

She couldn't watch him go. Despite what she'd told him, she *was* no longer sure what she wanted. Turning to the sea for solace, the dark watery depths drew her gaze. "Oh, Nick. What do I do now?" she whispered to the waves.

She stood there, staring at the sea, for what seemed an eternity until she was certain Vince had had enough time to get off the pier and up the hill. Then she turned and started home.

He was standing under the lone streetlight.

She walked off the pier and started to go past him. Then she stopped.

He was leaning against the post, watching her. Something was nagging at him, telling him that Lynn needed his help, despite her reluctance to admit it.

She brushed back her hood, letting her blond hair fly in the breeze. "Give it up, Vince."

"Give what up?"

"Whatever it is you're trying to do."

"I'm just trying to talk to you." He squared his shoulders and closed the gap between them. "What is it you expect to find out on the end of the pier?"

"How do you come up with such stupid questions?" Her tone was brusque and unyielding. She started walking and he fell into step beside her.

"It's not a stupid question if it has an answer." He glanced at her, but she kept her eyes straight ahead.

"When I'm out there, I feel as if Nick is with me." Her words were low, half muffled by the sounds of the ocean behind them.

They started up the path to the house. "Wouldn't you be happier with a flesh-and-blood man?"

"No!" she almost shouted. "No one can take Nick's place."

"That isn't what I meant. But you can love again. A person doesn't have only one chance at love in a lifetime."

"I could never love anyone else until I know for sure that Nick is dead."

He heard the fierce determination in her voice and found himself feeling sorry for anyone who had the misfortune to fall in love with her. "You are undoubtedly the most stubborn female I've ever encountered."

"And you are the most relentless male I have ever come across."

"There are times, like right now, that I wish Pete had never talked me into coming out to Garrett Cove."

She looked up at him. "And I wish you had never come. You do know what Pete is trying to do, don't you?"

"What?"

"He's playing matchmaker. I think he has some mistaken idea that you and I would be good for each other."

They had reached her back door. Without a backward glance, she walked into the house and disappeared from view.

He went to the garage and let himself in with his key. What she'd said made sense. No wonder Pete wanted him to ask her for the use of her garage. Pete *had* set him up. And baited him. Telling him that Lynn had been grieving and in a depressed state for a year and a half, telling him that everyone was so worried about her. That damn Pete knew he wouldn't be able to resist such a challenge. Pete knew he'd tangle with her over the grief thing.

He dropped down on a stool and felt his anger rising. He wasn't looking for a woman—for a relationship. That was the last thing in the world he needed now. But he'd like to help her—without getting involved.

Then a little voice asked him, *If you're not interested in her, why are you so angry?* He had to stop and think about that one. Was it more than just feeling sorry for her? After all, he knew what she was going through.

Then another thought struck him. If he was going to get involved with a woman, and it was a big "if," Lynn Frazer would be a likely choice. How did Pete know that?

He walked back outside. The light in the kitchen beckoned to him. Through the sheer curtain he could see Lynn moving about, probably fixing her dinner. He frowned. She was a pixie of a woman who didn't realize how sexy and desirable she was. Firm uplifted breasts teased at the front of her sweater. Small shapely lips drew into a sultry pout. And the way she tossed that long blond hair of hers behind her shoulders... He felt a stirring in his loins.

He knocked on the back door and saw her face peer through the window at him. She opened the door a crack. "What do you want now?" Her tone accused rather than questioned.

"Just to tell you I won't bother you anymore with unsolicited advice," he said. "I think you're right. If Pete really is trying to set us up, he's got the wrong two people. It would never work."

She frowned and he saw a flicker of something in the depths of her eyes that puzzled him.

"Good night," he said, and headed back to the garage. They were all wrong for each other, he told himself again. Too many problems. Now he just had to convince himself of that.

Four

A brisk morning breeze caressed Lynn's hair and face as she started down the driveway toward her shop. Loud cursing coming from the garage broke into her meandering thoughts. She stopped next to the garage and heard a loud thumping sound followed by more cursing.

Her curiosity aroused, she peered through the window and gasped. She knocked, but Vince didn't acknowledge her presence. Pulling open the door, she stepped inside just as he hurled a misshapen bowl against the wall. Several other lumps of wet clay littered the floor along with items that had fallen off their hooks on the Peg-Board.

"Are you all right?" she asked tentatively, not sure she should say anything after their encounter last night. But he'd said he wanted to be a friend. He'd said he would keep his opinions to himself. She ventured closer.

He rose from the stool, and the scowl on his face as he turned to her spoke volumes. "Can't get my rhythm going this morning, that's all. It's been a long time since I've thrown a pot."

She stifled a giggle. "Looks to me like you're throwing quite well." She gestured toward the scattered lumps of clay. "You're letting your anger take over and add to your stress, you know. You'll never do a decent piece that way."

"And I suppose you have a solution?"

"Sit down," she commanded.

He lowered himself onto the stool behind the wheel and quirked one brow. Without thinking of the possible consequences of what she was doing, she walked around behind him and grasped his shoulders, slowly massaging the tense muscles beneath her fingers—the same way she'd always done for Nick when he'd come home from a day of fishing, his shoulders knotted from hefting the heavy poles.

The heat from Vince's body radiated through the thin turtleneck shirt he wore. She inhaled the subtle aroma of maleness that mingled with the earthy odor of wet clay permeating the room. A day's growth of beard shadowed his face. Steadfastly ignoring the pulses of desire skittering uninvited through her body, she continued her rhythmic kneading of his shoulder muscles. She could feel him begin to relax under her ministrations. She couldn't stop now. It wouldn't do to let him know how being close to him, touching him, was affecting her.

She'd been too long without a man. That was all it was. But then she brushed that thought aside. She had to admit there was something special about Vince, something that stirred her blood and made her glad she was a woman. But she wasn't going to act on any insane impulses. She couldn't. Not when there was still a chance Nick could come back. She glanced at her wedding band. Until she knew for sure that Nick was dead, she would not take it off.

A sigh escaped Vince's lips as he twisted around. "You have a magic touch," he said, his tone indicating a much more relaxed state of mind than when she'd entered the garage. "I feel better already."

She stepped away from him, anxious to break the physical contact.

He dipped his clay-streaked hands into a bucket of water and then wiped them dry. Grinning self-consciously, he said, "You're right. Beating myself up isn't going to solve anything."

He stared at her a moment, then took a step nearer. She could see a glint of desire shimmering in his eyes. Mesmerized by the power he emanated, she didn't move when he grasped her shoulders and pulled her close.

His mouth hovered so near she could feel his warm breath. It seemed an eternity before his lips finally covered hers, hungrily exploring. The touch of his lips sent tendrils of need spiraling through her. She leaned into him, kissing him back, no thought of resistance entering her mind.

When he broke the contact with her lips, his gaze continued to hold her eyes captive. "I'm sorry," he said quietly. "I shouldn't have done that."

He released her and turned away, his shoulders and chest heaving. He stared into the corner of the garage, hoping she'd take the hint and leave. It wouldn't do for her to see just how much that kiss had affected him.

Why had he done it? Because he wanted to. That answer was easy enough. He'd wanted to taste her lips for days. What surprised him was her response, her participation. Surprised and puzzled him.

He heard the door close behind him. When he turned around, she was gone. Only the lingering scent of flowers from the fragrance she wore told him she'd been there. He stood by the window in the door and watched her slowly walk down the hill toward her shop.

Lynn turned around when she reached the bottom of the hill and looked back toward the garage. She could just make out Vince's head and shoulders at the window.

Her own heart still beat wildly. She watched him for a moment, wondering why she hadn't tried to stop him from kissing her. She knew she had to get over losing her husband before becoming involved with another man. Wasn't that the way things worked? With a sigh of frustration she strode quickly on to her shop.

By the time she opened the door she'd resolved again not to get involved with Vince Coulter—or any man.

Several times that morning she caught herself running her fingers over her lips as she relived that devastating kiss and felt the stirrings in her body the memory evoked. He'd said he was sorry. What did he mean by that? She preferred to think he was sorry he'd lost control. Just as she had. Her own response was every bit as incriminating. Maybe *she* should have apologized to *him*. She smiled at the thought.

Then a frown wrinkled her brow. Where did they go from here? She refused to dwell on the question.

The kiss was a mistake. She was sure of it. Twisting her wedding band on her finger, she vowed she wouldn't allow it to happen again. By touching him in the first place, intimately massaging his tense shoulders, she'd brought it on. Maybe she could explain to him... No, forget the explanations, she told herself. Just don't get into that kind of situation again.

By lunchtime she was convinced the kiss was an accident that wouldn't be repeated. All she had to do was avoid touching him again. She passed by the garage on the way to her house without longing to go in. When she opened the back door of the house and stepped into the porch, she noticed the unmistakable scent of shaving lotion still lingering in the air. He'd come into the house while she was gone and used the bathroom to shave.

Her first impulse was a sense of outrage that he'd dared to use her bathroom without her permission. Then guilt set in. How selfish she was, making him use the rest room down on the beach, with its icy-cold water, when her own little house was arranged with the bathroom conveniently located on the back porch. He already had the key to the porch. The latch she'd installed on the kitchen door would keep him out of the rest of the house.

Before she lost her nerve, she marched out the back door and straight to the garage. Vince was bent over the wheel molding a vase when she opened the door, walking right in without knocking.

He turned at the sound and a smile softened his features.

"I've decided to be neighborly," she said. "You can use the bathroom in my house. Just clean up after yourself. I don't provide maid service." With that, she hastily retreated.

Vince heard a timid knock on the garage door a few days later. "Come in," he called without looking up from the half-finished vase on the wheel.

He maintained his concentration on the evolving piece, slowly guiding the clay upward with his hands to fashion the neck and the rim of the vessel. Only as he was cutting the piece from the wheel did he allow himself to know that it was Lynn who'd come through the door.

What amused him was how her knock was always so tentative, as if she wasn't sure she should disturb him. The only time she'd come in without knocking was when she'd announced he could use her bathroom. He could feel her presence hovering behind him now. As she moved closer, he breathed in the delicate scent of her floral fragrance. Was it lavender? No. A subtle blend of some kind, he decided.

"You're making progress," Lynn said.

He spun the stool around and felt that tingle of awareness she awakened in him whenever he was close to her. She stopped in front of the shelves along the side wall, gazing at the rows of drying ware.

"I'll bisque-fire the first batch in a couple of days," he said. "Then we'll see what kind of progress I've made. It's been so long since I've thrown any pots I'm not so sure they'll hold up in the kiln."

"They look fine to me," she said. Then she spotted a pitcher on top of the damp cupboard and picked it up to examine it more closely. "Don't put this one back into the clay," she said. "Look at the distinctive shape. Look at the lines. It may not be as straight as normal functional ware, but there's a certain symmetry about it. I like it." She smiled a soft wistful smile.

"But it's not the kind of thing I'm attempting to do," he said, letting his voice show his exasperation.

"I know," she said quietly. "It's better. Somehow this one speaks to me."

He scowled. "You don't know what you're talking about."

"With the right glazing techniques," she said, "this pitcher could go in a gallery, instead of a craft shop, and outsell ten of your other pieces." She waved a hand toward the assortment of functional pottery on the shelves.

"But what if I can't get the right glaze on it?" he asked, his tone decidedly negative. "Then what do I have? A piece of junk only fit for the trash."

"I'm not saying the first piece you do will be a big success," she replied. "I'm only suggesting you try.

Do a little experimenting. That's what you're doing, anyway—experimenting with becoming a craftsman."

The words stung. He was aware of his own rising anger. "And you're not sure I can make it."

She stood in front of him, hands on her hips. "I never said that. Those thoughts are in *your* mind. You're the one giving up on yourself. Have a little faith."

He heard the challenge in her voice and fought back with the one weapon he had. "You're a great one to talk," he said. "You're giving up on life itself, hiding behind a dead husband, unable to get past a day without communing with him from the end of that damn pier."

"I don't go there every day," she said, her anger flaring.

"Just about," he replied. "And you're still wearing your wedding band. Someday you're going to have to accept his death and get on with your life."

"It's no concern of yours."

"And the kind of pottery I choose to make is a concern of yours?" he asked. "You sell pottery made by other craftsmen all the time."

She drew a breath as if to calm herself, and faced him directly. "The potters and I both make more money when the work is original," she said. "When it has that spark that says the person who made it is a creator breathing life into his designs."

"But a mistake isn't an artistic creation." He was almost shouting.

"You're the one who labeled this intriguing pitcher a mistake," she said, looking it over again as she held it carefully in her hands. Then she set it back down and stepped away with a thoughtful look on her face. "I say there's still a lot more artistic potential in you than you care to acknowledge." She punctuated her words with a nod of her head.

"I don't have the control I used to have," he said, angry at himself and at her for daring to point out to him his lack of will. "I can't do it." He stood up. "Get out of here. Leave me alone."

"You're scared. Admit it. You're scared." She lifted her chin and glared at him.

"All right, I admit it. I'm scared stiff I won't be able to make a living doing what I love to do." He glared right back. "Now are you satisfied? Now will you go away and leave me alone?"

"Okay. I'll go. Just don't throw away that pitcher." She marched out the door, slamming it behind her hard enough to rattle the window.

He picked up the pitcher, and the temptation to hurl it against the wall was almost overwhelming.

After a few deep breaths to bring his anger under control, he held the pitcher at arm's length, letting his artist's eye really look at it. Its squat irregular shape reminded him of a gourd. The bottom was flat, but the angle of the spout a bit skewed....

He set the pitcher on the turning wheel and worked with the lip for a few minutes, molding it, smoothing it, building it up in one thin place and working out the excess clay in another. A glimmer of excitement skittered through him.

Maybe she was right—about this one. Maybe the right glaze—a smooth, burnished surface perhaps? Like bronze.

He worked with the piece for a while longer, his enthusiasm mounting. At last satisfied that the pitcher had some potential, he set it on the shelf with the other pieces waiting for the kiln. After rinsing his hands in a bucket of water and drying them, he put on his jacket. The least he could do was apologize for shouting at her and sending her away.

Once out the door, he glanced down the hill toward the ocean and caught sight of a slim figure at the end of the pier. A sinking feeling coiled in the pit of his stomach. Communing with her dead husband again. Hiding from life. He turned back to the garage.

Then he stopped and swiveled around to face the ocean again. The realization hit him that he needed to talk to her, needed her to understand why he felt the way he did. That meant explaining to her what had happened back East on Long Island. Was he ready to tell her the whole truth? Or only part of it? Why had she become so important to him?

It wasn't just a physical attraction, either. Otherwise he wouldn't care how she felt. He wouldn't be upset that he'd sent her away in anger. And he wouldn't care that she was wasting her life waiting for some kind of sign that her husband was really dead.

Had the invincible Vince Coulter, a man who'd never considered a woman as necessary to his happiness, finally fallen in love, and with someone who couldn't let go of the memory of her dead husband? How could he compete with a ghost, especially when he had ghosts of his own?

Five

Lynn had no sooner returned from the pier and closed the kitchen door behind her when she heard the outer door open. Glancing over her shoulder through the window, she saw Vince stride to the inner door and open it, boldly walking into the kitchen. Her pulse quickened, his angry outburst earlier still very much on her mind. "I didn't say you could come in here."

"You going to throw me out?" he challenged.

She kept her voice calm while trying to assess his current mood. "If you've come to argue."

"I came to apologize for shouting at you," he said. "I know you were just trying to help."

She sighed. With this volatile man she never knew what to expect. "Apology accepted. Is that all?"

"Yes," he said. "No."

She waited, wondering at the apprehension in his eyes.

"Look, I..." He shrugged and backed away. "It doesn't matter. See you tomorrow."

"Wait," she said. Something puzzling in the expression on his face intrigued her. She made an instant decision. "Join me for dinner. We can talk."

He glanced around the kitchen, undoubtedly for signs of a meal in preparation. "The food's in the refrigerator, and I can just heat it up," she said, gesturing toward the microwave. "It'll be ready in a jiffy."

The beginning of a smile tipped the corners of his mouth. "I'll wash up."

By the time he returned to the kitchen she'd set the small table in the nook and the tantalizing aroma of hot fried chicken filled the room. She saw the pleased look on his face as she added potato salad from the refrigerator and a steaming bowl of baked beans from the microwave.

"Smells delicious," he said, taking the chair she indicated.

"Do you drink milk?" she asked, suddenly aware that there were many things about him she didn't know.

"Milk's fine."

She poured two glasses and set them on the table. "Help yourself," she said, trying to disguise just how nervous she was having him here. Whatever had possessed her to invite him into the intimacy of her small kitchen? He filled the room with his presence. She speared a chicken leg, then took salad and beans, willing herself to relax.

Why should she feel so uncomfortable sharing a meal with Vince? She'd known him almost two weeks, she'd been in his studio, they'd talked many times, yet this was the first time he'd been farther than the back porch. Had she been purposely keeping him outside?

Of course she had. Because he wasn't Nick. Because he was a man she was attracted to. Because she couldn't get him out of her mind, day or night.

"How long have you lived in Garrett Cove?" he asked, breaking into her troubled thoughts.

She raised her eyes to his and saw a strange sparkle. He was as nervous as she was! "Nick was living here in town when I married him—three and a half years ago. I was born just over in San Luis Obispo."

"And you intend to stay here?"

"Yes," she replied emphatically. "I could never leave here. Not after all that's happened."

"I didn't think I'd ever leave Long Island, either," he said with a frown. "And here I find myself on the other side of the continent."

"Wouldn't it have been easier to start over with supportive friends and family around you?" She thought of her own family and how hard they had tried to help her.

"No," he replied. "Just the opposite. My friends on Long Island either pitied me or told me I could still do the same kind of work as before, if only I tried harder. I couldn't tolerate those attitudes."

"And your family felt the same?"

"My father, a businessman to the core, always insisted I'd never make a decent living as an artist," he said, then hesitated. "He was the first one to say 'I told you so' after the accident."

She saw the haunted look in his eyes. "You couldn't help what happened to you," she said. "An accident is an accident."

His expression was tight with strain. "The accident was all my fault," he said, emphasizing the word "accident." He took a deep breath before going on. "I was clowning around, not paying attention to my driving. We'd just come from a gallery opening that was supposed to herald a momentous step in an illustrious career. You know the Greek theory of hubris—the gods shoot you down when you get too cocky? I clipped a guardrail and ran off the road that night, broadsiding a tree. Utter stupidity on my part!"

"And you haven't let yourself forget it for a minute," she added. "When are you going to forgive yourself?"

"Never. I'll live with the consequences of that night for the rest of my life. My brother died in the accident."

He glanced away. She felt the anguish in his words and just stared at him, at a complete loss as to how to respond.

Then he pulled up his sleeve and thrust his arm forward. A six-inch jagged scar, like a bolt of lightning, flared on his inner wrist, its ruddy hue setting it apart from the surrounding flesh. "This is my punishment for killing my brother."

She reached out and covered the scar with her hand. "You haven't dealt with your own grief, yet you're telling me to let go of mine."

"Oh, but I have dealt with it. I'm getting on with my life." He pulled his arm away from her hand. "Now that I've discovered I can still throw pots, I know I can support myself making pottery. I can mix the glazes and do whatever else needs to be done."

She couldn't resist an additional jab. "And see the potential in design. That slice on your wrist didn't sever the connections to your brain."

"I don't want to be an artist anymore, just a potter."

"Don't close yourself off from what you could be. Build a new life. A better one."

"I don't deserve anything more than what I'm aiming for. I need an income now. Besides, it takes time to develop the skills to make an artistic statement. I don't have that kind of time."

He'd said the words without the anger she'd expected. With a resignation that saddened her. She got up from the table and took a check from her purse in the living room, handing it to him. "I intended to give this to you earlier—before you ran me out of the garage. It's the first installment on the rest of your life. I've already sold a fourth of those pieces of yours."

His eyes widened as he stared at the check. "Almost enough to pay Pete back what I borrowed from him." He glanced up at her. "Uh...I haven't yet paid you any rent on the garage."

"Pay Pete first," she said. "One other thing. I've noticed you're not taking the time to go down to the café for lunch. I'll leave a sandwich and fruit in my refrigerator for you. You can come get it when you're hungry."

"You don't have to do that," he said.

"I want to. Can't have a starving artist on my hands. I'll leave the kitchen door unlocked." But only during the day, she added to herself. "You can put drinks, anything else you want, in the refrigerator too."

The haunted look left his face. A half smile softened his features. In that moment her impression of him changed. He was handsome, in his own unique manner. Besides being overtly masculine, in a tantalizing way.

How had he managed to become a part of her life in such a short time? She *cared* what happened to him. She cared that he hadn't exorcised his demons.

And he stirred delicious feelings deep inside her that should never be.

"Do you ever take a day off?" Vince asked, reaching for another piece of chicken.

His question surprised her, and she hesitated a moment before answering. "No, I don't. I keep my shop open seven days a week." She watched his eyes while he weighed her answer.

One brow lifted quizzically. "What if you're sick?"

"I post a sign in the window and go back to bed." She pursed her lips. "It doesn't happen very often."

"I think you ought to put a sign in the window tomorrow and play hooky, show me some of the countryside, like that rugged coastal area to the north." He gazed at her expectantly.

"I can't."

"You mean you won't." His eyes challenged. "What are you afraid of?"

"I'm not afraid of anything."

"Then go for a drive with me." He picked up the check she'd given him and waved it at her. "Pete doesn't get *every* penny of this. I'll buy us lunch along the way."

She met his even gaze. "I'll think about it. I haven't taken a day off in months."

And she did think about it—constantly—all the rest of the evening. And changed her mind countless times until she had to admit that she was afraid. Afraid of him. Afraid of the feelings he aroused in her. Yet . . . what would be so wrong with spending a day with him? She hadn't done anything simply for the fun of it in a long time.

About ten o'clock she clicked off the television movie she'd only half watched and heard Vince running water in the bathroom. She waited, listening for him to leave the house. Instead, she heard a knock on the kitchen door.

When she turned the latch and opened the door, he grinned at her. "I filled the van with gas tonight. Put your sign in the window and be ready to leave by nine in the morning." He turned and strode out the door toward the van parked by the garage.

She realized she had several choices. She could run after him and tell him she wasn't going. She could tell him in the morning when he came looking for her. Or she could go with him. Her traitorous heart made the decision.

The maroon van sped north on the coastal highway, a twisting, narrow, two-lane road built by convict labor between the two world wars. Lynn entertained Vince with stories of some of the local history as he drove. At least by keeping to neutral subjects she hoped to avoid the topics that sparked too personal a conversation. For a reason she wasn't ready to analyze, she wanted simply to enjoy this day and friendly company.

As she gazed at Vince's rugged profile, she realized there was one thing she was thankful for. In the van the two bucket seats in the front were far enough apart that their arms wouldn't accidently touch. In her little Honda they would have been sitting much closer together. Then Lynn glanced behind the seats. Vince's rumpled sleeping bag lay on a mattress. She felt a tightening in her chest. They were driving up the highway in his bedroom.

"I didn't tell you why I wanted to take a day off today," Vince said, breaking into her thoughts. "I fired the first batch of pottery. They're cooling right now. When we get back, we'll open the kiln. Then we'll see what kind of a potter I am."

"You're nervous," she said, the truth dawning on her. "Are these the first ones you've done since the accident?"

"Oh, I tried to throw some pots before I had the strength back in my wrist," he said. "What a mistake. They were utter failures."

"This time you decided you were ready," she said.

"I worked with a physical therapist for a while, until my money was almost gone." He sighed, keeping his eyes on the winding road. "That's when I knew I had to get away and make a new start somewhere else. So I called Pete and talked to him. He'd suggested before that I come to Garrett Cove."

"So Pete encouraged you to come," she put in.

"He told me about the summer crowds on the beach. About the nearby golf course and those big motels. And about your shop and how well pottery sold there." He paused. "He did keep one bit of information from me, though. He didn't tell me how pretty you were."

She was glad he had to keep his eyes on the winding road and couldn't see the flush in her cheeks. Somewhere back in her mind, a little voice reminded her she was making a mistake coming with him. She refused to listen.

The road was climbing again, from a stretch at sea level back to a high promontory, and she realized where they were. "There's a great view up ahead," she said.

He pulled the van off the highway and stopped short of the low rock wall. She climbed out and walked over to the wall, the sun shining from a cloudless sky, a stiff breeze blowing her hair into her face. She felt rather than saw him at her side. Concentrating, instead, on the scene below, she gazed down at the steep, brush-covered slope that dropped to the swirling gray-green water. The rocks jutting from the surf were surrounded by frothy white foam. Occasionally a cascading spray broke into the air with an iridescent shimmer. Gulls hovering overhead, drifting in the breeze, squawked out a warning. She breathed the clean ocean air and savored its salty twang.

"Too bad we can't get down there for a closer look," he said. "It's beautiful. So wild."

She smiled at the almost worshipful look on his face. His artistic sensibility was engaged. He might just do better here on the Coast, with new places to see and new artists to inspire him. He needed to meet the other artists in the area, too. She had a few contacts. She'd have to see to it sometime.

When they returned to the van, he opened the passenger door for her and grasped her arm to help her in. She felt the heat of his hand through the fabric of her sweater, just a gentle touch that radiated warmth to all parts of her body. Her eyes met his and he turned away, closing the door.

They ate their lunch at a roadside café before going in search of another promontory from which to view the ocean. They found one about twenty miles north. No other cars were there when Vince steered the van off the highway.

Lynn shivered as the breeze from the ocean tugged at her. An uneasy feeling crept over her. Vince had been unusually quiet during lunch, and he had looked at her with a warmth that had made her tingle all over. Now they were alone.

"Come on," he said, grabbing her hand and pulling her over the low rock wall and around some large boulders. She knew she shouldn't go with him, but couldn't stop herself. They found a trail that led to a spot out of sight of the highway, tucked behind an outcropping of rock and brush. The rains of the previous weeks had left a carpet of new green grass among the low bushes dotting the hillside.

She glanced back at the trail, then at Vince. Smiling, he pulled her toward him. The look in his eyes told her it wasn't the ocean that interested him.

"I don't think this is a good idea," she said, shaking her head to reinforce her words.

"I do," he whispered against her lips just before his mouth touched hers in a slow sensuous assault that seemed to go on and on. Powerless to stop him, her lips parted, granting him entrance, and he deepened the kiss, his arms crushing her to him, molding her body against his.

A kaleidoscope of conflicting emotions raged through her as she felt the hard evidence of his need. She wanted his kisses, wanted to feel his arms around her. Her heart beat wildly and ripples of desire consumed her as she returned his kisses, giving in to the delectable whirling sensations of her own need.

Yet it was wrong, all wrong. Her mind knew that. But her body wasn't paying any attention. She couldn't bring herself to give up the warmth of his lips and the heated awareness of his body clasped against hers.

She felt momentarily bereft when he pulled away from her and lowered her to the ground, where the scent of grass mingled with the salty air and tickled her nostrils.

The weight of his body pressed against hers as he lay half on top of her, his mouth joining with hers again. She gave in to her aching need and returned the fervor of his kisses.

It was only when his hand slipped under her sweater, hot against her cool flesh, exploring and finding the swollen peak of her breast beneath her bra that her reason began to assert itself. If Nick wasn't dead, she was still married.

She pushed against Vince's chest, turning her head away from the magic of his kiss. "No...no. Please stop."

He pulled back. "Are you sure that's what you want?" he said, his deep voice husky with passion.

"Yes." She didn't trust herself to say any more. Sitting up, she turned away from him and adjusted her bra and smoothed her sweater.

"Why?"

"You know why," she said, raising her eyes to his. What she saw alarmed her.

His pupils were dilated with anger. "No, I don't. I thought you were enjoying it as much as I was." The words came out in a bitter torrent. He grasped her arm and pulled her around to face him. "We'd be good together. Can't you see that?'' He was almost shouting.

She cowered under the verbal onslaught. ''No! I shouldn't have come with you today. I'm . . . I'm not ready for this.''

''How many years is it going to take before you are?'' His voice was low and hard. He stood up, towering over her. ''You could let go of Nick and get on with your own life. You're young and beautiful and desirable. Don't hide away with nothing but memories.''

She saw the hurt in his eyes and knew she'd let things go too far. Too far for both of them. ''You don't understand. I can't stop loving him just because he's gone. I feel such guilt each time I let you touch me or kiss me.''

''Guilt?'' He snorted derisively. ''You've done nothing to feel guilty about. Your husband is dead. Dead and gone.''

''You're being cruel. You of all people ought to know the power of guilt. You haven't given up your guilt over your brother's death.''

''But I caused the accident that killed Damon. You didn't capsize your husband's fishing boat.'' He reached down and pulled her to her feet. ''Let's get out of here.'' He released her hands and headed off down the trail toward the van. She followed him, brushing at the grass and twigs caught on her sweater and jeans.

On the drive back to Garrett Cove all her attempts at casual conversation were met with either silence or monosyllabic replies. She wanted to say something to ease the tension between them, but there wasn't anything that hadn't already been said. He didn't understand her feelings, probably never would. She hardly understood them herself. One thing she did know. Her own unfulfilled longing clamored for release. But that's all it was—a physical need. It couldn't be anything else.

Vince parked the van in its usual spot beside the garage. "I'm going to open the kiln," he said without looking at her. "You can come watch if you want."

She almost told him no, then decided that would be childish. She followed him through the side door into the garage, her mind and body in utter confusion. Fighting an overwhelming urge to touch him, she stopped several feet behind him and waited.

"I did the firing yesterday afternoon and evening," he said, his tone devoid of its earlier anger, "then cracked the door slightly before we left." He didn't say anything else as he opened the door of the kiln fully and began taking the pieces from the shelves, one by one, and setting them on a nearby bench.

He turned toward her with the squat gourdlike pitcher in his hand. "You were right. It does have potential." His eyes met hers for the first time since their disastrous encounter up the coast. They were still and dark—no anger, no passion.

She began to relax. "Now what will you do with it?"

"I have an idea that'll give it a unique finish. If it works, I'll show you when it comes out of the final firing." He set the pitcher on the bench and took the last of the pottery from the kiln.

"Did everything come out okay?" She surveyed the pieces on the bench. "What kind of glazes are you planning on using with this batch?"

"I'm going to experiment with several kinds I've never used before and find out what works the best," he said. "I've gotten this far. I threw the pots and fired them once. Now I go on to the next step. Then we'll see what kind of production potter I am."

He said the words without any air of confidence. He was scared—scared he wouldn't make it as a production potter. And she was pushing him to be even more. She wanted to put her arms around him and reassure him that he'd do just fine, that he had the skills and talent. But putting her arms around him was impossible now. From now on her goal had to be keeping a safe distance between them. If only he'd cooperate.

He faced her directly. "The next firing will be the crucial one. The real test. After I get the glazes on."

"You can do it," she said. "I have faith in you." She watched his eyes, wondering how those dark depths that were blazing with desire such a short time ago could now look so cold.

"One more thing before you go," he said. "I want to apologize for today. I was out of line."

She looked up at him. "And I apologize for not stopping you sooner."

He frowned. "I should have listened to you when you said it wasn't a good idea. But I thought I could change your mind. And I thought I had myself under control, that I'd be able to stop with a few kisses. I had no intention of going as far as I did, of forcing myself on you."

She stared at him, not sure what to say.

"I came here to make pottery, not to make love. I got sidetracked. I won't let it happen again." His words were uttered without emotion. And they drove through her like a razor-sharp sword.

Six

The door swished shut behind a departing customer, and Lynn glanced up at the clock. Almost closing time. She sighed. Maybe she ought to stop by the garage on her way to the house. See if Vince needed anything.

She hadn't seen much of him at all in the week since their drive up the coast. He was avoiding her, getting up earlier than she did in the morning. By the time she'd stumbled into the bathroom for her wake-up shower, he'd already been there, the scent of his soap and shaving lotion lingering in the moist air. He seemed to time his arrivals and departures to not coincide with hers. Deliberately. And it hurt.

And she'd stayed out of the garage on purpose. Avoiding him as he avoided her.

Thirty minutes later a shadow fell across the floor. She looked up in surprise to see Vince standing just outside the door, as if hesitating to come in.

She waited, her pulses fluttering.

He opened the door and crossed to her, holding out a bronze-tone pitcher like an offering. It was the squat little pitcher he'd wanted to throw away. She smiled and took it from him, setting it on the shelf in front of her. Then she stepped back and gazed at it. "I love it," she said reverently.

"Now we'll see if it'll sell," he said, his own voice full of skepticism.

"It will. I guarantee it."

"I'll bring the rest of the first batch tomorrow." He grinned sheepishly. "But I couldn't wait to show you this one."

"I'm glad." She smiled and gazed at the pitcher again. It was perfect, as she'd known it would be. When she turned back to Vince, he'd gone.

The next morning he was back.

"Hi," was her simple greeting, but her tone was soft, welcoming.

He answered with a grunt and set a box on the floor. She opened the lid and saw an assortment of vases, bowls, cups, pitchers—the kind of ware she got regularly from other production potters.

After bringing in a second box from his van out front, he approached her. "This is it," he said. "The ones that are worth selling."

"No more little bronze-tone pitchers?" She glanced at the pitcher on the top shelf of the display table that sat in the middle of the room.

"That's one of a kind. There won't be any more." He snapped out the words.

"You're not going to try to make any more distinctive pieces." It was a flat statement. She knew the answer. His words and attitude was unmistakable.

“I’m a production potter,” he replied with a scowl. “I told you that. That’s the best I can do now.” He laughed—a deep, throaty, mocking sound. “That pitcher was nothing more than a lucky accident, not likely to ever be repeated.”

She stared at him. “I don’t believe you. You’ve done it once. You can do it again.”

“Believe what you want,” he said bitterly. “But I know what kind of pottery I’m going to make.”

She leaned against the counter and suddenly felt very reckless, ready to challenge him again. “You’re trying to punish yourself by denying your abilities. What you suffered in that accident was punishment enough.”

“You don’t know what you’re talking about.”

She pursed her lips. “Oh, but I do. I talked to Pete a couple of days ago. He told me you took the full brunt of the impact when you broadsided that tree, that you had a broken leg, cuts and bruises, and a head injury that had you on the critical list for days.”

“I got what I deserved.” He strode toward the door.

She called after him, “Pete also said that there were four of you in that car, all clowning around.” He turned and glared at her. “If your brother had been wearing a seat belt like the rest of you, he wouldn’t have been thrown from the car and he wouldn’t have been killed. The other two passengers had only very minor injuries.”

He stood at the door, one hand on the knob. “He might still have died. He was in the front seat beside me.”

She advanced toward him. "Damon lived on the edge, tempting fate all the time. He refused to ever wear a seat belt. Pete said that, too. Your brother's life-style is not your fault. You didn't kill him. You don't have to punish yourself with guilt for the rest of your life."

"But I was driving the car!"

She kept her own voice under tight control. "Did you tell him to put on a seat belt?"

"Yeah—though I knew it wouldn't do any good."

She suppressed her urge to smile. "His refusal to wear a seat belt made his death his own fault. Not yours."

"But I caused the accident. He died. It has to be my fault."

"You're using your guilt as an excuse. You're not letting yourself be what you're capable of being." She put her hands on her hips and faced him squarely.

He towered over her, scowling. "Maybe I am. But it's my guilt. And I do know my limitations."

"I know your potential. I can see it in that bronze-tone pitcher."

"You're weaving fantasies." He marched out of the shop and climbed into his van without a backward glance.

She stared after him. Vince Coulter was not willing to take any risks. His damaged ego was too fragile right now. She stewed about it for the rest of the morning, then formulated a plan. She'd show that man what a lucky accident was worth!

Lynn slit open the envelope and took out the check, hardly glancing at the note that accompanied it. A huge smile of satisfaction spread across her face. She stuffed the check into the pocket of her windbreaker, pulled a chilled bottle of champagne from the refrigerator and uncorked it, then picked up two goblets and raced out to the garage.

She pushed open the door without knocking and surprised Vince as he was loading the kiln. He glowered at her at first, then saw the champagne bottle. His brows shot up. "What's going on?"

"We're going to celebrate," she said, setting the goblets on a table and pouring the champagne. She handed him a glass, then the check. Then she raised her own glass. "To your future."

He stared at the check, frowned and looked up at her. "What's all this about? I never sold anything to the Irvington Gallery in Los Angeles."

She grinned. "Yes, you did," she said. "That bronze-tone pitcher. Your 'lucky accident.'"

"You sent it to this gallery?" he asked.

"And they sold it in two days for ten times what I could have sold it for in my shop," she said triumphantly.

Vince shrugged. "This doesn't prove a thing." He set the glass down without tasting the wine. "Selling that pitcher was only another lucky accident," he said with a frown.

"You can make more pieces like that." She raised her goblet in a salute and took a sip. "The owner of the gallery is a friend of mine. She agreed with me that the pitcher was top quality. That it had a character all its own.''

''I can't count on lucky accidents to support myself.''

''I disagree. If you've done it once, you can do it again.''

''Why'd you send it down there?''

''Two reasons. Because I knew it would bring more money in the gallery—'' she smiled sheepishly ''—and to get temptation out of my way. I didn't dare keep it around. I was tempted to buy it for myself, but I couldn't afford to pay that kind of money for it.'' She indicated the check he held in his hand. ''I had to get the thing out of my shop while I still could.''

She watched his eyes, wishing she knew what he was feeling right now. His expression, she decided, was one of bewilderment more than anything else.

''Thank you,'' he said, picking up the goblet, ''for believing in me when I couldn't believe in myself. You've given me something I didn't have before. Hope.'' He clinked his glass against hers. ''Here's to the future.''

She smiled, glad he was beginning to see the potential he still had as an artist. But a little cloud passed through her mind. What if he *did* make it? What if he became as famous on the West Coast as he'd been on Long Island? Would he leave Garrett Cove? Did she want him to?

Vince paced the garage, glancing out the window every couple of minutes to see if any lights were on, indicating Lynn was up. He had to talk to her. It had been a week since she'd given him the check from the gallery, a week of soul-searching and experimenting for him.

But his conversation with Pete the evening before was what had him upset this morning. He'd stewed about it half the night. Now he had the ammunition to get back at her, and by golly he was going to use it.

The next time he glanced out the window, the bathroom light glowed in the darkness of early morning. He waited for what he thought was enough time for her to shower, then went outside, stopping short of the back door.

When the bathroom light snapped off, he charged into the house, confronting Lynn in the dimly lit kitchen. "Just a minute," he said. "I need to talk to you."

"Can't it wait until I get some clothes on?"

"No, it can't wait," he said. "I've waited all night as it is." He glanced at the fluffy terry robe that wrapped her slim figure. "Besides, you're covered up. This won't take long."

She sighed and flipped on the overhead light. "All right. I'll start some coffee." She turned her back to him and pulled the coffeemaker from its corner.

He watched her movements as she poured water and measured coffee, his mind conjuring up an image of naked flesh under blue terry. Her hair was still damp from the shower, and the scent of herbal shampoo wafted his way. The urge to put his arms around her and pull her close threatened to overpower him, and he had to do something to distract himself. He jerked out a chair and sat down at one end of the little table.

"If it's so important, you might as well start talking," she said. "You don't have to wait for me to finish here."

"I want your undivided attention," he replied, realizing he really wanted to watch her reactions.

She sat in the chair at the side of the table. "Okay. What's so important?"

"You and that ghost of a husband of yours." He hesitated as her eyes opened wide, then plunged on. "Pete told me last night that you've never even looked at the evidence your brother-in-law gathered after your husband died." He watched as her face turned pale.

"What if I haven't?" she asked. "That's no business of yours." She bounded from the chair. "I'm not going to listen to this."

He was on his feet immediately and grabbed her by the arm before she could escape to the other room. "Oh, no, you don't. You're not running from me this time. You're going to hear me out."

"I don't have to listen to anything." She hissed the words through clenched teeth.

"This time you do," he said. "You say it's none of my business? Well, I've decided it is."

She tried to tug out of his grip, but he grasped the other arm and held her in front of him. "Listen to me," he said. "You made me face up to myself. You made me see that I could still throw pots of artistic quality."

"That has nothing to do with Nick," she said, glaring at him.

"Yes, it does," he replied. "You butted into my life and badgered me until I faced up to my guilt and my fears. Now I'm going to do the same for you."

"It's not the same thing," she said, trying to wriggle out of his grasp. "There's nothing you can do."

"That's where you're wrong," he replied, tightening his hold. "I'm going to badger you in return until you finally look at the evidence, finally allow yourself to believe that Nick is dead. You have to stop being afraid to live without him. Even though there's no body, you can still bury him and your guilt and get on with your life."

"You're being cruel." She snapped out the words. "Leave me alone." She tried to turn away.

"Look at me," he said. He released one arm and grasped her chin in his hand, turning her head until her blazing eyes were directed right at him.

"You have a Late Death Registration," he continued, "issued by the court. Pete says such a document is very difficult to get, that the evidence has to be more than circumstantial. The judge believed Nick died that day. So should you."

"I can't," she said, "and there's no way you can force me to. I didn't see his body."

"Lynn! You're *never* going to see it!" he shouted. "And you know that as well as I do."

"Don't yell at me."

"And I always thought I was stubborn," he said. He let go of her chin and she pulled her arm from his grasp.

"Give it up, Vince. Nothing you can say is going to convince me."

He felt like shaking her and was glad he no longer had ahold of her, or he might have followed through on the urge. Then he realized the coffeepot had stopped gurgling. "The coffee's ready," he said. "Where are your cups?"

She reached into the overhead cupboard and slammed two pottery mugs on the counter. He poured the coffee and carried both cups to the table.

When he sat down across from her, he gazed into cold blue eyes. "Do something for me," he said in as calm a voice as he could muster. "Just go look at the evidence your brother-in-law accumulated. See what's there. You're never going to finish grieving for Nick unless you do."

"I'll look at it sometime," she replied, "but I'm not ready yet. I don't even want to think about that awful day. And you keep bringing it up, again and again."

"Lynn. A year and a half is long enough to live with a ghost. Give yourself a break. Take a chance on life."

"You don't understand," she said.

"Yes, I do," he replied. "You're afraid to face reality. Just like I was. I've confronted my fears. It's your turn."

Her eyes lifted to his. "What do you mean, you've confronted your fears?"

"I finally admitted to myself that I was afraid of the future. That I was hiding behind my guilt. I'm trying to forgive myself for my part in Damon's death, realizing that he has to share the blame."

When he saw her eyes brighten he forged ahead. "I'm consciously giving up my guilt, taking a risk," he said. "I'm doing what you told me I should do. And it's working. The proof's out there in the garage."

She smiled tentatively. "What do you mean? Are you making more little squatty pitchers?"

"Better than that," he replied. "I have some new things to show you. I'm even working with different clays. Come take a look."

She glanced down at her robe. "Later, after I've had a chance to dress and eat breakfast."

"Stop on your way to the shop," he said, standing. He refilled his coffee cup. "I'll return the cup later. And you think about what I've said." He headed for the door.

As soon as the door shut behind him, Lynn set her cup down and headed for the bedroom. She dressed and returned to the kitchen for her usual breakfast of cereal and toast. She thought about what Vince had said, the part about experimenting with new forms. She forced thoughts of Nick from her mind, as she usually did, except when she was on the pier. She'd think about him later.

Pushing open the side door to the garage, she stepped into the brightly lit interior and found Vince standing by a bank of shelves, rearranging the pieces sitting on the middle shelf.

He turned at the sound of the door and a smile lit his face. "Come look. Give me your honest opinion."

Lynn stopped at his side and gazed at the eight porcelain vases displayed there. They were exquisite! Each had a different shape, a different pattern and color combination of glaze decoration, a different impact on her own artistic sensibilities. She couldn't even begin to pick out a favorite.

"You've done it!" she exclaimed. "Each one is uniquely artistic in its own way. They're magnificent."

"I won't tell you how many I ruined in the process," he said with a laugh.

She smiled up at him. "That's not important. The results are what counts."

"Now, the big question," he said. "What will you do with them?" He looked at her thoughtfully. "Do these go to that L.A. gallery?"

"I have contacts in Carmel and Monterey, too," she said. "Why don't we promote you as a local phenomenon?"

"The potter guru of Garrett Cove?" He frowned. "I'm not sure about that. I had that kind of notoriety on Long Island. Don't think I want to go through it again."

"Then I guess we send them to the Irvington in Los Angeles and see what happens."

"I'd prefer that," he replied. "I'm really a very private person. I'd like to stay here, live a simple life and work in relative isolation."

"Won't Garrett Cove be too dull for you after you become rich and famous?" she asked.

"Rich and famous!" He laughed. "You're rushing things a bit, I think." He gestured toward the vases. "This is just a beginning. I have a lot of work to do. Besides, *you're* here in Garrett Cove."

She heard the tenderness in his words and looked into the dark depths of his eyes.

"I'm sorry I got so upset with you this morning," he said.

"I realize what you're trying to do."

He dropped a soft kiss on her lips, then stepped away from her.

At the gentle touch of his lips, her heart began a staccato pounding she was sure he could hear. Just that light contact was enough to set her pulses racing. Would it be so wrong to give in to the desires smoldering inside her?

Yes, she decided. She couldn't do it. She had to get her mind back on business. "I'll call my friend at the Irvington," she said. "I'm sure she'll want the whole batch. She's very impressed with your work."

"Thanks—for all you've done for me," he said, his tone sincere.

"I'm glad to help a friend—an artist in need."

"I wish you'd let *me* help a friend," he said. "A woman who needs to learn to live in the present, instead of the past."

"Don't start on that again—please," she said.

"I have to. You've done so much for me. I have to repay the debt."

"I can't just forget Nick."

"I'm not asking you to forget him," he said. "I'm asking you to acknowledge that he's dead. Nothing more."

"I can't."

"Take off that wedding band," he said, "and put it away. That might help."

She fled from the garage.

Seven

Lynn waited two days before venturing into the garage again, hoping Vince wouldn't bring up the subject of Nick. Vince was bent over the wheel, working on what looked like a teapot. She glanced at the shelf where all the new vases had been. They were gone. Panic struck her.

"The vases—where are they?" she asked. "What did you do with them?"

He turned around and smiled when he saw her. "In those boxes over there," he said, pointing to two cardboard boxes under a table.

"You had me worried for a minute."

He quirked one brow. "Oh? I was simply waiting for you to come to me."

She detected a subtle message in the tone of his voice. "I came for the vases," she replied. "Nothing else."

"If you'll wait a minute, I'll help you carry them down to the shop."

"You don't have to," she said. "I can take two trips or use my car."

"I want to help you."

There it was again, that subtle message. His words had a double meaning she was determined not to acknowledge.

"If you insist," she said with a shrug, "but it's really not necessary."

He finished off the rim of the vessel he was shaping, then cut the pot from the wheel. "This needs to dry a bit, anyway, before I add the spout and handle," he said. "I have plenty of time to help a... friend."

Lynn watched from near the door as he placed the pot on a slab on the table, then rinsed his hands in a bucket and dried them. She hardly recognized the old towel she'd given him when he'd first moved his things into the garage. It was stained from the clay. Then she realized it was one of the towels she and Nick had received as a wedding present, the blue ones that used to be trimmed with a delicate pink satin ribbon.

There she was, thinking about Nick again. She was doing far too much of that lately. And if he wasn't on her mind, Vince was. How had her life gotten so complicated?

Vince picked up one box from under the table, handed it to her, then picked up the other and pushed open the door with his foot. "Let's go."

She glanced at him ruefully. He'd become such a big part of her life and thoughts. And she hadn't a clue what to do about it.

Later that evening, as she tried to concentrate on the novel she was reading, she heard the back door open.

It had to be Vince heading for the bathroom. Then the kitchen door opened, and her muscles tensed. She put a marker in the book and closed it.

"Lynn. Are you in there?"

At the sound of Vince's deep voice, she relaxed a bit, but not completely. It was not like him to come looking for her in the house. But certain things were changing in their relationship, subtle things. He was deliberately crossing the invisible barriers she'd erected around herself, and she couldn't seem to prevent him.

"I'm in the living room," she called, not wanting to get up from the protective corner of the couch.

When he stepped into the room and glanced around, she realized he'd never been as far as her living room before. She saw the expression on his face when he spotted the slender vase decorated with lavender iris that sat on the buffet against one wall. His smile was the gentlest one she'd yet seen.

"You kept my favorite," he said. "My grandmother used to grow iris at her cottage on Long Island."

"I couldn't sell all of them," she said. "They were too beautiful."

"I'm glad you didn't," he replied.

He stood in front of her, so tall, so masculine. It felt strange, having him in her living room. He seemed to fill the tiny room with his presence.

He frowned as if in remembrance. "At first I wanted all those pieces to be gone," he said, "so I'd never have to look at what I used to be able to do.

Then I regretted my decision. I'm glad you saved one."

She smiled. "That's what I figured would happen sooner or later. Sit down."

He lowered himself to the middle of the couch just a short distance from her.

As she gazed at him, so close, the room suddenly seemed warmer. "Was there something you wanted?" she asked nervously.

"To see you," he said with a grin as he extended one arm along the back of the couch toward her. "I was pacing the floor out there, thinking about you—" the expression on his face became serious "—and I decided to see what you were doing tonight."

The pounding of her heart heightened the tightness in her chest. "Nothing much. Just reading..."

All her instincts told her she should send him away. Something was different about him tonight. He didn't have that look about him that signaled a willingness to do battle. She could handle the arguments.

His hand dropped to her shoulder and began a slow sensual massage that lit a flame deep inside her. Her lips parted as she glimpsed the glow of desire in his eyes. She needed to get up from the couch. Now.

But something kept her there. His touch? The look in his eyes? Or her own needs?

He pulled her into his arms, and she went willingly, closing her eyes and savoring the feel of being so close to him.

His lips found hers and his invading tongue sent shivers of desire racing through her. The questions in her mind changed slightly. Could she send him away now? If not, could she let him make love to her? Could she make love to him?

Behind her closed lids, she tried to conjure up an image of Nick. But instead, she saw the dark depths of Vince's eyes, the rugged planes of his face, his lean powerful physique.

She wanted him. It was as simple as that. And as complicated. But she'd deal with any problems later. Now, in his arms, she felt more complete than she'd felt in . . . She didn't remember how long.

His lips withdrew from hers and began pillaging her neck, her throat, and his hands went on their own exploration, finding and cupping her breasts. She could no longer deny herself his touch. Her own hands caressed his shoulders, crept around his neck, then tangled in the fringe of hair at his nape.

He unbuttoned her flannel shirt and undid the front closure of her bra. She drew in a breath as his lips traveled from her throat to her breasts. When his lips brushed her nipples, she shivered and pulled him closer. His touch was light and teasing, and it was driving her wild. She arched into him.

"I want you...and not just for now...forever...." His words were almost a moan.

She wasn't sure at first what he'd said.

"I love you," he added. "I want to marry you. To have you by my side . . . forever."

A warning reverberated through her brain. "No...no." She pushed at his chest. "Don't say that. You can't mean it."

He sat up and his gaze was as soft as a caress. "But I do mean it," he said softly. "Every word. I want you as my wife. I love you."

Too much. Too fast. She pulled her shirt together, covering her nakedness. "You can't love me. It's all wrong. I can't love you. Nick..." His name came out as a gasp. She stared at Vince. "Please...go away."

"Dammit, Lynn," Vince said, all the warmth gone from his voice. "Don't do this to us. We'd be good together. Don't you see that?"

He pulled her to her feet and then over to the bedroom door, which was standing open. "Nick's not in there anymore. But I could be—with you. Marry me. Let me help you deal with your memories of the past."

"No!" she said, letting the panic she felt into her voice. "That's not the way I have to do it. I can't make that kind of commitment yet."

He grasped her chin and held it rigid so she had to look at him. "I can't wait any longer," he said. "Can't you see I'm at the end of my patience?"

His anger gave her new strength. She pushed his hand away and drew herself up to her full height. "I'm sorry, Vince," she said. "I'm sorry I can't be the woman you need."

"'Sorry' doesn't cut it," he replied. "And you *are* the woman I need. You just don't know it yet."

She turned on him. "You're asking too much, too soon."

"It's not too soon for me," he said. "Seeing you every day and not being able to hold you, to make love to you, is driving me crazy. I don't know how much longer I can live like this."

"You're the one who came to me," she said, "with the silly idea of using my garage."

He laughed. "Boy, did that plan backfire."

"If being here is the problem, then I guess you'll have to go," she said. "Get your own place. Get out of my garage."

"That's not going to solve anything for us," he replied.

"You wouldn't have to see me every day," she said. "You wouldn't be sharing my bathroom."

He faced her squarely. "If I move out of your garage," he said, "I'll also have to move out of town. I can't stay in Garrett Cove and watch you tear yourself apart over a ghost." He turned and stomped out of the house.

"Then go!" she shouted after him.

She collapsed on the couch, tears welling up in her eyes and spilling down her cheeks. What had she done? He wouldn't really leave, would he?

Several hours later lights flashing across the front window startled her awake. She realized she'd cried herself to sleep on the couch and hadn't even gone to bed. But the lights...

When she got up and looked out the window, she gasped. Vince had backed his van up to the door of the garage and was loading boxes into the back of it. He was leaving.

The intensity of her feeling of loss surprised her. If Vince left, she'd be alone again. But wasn't that what she'd been afraid of all along? Why she didn't want to get involved with another man? She had intended to build herself a life so independent she'd never need anyone else again. That's what she'd been telling herself, over and over, since Nick had died. That way she'd never be hurt again.

Since Nick had died? Did she believe that now? Did she want to believe he was dead?

She huddled into the corner of the couch and pulled an afghan around her, letting her mind wander back over all the things she could remember that Larry had told her, things that were in that file she'd never read. Never had the courage to read, she amended. She let the agonizing details wash over her. Again and again. Her tears fell freely for what seemed like hours.

Glancing out the window, she saw that the lights in the garage were out. And the van was still there. "Vince, I *do* want you. I want to be able to love you." She spoke the words aloud into the blackness of the night. "I do want to believe that Nick is dead. I'm trying. I really am."

She dozed off again on the couch, unwilling to go to bed. Unwilling to let the van and Vince out of her sight.

The first rays of daylight were creeping into the room when she awoke from her restless unrefreshing sleep. The van was still there. Relief flooded through her. Maybe there was still time. But would he still want her?

She hurried to the bathroom and took a quick shower, realizing that Vince hadn't been inside yet. He could still be asleep in the van and planning to leave when he woke up. The thought brought back the dark cloud that had settled over her when he'd walked out last night.

Rushing out the door, she almost ran into Vince heading for the house. She stared at his tousled hair and sleepy eyes. "Don't leave," she said. "Not yet. Can't you give me a little more time? A few more weeks maybe?"

"No, I can't do that," he replied coldly. "I've given you all the time my sanity will allow. I made a decision last night. I can't work here any longer. I'm leaving Garrett Cove."

The finality of his tone sparked something inside her. She wasn't going to grovel or beg. She bit back the words she wanted to say. She had her pride, too. Besides, maybe he was better off without her. He could support himself now. She knew that. And her ghost, as he chose to call it, was still hovering in the background, though diminished in stature.

"Where will you go?" she asked.

"Maybe back to Long Island," he replied, his eyes dark and expressionless. "I'll send you my new address so you can forward any checks."

She looked up at him and tried to keep her tone casual even though she wanted to fling herself into his arms and beg him to stay. "I'm glad things are working out for you," she said. "And I hope you'll come back some day."

"No," he said with finality. "There're one too many ghosts in Garrett Cove."

"I'm sorry you feel that way," she said. "But I can't just change overnight."

"You've given me no sign that you're trying to change at all," he replied. "The passion's there, but not the love. You were ready to give me your body last night, but that was all. I want you to love me as I love you."

She couldn't deny his accusation. And she couldn't say the words he wanted to hear. Something was still not right in her own mind. Something unfinished.

"When are you leaving?" she asked.

"As soon as I'm packed and have your garage cleared out for you."

"I see." She turned back to the house and he followed her inside, stopping in the bathroom. She went on into the living room and sat down on the couch, clutching a pillow to her chest for comfort. She'd lost him.

The sound of the shower running tore her from her reverie. It felt right having a man in the house again. She'd miss him terribly.

Wasn't that what love was all about? Wanting to be with the person so much it hurt? That's what her horrible night had tried to tell her. She *did* love him.

Hurrying to the phone, she dialed her sister's number.

After a quick drive inland, she was sitting on the brocade couch in her sister's living room in a fashionable home on the outskirts of San Luis Obispo. Lynn glanced around the classically decorated room and smiled. Marrying a lawyer had given Carol all the material comforts.

But Lynn didn't envy Carol for that. She envied her for her good solid marriage, based on a foundation of love. Lynn wanted love, too. Vince's. If it wasn't too late.

Carol came in from the kitchen carrying a tray with teapot and cups. "Larry's on his way back home with the file. I'm glad you've finally come to your senses."

Lynn sniffed and tried to stem the tears that threatened. "I can't let him leave."

"I knew when I saw him in your shop that he was the man for you," Carol said. "I don't know why. Instinct, I guess. The way you looked at him."

Lynn gasped. "And just what makes you so all-knowing?"

"Remember," Carol replied, "I was the one who comforted you after several broken romances—before you met Nick. I saw the signs right after Vince arrived. I knew it was only a matter of time."

Larry burst through the front door just then, dropped a thick file onto Lynn's lap and sat down beside her on the couch. "Take all the time you want. Read every word if you have to."

Lynn smiled wanly at her brother-in-law. "I don't think that's necessary. But I do want to see what facts were presented."

"Here, look at this." Larry shuffled through the pages until he came to one. He pointed to the page. "Here's Pete's deposition. He was practically standing next to Nick when he went overboard."

Lynn read the words through her tears, then dried her eyes and looked at several more of the documents, coming at last to the judge's opinion. After reading that, she turned to the copy of the Late Death Registration and read what it said. Then she closed the folder.

Nick was dead.

She knew it at last. But there was something else she had to do before she could go to Vince—if he'd still have her. If he was still in Garrett Cove.

Hugging Carol, then Larry, she rushed out the door.

She drove to the nearest florist shop and astounded the surprised clerk with her request. Thirty minutes later the clerk handed her a funeral wreath. A yellow banner across it read "Nicholas S. Frazer—Lost at Sea."

The traffic between San Luis Obispo and Garrett Cove had never seemed so heavy. Lynn inched along behind a truck for a good two-thirds of the way. When she pulled into the main street of town, she saw immediately that Vince's van was no longer in front of her garage. She drove up the hill and parked in her driveway.

A glance through the window in the side door of the garage told her Vince had finished his packing. He wouldn't be back. She had her garage back now—whether she wanted it or not.

Opening the door, she stepped inside and surveyed what was left. The shelves were still in place. The benches and table were stacked neatly on one wall. The Peg-Board hung on the wall, but now it was empty of tools. Only the lingering odor of damp clay gave any indication of Vince's former occupancy.

She closed the garage door and went into the house. All signs of Vince were gone from the bathroom—his soap, shaving kit, shampoo.

He had well and truly left.

She hadn't figured on his leaving without saying goodbye. But he had.

She walked through the quiet house and into her bedroom. Staring at the quilt-covered queen-size bed, she tugged the gold wedding band from her finger. A jewelry box sat on top of the dresser. She placed the ring in the box and snapped the lid closed. Then she glanced at her finger. It looked so bare without that ring. She rubbed the place where it had been. But she couldn't back down now. Nick was gone and she knew it.

But so was Vince, her heart wailed.

She retraced her steps through the house and back outside, stopping at the car to grab the wreath from the seat. Then she walked down the hill and out to the end of the pier.

The gray-green water lapped against the pier in a comforting soothing rhythm. The ocean had become a great solace to her. She'd miss her solitary vigils here. But Vince was right. It was time to get on with her life.

As a gentle breeze teased her loose hair, she lifted the wreath to the railing, read the inscription one last time, then flung it as far as she could out to sea.

"Goodbye, Nick," she called aloud. "Rest in peace." A glint of sunlight sparkled on the lettering across the yellow ribbon.

She gazed at the ocean a moment longer, at peace with herself for the first time in a long time. Then she turned resolutely toward the shore. And stopped abruptly.

Vince stood on the pier, about ten feet away.

"I...I thought you'd left," she stammered.

"I went to tell Pete and Maria goodbye. Then I came back to tell you goodbye. And give you your key."

She stared at him, a glimmer of hope rising within her.

"Does that wreath mean what I hope it does?" he asked.

"Yes," she said. "I've buried Nick."

"Are you sure?"

"I saw the file. He's dead. I know it now, and I've accepted it."

She walked into Vince's outstretched arms. "I love you. I want you," she murmured into his chest. "Please, don't go away."

He tilted her chin upward. "You'll marry me?"

"Any time you want." She held up her ringless left hand.

A big smile lit his face and he gazed at her with eyes ablaze with love.

She sighed and pulled his head down till his lips met hers. This time she wasn't wishing anything was different. This time she was perfectly content in his arms.

MAGGIE AND HER COLONEL
Merline Lovelace

To my dad, Merl, who gave me his name,
a childhood filled with love
and a hopeless addiction to golf.

Chapter One

"Just who the hell is this Dr. Wescott, and where does he get off disapproving my test?"

Seated in the outer reception area, Maggie heard every angry word. She shook her head and shared a wry grin with the secretary perched behind a large modular desk unit. The older woman winked, then turned to listen with unabashed interest to the exchange taking place in the commander's office.

"Dr. Wescott is our new chief of Environmental Engineering and is waiting outside to discuss the issue with you when you calm down, Mac."

Her boss's measured tones provided a sharp contrast to the visitor's deep angry growl.

"I'm as calm as I'm likely to get over this. Bring him in."

The secretary answered the intercom on its first short ring. Gray curls bouncing, she nodded toward the open door.

Here we go, Maggie thought. She squared her shoulders to take full advantage of her considerable height and entered the inner office. She could tell from the glint in her boss's eyes that he was thoroughly enjoying the situation, the old reprobate.

"Colonel MacRae, this is Dr. Wescott. She joined our staff a week ago. One of her first projects was your proposed test."

Maggie had to admire the visitor's composure, even if she *had* decided to dislike him on principle. MacRae's blue eyes narrowed dangerously for a moment when she entered, and he slanted a sharp glance at Maggie's grinning supervisor. He showed no other signs of surprise that Dr. Wescott was not the man he expected, however, and took her hand in a firm grip.

Maggie felt a strange sensation as she looked up, and up, into the man's eyes. He was a linebacker in a blue air force uniform, for heaven's sake. She couldn't remember the last time she felt dwarfed by any man. At five foot eight in her stocking feet, she was usually at least eye level with her coworkers and acquaintances.

"Dr. Wescott, Colonel MacRae is commander of the armament division of Wright Laboratory here on base. He's concerned that you disapproved the propulsion test his lab wants to conduct and would like to discuss the project with you personally."

With that bland introduction, Ed Stockton sat back to enjoy the fireworks. He'd only worked with the young woman who now headed his Environmental Engineering department for a week, but he'd put his money on her, hands down. She'd made mincemeat of one of the other department heads who'd mistaken her blond good looks and laughing green eyes for those of a professional lightweight. The lady knew her stuff and didn't take any nonsense from anyone.

MacRae started his attack even as they moved to the conference table.

"Since you're new here, Dr. Wescott, you may not fully understand the implications of this test for Eglin Air Force Base and for the lab. It involves over a million dollars in reimbursable costs and is vital to the space program."

The hairs on Maggie's neck bristled. She could almost forgive this man for the unconscious chauvinism she'd overheard while she sat in the reception room. Most men, and women, of her acquaintance assumed engineers were of the male persuasion. But no one questioned her professional competence and lived to tell about it. Inwardly seething, she kept her voice level.

"Colonel, I fully appreciate the implications of this test for Eglin. The chemical you want to use as a propellant is highly volatile and has never been tested anywhere in the quantity you propose. Your people have done a poor job in addressing potential impacts in their environmental assessment."

Maggie seated herself at the conference table and laid the folder with her notes aside. She'd done some quick reading since the call had come to report to her boss's office. She had her facts down cold.

"The U.S. Fish and Wildlife Service has already issued a statement of concern over your test's threat to endangered species. Even if I wanted to override their objections, which I don't, Eglin would be slapped with a notice of violation. Not only would the Wildlife folks have scrubbed this test, but they might hold all our other tests hostage while we negotiated with them. This base is too important a test facility to the Department of Defense to allow a poorly planned, inadequately researched project like this to close it down, even temporarily."

Mac MacRae leveled a hard stare at the young woman across the conference table. She must have ordered her Ph.D. through the mail, he thought. With her mass of golden curls that tumbled wildly over her shoulders, she looked about eighteen. Only when he noticed the fine lines fanning out from the corners of her eyes did he revise his estimate of her age, if not her capabilities. Maybe she was old enough, but surely not experienced enough to make the kind of judgment she had.

His lips settled into a grim line, and he gave her his full attention. By the time she was halfway through her succinct review of the situation, he'd stopped seeing her curly hair and sensuous lips. Instead, he focused on clear green eyes that looked at him with distinct challenge and more than a hint of disapproval. He listened in silence, then sat back in his chair to consider the facts she'd laid before him.

Maggie refused to let MacRae's silence disconcert her. She held his gaze steadily and used the pause to take a mental inventory of the man facing her. Those penetrating blue eyes seemed out of place in a tanned face with a nose that looked like someone had taken a fist to it more than once. Or a shoulder, Maggie thought, in keeping with his linebacker appearance. She noted with some satisfaction the silver that liberally laced his dark hair. He wasn't as young as he looked at first glance, she thought, unknowingly mirroring MacRae's assessment of her. Although why that thought should give her satisfaction, she had no idea. She was so absorbed in her private review that she jumped at the deep gravelly voice.

"I apologize, Dr. Wescott. You've obviously put more effort into studying this project than I realized. I'll have my people redefine the test parameters. I'd appreciate it if you'd work with us closely so we can modify the test to satisfy all environmental concerns."

His response surprised Maggie. She'd had her hackles up and was ready for a long argument. Hard experience had taught her that some men were congenitally unable to give in gracefully to a woman. She would've bet her last dollar this hulking male was one of them. His reasonableness left her feeling slightly deflated.

Before she could frame a coherent reply, MacRae got to his feet and shook Ed Stockton's hand. He turned to take Maggie's hand again, and her pulse seemed to jump at the hard warmth that enveloped her palm. She was sure she only imagined that he held her hand longer than he had the first time. Tugging her fingers loose as nonchalantly as possible, Maggie used the excuse of gathering up her papers to put some distance between them. For some reason, this man disturbed her. Maybe it was his size. He was a veritable mountain, for heaven's sake. By the time she'd stuffed the report haphazardly into a file, he was gone.

"Just who was that masked man?" she asked her boss.

Ed Stockton laughed at her rueful grimace. "I've known MacRae a long time, Maggie. There isn't a more brilliant physicist or better commander in the air force."

"He looks more like a football player than a scientist," Maggie commented.

"You aren't exactly the stereotype Ph.D., either," Ed responded blandly. "Actually I think Mac did play football at the Air Force Academy. Now he's a test pilot, but one of the weird ones. He actually finds the science of what makes those tubes of steel fly more fascinating than the flying itself. He's brilliant, but when he has a hot project in the works, he's like a bulldog. The man's made my life miserable more times than I can count with his demands for range support for his propulsion tests. It did the old heart good to see him put in his place for once."

Maggie knew her boss well enough by now not to take him seriously. A senior colonel, Ed Stockton could give as good as he got and then some. His gruff voice hid a sharp precise mind and a total dedication to the air force. He needed both to command the nine-hundred-plus civil engineers, military and civilian, who were responsible for maintaining Eglin Air Force Base. The largest air base in the world, Eglin covered a land area of more than half a million acres and ate up most of the western half of Florida's panhandle. It boasted thousands of miles of roads and hundreds of buildings and test facilities.

Maggie was just beginning to appreciate the vast size of the base, as well as the scope of her job. As chief of Environmental Engineering, her responsibilities included anything and everything that might have an impact on the environment on that half-million acres. When she'd first arrived, she'd outlined a schedule to visit every hazardous-material site, fuel-storage area and restricted-test area on base. It would take her six months to cover them all.

Maggie had responded on impulse to the ad for an environmental engineer at Eglin. She'd worked for the government before on some classified projects in Washington and knew enough about the test business to win an immediate job interview. Unlikely as it seemed at first to either of them, she and Ed Stockton had hit it off from the first few minutes of the interview.

Maggie knew that her extensive credentials and her high-powered industry job she gave up to come to Florida had impressed Stockton. He'd asked her why she wanted to come to "redneck country," as he put, after working at corporate level for a major oil conglomerate in Houston. She'd responded that she needed a change and wanted to get back to field-level work. At Stockton's quizzical look, she added gently that she had personal reasons, as well, which were none of his business.

Maggie considered her private life her own affair. If the crusty colonel interviewing her wasn't satisfied with her professional credentials, she knew there were plenty of others who would be. Stockton was more than happy—with both her credentials and her feisty spirit, so like his own. He'd hired her on the spot and had enjoyed the reactions of the conservative local populace ever since she'd arrived. Just as he'd enjoyed MacRae's narrow-eyed appraisal of her. Ed leaned back in his swivel chair and regarded his newest employee.

"Work with MacRae on this test, Maggie. He's right about its importance. If there's a way to do it safely, let's find it."

"I'll give it my best, Ed, although I doubt I'll have much to do with the big man himself. He'll probably assign the task of convincing me to some lowly engineer."

"Possibly," Ed agreed. "Just don't be surprised if you find him taking a personal interest in this project. It's a big one."

Chapter Two

Maggie's next encounter with "the mountain," as she'd privately dubbed him, came sooner than either she or Ed Stockton had imagined. She ran into him, literally, the next evening.

She'd been invited by the chief of Natural Resources to join a nighttime expedition to one of the base's protected beaches. Natural Resources was responsible for wildlife and timber management on the sprawling Eglin complex. The chief of that division went about his work with a contagious enthusiasm. With Ed Stockton's support, he'd enlisted a local school to help with the annual turtle-hatching. Maggie listened with smiling skepticism as he explained how she could help.

"Really, Maggie, half the squadron turns out, as much to help supervise the kids as work the turtles. Most of the fun is watching the youngsters see nature at work."

"Come on, Pete, don't the folks in this corner of Florida have anything better to do on Friday night? Do you really expect me to believe you've got several hundred adults and as many kids coming out to watch turtles hatch?"

Pete smiled through his bushy beard. Now here was a man who fit his biologist image, Maggie thought. Unlike a certain hulking scientist.

"Not just watch," Pete protested. "We have to work them. The loggerhead sea turtles are one of the endangered species that are protected by law. But mama loggerhead isn't a very responsible parent, and that makes our job difficult. She deposits her eggs on Eglin's beaches, then swims off into the gulf. My people have spent the past few months building wire cages to protect the nests from predators."

Pete's earnestness won Maggie's interest, and she leaned forward to peer over his shoulder at the map showing the various nesting sites.

"The eggs are just now starting to hatch. Unfortunately, on cloudy nights like tonight, the baby turtles can't see the moon's reflection on water to guide them to the sea. They get disoriented, lose their way and die."

"I would think a couple of hundred inquisitive schoolkids would only add to the poor baby turtles' confusion," Maggie joked.

"Come out to Site 15 tonight with me and see. Trust me," Pete said, placing a hairy paw on his plaid-covered chest. "It'll be one of the adventures of your life."

Later that night, as the moon darted in and out of dark clouds, Maggie stood a short distance apart from a milling group of adults and preteens that Pete was organizing. She'd driven out with him and listened to his detailed explanation of the night's activities, but still felt a bit foolish among a bunch of strangers baby-sitting turtles of all things. She shivered slightly in her lightweight jacket. So much for balmy Florida nights and swaying palm trees, she thought.

Even the cool May night air, however, couldn't dampen her natural ebullience for long. She stood on a slight rise and caught her breath as the moon peeked around the edge of a cloud, bathing the beach with soft light. White sand, undulating dunes and the iridescent ripple of the waves washing in combined to make a magical seascape. Maggie drank in the serene beauty of the night, disturbed only by the excited noise of a dozen children trying to be quiet.

She turned toward the nest area, noticing that the kids had formed a line from the dunes to the shore. When they switched on their flashlights, a wave of high-pitched giggles and muted adult exclamations drifted across the night air. Despite herself, Maggie felt a thrill as she saw hundreds of tiny dark forms begin to make their squiggly way to the sea. She started to run down to join the line, but crashed headlong into a very large dark form coming from the side.

Hard hands gripped one arm and one breast, trying to keep her from falling. The hand on her breast shifted almost immediately to her other arm, but not before Maggie's startled glance had looked up, way up, into equally startled eyes.

Maggie's ready sense of humor overcame her momentary embarrassment. "I know you wanted us to work closely, Colonel, but isn't this above and beyond the call of duty?"

"Dr. Wescott, I'd have recognized you anywhere."

At Maggie's indignant gasp, MacRae added, "From the moonlight glinting on that wild head of hair."

His wicked smile told Maggie that he knew very well she'd thought he was referring to his quick but very thorough exploration of her breast. The thought of his hand on it brought an unexpected tingle to the very area he had pressed so briefly. She stepped back quickly out of his hold.

"What are you doing here, Colonel? Scouting out the next site to blow up with one of your super ray guns?"

Mac smiled down at her. "You've been listening to that old goat Stockton too much. I don't blow up every part of his precious range. Only the selected portions he grudgingly allows the rest of us to use. Actually I'm here in my other official capacity tonight. Those are my two boys over there, trying not to stomp too many turtles to death as they help 'save' them."

He waved in the general direction of the line of children. Maggie saw a couple of flashlights dance wildly in response. Even in the darkness, she guessed, his kids could pick out their giant of a father. She firmly suppressed a surprising twinge of disappointment at the thought of his having children. Of course he had kids, and he probably had a dainty demure little wife, as well. Maggie took a step away from him.

"I better get over there and help, too, or I'll lose my environmentalist badge."

Mac fell in beside her as she headed toward the line. Inexplicably, some of the adventure of the night had dimmed for Maggie.

"Dad, Dad, can me and Danny spend the night at Joey's?"

A sand-covered shadow ran full tilt toward them out of the darkness. Maggie barely avoided her second collision of the night, but Mac wasn't as lucky. He caught the youngster, who appeared to be about nine, under his arms and swirled him around in a shower of sand, wet jeans and giggles.

"Mind your manners, Davey. Say hello to Dr. Wescott. She works at the base, too."

Davey extended a damp sandy hand to Maggie. His grin, as he introduced himself, was a miniature duplicate of one she had seen smiling down at her just a few moments ago. Heavens, there were three of these males loose on society!

"Please, Dad. Joey's mom promised to make fudge tonight. Can we go?"

"Let me talk to her first, son, and make sure it's all right."

As the child dashed back to his place in line, Mac excused himself. "I need to catch Joey's mom before they overwhelm her. I'm not sure she knows what she's getting into with those twins of mine. They've been through half a dozen full-time housekeepers in the past few years. The latest has worked out only because she used to be a warden in a woman's prison."

He started to walk away, then turned back. "What the heck's your first name, anyway? I feel like we've passed the Dr. Wescott stage."

"I'll tell you, if you'll tell me what goes in front of the 'Mac' in MacRae."

For the first time, Maggie saw the big man slightly discomposed.

"It's Alastair, after my Scottish grandfather. Most of the folks who know me have managed to forget that. Mac'll do just fine. Your turn."

"Maggie, short for Marguerite. After my French grandmother."

He left Maggie with a smile. She wandered toward the line, thinking of their brief conversation. After their initial meeting, Maggie never would have imagined enjoying herself with the incredible hunk so much. She had just reached the point of wondering about the string of housekeepers when he was back.

"All clear. The boys are set, and I have an unexpected free evening. Do you want to go hatch turtles with me?"

The moon came out from behind a scudding cloud, lighting the beach and Maggie's night. She resisted an almost overwhelming urge to put her hand in the one he was holding out to her.

"Wouldn't Mrs. Colonel MacRae mind you going off to hatch turtles with another woman?"

Maggie was nothing if not direct. She had learned to be to succeed in a field still dominated by men.

Mac was equally direct. "My wife died in a car crash six years ago. It's just the boys and me." He looked out at the sea briefly, then deliberately lightened the somber mood. "Danny and Davey have been trying to marry me off for years to any woman who can cook. You don't have a diploma from a gourmet-cooking school tucked away with all your other degrees, do you?"

"Nope, you're safe."

"Good, come on, then. There's another nest a little way down the beach, minus kids. Pete told me about it. Incidentally he mentioned that he'd be here late. I told him I'd take you home if you want to leave before he does."

Maggie stared at him in wry amusement. The man sure moved fast for someone his size.

They spent the next hour alternately escorting hatchlings to the sea and sitting next to a small fire set in the protection of the dunes. Mac provided a thermos of hot coffee laced with rum. Obviously he'd done turtle duty before.

She found the man beside her fascinating. He laughed and joked easily with the other members of the small group. In between dashes to the sea, he kept Maggie amused with a light running commentary on the joys of parenting twin boys.

For his part, Mac couldn't keep his eyes off her mobile expressive face with those green eyes gleaming in the moonlight. Nor off her long legs and the firm tush outlined to perfection by her tight jeans. She had a light and laughing personality that attracted Mac even more than her trim figure. When the last hatchlings finally made their way to the surf, he took Maggie's arm and led her away from the small fire toward a Jeep parked at the edge of the dunes.

"Mac, I'm cold," Maggie protested, looking back longingly at the fire and the thermos of doctored coffee Mac had left with the remaining group.

"Me, too. We'll get warm in the car. My jeans are wet clear up to my thighs."

"That's a lot of wet," Maggie said, her voice solemn.

He grinned and helped her into the Jeep. Joining her, he turned on the ignition and the heater. Welcome warmth began to fill the cab, along with the soft strains of a country-and-western ballad from the radio.

"Better?" he asked.

"Mmm, much."

Maggie propped her knees up against the dash and leaned back in the seat, drinking in the sight of shadowed moonlight dancing on the sea and her tingling awareness of the man beside her. Idly she wondered if she'd have a chance to see Mac again once she started working with his people on the test project. She certainly hoped so.

Mac's low voice cut through the stillness. "I was impressed with your grasp of the issues on our propulsion test. For someone so new to the base, you've certainly picked up on our business quickly."

"I may be new to Eglin, but I'm not new to testing," she told him. "I worked in Research and Development on the Air Staff for a while before I moved to private industry."

"What made you come back to defense work?"

Maggie found that Mac's presence was proving to be a major distraction. That, and the way his arm stretched across the back of the seat. She had to think a couple of moments before she could come up with a response.

"It was time for a change," she finally managed.

"I'm glad," he said, and smiled.

At her inquiring look, his hand slid off the seat back and burrowed under the weight of her hair. It settled on her nape, and Maggie felt the tender rasp of his callused fingertips all the way down to her toes.

"I'm glad you needed a change, Maggie. I'm glad you're here."

Maggie swallowed and looked up to see his eyes glinting silvery blue in the moonlight.

"Me, too, Mac," she whispered.

With a lopsided grin, he moved his arm down to wrap it around her waist. His muscles barely shifted as he lifted her easily across the gearshift and into his lap. She half-sat, half-lay across his iron-hard thighs.

"I've been wanting to do this since turtle number twenty-seven," he murmured.

His dark head bent toward her, and Maggie felt his lips close over hers. He tasted of coffee and rum and delicious male. Letting her eyes drift closed, she savored the slow languorous way his lips moved over hers.

She smiled up at him when he pulled back moments later. "Why did you wait so long?"

Mac gave a little groan. The hand around her waist tightened as he fit her more fully against his chest, and her head angled back for his kiss. When she moaned softly in an unconscious echo, his tongue delved in to explore her mouth. Maggie's last rational thought was that she hadn't necked in a parked car since junior high. She hadn't realized what she was missing.

A long time later they surfaced. Mac tilted her chin up so he could see her face in the moonlight. With a grunt of pure male satisfaction he took in her half-closed dreamy eyes and swollen lips.

"Lord, you look great in the moonlight, woman. Especially with that hair of yours glinting that way."

When she only smiled in response, Mac ran his finger gently back and forth across her lower lip. Maggie had thought the feel of his lips on hers erotic. This finger business was about to drive her crazy. Instinctively she opened her mouth and captured his finger in a teasing nip.

"You little cat."

Mac bent her back over his arm as far as the truck door would allow and kissed her again. His hand started to move toward the zipper on her jacket, then stopped a tantalizing few inches away from her breast.

Dragging in a harsh breath, he lifted his head and dropped his hand to rest on the curve of her hip. "Lord, I'm sorry, Maggie."

She blinked. "Sorry?"

"I'm acting like some pimply teenager on his first date. I must be crazy, trying to grope you in the front seat of a car."

Flustered, Maggie stared up at him. She wasn't about to admit that she wanted to be groped, front seat or back. That she hadn't been kissed like that by anyone, pimply or otherwise, in this lifetime. That her nipples had tingled in anticipation as his hand started to open her jacket. She swallowed and tried to take in his next words.

"I can't believe I lost control to the point where I was ready to do something I'd wallop the boys for in a few years. Would it help any if I said you and the moonlight are a fatal combination and I couldn't help myself?"

A slow wave of embarrassment washed over Maggie as she listened to his apology. Here she was, a grown woman with a string of degrees, trading kisses with a man she hardly knew. In a Jeep, no less. Obviously, Mac hadn't expected her uninhibited response—any more than she had herself.

She shifted off his lap and scrambled awkwardly to her seat.

"I'd like to go home now."

"Maggie—"

"Now, please." Thoroughly mortified, and a little hurt by his rejection, Maggie stared straight ahead.

Mac studied her stony profile and cursed himself for being such a clumsy idiot. It wasn't as if he was totally out of practice. He hadn't been celibate all these years since Anne's death, but normally he managed a bit more finesse. He didn't know what it was about this woman now staring at the sea that started his hormones raging. Since his first meeting with her, he'd felt far more than a professional interest. That interest had ripened to a deep attraction as he'd watched her sparkle in the firelight and shimmer in the moonlight.

He'd responded to her looks as any healthy male would, but it was more than that. She'd put him calmly and efficiently in his place in Stockton's office. Instead of turning him off, he found himself intrigued by the brain behind the face. By the whole woman. When she careened into him tonight and he felt her firm breast in his hand, Mac had decided instantly to follow up on that promising lead. He just hadn't planned to let it go quite so far, so soon.

"Look at me, Maggie. Please."

He waited until she speared him with a cold challenging look. "I'm sorry. I didn't mean to come on to you like some sex-starved jerk. We're going to be working together closely for the next few weeks. I don't want you to be... uncomfortable around me."

Mac could have kicked himself as soon as the words were out. They sounded pompous and all wrong, and he could see that was just the way Maggie heard them. Anger quickly replaced the stony stillness on her face.

"Look, Colonel, I've never yet let private feelings interfere with my professional dealings, and you aren't the man to change that. If you're through beating your breast over this evening's fiasco, would you please take me home? Or shall I find another ride?"

Mac muttered a curse under his breath. Obviously he couldn't recover tonight. However, he hadn't risen to the top of his profession without learning his trade. Any good military man knew when to beat a strategic retreat and marshal his forces for another day. Without another word he drove the Jeep out of the tall dunes and onto the highway.

During the ride home Maggie stoked her simmering anger at the man seated next to her. So he was a world-class hunk who looked as good in his uniform as in the worn jeans he was wearing tonight. So he had a slow easy smile that crinkled his eyes. So some people thought he was brilliant. She knew better. The man was a jerk, just as he himself said, and the less she dealt with him the better. The fact that he'd stopped kissing her when she was warm and willing had nothing at all to do with the matter. At least that's what she finally managed to convince herself of by the time she'd soaked in a hot tub and buried her head under a mound of covers.

Chapter Three

Maggie wasn't sure whether it was the insistent ringing of the doorbell or the loud barking that woke her the next morning. She poked her head out from under the tangled covers, pushed a pile of hair out of her eyes and squinted at the clock.

It was only seven-thirty, for heaven's sake! And a Saturday morning, as best she could recall. What idiot was making such a racket so early? It took another few moments for the fact to penetrate that the ringing doorbell was hers and the barking didn't seem to be going away.

Muttering something that wouldn't have done much for her professional image, Maggie climbed out of bed. She searched among the jumble in her closet for a robe. She hadn't had time in the week she'd been here to unpack, but household chores were pretty low in her list of priorities. By the time she'd found a short beach robe to cover her nightshirt, the doorbell had begun to grate on her nerves, and she was seriously considering changing her opinion on animal euthanasia.

Her sleepy irritation changed to surprise when she opened the door of her rented condo. Three pairs of male eyes surveyed her. Four, if the huge creature who treated her to one more ear-splitting bark before plopping down on her doorstep happened to be a him.

"Mornin', ma'am." Mac's blue eyes twinkled down at her confusion. "I just collected the boys from Joey's house, and they swear three pounds of fudge barely kept them from starving to death last night. We're on our way to our favorite restaurant for breakfast. Since you're new in town, we thought you might like to join us for some local down-home cooking."

In answer to her skeptical look, one of the boys chimed in. "Honest, ma'am. Felix makes the best grits in town. Probably in all of Florida. Maybe in the world." Another enthusiastic bark seconded the boy's earnest opinion.

Maggie smiled down at him, then gave Mac an inquiring glance.

"This is Daniel." Mac ruffled one dark head affectionately. "You met David last night. They're otherwise known as the Terrible Twosome or, more politely, the Scourges of Northwest Florida."

"Aw, come on, Dad." Davey grinned up at him. "We're not that bad, at least not all the time."

Maggie suddenly realized that her front doorstep was not exactly the proper place to be standing in a short robe and carrying on an extended conversation. Not that she should be carrying on a conversation with these three males in a short robe at all. Correction, make that four males, Maggie amended as the big hairy beast sniffed a ceramic pot gracing her doorstep, then lifted his leg to drown her poor potted mums. Thank goodness they were artificial, Maggie thought. Gardening was another domestic task she had little interest in or talent for.

"Woof—bad boy!" three male voices chastised the dog in unison. The dog drooped his head in a semblance of repentance for a few seconds. Then a squirrel in the yard caught his attention and he bounded off.

"Woof, come back!" Davey yelled.

"Interesting name," Maggie said as the dog returned, tail wagging. She stood aside. "Why don't the bunch of you come in for a moment while I put on something more presentable?''

Mac's eyes told her that he found her eminently presentable, but he prudently kept silent as she led them into a light airy living room.

Maggie had fallen in love with this condo the first moment she'd seen it. Since it fronted the emerald-green waters of the Gulf of Mexico, the rent was high. She considered the spacious rooms well worth the price, though. At least they had seemed spacious until her three—four—unexpected guests filled them.

Mac caught her arm as she turned for the hallway. ''Please come, Maggie,'' he said softly. ''I at least owe you breakfast for last night.''

''You don't owe me anything at all,'' she began, only to stop abruptly as she noted two pairs of very interested blue eyes fixed on her and Mac.

''What happened last night, Dad? Did you put the make on Dr. Westly?''

Out of the mouths of babes, Maggie thought. She folded her arms and turned to watch how Mac handled this one. He got himself in. Let him get himself out.

''It's Dr. Wescott, Davey. And I guess I did come on a bit strong with her. Breakfast is my way of apology.''

Maggie had to admire MacRae's honesty with his sons, even if she didn't particularly like being the subject of it. She gave a silent groan as the boys turned their bright inquisitive eyes back to her. She forestalled the highly personal questions hovering on their lips.

''Apology accepted. And it's Maggie, guys. Give me a few minutes to get dressed, and I'll take you up on your offer of grits.''

''That's great, Maggie. But don't take too long, okay? You won't mess with all that female stuff, will you?'' Davey, or maybe it was Danny, managed to project a superb impression of imminent starvation.

"I wonder where they picked up that little bit of sexism," Maggie tossed at Mac as she moved past him.

Five minutes later she was back, dressed in snug jeans and a soft red sweater. Her only concession to "female" stuff was a red band that caught her long curls up in a wispy concoction Mac found utterly enticing.

He forced himself to repress the mental urge to pull that band slowly back out of her hair and watch the tawny mass spill across his arm. *Come on, man,* he told himself, *you're here to make amends, not make matters worse.* With that admonishment, he shepherded Maggie and his tribe out of the apartment and into his Jeep.

Maggie found herself amazed at the variety and scope of interest displayed by the two lively nine-year-olds. During the short ride their conversation ranged from the fate of the turtles hatched last night to hockey strategy to some strange rock group whose name seemed to be composed mostly of dead things. She sat back, content to enjoy their company and let the crisp Florida air fan her hunger.

An hour later the boys watched with open admiration as she pushed back her second empty grits bowl. It joined the litter of empty biscuit platters and gravy boats on the table.

"Gimme a break, guys," Maggie said, noting their expressions. "I'm a big girl. I need a lot of sustenance."

The boys and their father flashed identical grins. Maggie felt her heart thump against her full stomach. It must be heartburn from all this food, she thought. She couldn't be falling for three bothersome males who wouldn't even let a gal sleep late on Saturday mornings.

She sipped her coffee, feeling full and strangely happy in the midst of the noisy clatter of the restaurant. When she met Mac's look, he let loose with one of those slow easy smiles that started at the corners of his mouth and ended up lightening his blue eyes to silvery gray. It almost made Maggie forget where she was.

"Forgiven?" he mouthed at her over the boy's heads. She smiled back and gave a slow nod.

"At the risk of overwhelming you with MacRaes, would you like to fill the next couple of hours with fresh air, terrifying suspense and unmitigated violence? The boys have soccer practice in half an hour. They always perform better before admiring females."

"Daaad," the twins chorused, but they turned identical hopeful looks on Maggie.

Maggie rubbed her full tummy as if in deep thought. "I guess I need to do something to repay the guys for the best grits I've ever had. Sure, I can cheer them on for an hour or so."

Mac's thigh rubbed against Maggie's jean-clad leg as they sat on the hard bleachers. She found his taut muscles much more fascinating than the controlled mayhem that passed for kids' soccer. She retained barely enough consciousness of the game to return the twins' waves after each spectacular play, which, given the wild charges up and down the field, didn't happen too often. The bleachers were crowded with noisy parents, all no doubt hoping their offspring would work off some energy. Maggie noticed the speculative glances other parents had given Mac when he arrived with boys, dog and herself in tow.

Mac had returned several friendly greetings, but didn't linger beyond brief introductions. He wanted some time alone with the tawny-haired creature next to him—if you could consider being surrounded by yelling soccer parents on a crowded bleacher alone, he thought with a wry grimace. Actually the strategy worked better than he'd anticipated. From long years of practice he caught all the boy's more energetic moves while he kept his attention and gaze mostly on the woman beside him. She fascinated him more by the minute.

"We all appreciated not being kept waiting for 'female stuff' this morning," he told her, gazing down at her fresh glowing complexion. "The boys, because they were about to expire with hunger on the spot. Me, because I find you look even better in the light of day than in the moonlight."

"I'm not sure you ought to bring up the subject of moonlight. I'm still trying to sort last night out."

Mac winced at her directness. She leaned her elbows back against the seat behind them and studied him from under thick gold-tipped lashes. "You confused me," she added. "My own response to you confused me."

"Well, confusion is better than the disgusted looks I was getting last night." He grinned down at her, unrepentant. "Our housekeeper gets back tomorrow afternoon, Maggie. Would you have dinner with me tomorrow night? Just us, I promise. No boys or turtles or dogs."

Maggie gave him a long considering look. She should say no. Things were moving too fast with this man. He overwhelmed her, both physically and with his exuberant family. Besides, there was the project to consider. They might find themselves on opposite sides of a very nasty debate before too long. Despite all that, Maggie found herself nodding.

"Yes," she got out, right before an errant soccer ball rocketed toward their heads and they both ducked, laughing.

Chapter Four

After the game Maggie spent the rest of Saturday and most of Sunday at her cubbyhole of an office. She might hold a Phi Beta Kappa key from MIT and have a good ten years' experience in environmental issues, but the complexity of Eglin's operations awed her. Like any professional, she wanted to learn as much as she could as quickly as possible.

Late Sunday afternoon she found the folder on the laboratory test under a stack of files. Although she felt comfortable with her initial assessment, she decided to go through the documentation again. Her growing personal interest in the man behind the test had nothing to do with it, she told herself. This was business.

The new chemical proposed as a propellant could make a major difference in the Department of Defense space program. Although highly volatile, it was inexpensive to formulate and readily available. Maggie had read a lot about it, had even been involved in another minor experiment involving it a few years ago. But this test represented a major milestone in its practical application. She spent a good hour rereading the report and doing her own analysis of the test parameters.

She sat back in her chair, brow furrowed and doubts still unresolved. The propellant was incredibly dangerous, more so than most of the exotic explosives and chemicals tested at Eglin. Maggie knew commercial concerns were just beginning to consider it as a possible source of power, but no one had figured out how to reduce its volatility to safe levels yet.

As she reviewed possible test impacts, Maggie began to appreciate just why Eglin Air Force Base covered an area larger than a small state. The test business involved a lot of unknowns—dropping bombs or firing missiles for the first time and recording their properties. The fliers and engineers required a large safety footprint for their tests. Unfortunately the footprint included habitats of several endangered species, highways that had to be closed during tests and encroaching civilian communities. All of them had to be considered in the environmental analysis for each major new test. Mac's staff hadn't adequately addressed all the environmental impacts if this propellant lived up to its dangerous potential.

She made a few hasty notes and stuffed the folder into her tote to take home with her for yet another look. She put the other folders back in her drawer and glanced at the wall clock. She wanted plenty of time to prepare for her dinner date this evening with her enigmatic colonel.

If Mac's soft whistle when she opened her door to him later was any indication, her preparation time had been well spent. She felt the impact of his glinting approval from her hair, held up with combs on top of her head, down the length of the shimmery green silk pantsuit to her high-heeled sandals.

"I'm not exactly sure how anyone encased in cloth from neck to toe can manage to look mostly undressed, but you come close."

"I think I'll take that as a compliment," Maggie said, moving aside to let him in. "Wearing outrageous clothes is one of the few advantages a tall woman has in life over the dainty types."

Maggie smiled to herself as she turned to shut the door. She'd bought the outfit because of the way the silk clung sensuously to every curve. She didn't have that many of them, and if this little outfit helped Mac notice the few she had, it was worth every penny.

Mac would have disagreed with her assessment of her attractions had he known it. His eyes roamed appreciatively from her slender hips to her small high breasts. The jade-green tunic outlined them clearly, hinting at the nubs in their centers before falling in graceful folds. Surveying the way the fabric moved as Maggie did, Mac's feelings underwent a subtle change. From masculine appreciation, he began to experience a possessive desire to keep Maggie's curves to himself. He felt a surprisingly primitive urge to wrap her in a shapeless blanket so that only he knew what was beneath.

Unaware of his thoughts, Maggie turned to pick up her small gold purse. Mac barely stifled a groan when the silk outlined the delicious curves of her derriere as she leaned down. It was with a somewhat grim expression that he escorted Maggie to his car.

He managed to relax over dinner. The sight of Maggie demolishing a grilled red snapper, a generous portion of steamed rice and half a loaf of crusty French bread, along with a bottle of perfectly chilled chardonnay, restored his balance.

Maggie sighed as she leaned back in her chair. "That was heaven."

"It's nice to share a meal with someone who appreciates it," he responded, lifting his wineglass in her direction.

"Which is a very tactful way of saying I eat too much." Maggie laughed. "I guess being tall has another advantage, besides allowing me to wear outrageous clothes. It takes a lot more to fill me up. And I can enjoy every morsel." She grinned unrepentantly over the rim of her wineglass.

"Yes, and I can think of at least one more advantage." At her inquiring look, he stood and held out his hand. "I've been looking forward to dancing with someone whose nose won't tickle my belly-button. Come dance with me, Maggie m'girl."

Mac decided he liked the feel of the woman in his arms. Very much. She fitted him perfectly. Ignoring the glances other men in the room directed at Maggie, he enjoyed the feel of her warm flesh through the smooth material as he moved his hand slowly up and down her back. To distract himself from what he could feel at her front, he nuzzled a soft tendril of hair that had escaped from the topknot and resumed their lighthearted dinner conversation.

"So where did you work before coming here? You mentioned the Air Staff."

Held closely against Mac's hard body, Maggie had difficulty remembering her own name, let alone her career history. Only after she'd shifted away from the warm cradle of his thighs could she collect her thoughts.

"Mmm, yes. I worked on the Air Staff in Washington for a year or so. It was exciting, but I didn't care much for the paperwork. I decided I liked fieldwork better.

"Houston was next," she murmured into Mac's obliging shoulder. Really, it was amazing she could talk at all. She found herself reveling in the sensation of dancing with someone whose shoulder was just the right height to rest her head on. Even with her high heels, the mountain retained his majestic proportions.

"How long at Houston?" he asked, his voice low, his breath teasing the wispy curls at her ears.

"Not quite two years."

"So why did you leave there to come here? That job must have paid twice what the government could pay you."

Maggie smiled into Mac's shoulder. "I think I had this conversation once before with Ed Stockton. The same answer still holds. There's more to life than money. I wanted to get back to hands-on environmental work, and Eglin has plenty of that."

Maggie leaned back in his arms to look up at him. Mac barely managed to suppress a groan as her breasts brushed against his chest. Damn that silk! He could feel the peaks of her breasts clearly through the material, distracting him so much he almost missed her soft words.

"My needs in life are pretty simple, Mac. Some nice clothes, a good car and a challenging job, in reverse order, about sum them up."

"Isn't there something missing from that list? Like a home and a family? Someone to cook for you?" he teased.

Much as she liked him, Maggie's habit of keeping her private life private was too ingrained to give Mac anything other than the barest details.

"I've come close once or twice," she admitted lightly. "But every time I thought I'd found Mr. Right, he turned to be Mr. Wrong. Enough about me. What about you? What's on your list?"

"My priorities are pretty simple, too," Mac answered as he moved them in time to the slow dreamy tune. "The boys and the air force, not in reverse order. I'm lucky. Between those two devils and the demands of a military career, I've never been still long enough to be bored."

"And that's enough? What about someone to talk to in the night? About things besides soccer or Boy Scouts, I mean? Don't you want to marry again?"

"What makes you think husbands and wives talk in bed about anything other than Boy Scouts and grocery lists and who's going to take the kids to the dentist?"

At her mock scowl, he shrugged. "Like you, I've had a few close calls over the years. Being single and so physically big make me a real target it seems. But so far, it's just me and the boys. And Woof."

Maggie buried a small sigh of satisfaction in the fabric of Mac's shirt. She was glad Woof and the boys, and no one else, were taking up his time.

Mac led her around the dance floor a couple of more times, then leaned down to whisper in her ear, "Let's go, Maggie. I don't think I can take one more man sliding his eyes over you in that slinky getup."

Maggie gave silent thanks once more to Nieman Marcus for her outfit and smiled her readiness to leave.

She promised herself another shopping trip when Mac closed the front door of her apartment and growled, "Come here, woman. That thing you're wearing has been driving me nuts all evening."

Maggie allowed Mac's big hands to pull her close. He propped his shoulders back against the door, forcing her to put her palms on his chest and lean heavily against him. Her body was plastered against his from shoulder to knee.

"This is much better," he said, rubbing his hands up and down her back. He bent his head to taste a spot on her neck bared by the upswept curls.

Maggie kept her eyes closed. She kept her hands still where they pressed against his chest. But she couldn't keep her nipples from tightening as Mac rubbed her front against his, or a hot streak from shooting through her when his moist tongue left her neck and pushed gently into her ear.

Good grief, she thought, how did such a mountain manage to create such delicate shivers in every nook and cranny of her body? Then she forgot to think at all as his mouth took hers. He shifted her weight against his right arm. With his other hand he reached up to tug loose her curls. With a grunt of pure male satisfaction, he lifted his head to watch her hair spill down in a tumbling mass. That basic task done, he looked into her eyes.

"I want you so much it hurts, but I suspect you won't accept grits as a peace offering if I come on too strong again. So from here on out it's your call. You set the pace, Maggie. Tell me what you want."

She opened her eyes and gave him a clear direct look. "I want you, Mac. It'd be nice to get you and grits, too, but I'll settle for you."

"That's all I needed to know."

With an easy movement he bent and scooped her up in his arms, then headed down the hallway toward the bedroom.

Chapter Five

Maggie reveled in another totally new sensation as Mac carried her through the dim hall. Being carried was even more exciting than having a shoulder at just the right height to rest her head on while dancing. As best she could remember, no man had ever tried to hoist her off her feet before. *Talk* her off her feet and into bed maybe, but nothing quite this physical. She began to appreciate that there was a lot more to this seduction scene than she'd experienced before. She rather liked it, she decided, enlivening the short trip down the hall by exploring Mac's conveniently placed ear with her tongue.

Mac reacted to her explorations with satisfying directness. He dumped her on the bed with more haste than finesse and was beside her before she could catch her breath. This time his kiss was fierce and hot and demanding. Maggie kept her eyes closed once more, but now her hands roved as feverishly as his. She plucked distractedly at the buttons on his shirt, not content until she'd undone enough to slide her hands inside. Crisp hair curled over powerful chest muscles, teasing the tips of fingers. She delighted in the touch and the scent of him, strong and hard and very male.

When Mac slipped his own fingers under her satin tunic and shaped one aching breast, Maggie gasped. He slanted his mouth across hers more firmly, demanding her response. With a slow sure movement he pulled her body under his and pressed her down into the thick comforter.

"Your body fits against mine as well horizontally as it does vertically," he murmured. "I like being able to kiss most of the important spots without getting permanent spinal damage."

Maggie's breath slammed out of her as Mac suited action to words. With a quick bend of his head, he closed his mouth over a breast. She felt him hot and wet through the silk. When his teeth took the nipple and teased it into taut stiffness, a shaft of pure sensation shot through her.

He found the side button of her pants and slid them and her lace panties down to her ankles. With a muttered curse, he sat up to fumble impatiently at the tiny straps of her sandals. He finally pushed shoes, slacks and panties off in one tangled mass. Maggie reached for him and he turned back to her, but he caught both her hands loosely in one of his and stretched them over her head.

"Let me look at you, Maggie. Let me drink in the sight of those long luscious legs and gorgeous gold curls."

Maggie blushed in the half-light. She felt indescribably wanton with her lower body naked and exposed to the cool night air, not to mention his decidedly hot stare and her satin tunic sliding sensuously over highly sensitized nipples. She twisted her hands free and undid the last of his shirt buttons.

"Your turn, Mac. Let me look at you."

She pushed his shirt off shoulders so broad they blocked out all the light from the hallway when he leaned over her. Her hands fumbled at his belt buckle. With an impatient movement, he got up to rid himself of the rest of his clothes. Maggie gave in to the pleasure of watching him, then quickly pulled off her last piece of satin.

She lay back and let her eyes rove with hungry appreciation over his massive body. He fumbled in his pants pocket for a small foil package and turned away for a moment. A warm glow lodged just under her heart at his unquestioned willingness to take responsibility for her protection. When he turned back, she eyed his rampant manhood in the dim light and bit back a grin. The man certainly ran true to size!

She wondered briefly if it was possible to have too much of a good thing, then gave up all attempt at rational thought as Mac lowered himself to her side. One of his legs nudged her apart, and he slid a callused palm down her belly. His fingers tugged playfully at her nest of curls, then buried themselves in her wet heat.

Maggie arched against him. Her breathing changed to shallow panting gasps as he moved his fingers in and out, slowly, deliberately, while his thumb explored the sensitive little nub at her core. His hands tantalized and roused her to fever pitch. When he lowered his head and took an aching nipple into his mouth once more, Maggie thought she would explode.

"Not yet, Maggie my sweet," he whispered. Removing his hand, he positioned himself atop her body. "First I want to feel you all around me."

Holding her head still with both hands, watching her eyes in the dim light, Mac pushed himself into her welcoming warmth.

Long hot moments later, after his hands and his mouth and driving manhood had taken her to incredible heights of sensation, Maggie gave a hoarse cry. Waves of pleasure swamped her, and the darkness behind her closed lids shattered into splinters of bright light. Mac echoed her panting cry as her tightness gripped him in rippling waves. He muffled his shout of satisfaction against her neck and thrust deeply, following her over the edge.

Hours later, or so it seemed to Maggie, she roused herself enough to run light fingers through the dark head resting on her breast. Mashing it to a pulp, really. Even with most of his weight on his forearms, Mac crushed her into the mattress. She wiggled and tried to shift to a more comfortable position, only to have him lift his head and grin down at her.

"So soon, Maggie m'girl? Without even a nourishing snack to sustain your energy? Well, we fly-boys aim to please. If you're ready, I'll do my best."

"You big lummox, stop grinning or I might force you to make good on your boast." Maggie tried again to shift him. He let himself be moved off her body only enough to insert his hand between them and cup her breast.

"Boast? I never boast. But I need sustenance after a good workout even if you don't. I think a little midnight feeding will do it."

Before Maggie understood his meaning, he'd lowered his head and began a slow sweet suckling at her breast. His hand pushed the firm mound up so his mouth could draw at the nipple, then covered half her breast with hot wetness.

In total amazement, Maggie felt streaks of heat shoot through her again. And again, when he woke her up an hour later. Only after he'd pulled her on top of him and made her take her bedsprings to the limit of their endurance did he fall asleep himself.

She awoke again just as gray dawn was beginning to lighten the room. Without having to reach across the bed, she knew he wasn't there. She lay quietly, her eyes closed, while a series of incredibly erotic visions danced behind her eyelids. Lord, she hadn't really moaned like that, had she? Her raw throat and the tenderness between her thighs mocked her own denials.

She was about to bury her head in the covers at the thought of some of her more energetic activities when the unmistakable scent of fresh coffee reached her.

Heavens, he was domesticated, she thought. Untangling herself from the bedclothes, she slipped on the faithful short terry robe and padded down the hall to the living room. She pulled up short at the sight of Mac, slacks riding low on lean hips and shirt hanging open to display that massive chest. He was leaning casually against her desk with a steaming cup of coffee in one hand and an open folder in the other. Even from across the room, Maggie could see it was the propulsion-test folder.

The warm greeting bubbling on her lips died. Her eyes fastened on the folder in growing consternation. Was that what all this was about? Had he wined and dined and put on that admittedly spectacular bedroom performance to change her mind about that damned test? Doubts swamped her, even as Mac looked up and met her suspicious gaze.

His own slow smile of greeting died. There was no mistaking the direction of her thoughts as her eyes moved from the folder to his face. He watched her thoughtfully for a few moments, then greeted her in a neutral tone.

"Morning, Maggie."

If the woman had a problem, he wasn't going to help her with it. She could darn well spit it out.

"I see you make yourself at home, MacRae. Anything else you'd like access to? After my body and my private reports, that is?"

Whew! When she let loose, she did it with both barrels. Mac told himself to stay calm. There was nothing in this report he hadn't already seen. It was government property, for Pete's sake. Hell, he had a copy of it on his desk at work. Maggie's own people had sent it over, as she'd remember if she hadn't been so busy jumping to her angry conclusions.

Still, Mac knew he shouldn't have just picked it up and started reading while he waited for her to awake. He also knew he should apologize, but rational thought warred with stung male pride. The woman had just spent the night in his arms. How the hell could she think what she so obviously did?

Pride won. Setting his mug down with a thump that sloshed coffee over onto the damned report, he started across the room toward her. When she backed away from him nervously, he stopped short. His jaw tightened ominously.

"Dammit, Maggie, that report isn't private. I've seen it several times. It was lying open on your desk."

"The point is, it was on *my* desk, MacRae."

Even as the words tumbled from her mouth, Maggie knew she was making too much of the whole thing, but she couldn't help herself. She hadn't had that many lovers during her otherwise adventurous thirty-three years. But based on her limited experience, she thought what she and Mac had shared last night was special. It hurt to think it may not have been so special, after all, but something rather sordid. Angry and confused, she wrapped her arms around her waist.

Mac gave her a long hard look, then began buttoning his shirt.

"Fine, it's your desk. Nice to know you think I'm the kind of guy who has ulterior motives for sleeping with a woman, Maggie. You'll understand if I don't hang around for any more of your flattering comments. I have to get home before the boys wake up and put two and three together."

Miserable, Maggie stood stiff and silent as he gathered the rest of his clothes. When he let out an exasperated sigh and stopped in front of her, she set her jaw in mulish lines.

"Maggie, this is crazy. We need to talk this out."

"I don't want to talk right now," she said to the solid chest blocking her view. "Right now, all I want is for you to leave. It was fun, MacRae, but don't overstay your welcome."

Mac's breath hissed in at her flippant words. "Why the hell is it that every time we get together, it starts with magic and ends with an argument?"

When she refused to respond, he yanked the door open. "I'll talk to you later when we've both had time to cool off."

He was gone before Maggie had a chance to think of a suitably devastating response.

Chapter Six

Cool off indeed, Maggie fumed all through her quick breakfast and preparations for work. She didn't need to cool off, she needed space. Lots of it. She needed time away from a certain Colonel MacRae and his overwhelming presence. She needed...Maggie sighed and shoved the folder into her briefcase. What she needed was to put the whole incident into perspective.

It didn't help that she knew Mac was right, that she had overreacted. She felt slightly disgusted with herself as she wheeled her Jag through the crisp morning air. She knew darn well that much of her anger had stemmed from a combination of surprise and old-fashioned embarrassment. She'd never responded to any man the way she had to Mac. In the privacy of her car and her thoughts, the memory of their activities the night before still made her blush.

The early-morning drive helped her relax. It took half an hour to reach the base from her rented condo in the little resort village of Destin. The most enjoyable stretch of her drive began when she crossed the high bridge spanning the channel connecting Choctawahatchee Bay to the Gulf of Mexico. Ahead of her was Santa Rosa Island, with its rolling dunes, feathery sea oats and blinding white sand. Emerald-green gulf water sparkled on the left, while the huge bay stretched to the horizon on the right.

The sunlight dancing on the water and the smooth rush of waves washing the shore restored Maggie's usual good humor. By the time she pulled the Jag into her parking slot behind the long low World War Two-era building that held her office she had her ready smile back in place.

"Morning, team," she cheerfully greeted her small staff, who were assembled for their daily meeting. As she edged her way through the crowd in her tiny office, which had to double as a conference room, Maggie firmly suppressed a fleeting image of the spacious corner office in the Houston high-rise she'd left behind.

"Okay, we've got a lot to cover this morning. Let's start with the reds."

Within days of her arrival, Maggie and her staff had devised a color-coded system for dealing with the avalanche of issues facing them. Red signaled a potential hazard that required immediate attention to avoid danger to health or welfare; yellow, a hazard that could result in action against them by a regulatory agency but wasn't imminently threatening; blue, a task they felt needed attention but could wait; and green, a purely administrative requirement. The fact that Maggie firmly refused to waste her small overworked staff's talents on greens had won their immediate loyalty.

"We found a couple of more transformers leaking PCB last week, Maggie," said one. "I'm going out with the folks from the exterior electrical shop this morning to replace them. I'll try to get the shop to move a little faster on completing the survey."

Maggie nodded her approval. PCB, or polychlorinated biphenyl, was a highly toxic chemical compound used extensively in electrical transformers before its cancer-causing characteristics were fully understood. Eglin, like most cities across the nation, faced massive challenges in recording and replacing older transformers. The base was almost a year late in completing the survey of the hundreds of transformers used to channel power at all the test sites scattered across the half-million acres. Higher priorities had eaten away at the money and time needed for the survey, even with an extension. They only had a few more months to get it done before the extension ran out and they faced heavy fines.

"Do that, Jack. I know the shop is as strapped for manpower as we are, but we've got to get that survey done. Let me know how it goes."

An intense young woman opposite Maggie spoke up. "We found some seepage on Site 22 last week. I think it may be an abandoned underground storage area."

Maggie grimaced. Burying was the accepted method of disposing of toxic waste twenty, even ten, years ago. The nation was just beginning to understand the effects as toxic waste escaped from rusted containers and seeped into the ground. With all the tests conducted at Eglin over the years, they had dozens of known underground storage sites and probably as many that were never properly recorded.

"How bad is it?" she asked.

The woman looked at her notes. "There's a small pool of greenish liquid, with bubbling at one edge. I'm going out with the Bio-environmental folks from the hospital this morning to take samples for analysis."

Telling her she'd join them, Maggie finished her short meeting. She was on her way back from the washroom, where she'd changed her linen skirt and high heels for the jeans and rubber wading boots she kept in her office, when her intercom rang.

"Dr. Wescott, it's May in Colonel Stockton's office. The boss just got a call from the lab. They'd like you to meet with them this morning to go over the propulsion test."

"I can't do it this morning, May. See if you can set it up for this afternoon and call me back. I'll be on my beeper."

Maggie replaced the phone with a twinge of guilt. She could've rearranged her schedule. After all, the test was a top priority. But the small act of defiance somehow made her feel better about last night. With a cheerful nod to her crew, she clumped out of the office and went off to explore the green slimy gook.

When she entered the armament lab's paneled conference room later that afternoon, she was once again in her skirt. The soft cream-colored linen was paired with a gold-patterned silk blouse and high-heeled sandals. A long strand of cultured pearls gave her added dignity, she thought. She suspected she'd need all the professionalism she could muster for this meeting.

The half-dozen or so men present stood up as she entered. A couple of them, including an older distinguished-looking man who should have known better, stared outright. She wasn't quite the type of engineer they were used to dealing with, if Maggie read their assorted expressions right. Well, here we go again, she thought.

"Good afternoon, gentlemen, I'm Dr. Wescott." She moved to an empty chair on one side of the long polished table. Setting her briefcase down, she went around the room to meet each man individually. Pleasantries done, she sat down and looked inquiringly at the man who'd introduced himself as Dr. Ames, the lab's deputy director. It was their meeting, she thought. They could darn well take the lead.

The older man shook his head slightly and squared his tweed-covered shoulders. "Ah, Dr. Wescott, Colonel MacRae asked me to get the propulsion team together so we could discuss your objections to the test. I'm not sure we understand some of your concerns."

"My team's concerns were detailed in the draft report they sent over several weeks ago," Maggie responded coolly. Then, with a small sigh to herself, she relented. Ames probably hadn't even read the report. Besides, she preferred a cooperative mode of operation. "However, I appreciate the chance to discuss the project in detail with you. I understand it's an important test for Eglin, and I'm part of the team now."

"Good. We've set aside an hour for Major Hill to brief you and answer your questions."

Ames settled himself with a condescending smile into the chair at the head of the table and nodded to the young major standing by the podium. Maggie decided to ignore the pompous deputy, and turned to the man who should really know what this project was all about.

Three hours later, the once immaculate conference table was littered with coffee cups and scattered papers. Discarded suit coats lay over the backs of chairs and various charts filled a large corkboard. Major Hill had abandoned his canned briefing and was standing by a built-in blackboard, scribbling notes as the group worked their way through one particularly complex chart covered with annotations and formulas.

Mac entered the conference room through his office's connecting door. He stopped short at the sight of Maggie and his deputy bent over the table, trying to read one of the chart's more obscure formulas.

Waving the other men back into their chairs as they started to rise, he leaned against the wall and waited patiently for Maggie and Ames to finish. His eyes passed over the way the soft linen clung to her delectable tush, and he shook his head in despair. Her wardrobe was wreaking havoc with his self-control.

"Dr. Wescott."

Mac greeted her gravely when the pair finally finished examining the chart and straightened up. His firm handshake held Maggie's until she tugged it free.

"Colonel MacRae." She nodded curtly.

His small private smile gently mocked her. He held her gaze for a moment, then turned an inquiring look on his deputy.

"We're getting there, Mac," Ames responded heavily. "We've resolved most of the minor questions and are just getting into some of the major issues. Dr. Wescott has some valid concerns.''

Mac bit back a smile at his deputy's reluctant admission. Ames had been a brilliant scientist in his time, but he'd peaked a few years ago. Now that he was close to retirement, he filled his time more and more with administrative duties and less with the research that was the lab's lifeblood. Mac bet Maggie had probably given him a real run for his money.

''Good. I won't interrupt you, then. Dr. Wescott, if you would, please stop by and see me before you leave.''

Maggie tried to think of some important meeting she had pending, but Mac was gone before she could tell him he could go whistle Dixie—professionally speaking, of course.

It was several hours later when the group in the conference room finally gathered up their assorted papers. Maggie had a pounding headache and was in no mood to face Mac. She knocked irritably on his office door, then entered without waiting for an answer.

He was on the phone and waved her to one of the soft leather chairs in front of his desk. Maggie tossed her briefcase down but was too restless to sit. While Mac finished his conversation, she prowled around his roomy corner suite. It had most of the trappings of a military commander's office—the requisite set of flags, a large conference table, a computer on the credenza—but few of the plaques and memorabilia most military personnel liked to display. The only real personal touches were a small picture of Mac giving a thumbs-up in the cockpit of some sleek lethal-looking jet and a picture of him with the twins, their laughing faces surrounded by bright blue sky and a tangle of fishing tackle.

His call finished, Mac watched as she settled herself with a deliberate touch of defiance in the chair across from him. His small sigh wasn't lost on Maggie.

''I take it this isn't a good time to talk about what happened last night,'' he said.

He leaned back in his massive desk chair. It probably cost the government a fortune to build one big enough to keep from folding under his bulk, Maggie thought nastily.

"No, it's not," she snapped. "I just spent five difficult hours with the lab's best and brightest. And I'm tired."

She stopped abruptly as she remembered just why she was so tired. She hadn't gotten much sleep last night. A quick glance at Mac's glinting eyes told her he was remembering, too.

"Look, Mac. I'll do my best on this damn test. Just get off my back."

Maggie bit her lip in real chagrin. Her words conjured up another decidedly erotic memory, and hot blood crept up her cheeks. She ignored the wide grin spreading across Mac's face. She got to her feet and reached for her briefcase.

"Maggie, we need to talk."

She turned at his quiet words. "Not now, please. I'm still sorting out last night in my own mind. I know I overreacted to your reading the report this morning, and I apologize for that."

Mac felt a spear of relief in his gut. He'd worried that the damn report would stand between them like a wall. Maggie's candid apology eased his tense neck muscles, but her next words had them tightening into knots again.

"I think we've both moved too fast, Mac. We need to slow this—this relationship down a bit. Why don't you call me later in the week and we'll find a time to talk?"

Pure unaccustomed anger surged through him. He wasn't about to let her get away with this call-me-sometime crap. Not after last night. She'd given herself to him totally, and his every instinct told him she wasn't the kind of woman to do that lightly. He forgot his promise to let her set the pace. He forgot his own determination not to rush her, as he had that night in his truck. He wanted to pick her up, carry her to the couch in the corner of his office and show her just how slow she thought she could take it. Only the sight of her white face, with faint blue shadows of fatigue under her eyes, stopped him.

"All right, Dr. Wescott. You've got your reprieve. But don't kid yourself that either you or I have much control over what's happening between us. Now go home and get some sleep."

He handed her her briefcase and very nobly resisted the urge to kiss her unconscious. She left with a definite flounce of cream-colored linen.

Mac watched from his office window as she crossed the street in front of the lab and climbed into her Jag. The sleek green sports car was the number-two priority in her life, he recalled. He was thinking seriously about rearranging her priorities, not to mention her clothes and her hair and her bedcovers, when his deputy, Dr. Ames, knocked on the door.

Turning, Mac greeted the older man. "Still here, Jim? Did you get everything resolved?"

"Not quite. We're going to have to modify the test significantly. That Wescott woman is stubborn as hell."

Mac made no comment. He wasn't about to argue about Maggie with anyone.

"Ed Stockton should have known better than to let her exercise veto power over this project."

"Why?" Mac asked coolly. "I've seen her credentials. She's certainly better qualified than some of the folks we've had reviewing our proposals."

"Oh, on paper, she looks good," Ames allowed.

Mac was thinking of a few other things she looked good on, as well, such as rumpled bedclothes, when Ames's next words caught his attention.

"Don't you think it's rather coincidental that she left a plush job with a corporation that's very much against alternate energy sources to come here? And one of the first things she does is put the kibosh on our test?"

Mac regarded his deputy steadily for a long minute. "What are you implying, Jim?"

"I'm not implying anything. I just find it interesting that this particular propellant has a lot of potential for commercial use. If our test succeeds, it could cut into the oil companies' profits. Be a threat to Dr. Wescott's former employers."

"We got the draft report challenging the test over a month ago, well before Dr. Wescott's arrival. Did the final signed report differ from the draft substantially?" Mac kept his voice level, fighting his rising anger.

Ames fidgeted with his tie. "I didn't read the draft myself. Major Hill briefed me on the key points. The final report included essentially the same issues, but in much more detail. Someone put a lot more work into that final product."

"Maybe if we'd put as much effort into our initial test design, we wouldn't have the problem we have today," Mac responded. "Stay with it, Jim. Let me know how you work out the remaining issues."

When his deputy left, Mac turned back to the window. The green Jag was gone. Ames's suspicions simmered at the edges of his mind, but he refused to accept them. Instinctively he knew the laughing smiling woman that was Maggie wasn't involved in anything like what Ames hinted at. He also knew that his deputy was out of touch with current technology-sharing. Transfer of the technology developed by the air force to commercial use was a side benefit of their work. Mac knew his staff had already shared information on this particular propellant at a recent consortium of military and civilian scientists. There was enough material about it now in the public domain to preclude the big energy concerns from trying to sabotage their test.

Still, Ames had made Mac realize there was a lot he didn't know about Dr. Marguerite Wescott. Such as why she'd really left Houston. And why a woman with her credentials would be content with field-level work. They'd talked about a lot of things during dinner the previous evening, but most of it was lighthearted banter, the kind men and women engage in during the first part of any courtship dance.

After what they'd shared last night, Mac wanted to know more, a lot more. He wanted to know the woman beneath the easy smile and mop of curls. He didn't like the thought that there were still parts of Maggie he wasn't privy to. With a determined snap, Mac turned off his office lights and left.

Chapter Seven

"Hey, Maggie!"

A loud bark almost drowned the enthusiastic yell. Maggie turned to see the twins waving energetically from the other side of the small cove. She waved back, then waited while Woof bounded toward her along the narrow strip of beach, with Davey—or was it Danny?—dragging behind on his leash. The other twin and a short stout woman followed in their sandy wake.

"Ugh, hello, Woof." Maggie tried to keep the massive paws off her chest and the wet slurping tongue off her face. She held him at arm's length while Davey/Danny struggled to reduce the dog's ecstatic greeting to a wagging tail, though even that furious action threatened to knock them both over.

"Whatcha doin' here? This is our favorite spot. Woof loves the water, but Dad says we can't let him loose where people go, so we always come here."

"I can understand why." Maggie smiled down at the boys while she held her shirtfront out with both hands to shake off the wet sand. Splotchy paw prints decorated the once pristine white cotton.

"I'm here checking some erosion along the shore, and no, I didn't know it was your favorite spot."

"Mrs. Harris, this is Maggie Westlake. Remember, we told you? She likes grits." The boys knew their manners, even if they couldn't remember names.

"Maggie Wescott." She smiled at the older woman and held out her hand. As her fingers were encased in a hard grip, Maggie suddenly remembered Mac's saying his housekeeper was a former prison warden. Clearly this was she.

"Hello, Dr. Wescott. Colonel Mac mentioned he had dinner with you last week."

If the older woman knew that the dinner date had lasted until morning, her bland expression gave no sign. Nevertheless, Maggie felt a surge of self-consciousness as the woman's bright eyes assessed her from head to toe.

Luckily she was spared the necessity of answering when one of the twins tugged on her sleeve.

"You wanna come with us, Maggie? We've got a special place down the beach and nobody knows about it 'cept us and Mrs. Harris. We'll show you some real neat stuff."

Maggie glanced at her watch. After a long morning in her deserted office catching up on paperwork, she'd intended to spend a few hours checking for herself the erosion along Eglin's north shoreline. She'd become so absorbed in taking notes and clambering over uprooted tree stumps that she'd forgotten the time. It was too late now for the errands she'd planned to run this beautiful Saturday afternoon. Tossing aside her plans, she gave herself up to the boys' bubbly companionship.

"Sure, I'd love to see something special. If you guys and Mrs. Harris don't mind sharing it."

"Nah, she doesn't mind, do ya?"

The older woman's plump face lost its blandness when she smiled down with genuine affection at the twins. "No, I don't mind at all. Why don't you two and Woof lead the way?"

Maggie admired the woman's strategy as the boys and Woof charged down the beach, wildly splashing through the shallows. She fell in beside Mrs. Harris, and they followed at a more leisurely pace.

"We walk along this beach almost every afternoon," the older woman said. "I thought it would take some of the edge off their collective energy, but the air and the water only seem to revive them after a tough day at school. They especially love coming here on weekends when they don't have homework hanging over their heads. My name's Kate, by the way."

"Please, call me Maggie. The boys do."

"Yes, I noticed. They talked a lot about you after the soccer game last weekend." Kate cast her a shrewd look. "They like you. So does Colonel Mac, unless I miss my guess."

Maggie blinked at the woman's bluntness. She bit back the quick retort that evidently the colonel didn't like her all that much. He hadn't called in five and a half days—not that she was counting.

"I like the boys, too. They're lively and bright."

The woman beside her snorted. "Too lively on occasion. It's a good thing I've still got my nightstick. It's the one souvenir I took with me into retirement. I keep it hanging on a very prominent peg in the kitchen. So far, just the threat of it has worked."

Maggie chuckled, then asked, "How long have you been with them?"

"Well, I came down here a couple of years ago. I'd just retired from the Federal Bureau of Prisons and thought I'd just laze the rest of my days away in the sun. That lasted about a week. Luckily, Colonel Mac advertised for a housekeeper about the time I started counting damp spots on the walls for entertainment."

By the time they caught up with the twins, Kate had Maggie laughing delightedly with stories of her days "in the pen," as she termed it.

"C'mon, Maggie, look here!"

Two pairs of excited blue eyes and two very wide grins told her this was the special place. Maggie looked around the small cove with interest. A fallen tree edged the bank and scrub littered the narrow beach, but try as she might, Maggie couldn't see what held their interest.

"Here, right here."

Danny, yes, she was sure it was Danny, pointed. He was the one with the single dimple in one freckled cheek. He grabbed hold of her hand and together they waded toward the north end of the cove, where the water of the bay lapped right up against the rugged shore. It wasn't until they were almost upon it that Maggie noticed the indentation halfway down the bank.

"It's a cave. Dad says Indians used to camp here in the old days. This was one of their hiding places. See, it goes way back behind the bushes and has all kinds of neat stuff in it."

Danny pulled her closer to the hole and bent his body half into the shadowed darkness. Maggie resisted the urge to pull him out. So far she hadn't seen any snakes or wild creatures in the area, but she didn't much care for dark holes, inhabited or otherwise.

"There're bunches of arrowheads in there and some old pot bits," Davey explained while his brother continued to root around in the cave. Danny emerged, grimy but triumphant, gripping some small stones. He took Maggie's hand and poured them into her palm. Sure enough, they were arrowheads.

Maggie didn't know much about archaeology, but she did know that northwest Florida has been home to several prehistoric tribes. They'd hunted the vast forests and fished the rich waters of Choctawahatchee Bay. In fact, the bay was named for one of the early tribes. There were several major historical sites and hundreds of minor finds scattered across the Eglin complex.

Her staff had briefed her about the consultant from Florida State University who was on call for archaeological matters. He was supposed to help catalog finds and do the necessary paperwork whenever there was any test activity that might affect a historical site.

"Dad says we can't take them 'cause they have to be registered or something. But we can play with them if we're careful."

Maggie knew there was a whole storeroom of as yet uncataloged artifacts somewhere on base. But archaeological-consultant fees ranked low on the list of the base's priorities.

"Go ahead, look inside and see how many there are."

"Ah, no, thanks, Davey. I'll take your word for it." No way was she going to stick her head or any other part of her anatomy into that hole.

"Chicken!" Dave taunted over Maggie's laughing protests. His twin took up the refrain, with enthusiastic accompaniment from Woof. Mrs. Harris added her voice to the general cacophony, telling the boys to lay off. Then a deep voice interrupted them all.

"You have to learn to take a lady at her word when she says no, boys."

"Dad! You're home."

The boys scooted up the bank, Woof at their heels, and threw themselves at their father. Mac wrapped a big arm around each of them, only to let go to ward off Woof's happy greeting. The boys shouted with laughter when Woof managed to sneak in a wet swipe at their father's face on one of his bouncing tries.

Maggie watched the four of them. Whatever else the exasperating man might be, he was a good parent. Their unabashed joy in each other shone through like a beacon.

She and Mrs. Harris climbed the slight bank as Mac finally calmed dog and boys.

"Hello, Kate. I expected to find you and the boys here, but I didn't expect to find you had company."

Maggie sucked in her breath as the corners of Mac's mouth pulled up in a slow easy smile. Damn, one smile and he could make her forget five and a half days without a call—almost.

She started to return his greeting, only to lose his attention to a demanding nine-year-old.

"Did you fly the F-15 back, Dad? Did you? How'd it handle?"

"Yes, Dave, I flew it back. And it was worth waiting a week for. It cuts through the air like the Eagle it's named for. Come on back to the house and I'll tell you all about it." He ruffled the boy's hair, then turned to Maggie.

"Why don't you come back with us? I smelled something delicious when I passed through the kitchen on my way out here." His twinkling eyes told her he knew very well she could resist *him,* but probably not the offer of food.

"Yeah, please come, Maggie," said Davey. "Mrs. Harris made lasagna. You'll like it better'n grits, even."

"How can I pass up an offer like that? But I left my car parked back up the beach. I better go get it."

"We'll go with you, so we can show you the way."

The boys slithered eagerly back down the bank. Mac managed to grab Woof's collar just in time to keep him from joining them. He could just see Maggie driving down the road with a big hairy hound sticking out of the sunroof of her Jag.

"See you at the house." He smiled and turned to join a very interested Mrs. Harris.

By the time Maggie made it back to her car, answered the boy's excited questions about just how fast the Jag could go and followed their somewhat disjointed directions to their bay-front home, she'd managed to get a few questions of her own answered. So Mac had left unexpectedly for California to participate in some special test at Edwards Air Force Base. So he just got back this afternoon. So maybe that was why he hadn't called. . . .

Chapter Eight

Three hours, two helpings of lasagna and a long laugh-filled game of Monopoly later, Mrs. Harris sent the protesting twins to bed. She went upstairs herself soon after, with only one or two significant glances and a slightly smug grin.

Mac poured brandy into large snifters and led Maggie out of the cluttered den to the deck that ran the entire length of the back of the big house. The last rays of the sun streaked through dark clouds drifting above the bay. With a contented sigh, Maggie slouched down in a redwood lounge piled with weather-beaten cushions and stretched her long jean-covered legs out to rest on the deck rail. Woof immediately plunked his massive head down on her knees. Two soulful eyes gazed up at her in the dim light until she got the message and began to scratch behind his ears.

"I'm sorry I didn't get a chance to call before I left for California. I didn't like leaving things unsettled between us. I thought the conference would never end."

Maggie turned her head to study the man next to her. He was as relaxed as she in a huge battered chair. His face was hard to see in the fading light, but she could feel his eyes watching her.

"It was a long week for me, too, Mac." Her admission surprised her. "I half expected you to call to make sure Ames and I hadn't killed each other trying to resolve the rest of the test questions." She could see his white teeth as he smiled in the gathering darkness.

"Well, *you're* still alive. Is he?"

"Barely. The man is more stubborn than I am. We still haven't closed on one or two issues," Maggie warned softly. "If we don't resolve them this week, you may have to scrub the test."

"To tell you the truth, I'm sick and tired of that damn test," Mac grumbled. "I'm still carrying the scars from your raking me over when you found me reading your report. I was hurt by your thinking I'd had an ulterior motive for sleeping with you."

"I'm sorry, Mac," Maggie murmured as she swirled the brandy around in the heavy crystal goblet and scratched Woof's shaggy head absently. "I knew there wasn't a thing in that folder you hadn't already seen, but I was too upset to admit it. I'm not normally a suspicious person. I don't know what it is about you, about us, that makes me overreact so."

Mac grinned at her. "I've noticed that your emotions do run a bit high. Seems like every time we've been together, I've had to beat a hasty retreat. That's not a very satisfactory state of affairs for a military man."

"Well, why don't we declare a truce?" she asked lightly.

"Nope. No truce. A truce implies both parties shake hands, retire from the field of honor and go their separate ways."

"A cease-fire, then? An end to hostilities."

"Not good enough. Nothing so imprecise for us."

"Well, for heaven's sake, what *do* you want?" Maggie asked, exasperated.

"I won't settle for anything less than unconditional surrender."

Maggie bristled. She'd been her own woman too long and was too comfortable in her independence to accept his casual ultimatum.

"Whose surrender? Yours or mine?"

"What difference does it make?" Mac asked with a low chuckle. "If it matters, I give!"

He rose, then reached down to pull Maggie to her feet. Taking the glass from her suddenly nerveless fingers, he sat back on the rail and pulled her between his legs. Maggie gave a devout prayer that the railing was up to holding his weight before he tugged her head down to meet his.

A loud slurping sound brought them both back to consciousness long moments later.

"Woof, for Pete's sake, get away from that brandy!"

Mac eased her out of his arms to move toward the dog. Pulling a crystal goblet off the end of a long hairy nose, he shooed the grinning hound into the house.

Maggie waited silently in the dark while he tended to the dog, using the brief respite to try to settle her spinning senses.

"Come on, I'll take you home." His shape materialized beside her in the dark.

"You don't need to. My car's here."

Mac took her chin in his fingers and turned her face up to his. "We'll come back for it in the morning."

If there was a question in his words, Maggie didn't hear it. She heard only quiet conviction.

"You've filled my mind all week, Maggie. When I saw you with the boys this afternoon there on the beach, I felt like I'd truly come home. I've been aching to hold you in my arms all evening. Let me take you home."

With a sense that she was committing herself to something she wasn't quite ready for, something deeper and stronger than she'd ever felt before, Maggie nodded slowly.

With that nod, she knew she'd crossed a line, one she'd had in front of her throughout her varied personal and professional life. She'd always kept things light and kept herself on the move. Even the upwardly mobile and short-lived fiancé hadn't drawn the unspoken commitment from her Mac had. In fact, one of the main reasons she'd left Houston was to distance herself from the man who'd started pressuring her to put down roots, to take her position in the corporate world more seriously. Yet here she was, less than two weeks after meeting Mac, driving through the dark to a night of loving in his arms. Throughout the long trip back to her condo, she wondered just who had surrendered to whom back there on the deck.

As they rolled silently through the glowing Florida moonlight, Mac, too, examined his feelings, trying to understand the fierce satisfaction he felt to have this tousled, exasperating, wholly fascinating creature beside him. When he'd seen her there on the beach, laughing with the boys, a sense of absolute certainty had jolted through him. He wanted this woman—in his bed and in his life. Tonight he'd try to make her want him, too.

He smiled when he closed her condo door behind them. She stood uncertainly in the middle of her living room, looking at him with a slight frown.

"Don't worry so, Maggie. I won't ask anything of you you're not prepared to give."

"Damn that smile," Maggie said with a resigned sigh as she walked into his open arms. "It constitutes a lethal weapon."

Mac let her set the pace as she explored his lips. He contented himself with running his hands over the rear so obligingly at arm's reach and available to him in the tight jeans.

His smug confidence that he could control the pace shattered when she ran her hands down his chest, then lower still. When they moved slowly, deliberately, over his manhood, Mac sucked in a quick breath and pulled her hands away. Maggie tugged them free and went back to her erotic massage. The bulge in his jeans turned rock hard under her hands. Mac stood it as long as he dared, then groaned and pulled her hands away once more, this time twisting her arms behind her back and holding them there with a gentle grip.

"Maggie," he said on a shuddering breath.

"Don't worry, Mac," she looked up at him with a teasing glint in her green eyes. "I won't ask for anything you're not prepared to give."

That did it. With a low growl, Mac had her flat on her back on the soft carpet. Her arms were still twisted behind her back, causing her breasts to arch up invitingly toward him. Mac gave her a mocking smile that promised retribution, then bent his head and took one nipple into his mouth, his teeth worrying it until it grew hard. Maggie gasped as he continued to nip and suck at her aching breast through the soft cotton shirt. She tried to free her hands.

"Oh, no, Maggie m'girl. Not yet. I owe you for that little bit of teasing."

Mac pushed one heavy leg between hers and used it to pry her thighs apart. His free hand roamed down her front, to the deep jean-covered V between her legs. Maggie held her breath as he cupped her mound and ran his fingers along the seam of her jeans. She felt the heat of his hand even through the thick material. And it felt wonderful.

Mac, too, could feel her heat. For a few moments more he struggled to hold on to his own control as his hand shaped and stroked her femininity. He bent down to still her thrashing head and capture her soft moans in his mouth. All vestiges of playfulness disappeared. He gave in to the deep primal need of the male to cover his mate.

Maggie lay helpless as he released her arms and methodically removed both her clothes and his own. He made undressing a new erotic experience as his mouth touched everywhere his hands uncovered. By the time he had taken the few seconds to protect her and had repositioned himself at the juncture of her thighs, she barely had the strength to lift her legs around his waist as he directed. Mac tried to cushion her on his arms as he moved into her in long sure thrusts. Her back was spared, but her hips ground against the carpet with every move.

Mac took a handful of soft curly hair in both fists and held her head steady so he could look down into her face. He could tell by her soft moans and the gathering spasms of her satiny sheath that she was near her peak. For some reason, it was vitally important to see her face when he brought her to pleasure. Only after she'd arched under him and he'd seen, as well as felt, her shattering climax, did he allow himself to close his eyes and follow her over the edge.

Chapter Nine

"Well, I see the mountain has come to Muhammad," Ed Stockton tossed at her with a grin several weeks later. They'd just finished a meeting on a new education center to be built on base. Unfortunately the chosen site was right in the middle of a nesting area for red-cockaded woodpeckers, one of Eglin's endangered species. The meeting had been lively, to say the least, and Ed was glad it was over so he could turn to more interesting matters.

Maggie didn't pretend to misunderstand his sly comment. She stopped gathering up her papers to grin back at him. "Let's just say we met on the road to Mecca."

Ed had teased her once or twice about her pet name for Mac—the mountain—since the rumors began that she was seeing the lab commander on other than business. This was the first time she'd acknowledged their relationship publicly.

"The word is you and MacRae are making all the local hot spots together, kiddo."

"What there are of them," Maggie laughed back. In addition to the various official functions on base Mac had taken her to, they had explored the rich fare in their corner of northwest Florida. Under the twins' enthusiastic tutelage, Maggie had been given a crash course in the local haute cuisine.

Quick visions of restaurants with paper place mats and plastic baskets piled high with shrimp and mouth-watering fried amberjack filled Maggie's mind. Mac had taken them all out to various local eateries, seeming to derive as much enjoyment from watching Maggie and the boys together as from the food itself. Mrs. Harris enjoyed the treats, too. She ate the local fare heartily, but insisted they all go "home" for dessert. Somewhere in her long career she had picked up a fatal weakness for gooey, saccharine-sweet confections, and always had something freshly baked in the pantry. Maggie and Mac discreetly scraped off layers of frothy icing and passed the goo to an appreciative Woof rather than dampen Kate's pride in her culinary achievements.

But the desserts were nothing compared to the sweetness that followed when Mac drove Maggie home. When it wasn't too late, when one or the other of them didn't have an early conference or a flight, or the boys weren't expecting him back, Mac would stay the night and they would make long lingering love. Other times, when he couldn't stay, they shared more kisses and heavy breathing than anything else.

"Jim Ames was over here yesterday. He mentioned that their big test is set for next week." Ed Stockton's voice interrupted Maggie's private thoughts. She frowned.

"Yes, I know. It was a struggle getting them to agree to all our conditions. The last issue was the height of the dike around the ignition site. Mac approved the change—and the associated costs—over Ames's objections."

"Ames was also asking a lot of rather strange questions," Ed continued after a pause. "Like why you left a big oil conglomerate to come to this little corner of God's country. Particularly when we're about to test a new energy source that might make your former employers very, uh, nervous."

Maggie stiffened and turned slowly to face her boss. She let the implications of what he was saying sink in fully before she answered.

"And what did you tell him."

Ed blinked at the ice in her voice. "Hey, hold on there. Don't shoot the messenger. I told Ames he was nothing but a fussy old woman— Oops, sorry!"

Ed had a tendency to forget that some of the old euphemisms were taboo in the current more sensitive work environment. Maggie usually didn't hesitate to correct any of her crusty old boss's lapses, but this one she let slide.

"I just thought you'd want to know what you're dealing with."

Maggie gave him a hard clear look, then nodded. She walked back through the bustling yard to her office, for once not noticing the activity teeming around her.

Industrial espionage—that's what the old fart was implying. She thought indignantly of all the hours she'd humored the man, maintaining a polite respectful demeanor even when he asked the same question for the third or fourth time. Despite herself, she couldn't help wondering whether Mac knew of Ames's suspicions. Surely, he himself didn't think that about her, not after all they'd shared.

Mac came by early that evening to pick her up for a formal function at the base. He could tell something was wrong as soon as she opened the door. She'd caught her hair up with glittering rhinestone combs, and was wearing a long slinky red thing that almost covered her tall frame, except for the slit up one side that appeared to go all the way to her armpit. It was an outfit only someone with Maggie's long lithe beauty could carry off, and one that made Mac's mouth go dry. The look that should have gone with that getup was sultry and smiling. Instead, there was a slight furrow on Maggie's brow, quickly erased as she took in his full glory.

"Lord, Mac. I didn't think they made uniforms with padded shoulders like that," she teased.

"It's the shoulder boards. And this damn cummerbund. They make a man look like he's all trussed up."

Not hardly, Maggie thought, as she feasted on the sight of Mac in his dress uniform. The short tailored jacket of midnight blue sported a glittering array of medals, topped by shiny wings. It fastened with a single button at his trim waist, showing a deeper blue cummerbund, pleated white dress shirt and a jaunty satin bow tie.

"Is this the same man whose standard dress is worn jeans and old sweatshirts?" she asked with an awe that was only half-pretended.

"One and the same, Maggie m'girl. I'll prove it."

And he did, with a kiss that left them both breathless. Maggie was still trying to steady her racing pulses when he put a finger under her chin and tilted up her head.

"Your dress is spectacular—what there is of it—and I love your hair up. The only thing missing is the smile in your eyes. What's the matter?"

Maggie wasn't ready to talk to him about Ed Stockton's disclosures, nor the doubts they raised in her. Not now, with a big function ahead of them. Later, she thought. Later they'd talk.

"Nothing, Mac. I'm a little nervous about tonight's do, I guess. I haven't been to one of these before."

The Maggie he knew wasn't nervous about anything. Mac decided not to press the issue until they had time to thrash out whatever was bothering her. Later, he thought.

"Don't get your hopes up, honey," he warned as he escorted her outside. In honor of the occasion he'd brought his little sports car instead of the Jeep. "The Air Force isn't very old. We're the baby military service, don't forget. We're still feeling our way between ironclad British-mess traditions and fighter-pilot free-for-alls. What you'll see tonight will probably be a mixture of the best and the worst of both."

His words proved prophetic. Maggie couldn't remember ever attending any function where dignitaries were marched to a noxious-looking grog bowl for real or imagined slights. Everyone forgot the rules of the mess in the general hilarity and camaraderie that filled the ballroom. She laughed at the silly rituals and was moved to tears by the guest speaker. The former POW spoke quietly about his experiences in Vietnam. Looking around the room during his stark moving speech, Maggie noted fierce feelings of pride on the faces of the men and women in uniform as they listened to their comrade-in-arms. With a rush of indefinable emotion, she took in Mac's clenched jaw and intense eyes. The speaker finished with a simple prayer for the warriors left behind.

Mac held her close against him as they danced after the official part of the evening ended. Even when the music sped up and the younger couples around them gyrated across the floor, he held her close and moved to his own beat. They were among the last to leave.

If Maggie thought the long dinner, the numerous toasts and the intimate dancing had made Mac forget her earlier pensiveness, she soon learned her mistake. When the door of her condo closed behind them, he led her over to an armchair and sat down, pulling her onto his lap.

She was going to have to invest in some sturdier furniture, Maggie thought as the chair creaked ominously under them.

"Okay, now tell me why your eyes have had a shadow in them all night."

She looked up at him, surprised. She hadn't even thought of Ames's ugly insinuations for whole hours at a stretch tonight. How in the world had Mac seen through her laughter and tears to the worry beneath? She took a deep breath. Better to get it out than let it fester. Besides, it wasn't her nature to dissemble or hide her feelings for long.

"Ed Stockton told me Dr. Ames seems to think I have some ulterior motive in my objections to the propulsion test. Something to do with loyalty to my former employer."

Mac cursed his bumbling deputy roundly. "Ames is a fool, Maggie. You probably talked circles around him, and he reached for something to justify his own inadequacies. The test is a go for next week, isn't it?"

She nodded, a troubled frown creasing her brow.

"My people resolved every one of your objections, didn't they?"

She nodded again. "I had my deputy review the proposed changes, as well—he's the one who wrote the original draft report. He's satisfied with the new parameters."

"So that proves you're not trying to sabotage the effort." Mac ran his thumb lightly along her furrowed brow. "Don't let Ames's dithering bother you."

Maggie let her breath out on a ragged sigh. "I'll be glad when the darn thing's done. It seems as if this test has been hanging over us forever." Swallowing, she looked up at him. "It's still awfully dangerous, Mac."

"That's the nature of the test business," he reminded her quietly. "You know that as well as I do. We're pushing the edge of the envelope, stretching into the unknown with every new plane we take up, every new chemical or explosive we test. All we can do is ensure all possible safety factors are considered."

Maggie huddled against Mac's solid chest. She wanted desperately to believe his steady measured words. Normally she wouldn't have let a man like Ames bother her in the least. She had supreme confidence in herself and her professionalism. But she felt vulnerable lately, as if by giving in to Mac, she was laying open a part of herself that had been hers alone up till now. Her confidence had developed a soft spot where he or anything to do with him was concerned.

"Look at me, Maggie," Mac's quiet voice commanded. "I refuse to let you be bothered by Ames. Forget it. Forget him!"

Maggie couldn't hold back a smile at his crisp order. "Yes, sir!" She tried to sit at attention in his lap and give him a smart salute.

Mac groaned as her fanny wiggled against him and held her still. They both forgot Ames and the lab and the test and their own names for a good long time.

In fact, Maggie managed to push the propulsion test to the back of her mind. She'd done everything required by law or common sense to protect the environment and the people involved, and had other equally demanding projects to occupy her energies. Added to her pressure at work, Mac had given her some more things to fill her mind, not to mention her body and her heart. He'd begun to get downright grumpy about the evenings he couldn't stay with her and had to leave for his own home. And in a man as big and normally even-tempered as Mac, grumpy was definitely a state to be reckoned with.

"Something's got to give, woman. I don't like crawling out of your bed and sneaking back into my home like an adolescent."

Mac nudged Maggie out of her sleepy lethargy and settled her boneless body in the crook of his arm. She snuggled into his warmth contentedly, wishing he'd let her just drift off to sleep. They'd had this discussion several times already.

"I love you, Maggie."

That got her attention. Her heavy lashes fluttered open to find him staring down at her, a determined expression in his eyes.

"I hate leaving you at night. I want us together, in our own bed, every night. I think we should get married."

As proposals go, Maggie had had better, but none that tempted her as much. None that called out to her heart to grab hold of something permanent, something wonderful. She wanted desperately to say yes.

"I... I think we should think about it." She forced herself to meet Mac's eyes. "I think I love you, too, Mac. But I've thought I was in love before, and it didn't work out. We owe it to the boys to take this slowly."

Mac's eyes narrowed. "Don't use the boys as an excuse. This is between us. And what's between us deserves better than this sneaking around. I want to marry you."

Some of Maggie's independence reasserted herself. After all, it was her bed and her bedroom and her life.

"You need to work on your technique, Colonel. Men usually ask women to marry them, not order them." She tried to slip out of bed to put some distance between them.

"Oh, no, you don't." Mac pulled her back easily. "I want an answer, however the question was or wasn't phrased."

"I told you, I need to think about it!" she snapped. At his hurt look, Maggie relented. "Mac, you don't understand. I... I'm nervous about marriage. I came really close once, and when I did, a trapped feeling overwhelmed me and I bolted at the last minute. I left a good job in Houston because I just wasn't ready and my fiancé was."

Well, at least now he knew why she'd come to Eglin, Mac thought. For a long moment, he studied her. He knew her too well to think she was being coy. It hurt him more than he was prepared to admit that she had doubts when he had none at all. He'd known she was the one he wanted in his home and his heart from the moment he'd seen her up to her knees in water, poking in that dark hole with the boys.

"Okay," he said finally, levering himself off the rumpled bed. "Think about it. But think hard, Maggie m'girl. I may be big, but I'm not particularly slow or patient."

He reached down, took a handful of her hair in one fist and held her steady for his kiss. When he left, closing the door carefully behind him, he was breathing as fast and as painfully as she was.

Chapter Ten

Maggie was learning. She followed Mac's orders and thought hard over the next few days. She remembered her feelings of panic when her former fiancé had pressured her, although not quite as forcefully as the mountain had. She remembered how she'd run from him and her Houston job to escape her feelings of being trapped. And she compared those feelings to the intense urge she felt to accept Mac's hand and heart.

She didn't feel trapped with Mac, she felt...confused. Ten years or more of lighthearted wandering wherever her will and her talents took her were at stake. Suddenly they seemed trivial compared to what she suspected she might find with Mac and his two, correction, three, holy terrors.

Maggie had just tossed another page of doodles into her overflowing wastebasket when the crash phone rang. With Eglin's active flying mission, there were usually one or two in-flight emergencies a day, most of which ended routinely. Maggie or one of her staff monitored every call on the crash line. If the incident being reported turned out to be serious, they needed to respond. She picked up the receiver quickly.

"This is the Eglin command post. We have a report of an explosion on the range. The base commander has directed the disaster-response team to assemble immediately at Base Operations. Acknowledge."

Maggie's heart turned over in her chest. Telling herself not to panic, she waited until the command post rapped out her office code, then responded with the approved call sign.

Don't let it be the propulsion test! Dear Lord, please don't let it be the test! Her mind screamed the silent prayer as she grabbed her boots and jeans, slammed her office door shut and tore off her skirt and slip. Her fingers trembled, fumbling on the snaps. She grabbed her hard hat and was just pulling the thick disaster-response team checklist out of the bookcase when her intercom rang. She started to ignore it, but a quick glance told her it was Ed Stockton's direct line.

"Maggie, we just got a call. There's been an explosion."

She sucked in her breath. "Yes, I know. I just took the notification from the command post. I'm on my way out the door."

"Did they tell you the location or nature of the accident?"

"No." Maggie's last hope died at Ed's flat hard tone.

"It was Site 32. The propulsion test. Something went wrong."

"I was afraid it was," she rasped out. "Ed, Mac's out there!"

And Jack, her deputy, along with a lot of other people, she thought. She swallowed her gut-wrenching fear. Gripping the phone so hard her hand hurt, she forced herself to ask. "Any report of casualties?"

"Not yet. The fire department's on the scene right now. The chief himself went out for this one. He'll do whatever's necessary until the disaster-response team gets there."

Ed's words recalled Maggie with a jerk. "I've got to go. The team's assembling at Base Ops now. I've got our van with the radio in it. Please, please, let me know if you hear anything."

She knew the fire chief would be in direct contact with Ed, probably before he even called the command post to update them.

"Will do, Maggie. Be careful, okay? You know better than anyone how dangerous this may be."

She didn't need that reminder, Maggie thought as she forced herself to drive the speed limit the short distance to Base Ops. She knew it would take longer for the rest of the team to arrive, some coming from the hospital all the way on the west side of the base.

Please let Mac be okay, she prayed over and over in an unconscious litany. *Let me see him again.* They hadn't been together since Mac had delivered his marriage proposition three nights ago. Maggie refused to call it a proposal—it had really been more of a command—but it had filled her mind almost to the exclusion of everything else. She rubbed her eyes with a fist to hold back the threat of tears.

Forcing her personal fears from her mind, she made herself focus on her professional responsibilities. Mentally she reviewed everything she knew about the test. She'd gone over it with Jack again just this morning. Since he'd done the original analysis and wanted to cover the actual test, she'd agreed. Maggie refused to give in to the sick guilt that threatened to swamp her. She should have gone out to the test site, instead of Jack. He knew the test, knew all the properties of the chemicals they were using, knew the dangers. But it was her responsibility. And Mac may be hurt.

By the time she reached Base Ops and unloaded her gear, she had forced herself to an icy calm. She'd practiced with the disaster-response team a couple of times since coming to Eglin. The team took their responsibilities with deadly seriousness. Their practices were frighteningly realistic. They had to be. Eglin had an active flying mission and the population of a medium-sized city. Any type of accident could happen, from gas-main explosions to fires to airplane crashes. The exercise-team chief enlisted schoolchildren, wives and on-base civilians as participants in simulated bus crashes, hostage situations and major explosions of all types. Hospital personnel painted gory injuries on the players. The more realistic the better.

Their practice stood them in good stead now. As the various team members assembled, they ran through their checklists with brisk efficiency. The on-scene commander briefed them on what he knew, which wasn't much more than what had been relayed by the command post. Each team member then described what he or she knew of the test and the site. Maggie forced herself to detail calmly the environmental hazards to the other team members. Everything inside her wanted to scream at them to get on with it, to move faster. Her rational mind knew the danger of plunging blindly into an accident site. But emotionally, she wished she could jump in her van and take off without waiting.

After what seemed like hours, but was only minutes, the on-scene commander directed the team to an entry control/safe point coordinated by radio with the fire chief. Maggie ran to her van, accompanied by the chaplain and two bioenvironmental techs. Her four-wheeler could handle the rough range roads easily. She wheeled the van into the convoy of vehicles that drove off the main base, led by a police car with its siren screaming.

She kept the radio tuned to the fire-station crash line all during the long ride to the site. The firefighters were real pros, and the chief especially so. He kept chatter over the open radio to a minimum. Their lines were unscrambled and often monitored by civilians off base. There was no need to panic the general populace until they knew the scope of the disaster.

"It's Jack. Thank God!"

Maggie all but shouted as her van pulled up to the circle of police cars and fire trucks gathered at the entry-control point. Even from a distance she recognized her tall bearded deputy. Before the van had completely stopped rolling, Maggie slammed it into park and leapt out. As she ran toward Jack, she could hear the roar of flames and smell the sharp acrid scent of smoke in the air. Tall pines blocked the accident scene from sight.

"Jack, are you okay?" She grabbed his arm.

"I'm fine, boss. I wasn't on-site when it happened. I'd just come back to my car for some notes I needed."

"What happened? How bad is it?"

"It wasn't the propellant, Maggie. The stuff hadn't even been unloaded from the containers."

Maggie clutched his arm hard in relief. All during the long drive to the site, she'd dreaded hearing reports of toxic clouds spreading over the area.

"It was some kind of a freak accident. The crane lifting the firing tube into place snapped a cable, which in turn whipped into the mechanized loading vehicle. From what I can gather, sparks ignited the vehicle's fuel and caused the explosion. I wasn't there, though. The fire chief has the real poop."

Maggie glanced over to where the chief was briefing the on-scene commander. She turned back and asked the question eating at her soul.

"Jack, did you see Colonel MacRae before or after the accident?"

Jack shook his head slowly. He, like most of the engineering squadron, knew Maggie was dating the lab commander. Maggie caught back a ragged sob, then made herself take several deep breaths.

"The chief might know something," Jack volunteered. "He just came out of the accident area a few minutes ago."

Maggie knew she couldn't interrupt the fire chief as he huddled with the on-scene commander, but she watched them closely. When the commander turned away to take a radio call, she approached the sweating helmeted fireman.

"Chief, Colonel MacRae was supposed to be on-site for the test. Have you had contact with him?"

The stocky grizzled man turned to face Maggie. He admired and respected this vibrant young woman. She'd ridden with his fire crews during a couple of exercises and had spent a full day with his hazardous-materials team. If Maggie's own credentials hadn't already won his professional respect, her willingness to listen and learn from his people would have done it.

"Sorry, Dr. Wescott. I haven't seen him. There's still a lot of confusion in there." He nodded toward the flames they could see leaping above the treeline. "We should hear something soon."

He turned away to answer a call from the on-scene commander. They talked for a moment, then the commander called his team together. Maggie knew the man in charge both personally and professionally. She and Mac had been seated beside him and his wife at more than one social function. Maggie gave grateful thanks that he'd been in the job for more than two years and knew his stuff.

"Okay, this is what we have so far," the commander said. "A vehicle fire and explosion occurred just north of the control center at Site 32. Burning fuel sprayed several workers in the area. The fire crews have stabilized at least two people with severe burns, but there may be more."

He nodded to the senior medical rep. "Doc, make sure your folks call back for more burn-trauma kits, just in case. Additionally, the fuel ignited both structural and brushfires that are still burning. The lab folks moved the propellant and main rocket fixtures off-site immediately and they're out of range. Thank God we don't have that to worry about. But there may be other chemicals stored or brought out for the test. Fire crews are surveying the area now."

He took a deep breath, then finished with, "There were several lab and range control crews on-site. We're trying to get a firm head count. I'm going in with the chief now. Doc, you better come with me. The rest of you wait until I call you in."

Maggie bit her lip in an agony of frustration. Now that her worst fears of a major chemical disaster were allayed, every nerve and fiber in her body screamed for word of Mac. She forced herself to review again her disaster-response checklist, going over the sections on chemical and natural fires. Together, she and Jack added to the grease-pencil annotations on the checklist. She'd have to either call or fax a detailed report to both state and federal environmental agencies as soon as the imminent danger passed.

"Dr. Wescott, over here, please. Major, you, too."

Maggie looked up to see the on-scene commander returning. She and the senior bio-environmental medical engineer hurried over.

"Look, there are some barrels burning close to the control center. We couldn't find any lab folks who knew what they contained. The senior test engineer is one of those seriously injured. The chief has what markings his people could get off the barrels. I need you to get with him immediately and see if you can figure out if we have a danger of a secondary explosion on our hands."

Maggie and the young major hurried over to the worried fire chief. "What do we have?"

"I think they're chemical-waste containers, waiting to be transported to main base for disposal. I've called the numbers into the National Emergency Materials Center, but I need you to take a look and see what you think."

Maggie knew the twenty-four-hour hotline should respond within minutes. But even those few minutes could be too late for the people facing the danger of a secondary explosion. She pulled out her own copy of the materials directory and frantically scanned the listed agents that contained the numbers the chief cited. All were flammable, but should burn steadily, not explode. The men around her sagged with relief at the news. The call from the center confirmed her numbers a few minutes later.

"Thank God," the chief muttered. He picked up his hand radio and barked a series of short orders.

"The fire crews have contained most of the fires," the on-scene commander told his assembled team less than fifteen minutes later. "I'm moving the command post forward. Get your stuff. Public Affairs, you need to leave someone here to handle reporters. I don't want them on-scene until we ID the injured. Call me if anyone gets too persistent about wanting to film the scene. I want to clear it before you bring anyone forward. The rest of you gather your gear and move up."

Maggie, with Jack crammed between her and the chaplain, maneuvered her van over the bumpy road leading to the test-control facility. Several ambulances passed in the opposite direction, moving back toward the main road with lights flashing and sirens wailing. As soon as Maggie's van reached the site, the chaplain jumped out to hurry to the small triage area set up.

Maggie and Jack stood back to observe the devastated control facility and its surrounding area. Flames had scorched the earth all around and peeled the paint from the main metal building and its adjacent utility sheds. Electrical lines hung loose and snapping on one side of the building. Maggie directed Jack to get on the radio to the architectural section back at the main base. They needed a general idea of the floor plans of the main facility so they could check for underground drains that might carry burning fuel. While Jack was on the radio, Maggie desperately scanned the crowd of hurrying people.

She identified firefighters, security police, disaster-response team members in their distinctively marked hard hats, medics and a couple of frantic-looking civilians huddled to one side of the site. But, try as she might, she couldn't see any figure that came near Mac's dimensions.

She shivered with gut-wrenching fear when the chief approached her, his face grave.

"The doc just confirmed that Colonel MacRae was one of the injured. His burns aren't too bad, but he inhaled a lot of smoke pulling one of the crew out from under some burning debris. They've already transported him to the hospital."

He reached out a hand to steady her as she rocked back on her heels. "I'm sorry—I wish I could tell you more about how he is. But maybe Doc—"

Maggie was racing toward the clump of medics before he could finish.

The doctor assured her that Mac's condition, although critical, was stable. He was unconscious, and they feared lung damage. The doc couldn't, or wouldn't, say more, but he did add that the hospital commander, a noted surgeon, was already with the emergency-room crew awaiting the ambulances. Mac would be in good hands.

Maggie worked frantically with Jack to cover her checklist items. She guessed it would be at least three or four hours until the initial assessment was complete, and then there'd be days and weeks of investigative reports. But Jack could handle it from here.

The on-scene commander took her report, agreed Jack could handle the cleanup, then arranged a ride for her back to the main base in one of the police cars. With a grim shake of his head, he returned to the business at hand.

Chapter Eleven

"Maggie!"

The thin wavering cry greeted her as she got off the elevator and hurried down the pale hospital corridor toward the intensive-care unit. She recognized Davey's voice even before two figures came hurtling toward her from a small waiting room to one side. She knelt down to hug one small body in each arm.

"Don't cry, Danny," she whispered to a dark head buried in her shoulder. "I talked to the doctors downstairs. They're sure your dad will be okay."

Actually, the hospital commander, whom she'd met at a couple of parties, said he was sure Mac would pull through. Something about his being a tough son of a—

"Maggie, they say Colonel Mac has burned his lungs. That he's on a respirator." Mrs. Harris joined the group in the middle of the hallway. Maggie held out her hand and Kate gripped it hard.

Maggie loosened her hold on the twins. "Come on, troops. Let's get out of the hallway before the hospital orderlies sweep us up and out."

When the small group were seated in the waiting area, Kate wadded her handkerchief into a tight ball. "Did you say you talked to the doctors, Maggie?"

"Yes. The hospital commander stopped me on my way up here. He'd just checked on Mac and said he was doing as well as could be expected. I guess that's medical jargon for hanging in there. He's well enough for them to allow me a quick visit, anyway. Have you seen him?" she asked the boys.

"No, they wouldn't let us in," Davey answered waveringly. "The nurses have been real nice, though," he added after a quick swallow. "They come out every so often to let us know how he's doing."

"Well, I got the okay from the big man himself, so I'll go check. I'll see if they'll let you in."

Maggie wiped her finger gently across Danny's cheek to catch a lingering tear. She ached to kiss them both, but wasn't sure just how nine-year-old boys felt about kisses. She contented herself with one last ferocious squeeze.

The nurse in charge led her to one of the six beds that formed an open circle in front of the monitoring desk. Maggie wasn't prepared for the sight of Mac lying so still and helpless. He had a respirator tube taped to his mouth and various intravenous lines running into one arm. Gauzy tentlike structures covered both arms almost to his shoulders. A light gauze pad ran down one side of his face, from forehead to chin.

"Oh, Mac," she whispered. She wanted desperately to hold his hand, touch some part of him, but was afraid to disturb any of the bandages or cause him pain. She looked helplessly at the nurse standing on the other side of the bed.

"Don't worry," the woman said with a sympathetic smile. "He's doing fine. They've already decided not to send him with the others to the burn center in San Antonio. All these tubes make him look a lot worse off than he is."

Maggie smiled her thanks as the older woman turned to leave. She spent the next few minutes in a chair pulled up close to Mac's side, whispering softly to him. She could never recall afterward just what she tried to tell him in those first worry-filled moments.

The boys and Kate waited for her anxiously, along with a gathering crowd of Mac's co-workers and friends. Several officers who knew Mac were there already, some with their wives. The Eglin commander, a major-general almost as big as Mac, arrived within a half hour. He spoke to each of the boys and to Maggie and Kate after he'd taken a quick look in on Mac. The boys were allowed one short visit, which they took surprisingly well, before agreeing to go home with their friend Joey's dad.

Time passed in a blur for Maggie after that. It seemed as if there was a constant stream of folks coming to inquire about Mac. A surprising number knew her and knew of her relationship with him. Finally, late that evening, the traffic died down and it was just Kate and Maggie. They were allowed brief visits on the hour. Throughout the long night, the two women took turns making trips into the intensive-care unit, and their shared worry brought them closer.

Maggie spent her short spells at Mac's bedside perched on the edge of a hard chair, whispering soft nonsense to the accompanying hum of the hospital machinery. She finally worked up the nerve to touch him gently on his sheet-covered thigh. With every light stroke she thought about their last conversation, when he had told her he wanted them to marry. And with every stroke, she knew that was what she wanted, too, more than anything else in the world.

The same pattern repeated itself the next day. Kate convinced Maggie to bring some things to the house and stay with her and the boys, rather than make the long lonely drive around the bay to her Destin condo. She moved into a spare bedroom and managed to keep Woof out long enough for a brief nap in the afternoon before heading back to the hospital.

Mac's father arrived that evening. Maggie would've felt awkward if he hadn't greeted her with a warm twinkle in his blue eyes, which looked so like his son's her breath caught in her throat.

"So this is the little girl Mac's told me about." He grinned. The older man carried his years well on his big frame. "I understand you're soon to become part of the family," he added, taking her hand in both of his.

Maggie nodded slowly, but without hesitation. Another line crossed, she thought. "If he still wants me. I'm afraid I've given your son a rough time."

"Good," his loving dad replied with deep satisfaction. "Nothing worthwhile is ever easy in life."

He spent several hours at the hospital before Maggie convinced him to go home with Kate for the night.

Much later, when the hospital had settled into that peculiar somnolent state during which patients rested and the staff worked quietly, Maggie went in for her hourly visit and found Mac awake. He tried to grin at her around the tube taped to his mouth and failed miserably. It was the most gorgeous grimace Maggie had ever seen.

"Hello, Mac." She smiled down at him. "'Bout time you decided to rejoin the living." She sat down and began what by now was an unconscious light stroking of his thigh. "Kate and the boys and your dad were here earlier. They're all okay," she told him. She knew the boys would be his first concern.

"How...how long?" he managed to get out around the tube.

"Two days now. I'm not sure how much you remember. There was an accident, a cable broke and hit a vehicle."

Mac nodded. He remembered everything. Including the screams of the man trapped under the burning vehicle.

"Three men were hurt. They're still not sure if the one you pulled out will make it. They were all taken to the burn center in San Antonio."

He lifted one singed brow in query and nodded at his arms, still under their light gauzy tents.

"You've got second-degree burns on both arms and on one side of your face. The doctors were afraid you'd seriously damaged your lungs, but it's not as bad as they first thought. They'll give you the details now that you're awake."

She turned to alert the nurse of Mac's consciousness. A swarm of medical specialists soon surrounded him, and Maggie retreated to the waiting room. Alone in the dim light, she huddled in one corner of the couch. She drew up her legs, rested her folded arms on her knees and gave way to the tears she'd held back all those terrifying hours.

When she finally went back in to see Mac, he was asleep again. She looked at the tube taped to his mouth and wished with all her heart it was gone, so that she could hear her mountain rumbling in her ear again.

Chapter Twelve

A week later, Maggie almost wished the tube was back in Mac's mouth. He'd turned out to be a terrible patient, one of those men who were never sick and didn't believe anyone who tried to tell him his body needed time to heal. He responded gruffly to the nurses' orders and was extremely vocal in his opinion of the food they served. He told the doctors not to order any drugs or painkillers after just two days. If his burns pained him, he wouldn't admit it. As Maggie came up for her afternoon visit, she could hear his deep gravelly voice halfway down the hall.

"I don't care what the doctor says—I want up! I refuse to use that blasted bedpan again."

"Colonel, you can't, ah, do anything for yourself with those bandaged hands. This is better for you until—"

"I'll manage, dammit!"

Maggie shook her head at his clenched jaw and angry blue eyes as she strode into the room. Two young nurses turned to her with palpable relief. The ward staff had learned quickly she was the only one who could control their patient. The two nurses gave her a thankful glance and left.

"For heaven's sake, Mac, act your age. You've got to stop terrorizing those lieutenants. They're just trying to do their jobs."

Mac watched her toss down a pile of magazines and stand at the foot of his bed, hands on her hips. The sight of her pile of curls tied up with a blue silk scarf and matching soft silk shirt made his frustration level rise dangerously.

"They can damn well go ply their trade on someone else," he grumbled. "And take their bedpan with them."

"You know you can't do anything for yourself with those bandaged hands," Maggie tried patiently.

"Oh, yeah?" His grumpy look was replaced by a decided leer. "Wanna bet? These bandages are the only things that stand between you and being kissed senseless. I think I can manage at least a demure peck or two, even with them on. Come here."

"No way! The last time I got close, you ended up showing your buns to the general's wife when you tried to wrestle me onto the bed just as she came in. Nice conduct for a senior officer!"

"Maggie, come here."

She eyed him for a long moment, then gave in to the soft command. Better the bed than his trying to chase her around the room.

He sighed as she settled gingerly next to him in the wide hospital bed. "I've been waiting for you all afternoon," he said, nuzzling the golden head beside his on the pillow.

Maggie sighed. She relaxed contentedly and let the scent and feel and warmth that was Mac surround her.

"By the way," he added with seeming casualness, "Dad was here again this morning. He wants to know what we want for a wedding present. Does he know something I don't?"

Maggie looked up into his face in dismay. It was her own fault, she told herself. She should have said something sooner.

She'd been trying to bring up the subject of their future ever since Mac had regained consciousness. She wanted desperately to tell him that all her wanderlust was gone, burned up in the flames that almost took him, as well. To her dismay, she'd discovered that taking a man up on a marriage offer he hadn't renewed was a little tricky. She and Mac had had precious few moments alone since he'd been moved out of intensive care to a private room. It seemed the man knew half the people on the darn base. Someone was always there, even late in the evenings.

Well, it looked like her future father-in-law had made the first move for her. As long as they had a few moments alone now, she might as well follow up.

"Your father seemed to know about your rash offer, or rather, order, of marriage. If the order still stands, Colonel, I want very much to marry you," Maggie told him softly.

"Dammit, woman, you picked a fine time for this!" he roared.

"What?"

Maggie bounced off the bed. She'd have whacked the jerk with his own bedpan for startling her so if she wasn't so confused by his response.

"Hell, woman, I've been aching for you ever since I regained consciousness and found you stroking my thigh. Do you have any idea what that does to a man who's numb everywhere but one particular unburned spot? The nurses are going to have to build another little tent pretty soon to cover the evidence of my frustration."

Dumfounded, Maggie gaped at him.

"And then you have the nerve to bring up marriage when I can't even take you in my arms and kiss you and...do all the other things a man should do when the woman he loves says she'll marry him."

"You idiot," Maggie shouted. "First you order me to marry you, now you won't even take yes for an answer when I give it. Well, I've got news for you, Alastair Duggan MacRae—yes, your father filled me in on the Duggan—we're going to be married and that's that. The boys are already planning the ceremony."

Maggie took devilish satisfaction in Mac's surprised look. "They're part of this, too," she went on. "They've got a great idea for a guitarist for the reception. Someone with a safety pin in his ear, I think." She ignored his low groan.

"And Kate is already designing the cake. She's got visions of a pile of sweet gooey frosting five layers high."

This time she grinned at Mac's long moan. She was beginning to enjoy herself.

"Your dad is making reservations for the honeymoon. It's a toss-up between Disney World and fishing in Michigan. The boys are torn, but I think the vote is going to be for Disney World. Kate's never been there, you see."

Maggie's green eyes sparkled in pure mischief. She imagined there wouldn't be many times she'd have her mountain lying helpless. She enjoyed the rare sensation of having the upper hand.

Mac gave her a long-suffering look.

"And if you don't behave yourself and follow the doctor's orders we may line up Woof to stand in for the groom. He's about the same size, but has a much better disposition."

The corners of Mac's mouth turned up in his slow, lazy, incredibly sexy smile. Maggie thought she might drown in the flow of emotion that washed over her. Lord, she loved that smile. Not to mention the hunk of male that went with it.

"Well, you may think you have all the details covered. But I've got news for you, too. *I'm* going to pick out the wedding dress."

And he did. It was a loose, baggy creation with yards of netting that somehow managed to hang on Maggie's every curve.

PRAIRIE SUMMER
Alina Roberts

To all my friends at
Colorado Romance Writers.
Together we can.

One

Nearly doubled over, Casey wrestled with the trunk, trying to hoist it out of the car. With her neighbor's help last night, putting it in had not been that difficult. Now, however, she couldn't lift it by herself. She would have to unpack part of it, she decided unwillingly, making several trips, instead of one. Having already unloaded the other luggage, she was anxious to finish.

Dusk had settled, softening the rough edges of the Colorado landscape with a lavender haze. She paused for a moment, absorbing the harsh beauty of the land. It wasn't an easy kind of beauty, but the kind that demanded a response.

A deep voice, coming from behind her, startled her. "Let me help you with that."

Casey swung around to face a tall—he must have been well over six feet—commanding figure. She let her eyes travel upward until she encountered a pair of startling blue eyes set in a deeply tanned face.

She flushed. Fear made her voice sharp. "You startled me."

"Sorry." A smile touched his mouth briefly. "I'd like to see the new owner. A Mr. K. C. Allen."

"I'm K. C. Allen," she said, and enjoyed the surprise in his eyes. "Katherine Colleen Allen. Casey for short. Now that you know my name, who are you?"

"Matt Reilly. We're neighbors."

She took the hand he offered. Calluses rasped against her palm. She turned back to the trunk.

Large hands gripped her arms and firmly set her aside. With no visible effort, he hefted the trunk onto his shoulders and started toward the house.

"Where do you want this?" he called.

"Just inside the door." She ran in front of him to open it. "Thanks. I couldn't have managed on my own."

Depositing the trunk to one side, he looked about. "I see old Zach left a few things."

Casey nodded. The house was partially furnished. A rocking chair and an uncomfortable-looking couch occupied most of the small living room. A round table and two folding chairs filled the small kitchen. She smiled, remembering the old-fashioned trundle bed in the only bedroom, which her son, Robbie, now occupied.

"Did you know Mr. Morrow?" she asked at last.

"Everyone knew Zachary Morrow. He's practically a legend around here," Matt said. "Just before he died, he asked me to give this to the new owner." He laughed briefly. "At the time, I had no idea it would be . . ."

He handed her a sealed envelope. Casey fingered it curiously, eager to see its contents but reluctant to open it in front of a stranger.

"Yeah, Zach was a real character," Matt continued. "He prided himself on being eccentric."

"How so?"

Matt waved a hand about. "His near-poverty existence, when it wasn't necessary. His shutting himself off from the rest of the world, except for a few friends. His dogged determination to hold on to this piece of land, even though he couldn't take care of it. His insistence that the prairie dogs be left alone."

"He was within his rights," she defended her benefactor, remembering the instructions from Zach's lawyer that she was to continue letting the prairie dogs make their home on the land. "As for protecting the prairie dogs, I think he deserved to be commended, not condemned."

"Of course he was within his rights," Matt agreed impatiently, "but it made it hard on his friends who wanted to help him. And those prairie dogs cost his neighbors a bundle of money, not to mention a pack of trouble."

"Perhaps he thought that help might cost him his independence and freedom," Casey countered. For some perverse reason, she wanted to needle this man, who gave the impression of too often having everything his own way. "And I'm afraid I have to side with Mr. Morrow about the animals."

"Not another one," he muttered.

"Another what?"

"Save us from the world's do-gooders," he groaned. "You people create more problems than you solve."

Stung, she retorted, "I'm an artist, not an environmentalist, Mr. Reilly." She saw him glance at the stack of canvases that leaned against the wall.

"You're not here by yourself, are you?" he asked.

"No," she said quietly. "I have a six-year-old son. It was a long trip, and he's already asleep. Is there anything else?" Her voice betrayed her exhaustion, and she struggled to keep it steady.

"Yes, I want to buy you out. Your strip of property would—"

"I'm sorry. There's no question of my selling. We intend to make our home here." She stood in a gesture of dismissal. "Now, if that's all you have to say, I'm very tired, and I still have a lot to do."

"That's not all by a long shot. You can't live here. You and a child alone."

"I'll do whatever I have to."

During the two years since Dave's death, she'd had to struggle to remain independent. Though they couldn't afford it, Dave's parents had offered to help out. She'd refused, determined to make it on her own. And she had. She wasn't about to give that up now. "If you'll excuse me." She looked pointedly at the door.

"It's late," he said. "But I'll be back. You don't understand what you're taking on."

She didn't trust herself to answer that.

"Till tomorrow then." He slammed the door behind him.

Casey stared after him, startled more by her reaction to him than by anything he'd said.

Odd that a total stranger should affect her so strongly. Of course, she had nothing to fear from him. The house and land were hers. No one could force her to sell against her wishes. Resolutely she put Matt Reilly out of her mind.

The letter, forgotten during her confrontation with Matt, now beckoned to her. Ripping it open, she stared at it.

Dear Katherine,

I was sorry to hear of your mother's death. I've known her since her birth. She was very special to me. I'd hoped that you and I would meet one day, but that now appears impossible. Please accept this gift in memory of her. As you know, I let the prairie dogs make their home on this land. I've done it all my life and have never regretted it. Please take care of them.

Sincerely,
Zach Morrow

Tears shimmered in Casey's eyes as she read the letter once more, pausing over the mention of her mother. How she wished she'd known Zach Morrow. She was sure she would have liked him.

He'd left her with a charge, and she intended to honor it. Wiping the last smudges of tears away, she looked around, trying to understand the man who'd lived here for more than fifty years.

Neglect and time had taken their toll on the house and its furnishings. Dust coated not only the sparse pieces of furniture but seemed to be embedded into their surfaces.

Obviously Zach Morrow had spent little time inside. Perhaps she would find the answer outdoors. Despite her exhaustion, she wandered outside, looking for clues to the character of her mother's godfather.

Red and purple streaked the summer sky, providing an impressive backdrop for the craggy peaks of the Rockies. Clumps of grass dotted the ground. A cacophony of sound greeted her as a flock of sparrows gathered in the huge cottonwood trees that shaded the house. A smile erased the tiredness from her face as she listened to their chatter.

"So this is what you're about, Zach," she said. "I won't let you down."

Inside once more, she felt her smile vanish as she looked about at the shabby interior of what was now her and Robbie's home. Her head reeled with all that had to be done. Chipped green enamel on the kitchen cabinets showed glimpses of what might have been lovely hardwood beneath. Uncovering it would require hours of tedious stripping and sanding. The oak plank floor, too, would need refinishing. Suddenly she smiled. *One step at a time*. Her mother's words repeated themselves in her mind as they had so often in the past. *Not everything can be done at once,* her mother would say to the young impulsive Casey whose impatience often led her to tackle more than was reasonable. Or more than she could handle alone. Never one to refuse to try anything, Casey often leapt before she looked.

This time, though, she faced a very real limitation—money. Or the lack thereof, she amended wryly. Two thousand dollars was all that remained of selling everything to pay off Dave's medical bills. The small amount from his life insurance had to be kept in reserve.

She and Dave had married straight out of college. They'd planned to set the world on fire, she with her art and Dave by opening his own computer-software business. She postponed her dream of illustrating children's books and took a job as a commercial artist to help with the bills until his business was rolling.

Four year later, just when his business *had* started to pick up considerably, Dave had developed a brain tumor that left him too ill to work. As the disease progressed, she left her job to care for him. When he died, she struggled to make a living for Robbie and herself, once again shelving her dream. She'd learned something since Dave's death—she was a survivor.

Characteristically, Casey refused to feel sorry for herself. Now, with this mortgage-free house, they would have no worries about rent. She had noticed the good-size garden plot; perhaps next summer she could supplement their food budget by raising vegetables. She added that to her list of things to do—find out what grows well here.

The first order of business would be to give the house a thorough cleaning. A minimum of unpacking, though, was all she could manage now.

Sponging off in the shower in the closet-size bathroom, she realized how primitive the plumbing was and prayed it would hold out. The pressure was feeble at best, and pipes sputtered ominously in protest against their unaccustomed use.

Dressed in thin cotton pajamas, she slipped gratefully beneath the sheets. Even the lumpy mattress felt good. What a blessing Mr. Morrow had an old-fashioned trundle bed that she and Robbie could both use. Someday she would add another bedroom. Until then, they'd have to make do with what was there. The gentle cadence of Robbie's soft steady breathing lulled her to sleep.

The next morning, she rubbed her eyes crossly. Matt Reilly had plagued her dreams, taunting her in them, just as he'd done the night before.

Her expression automatically softened as she gazed down at Robbie. Impossibly long red-gold eyelashes fanned lightly freckled cheeks; one small hand gripped a much-loved toy unicorn while the other formed a dimpled fist, pushed up against his chin.

Her marriage to Dave had been achingly brief, but she'd never regretted their time together. And he'd left her a precious legacy—Robbie. Careful not to wake the little boy, Casey stepped gingerly over the lower bed and slipped into a short robe. A quick shower—she dared not strain the capacities of the hot-water heater with its low water pressure—and fresh clothing saw her ready for the day. Padding out to the kitchen, she surveyed the remainder of the groceries they'd bought early yesterday morning—a third of a loaf of bread, two bananas and half a quart of milk. Breakfast would deplete their meager supplies. She added grocery shopping to her list of things to do.

"Mom, where are you?"

"Right here, honey," she answered, hurrying back into the bedroom. "Hey, sleepyhead. I thought you were going to be the first one up and out exploring this morning."

"Is it too late?"

"No, sweetheart, it's not late at all." She tugged on the tail of his pajama top. "Come on and help me put this bed back together."

Why is it things slide out so much more easily than they slide back in? she wondered in exasperation. After trying for the third time to make the latch work, she finally plopped down on the bed, pulling Robbie with her.

"We may just have to leave it this way." She pulled a comic face at him, ignoring the knock at the door as she surveyed the bed.

"It seems I've found you struggling with inanimate objects again," an amused voice said from the doorway. Casey stood and faced the man who had so disturbed her sleep last night. "Do you always walk into other people's homes uninvited?"

"Only when my knocks go unheeded. I *did* call out several times. Can I help?"

"We were trying to put this thing—" she pointed to the bed "—back together, but it won't budge."

"Let me take a look." He maneuvered the sliding mechanism and, within seconds, had the trundle bed back in place.

"Thanks."

"You're welcome." He turned to Robbie. "Hi. What's your name?"

"Robbie. I'm six years old, and I go to school."

"Glad to meet you, Robbie. I'm Matt."

"How old are you, Matt?"

Casey intervened hastily. "Robbie, that's none of our business. Why don't you go get washed and dressed?"

"That's all right," Matt said easily. "I'm thirty-four, Rob. A bit older than you."

Snatching some clean clothes from the stack on the floor, Casey bundled them and her son into the bathroom.

"We can talk out here," she said, indicating the living room.

Following her out of the room, he looked at the sagging sofa and then leaned against the wall. "You said last night you and your son were alone."

She nodded.

"Your husband?"

"He died two years ago."

She tried not to notice the compassion in Matt's eyes. She didn't need that. All she wanted was a chance to make a new life for herself and her son—on her own.

"I can't give up this place," she said, anticipating Matt's next words.

Robbie wandered into the living room. "I'm hungry."

"We'll have breakfast in just a minute. We'll eat picnic-style, okay?"

"Okay!"

Casey felt Matt's gaze on her and wondered what he was thinking. Probably deciding how to convince her to sell her property.

His next words confirmed it. "I'll leave you to your breakfast. But I'll be back. You don't know what you've taken on." And with that, he left.

Robbie was standing at the window. "Look." He pointed to the gray gelding that Matt mounted. "Isn't he wonderful?" he asked. Casey didn't know if he meant the horse or its rider.

"It's a beautiful horse," she agreed, preferring to think that Robbie's enthusiasm was directed there. "We'll probably see a lot of horses here."

"Could I have a pony? Please. I'd take such good care of it."

"You know I'd get you one if I could. There just isn't a way right now." Seeing his disappointed look, she added, "Maybe if I can get a job or sell some of my paintings, well, just maybe, we could swing a pony later on."

Robbie appeared content with that, accepting her half promise with touching faith. It was dangerous letting him believe that she could do anything. She'd tried to point out that there were some things she couldn't do, but Robbie refused to believe that.

A lump formed in her throat as she watched him. A fierce love swelled up within her, making her want to hold him close, to know he was safe and secure. After Dave's death, her instincts to overprotect came all too easily. She had to fight against smothering Robbie.

Two

Every cow they passed, grazing on the seemingly endless range, elicited a delighted response from Robbie as Casey drove to the town of Little Falls. He swung his head back and forth, so as to not miss anything.

"Look, Mom! What are those little hills?" He pointed to a cluster of small mounds.

She followed the direction of his finger. "Prairie-dog holes. Prairie dogs tunnel underground and make their homes there. We'll see a lot more of them while we're here."

Casey relaxed and enjoyed the countryside, a palette of summer pastels. The sun cast a silvery edge over the heat-cured prairie grass. How she would like to paint it—a graceful windmill, a weathered barn, a pond shimmering in the sunshine. She listed the colors she would need for such a scene—burnt sienna, ocher—then laughed at herself. Here she was planning a painting when she had a hundred more important things to do.

Little Falls came as a pleasant surprise. Cottonwoods and aspens shaded wide streets; petunia-filled planters punctuated the street corners. A small park occupied the center of town. A family town, she decided approvingly. A place to build a home and raise a family. She easily located the elementary school—she'd learned that school started in four days—and registered Robbie in the first grade. A trip to the library netted a stack of books on gardening, plus a smaller number dealing with local wildlife. She'd have liked to browse longer, but Robbie's impatient glances toward the door persuaded her to postpone further reading.

On their way to the grocery store, they received several friendly nods. Casey gave shy smiles in return, while Robbie kept up a constant stream of chatter and questions. With careful shopping, she managed to buy what they needed and still keep within her budget.

While checking out, she spied Matt Reilly's tall figure striding across the street. Balancing a big sack of groceries in each arm, she urged Robbie, who was ogling a candy display, out of the store. As they headed toward the car, she shifted the bags slightly to ease the ache in her arms. The distance to the school, where she'd parked, was farther than she remembered. Robbie skipped happily beside her, intent on his game of not stepping on any lines in the pavement.

"Step on a crack, break your mother's back," he chanted.

Just as she decided the heavy sacks might indeed break her back, a familiar voice called to her.

"Mrs. Allen, it appears I'm destined to be your white knight," Matt said as he caught up to her. Without her quite knowing how, he relieved her of her groceries.

"I can manage," she said coolly, thinking that white knight was not how she regarded him at all.

"Are you always so gracious, or am I the only one who merits such treatment?"

She blushed guiltily, knowing she deserved that. "Thanks for your help," she managed at last. "Those sacks were heavier than I realized." She smiled in an effort to be more friendly.

He stowed the groceries into the back seat of the car. "I'm glad I ran into you. I wanted to apologize. I'm afraid I wasn't very neighborly last night or this morning."

"That's all right. You were disappointed about the land."

"I admit I'd like to buy your land, but that was no reason for me to snap at you like I did."

She extended her hand to find it covered by a much larger one. "Apology accepted if you'll accept mine. I'm sorry I overreacted."

"I'd like to talk to you about your land," he said. "Perhaps we could have dinner together. Tonight?"

Casey felt a keen stab of disappointment. He hadn't been trying to be friendly, after all. He still wanted her land. He was just trying another approach.

"No, thank you," she said stiffly. "Sorry to disappoint you, but my property is still not for sale."

"I didn't mean—"

"I know what you meant."

"There's something else," he said.

She eyed him suspiciously. "What?"

"The condition of your fences. If my cattle come to harm on your property, you'll be responsible." He paused. "Look, I'd like to help."

"Help who? Yourself or me?"

"You," he said, obviously curbing his impatience. "You can't string fence by yourself."

"Why not?"

"Independence is fine for those who can afford it. Just make sure you can," he said, clearly annoyed. "*My* fences are in order. *Yours* aren't." With that, he turned on his heel and strode off.

Casey glared after him.

"One more stop," she announced to Robbie who'd been checking out a squirrel scampering up a tree. "The hardware store."

Finding the store proved easier than determining what she needed for repairing fences. Finally she approached the young clerk and explained her problem.

"Kyle Bridges, ma'am," he introduced himself.

"Casey Allen."

Kyle showed her the reels of barbed wire and wire cutters. When she asked how to use them, he looked at her in amazement. "*You're* not going to put it up, are you?"

"I certainly am." Realizing he was not to blame for her problem, she apologized for her harsh-sounding reply. "Could you ring this up, please?"

Paying for the wire and tools left a big hole in her cash. But all she could hear was Matt Reilly's voice, challenging her independence.

The next day, while Robbie was busy exploring the property around the house, Casey wearily pushed a strand of hair back from her forehead. Taut muscles groaned in protest as she heaved yet another spool of wire. Though she wore leather gloves, she was careful to grip only the wire, avoiding the barbs spaced along it. She knew how easily they could bite into and tear soft flesh with only the briefest contact. Her left palm was still sore where she'd inadvertently caught it against one of the barbs.

Staggering with fatigue, she half-carried, half-dragged the spool of wire to the next fence post. Unwinding a long section, she started to tack the wire to the post. When she paused to push back her hair she saw Matt dismounting from his horse.

He covered the distance between them in a few long strides, then leaned against a post and watched.

Irritated at having him see her hot and disheveled, she dropped the wire cutters. As she stooped to pick them up, she found him standing over her.

"That wire wouldn't keep out a sick kitten, much less a fifteen-hundred-pound cow," he said.

She ignored him and tried to pull the wire taut. It persisted in remaining slack. Annoyed, she turned away. Taking a metal staple from her pocket, she started to hammer it to the post. His nearness made her clumsy, causing her to drop the hammer this time. Their hands touched as they both bent over at the same moment to retrieve it. Even through her leather gloves, she imagined she could feel the warmth of his fingers. She drew her hand away swiftly, afraid he might sense her reaction.

She finished securing the wire to the post and started toward the next one. Despite her best efforts, the wire still sagged when she attempted to tack it to the second post.

Matt followed her. "Wire should be tacked to the far post and then to the first one so that it can be pulled tight."

Exhaustion and his presence combined to make her even clumsier. Tugging at the wire with all her strength, she didn't watch her footing and caught one boot in the coil of wire on the ground. She lost her balance and toppled over backward.

Matt stood looming over her, concern mixed with amusement on his face. *If he dares laugh,* Casey vowed silently, *I'll*...

Her thought went unfinished as he reached out a hand to help her up. She glared at him, irrationally feeling it was his fault she'd fallen. She stared at the outstretched hand, tempted to ignore it.

Common sense battled with defiance and won. She accepted his hand and was immediately, if not gently, hauled up against a hard chest. She felt at home there in his arms, pressed against him. Aghast at the direction of her thoughts, she pushed away. She was freed, not, she guessed, through any efforts of her own, but because he had decided to release her.

"Thanks," she muttered.

He quirked an eyebrow at her less than gracious tone but said nothing. Instead, he shrugged off his leather vest and began unbuttoning his shirt, then tossed them both to the ground.

"What...what're you doing?" she stammered, disturbed by the sight of his bronzed chest, matted with light brown hair.

"Finishing this string of wire."

"It's my problem, and I'll handle it." She kept her eyes fastened on the brown column of his neck, refusing to meet his gaze.

"Like you just did?"

"Okay," she agreed reluctantly. If he were determined to help, she might as well take advantage of it and learn from him. "What should I do, boss?"

Matt spared her a moment's glance, indicating he wasn't deceived by her show of meekness. "Make some lemonade." He tweaked her nose. "And you might wipe that smudge of dirt off your nose."

Aware of just how grimy she must appear, she flushed. Her hair curled about her head in a riot of red and gold; sweat, mixed with dust, streaked her face. Her clothes were coated with dirt and wet with perspiration.

But she wasn't leaving yet. Not until she'd watched him string the wire. If she was going to make a home here, she had to know how to take care of the land, as well as the house. She studied the way he stretched the wire, how he positioned the metal staples.

After several minutes, Matt picked up his shirt and wiped his face. "I thought you were making lemonade," he reminded her.

"I'm going to." Conscious of his scrutiny, she walked toward the house. From behind her came the sound of soft laughter. She steeled herself not to turn around. She took a quick look in the backyard and noticed Robbie playing happily with the Lego set his grandparents had given him for his sixth birthday. So much for exploring, she thought wryly. Once inside the house and the safety of the bedroom, she peeled off her clothes, snatched up clean ones and marched into the bathroom.

Praying that the temperamental plumbing would behave, she turned on the shower and was relieved to find a tepid, if not hot spray. She scrubbed herself quickly and shampooed her hair, then let the water soothe her aching muscles. The stiffness eased somewhat and, regretfully, she turned off the water, knowing it would soon turn cold. She rubbed herself dry and slipped on the fresh clothes. Feeling more equipped to face the irritating Matt Reilly, she squared her shoulders and headed into the kitchen.

In a few minutes, she'd made the lemonade, set the pitcher and two glasses on a tray and carried it outside to the porch.

Matt joined her. She was relieved to see he'd put his shirt back on, though it remained unbuttoned.

"That section is finished," he said.

"Thanks." It seemed she was thanking him for something every other minute. But that was going to change. She would learn how to string fence, take care of the land and anything else that meant making a home for herself and Robbie.

"There's still a lot to be done. Zach let the whole place go—" he glanced around "—inside and out. Your work would be a lot easier without the tunnels caused by the prairie dogs. It weakens the ground so much the fence posts can't be driven in straight."

Frowning, she thought it over. "Can't I place the posts around the mounds?"

"Not and have them evenly spaced."

"Well, I'll just have to do the best I can, won't I?"

"Look, Casey, I know you like prairie dogs. All city folk think they're cute furry little creatures. What they don't realize is the damage they do to the land. It's not just the ranchers who don't like them. They destroy crops, too."

"So the farmers don't like them, either?"

"You got it." He finished buttoning his shirt. "Aside from everything else, they're competitors for the food. Did you know that thirty-two prairie dogs forage as much as one sheep? Two hundred and fifty can eat as much as a cow. In a drought, with every blade of grass worth more than gold, that can be disastrous. Not only to the ranchers, but to all those who depend upon them."

"But I can't just destroy them!"

"*You* wouldn't have to do it."

She recoiled in distaste at his implication. "I think we'd better agree to disagree on this subject."

"We're not finished with it," he said, "not by a long shot." Still he didn't press her anymore and gestured to the wicker chairs they were sitting on. "Zach made these himself. Collected the reeds, washed them and wove them into chairs."

Casey looked at the chairs with new interest. "He must've been very talented."

"He was."

She sighed tiredly and felt more than saw his scowl as he studied her.

"Look at you. You're exhausted," he accused.

"What was your first clue?" she asked, smiling.

He didn't return the smile. "Look around you. This old ruin of a place needs money, work and someone to put it to rights. Someone who knows what he's about."

"And you've looked me over and decided I don't measure up," Casey said, her good humor vanishing. "Well, let me tell you something, Mr. Reilly. I intend to live here and turn this old ruin, as you call it, into a home."

"Even assuming that you could fix up the house," he said, his tone indicating he thought she clearly could not, "what about the land? You can't even handle repairing fences. How're you going to clear the land? Haul away the junk that Zach had been collecting and storing for years? Do you have any idea at all how to make the land pay?"

Dragging a hand through his hair, he didn't wait for an answer. "Obviously not, or you wouldn't continue to let the prairie dogs destroy it. Why don't you admit you can't do the work, and sell out before it does you in? You're exhausted after stringing one fence."

"If this is such a ramshackle property, then why do you want it? You don't look like the kind of man who collects rundown houses and useless properties."

"I need this parcel of land to connect my two pieces of property. As it is, they're virtually cut off from one another. Adding this to our property would give us an uninterrupted range. Everything, from watering to roundup, would be simplified. I'd give you a fair price," he added. "More than market value."

Casey shook her head. "We don't have anywhere else to go. Such as it is, the house is mortgage-free. You probably don't have any idea of what it's like to worry about the rent due each month. I do, and believe me it's not pleasant." She stood. "Now, if you're finished, I won't keep you."

He stood, also, closing the gap between them. When the kiss came, she was too shocked to protest. It was hard and fast, as though he couldn't help himself.

Her hair tumbled about her face, and she stared up at him. "Why?" she whispered.

"I don't know," he admitted, looking no happier than she felt. Even so, his hands slipped to her shoulders, urging her closer.

She felt the warmth of his fingers seep through the thin cotton of her shirt, causing her to tremble with unexpected pleasure.

Conscious of his nearness and wary of her own reactions to it, she broke free. She backed away, anxious to widen the space between herself and Matt. Perhaps that would rid her of the breathlessness she was afraid was all too apparent to him.

Matt jammed his fists in his pockets. "I'll be seeing you."

She watched as he rode away and wondered why she wasn't angry. Anger, she understood. But the warm fluttery feeling in her stomach had nothing to do with anger.

Three

Casey rubbed the back of her neck and scowled at the coil of barbed wire. Her efforts at stringing fence today were proving no more effective than they had yesterday or the day before that. She shaded her eyes against the harsh glare of the sun to scan the field for Robbie. He'd gone exploring again but promised to stay in sight. A smile erased the scowl as she saw him running toward her.

"I brought you a present." Panting hard, he skidded to a stop in front of her.

Her smile widened as she took in the grubby hand clutching a bedraggled bouquet of dandelions. She knelt down to plant a kiss on his dirt-streaked cheek. "They're beautiful. Thank you."

"Do you really like them?"

"I love them. We'll use them for our table centerpiece tonight. Did you have a good time?"

"It was great." In the rapid change of subjects that only a six-year-old can manage, he asked in the next breath, "Can I help make dinner tonight? I'm a good hamburger-maker."

She laughed and ruffled his hair. "The best," she agreed. "And a pretty good hamburger-eater, too."

"Guess what I saw in the field behind the house?"

Her head swirled under yet another change of subject. "What?"

"A bunch of little animals. They look sorta like squirrels. Only they didn't live in trees like the squirrels back home. They were standing by little holes in the ground."

"Those are prairie dogs."

He shook his head. "Squirrels can't be dogs."

"These aren't *real* dogs," she explained. "Prairie dogs are like squirrels, only they live underneath the ground. Remember the little mounds we saw on the way to town?"

She took his hand. They tramped over the grass-tufted ground until they came to a cluster of small mounds of earth. "This is called a prairie-dog town." She pointed to the holes. "And those are the prairie dogs' homes."

Robbie pulled his hand free and squatted down to peer into the holes. "I can't see anything."

"They probably heard us coming and are hiding." She hunkered down beside him. "See the little marks around the holes?"

He nodded.

"Those are made by their noses."

He touched his own nose. "They put their noses in the dirt?"

Casey laughed. "Just about. They use their noses to push the dirt into a mound around the hole. That helps protect their home when it rains and also gives them a lookout place."

"What's a lookout place?"

"One prairie dog acts as a guard and keeps watch for other animals that might hurt his family and friends."

Her knees were becoming stiff, and she stood and pulled Robbie up with her. "I guess we scared them all off. Maybe we can see one another day."

"How come you know so much about prairie dogs?" Robbie asked as they trudged back to the house.

"I did some reading about them last night. A lot of people around here, like Matt Reilly, don't like prairie dogs. The ranchers want to get rid of them. I want to understand why."

"I'm going to learn to read in school."

She hugged him to her. "I know." Casey checked her watch. "It's five o'clock, and we haven't even started dinner! Race you home!"

She started running toward the house, but hung back to let Robbie outrun her, his short sturdy legs churning up the ground.

Robbie stopped abruptly. "Mom, look." He pointed at an approaching horse and rider.

Matt Reilly. What was he doing here?

"Good afternoon, Casey. Good to see you again, partner." He dismounted and put out his hand to Robbie.

Robbie reluctantly grasped it. "Hi, Matt." Though polite, the words lacked warmth.

Matt bent over and put his hand on Robbie's shoulder. "Something wrong?"

Robbie squirmed away. "Nothin'," he mumbled.

"I thought we were friends."

"Mom said you don't like the prairie dogs!" Robbie burst out.

Matt sighed heavily. "So that's it." He leveled a look at Casey.

"I just told him the truth," she defended herself. "Can you deny you think they're nuisances and want to get rid of them?"

"No, I can't."

Robbie turned an accusing glare at Matt. "I like prairie dogs. I don't like *you.*"

Matt squinted as he studied the late-afternoon sun. "I wish you did like me, Robbie, because I like you. I even like prairie dogs. But I also like cows and horses."

"So?"

"So sometimes what's good for one animal isn't good for others. In this case, the prairie dogs make the ground dangerous for the horses and cattle.'' He held out his hand. ''Come on. I'll show you.''

Robbie hesitated only a moment. Then he took the large tanned hand.

Matt waited for Casey to follow. ''You, too.''

Reluctantly she joined them. They retraced the path she and Robbie had taken. When they came to the edge of the prairie-dog town, Matt stopped.

''Shh,'' he whispered. ''If they hear us, they'll disappear into their holes.'' He crouched down.

Robbie followed his example. ''See that big one?'' Matt pointed to the buff-colored rodent that stood sentinel on the crest of his burrow.

Robbie nodded.

''He's the watchdog. When he senses danger, he'll warn his friends.''

Casey squatted beside them. ''He barks a warning,'' she explained.

''Not exactly a bark,'' Matt contradicted. ''Wait—you'll see what I mean.''

A prairie falcon swooped from the sky. The lookout gave a sound like a shrill whistle. Then he jumped into the air and bent backward so that his head nearly touched his rump. Immediately all the prairie dogs scurried into their burrows.

Matt stood and brushed the dust from his jeans. ''That was a back flip. It's like when someone yells 'Fire' to us. It's the prairie dogs' way of signaling danger.''

''Wow. That was neat.'' Robbie peered at the now empty field. ''Will they come out again?''

''Probably not for a while, though a brave one may venture out a little later. They're pretty cautious and wait to make sure it's all clear before they leave their homes.'' Matt took Robbie's hand and led him carefully between the mounds of dirt. ''All we can see are the holes. But underneath the ground there are tunnels connecting the holes to each other. What do you suppose would happen if a horse stepped in a hole?''

Robbie frowned. ''Would he hurt his leg?''

''Probably. In fact he'd break it. When a horse breaks a leg, sometimes he doesn't get better.''

''Never?''

Matt exchanged a glance with Casey. ''Most horses don't recover from broken legs. Now can you see why some of the other ranchers and I don't like prairie dogs on our land?''

The frown furrowed deeper as Robbie thought on it. ''Yeah. But isn't there enough land for the prairie dogs *and* horses?''

''That's a good question. One a lot of people have been asking. But so far we haven't come up with an answer.'' Matt slanted another look at Casey, who'd remained silent during the exchange. ''What do you think?''

''I don't know,'' she admitted. ''I guess I have the same question Robbie has. Why *can't* we share the land?''

''Don't you think we've tried?'' Matt hooked his thumbs through his belt loops and rocked back on his heels. ''It's not black and white. Once you've been here awhile, you'll understand. Maybe you ought to take a hard look at both sides.''

She looked up at the tall man regarding her quizzically. ''Maybe I ought to.''

''Good.'' He threaded his fingers through his hair. ''Rob, I hope you'll try to understand, too. Sometimes it's hard, but I think you're big enough to try.''

Robbie expanded visibly under Matt's praise. ''I'll try, Matt.''

''That's all I ask.''

Robbie scampered off in front of them, heading to the house, leaving Casey alone with Matt. They walked back to where he'd left his horse, his arm draped around Casey's shoulders. She willed herself not to react to the casual gesture, but couldn't help the tiny frisson of pleasure that skittered down her spine.

"He's a good kid," Matt said.

"Yeah, he is. Thanks for what you said to him. Maybe someday he can understand most things have more than one side."

Matt nodded, about to speak when a rider, coming from the east, hailed them. "Hey, Matt!"

Casey looked at the sandy-haired woman and then at Matt. The resemblance was unmistakable.

"My sister, Lisa," Matt said.

Lisa Reilly dismounted with practiced ease. She walked over to join them. "Introduce me, Matt."

Her brother obliged and Lisa stuck out her hand.

Casey grasped it, not really surprised to find it almost as hard and callused as Matt's.

"I'm glad you're going to be living here, Mrs. Allen," Lisa said. "Zach's place has been empty too long."

"Thank you. And please, call me Casey."

"Casey it is, then. Matt told me we had a new neighbor. He didn't say much else, though." She chuckled. "I can see why—now."

Blushing, Casey turned to find Matt watching them, a frown creasing his forehead. Probably he disapproved of his sister's fraternizing with the enemy.

"I have to go," Matt said abruptly. "I'll see you later, Lisa." Then he turned to Casey. "Think about what I said. My offer still stands."

She watched as he mounted the big gray and rode off, his easy grace unsettling her.

Lisa regarded her quizzically. "What was all that about?"

"Your brother was lecturing me on prairie dogs. Seems he doesn't like them."

"Not many people around here do," Lisa agreed. "But that's not what he meant, was it?"

Casey shook her head. "He wants to buy me out. I refused."

"Oh, that," Lisa dismissed. "Matt's had that idea for years. But he wouldn't let it make any difference in how he treats you."

Casey chose her words carefully. "Perhaps you and he see things differently."

"Sure we do. Matt's ambitious and a hard worker. Me, I'm basically lazy. But I get things done. My own way."

Remembering the work-roughened hand, Casey doubted Lisa was lazy.

"You inherited this place from Zach Morrow?" Lisa asked.

"He was my mother's godfather."

"I'm sorry about old Zach, but I'm glad it brought you here." She grinned. "Matt mentioned a little boy?"

"My son, Robbie. He's wonderful. But I could be a little prejudiced." Casey smiled, thinking she was a *lot* prejudiced. "He'll be starting first grade tomorrow."

"This is a great place for kids." Without pausing for breath, Lisa added, "Come to dinner tomorrow night."

Surprised at the invitation, Casey hesitated. "I don't know, Lisa. There's Robbie, for one thing. And I'm not sure your brother would approve."

"Matt doesn't carry grudges," Lisa said confidently. "Besides, I make my own decisions. And Robbie's invited, too. How about it?"

"Dinner sounds wonderful," Casey said.

"Six be all right? Don't want to keep your little boy up past his bedtime."

"Perfect."

"Great. I'll see you then."

Casey watched her ride away. Maybe, just maybe, she'd found a friend.

Four

Casey savored the last bite of baked Alaska. "Delicious. Everything was, Lisa. Especially the steak."

Lisa looked pleased. "We raise the beef ourselves. Matt's always experimenting, trying to improve the herd. Make the meat leaner and still keep it tender."

"Does everyone around here ranch?"

"Just about. There're some farmers, too. Those who aren't ranchers or farmers sell supplies to them. We're all one big happy family."

"Except if you happen to like prairie dogs," Casey murmured.

"Hey, I *like* prairie dogs. I just don't like what they do to the land," Lisa said. "But forget about them right now. Tell me what you're doing to the house."

When Casey mentioned she planned to strip the kitchen cabinets the next day, Lisa immediately offered to help.

Lisa arrived just as Robbie left for school. She was dressed in jeans and a T-shirt that read, "Now that I've got it all together, what will I do with it?"

Armed with a scrub brush and an electric sander, she struck a comic pose. "Ready for orders, chief."

Casey burst out laughing. "Where did you find that shirt?"

"Matt had it especially made for me. He was always teasing me about the self-improvement courses I was forever taking. He said, very nastily I thought, that he couldn't see they'd done any good. I told him I had it all together. Hence, this."

"You and Matt are close?" It was half question, half statement.

"We've always been close. Of course, Matt's quite a bit older. Kind of raised me."

"He's a difficult person to know," Casey ventured.

"He is that," his sister agreed. "I think I know him, and then he does something that makes me realize I don't know him at all. There are so many parts to him. He's much more complex than I am." She shook her wire scrub brush at Casey in mock warning. "If you get me gabbing, we'll never get any work done. Lead me to it!"

Together they went inside. Lisa looked about in admiration. "You've accomplished wonders already. I remember it as very dark and depressing. It seems light and airy now."

"You're good for my morale. I did away with those heavy velvet curtains and hung plants in the windows."

They worked steadily for the next two hours. Slowly, a honey-toned birch appeared from under the layers of enamel that coated the kitchen cabinets.

"Why would anyone cover this with paint?" Casey wondered aloud. "You hardly ever see real wood anymore. It seems a shame to hide it."

"Zach Morrow was a strange old bird," Lisa said. "We never knew why he did half the things he did." She sighed, then changed the subject. "Hey, are you going to be coming to the town fair? I'm in charge this year." She pulled a face. "We're always trying to find new booths to raise money for a much-needed hospital. People get so tired of the same old thing year after year. I've got two weeks to come up with something that'll knock their socks off. Any ideas?"

"What about a portrait booth?" Casey suggested. "Perhaps a caricature one."

"That'd be great. We've never had anything like that before." Lisa frowned. "But we'd need an artist. One who was willing to work for free."

"I might be able to do it," Casey offered. "I've done a bit of caricature work before. It wouldn't cost much for the supplies. We'd need paper and charcoal. Pastels, if we want color."

"That's wonderful! To be able to draw, I mean." Lisa laughed. "Guess I'll just have to stick with my camera."

"Don't get the wrong idea. I'm not really a portrait artist. What I'm talking about are just quick impressions. Nothing fancy."

"All the better. We couldn't charge very much, but even so, we should make a nice profit." Lisa turned off her sander. "If I keep this up without a break soon, I'm going to start vibrating. Casey, I know we just met, but I feel like we're already friends. Matt's throwing a birthday party for me Friday night. Can you come?"

"You're sure I won't be barging in?"

"Are you kidding?" Lisa laughed. "Half the county will be there. Please say you'll come."

"It sounds great. I'd have to bring Robbie, though."

"No problem. We'll put him down in one of the bedrooms. He'll probably sleep through the whole thing."

Cleaning up after Lisa had gone, Casey wondered what she could get Lisa for a present. With no extra cash, she'd have to make something—perhaps a watercolor.

She was still puzzling over it when Robbie burst into the kitchen. She *thought* she'd heard the sound of the school bus a few minutes earlier.

"Hey, Mom!" he said excitedly. "Can I have a prairie dog for a pet?"

"A pet? I'm afraid not, honey."

"Why not?"

"Prairie dogs are wild animals. As cute as they are, they wouldn't make good pets." Seeing she wasn't getting through to him, she searched for an answer he could understand. "And they'd be unhappy away from their families and friends."

"I guess you're right. I was watching one just now when I got off the bus. He has a white tail. I named him Ralph."

"Ralph?"

"That's right. Ralph. Wanna see him?" He tugged at her hand, urging her to follow him.

She let him lead her to the field on the other side of the road.

"There he is!" Robbie whispered, pointing to a plump ginger-colored prairie dog cautiously peering out from his burrow.

"How can you tell that's Ralph? They all look the same to me."

"'Cause Ralph has a nicked ear. Look."

She stared hard and noticed the small slit in the rodent's right ear. "How did you ever see that?"

"I like to watch him. I saw him yesterday when I got off the bus. He's braver than the others."

"I see what you mean." Casey hunkered down and watched as the plucky little animal came out of his hole, looked around, then contentedly began chewing on a juicy thistle stalk. "But you know that Ralph wouldn't be happy living inside, don't you?"

Robbie nodded sadly. "Yeah." Then he brightened. "Could we come out here and watch him every day? That'd be almost as good."

She grinned at his enthusiasm. "I think we could manage that. Hey, what do you say to dinner?"

"I say yes!"

"You're going to be bigger than me soon," she teased.

"Even bigger," he boasted.

Four hours later, after she'd checked on Robbie, who'd fallen asleep halfway through his bedtime story, and cleaned up the kitchen, she sat at the kitchen table, the book on prairie dogs propped in front of her. With growing indignation, she read how some farmers had started exterminating prairie dogs with poison.

But, could she really blame them? Everything she read only confirmed what Matt had already told her. How could she defend the small animals, delightful as they were, when they threatened the livelihood of so many people?

She slammed the book shut and glared at it as if it were the cause of the headache that had been nagging at her all evening. She felt caught between two opposing forces, each good, each right in its own way.

"Oh, Zach. What have you gotten me into?"

"Lisa," Matt called. "Casey's here."

Radiant in a yellow halter-style dress, Lisa bounced into the spacious front hall. "I'm so glad you could make it," she said, her smile encompassing both Casey and Robbie.

"So am I," Casey said. "You look terrific." She handed Lisa her present.

Lisa opened it eagerly. "I can't wait. Matt says I'm like a kid at parties. Especially my own. But I do love surprises." She lifted the watercolor from its protective tissue and caught her breath. "It's beautiful, Casey. Did you paint it?"

Casey nodded. Instinctively her eyes sought Matt's, seeking his approval.

"You have quite a gift," he said quietly.

She wondered at the shadow in his eyes before Lisa leaned forward to kiss her cheek.

"Thank you very much," Lisa said. She pulled Casey into the room and introduced her and Robbie to everyone, showing off the watercolor as she did so. Robbie literally ate his way around the room, helping himself to all the goodies Lisa had laid out. Casey smiled indulgently. It wasn't often Robbie got to eat to his six-year-old heart's content. After a while, between bites, he was yawning hugely. Noticing it, Lisa said, "Come on, kiddo. Let's you and me go find a nice room where you can have a nap." She took his hand and led him, almost without protest, out of the room.

Amazing, thought Lisa, how well her son took to the Reillys. He seemed perfectly willing to do their bidding. Her head spinning from meeting so many new people, she decided to look for a quiet place to sit down.

She wandered out onto the patio and sank onto a wicker couch. Digging a pencil and small sketch pad out of her purse, she began to doodle. The lines took shape until a familiar face smiled back at her. Even with the addition of horns, Matt Reilly was unmistakable.

She stared at the paper, unbelieving. How had her doodling turned into Matt's handsome mocking face? Drat the man. He was disturbing her thoughts, her dreams, and now, even her art. She tore the paper off the pad, intending to throw it away. But then she stopped herself. Even with the horns, it *was* a good likeness. In fact, the horns lent it an interesting if somewhat sinister distinction. Casey giggled. Did they reflect how she saw him? Ha! Wouldn't an analyst have fun with that one.

Something blocked her light, and Casey looked up to see the subject of her drawing. She gulped and hoped her face didn't give her away. Casually she folded the paper in half and started to slip it into her purse.

Matt sat down beside her. "May I see?"

"It's n-nothing. Only doodling."

"I'm sure even your doodles are beautiful." Gently he took the picture from her fingers. Unfolding it, he paused, then chuckled. "If all your caricatures are as successful as this, you'll be the biggest money-maker at the fair."

"Please, Matt. I didn't mean . . ."

"You didn't mean to draw me or you didn't mean to draw me with horns?"

Fortunately Lisa appeared just then, balancing two plates piled high with delicacies. She handed one to Casey, then demanded, "What's wrong?" Without waiting for an answer, she turned to Matt and demanded, "What have you been doing to Casey? I can tell she's upset."

"Nothing," he said blandly. "She's been showing me an example of the caricatures she'll be doing at the fair." He handed Lisa the picture. "What do you think?"

Upon looking at the picture, Lisa burst out laughing. "Why don't we display this? It'd be great publicity for the fair and Casey's booth."

Appalled, Casey objected. "But people might think their pictures would have horns or something similar. And Matt might find it embarrassing."

"Oh, I wouldn't find it embarrassing at all," he said unhelpfully. "I think they make me look...distinguished."

"See?" Lisa said to Casey. "People will love it. Matt's so well-known. This'll advertise the fair in a spectacular way." She looked at Casey intently. "You don't mind, do you?"

"No, of course not," Casey lied weakly. When Lisa began to walk away, she glared at Matt. "It serves you right," she hissed.

He only grinned in a maddening way, seeming not at all put out. "Lisa," he called after his sister, "take care of that picture. It's the only portrait I'm likely to have of me."

"It's certainly the only *realistic* one you're likely to have," Casey muttered. "Any other artist would probably try to make you look pleasant—you'd be totally unrecognizable."

"You *are* in a mood, aren't you? Here, have some food." Before she could protest, he popped a meatball into her mouth.

Caught unaware, she almost choked on it. "I'll feed myself, thank you." She started to get up. "I'd better check on Robbie."

Grabbing her wrist, he forced her to stay seated. "Robbie's sound asleep. So there's no reason for you to run away."

"I'm not running away."

He raised his eyebrows.

"I'm not."

"No? Then stay and keep me company for a few minutes."

"I think I prefer more congenial company," she retorted, trying to twist her arm out of his grasp.

Matt's grip gentled. "I'm sorry. I shouldn't tease you. I'd really like your company."

She glanced at him uncertainly. "I don't know..."

"Good. Let's declare a truce. Deal?"

A smile edged the corners of her mouth upward. "Deal," she said, and put her hand in his.

He traced the fine network of veins visible beneath her skin. "You're trembling."

"No...I mean, it's a little cool." Immediately she regretted her lie, for Matt wrapped his arm around her, drawing her closer to him.

"Better?"

No! It was worse. Much worse. But she could hardly tell him that. "Yes, thank you."

"Sure?"

"Hadn't you better get back to your guests?" she asked, instead.

"I don't think I'll be missed." Leaning forward, he kissed her lightly. Unthinkingly, she returned the kiss, arching toward him. When Matt skimmed his knuckles along her cheek, she felt a dart of pleasure, entirely out of proportion to the simple caress.

When Matt drew away she took an unsteady breath and touched her lips experimentally. They were still warm. She stood. "I need to..." She turned and fled, thankful that he made no attempt to stop her, and walked straight into Lisa.

"Are you all right?" Lisa asked.

"Sure." Casey managed a small smile. "Why wouldn't I be?"

An unfamiliar voice interrupted. "Lisa, great party!"

"Thanks, Sam." Lisa turned to Casey to make the introductions. "Casey Allen, Sam Meacham. Another neighbor."

Sam Meacham's expression, friendly until now, hardened into an unwelcoming glare. "I hear you're camping out at Zach's place."

Casey nodded, puzzled by his sudden animosity. "It's our home now," she corrected.

"Rumor is you're as crazy as Zach, letting that vermin destroy the land."

"If you mean I'm letting a few animals make their home on my property, then yes, I am."

"Those animals are ruining good land for miles around." He wiped a beefy hand across his mouth. "Your land borders mine on the north. If one of my horses or cattle comes to grief on your land, I'll..."

"That'll be enough, Sam." Matt appeared suddenly. "Mrs. Allen just moved here. It's up to the rest of us to make her feel at home."

"Just as long as she knows the score." Sam Meacham stalked off.

Unconsciously Casey moved closer to Matt. "I'm sorry," she said, noticing the stares they'd attracted.

"I was just introducing Casey to Sam when he started in on her," Lisa said. "Gosh, I'm sorry, Casey."

"It's all right." She drew a shaky breath. "I guess I'm not too popular around here."

"Don't judge all of us on the basis of one man," Matt said. "Sam's not really such a bad guy. He's worried about his stock. We all are."

"I figured out that much by myself." She glanced around at the other guests. "Does everyone here feel the same way?"

He followed her gaze. "Some do. But not everyone. You have to realize that most of the people here make their living from the land in one way or another. It's only natural they want to protect it."

"I understand. I only wish they understood how I feel."

The reassuring words she'd hoped to hear didn't come.

Later at home as she helped Robbie undress for bed, Casey reflected on the evening. It had been an unsettling one, in more ways than one. Sam Meacham's venom could be dismissed more easily than her own instinctive turning toward Matt. How she had allowed that to happen, she didn't know. He aroused feelings in her she thought she'd buried with Dave. Sheer physical appeal, she could have handled. But it was more than that...

He was an attractive man. And a disturbing one. A dangerous combination. She'd do well to steer clear of him. Dave's long illness and death had left her too vulnerable to risk her heart again.

She concentrated on remembering that Matt was only interested in her property. Besides, he was probably no more interested in a relationship than she was.

Two sleepless hours later, she acknowledged she'd been lying to herself. She *would* do well to stay away from Matt Reilly. Not because he wanted her property. But because it would be all too easy to give him her heart.

Five

A week later, the day of the fair dawned clear and hot. Casey found herself as excited as Robbie, and not a little apprehensive at her part in it. She still agonized over the caricatures. Would people like the humorous drawings of themselves, or would they be offended by the sometimes unflattering exaggerations?

Her caricature of Matt, displayed in the hardware store, had received wide attention and publicity. She'd learned from Lisa that Matt had taken a great deal of good-natured kidding as to what had inspired such a rendition.

Casey had come in for her own share of teasing and curiosity. She'd parried the questions and speculations with a smile and shake of her head, unable to put into words her feelings about Matt, not even to herself.

"What are you thinking about?" Robbie asked as they drove to the fairground.

"I was just daydreaming," she said. "Grown-ups have dreams, too, you know."

"Do you like Matt?"

Casey let out a long breath. "Of course, I like him."

"Good," said Robbie. "So do I."

Preoccupied as she was, she almost missed her turnoff. Scores of people were milling about, setting up booths, laughing, sampling refreshments. Casey looked around in bewilderment, unsure of where her booth was and just what she should be doing.

She smiled in relief as Lisa approached, waving gaily. "Casey, thank goodness you're here! I've got a million things to do and no one to help."

At Casey's pointed look at all the people, Lisa laughed. "They're not here to help. Most are just here pretending to be a part of things. They're useless if you ask them to actually do something."

Casey saluted smartly. "What are your orders, Captain?"

Lisa ran her fingers through her hair. Stray wisps escaped their confining clasp. "Not captain. More like a drill sergeant."

At that moment, Matt joined them and took a hard look at Lisa. "How long have you been here?"

"Three hours."

"I thought so," he said, pushing her down onto a nearby chair. "Stay there. You won't be fit for anything if you don't take it easy."

"But the booths," she protested. "I need to show Casey where to go."

"*I'll* show Casey. You've done wonders, Lisa, but now it's time to let others have a chance."

She sank back. "You're right. It's just that I wanted everything to be perfect."

Matt turned to Casey. "Come on." He relieved her of her supplies. "I'll help you set up your booth." Taking her arm, he guided her and Robbie to the stall. She'd brought a small easel, a large tablet of heavy paper, and her pencils and pastels.

With a minimum of effort, Matt set up her easel and tacked up the poster she'd made to advertise her booth. Noting the exaggerated noses, eyebrows and ears that adorned it, he grinned at her. "No horns?"

She grinned back. "Only for those who've earned them."

Their exchange held no rancor now, only a shared amusement. She felt carefree and happy. "Do you think people will like these?" she asked, waving a hand to indicate the extravagant features.

"I wouldn't be surprised if your booth is the biggest draw we have."

She warmed at his words. To hide her pleasure, she busied herself arranging her equipment.

Robbie, who'd been remarkably silent until now, asked, "Will you do me, Mom?"

"Sure thing, Rob," Matt answered for her. "You can be the first customer."

Casey began to sketch her son quickly. Swift strokes outlined his face and put in angelic features. She chose to accentuate his freckles, which were, in reality, only the briefest dusting of gold, and his cowlick, which remained stubbornly erect.

Matt refrained from watching, and she silently thanked him for that. Satisfied with the caricature at last, she handed it to Robbie.

"Hey, it's me!" he said. "I look funny!"

"You're supposed to look funny," Matt said. "May I?" He held out his hand, and reluctantly she gave it to him.

Casey watched his expression anxiously as he studied the portrait.

He smiled. "It's perfect."

Lisa joined them and pounced upon the picture. "We should pin this up. It'll be a great advertisement for your booth."

Casey grinned, and Matt ruffled Robbie's hair. "All right with you, Rob, if we borrow your picture?"

"Sure. Where will you hang it?"

"I think at the fairground entrance," Matt said. "That way everyone will see it."

Pleased at their praise, Casey began to feel more confident. "I guess I'm ready for business."

"I wanted to be your first customer—" Lisa paused to smile at Robbie "—but I'll be the second, instead." She promptly sat down and struck an exaggerated pose. Casey and Matt exchanged glances, then Casey said with a pretended frown, "I don't know if I can do you, Lisa."

"Why not?"

"You're too perfect," Matt put in. "There's nothing to caricaturize."

Lisa pretended to preen herself, accepting this at face value. "Well, there is that, I suppose."

Matt hooted with laughter.

His sister poked him in the arm. "Ignore him, Casey," she instructed. "Just draw me as I am—beautiful."

Casey chose warm tones to highlight Lisa's golden coloring. Her initial hesitancy gone, she drew boldly and quickly. Lisa's ready smile appeared, her large eyes winked back at Casey. With increasing daring, Casey transformed Lisa's blond hair into a tawny mane, giving Lisa a catlike quality.

When she saw the portrait, Lisa clapped her hands in delight. "It's not what I expected at all. It's even better." She paid her money and carried it away to show off to everyone.

Casey's customers began to line up. Some approached her timidly, others cockily, with directions as to how they should be drawn. She merely smiled and drew what she felt. Everyone appeared satisfied, if surprised, with the results.

She worked steadily all day, stopping only when she needed to grab a bite to eat. Matt and Lisa took turns showing Robbie around the fair. And when the boy wasn't with them, he sat near his mother, fascinated like everyone else, by the work of her clever fingers. The money accumulated quickly.

When Lisa came to collect it at the end of the day, she gasped at the amount Casey had made. "I knew you'd do well—I just never dreamed *how* well," she said, giving Casey a quick hug. "You've brought in over five hundred dollars!"

Casey flushed in pleasure.

Matt joined them, hooking an arm casually around Casey's waist. "I think the artist deserves a reward."

"What kind of reward?"

"Are you game for a horseback ride, or are you too much of a city slicker?"

"City slicker? Them's fighting words," she said, trying to look fierce. "Of course, I'm game."

"Great. Be at my place at nine Monday morning."

That evening and all day Sunday, Casey pondered Matt's changed attitude toward her. Maybe, just maybe, he was beginning to feel something different for her. A smile tugged at her lips as she considered the possibility. Not that she could afford to get involved with anyone right now. Still, the idea persisted.

No longer did she feel as if he was trying to force her to sell her property to him. In fact, he'd been helpful and even concerned that she make a go of it. Had his feelings changed at the same time hers had? Or was he merely playing a game with her for reasons of his own?

No. She refused to believe it. Whatever Matt Reilly did would be straightforward and aboveboard. He could be a formidable enemy, but he would be an honest one.

The next morning, after she saw Robbie off to school, Casey was having second thoughts about her decision to go riding with Matt. She hadn't been riding in years, and that had only been on park trails.

Despite her misgivings, though, as she drove to his place, she was excited. This would be their day, one for her to look back upon and cherish. She arrived just as Matt was leading a bay mare from the barn.

"Are you ready?" he asked.

"As ready as I'm likely to be," Casey muttered, eyeing the mare warily.

"Come on," he teased. "You're not afraid of old Tess, are you? She's as gentle as a rocking horse."

"Rocking horses have been known to throw people."

Matt tethered Tess to the rail. "Just pet her, like you would a dog. She loves having her neck scratched."

Tentatively Casey stretched out a hand to stroke the mare's neck. Tess whinnied in pleasure. "Wow. She likes it." More boldly now, Casey stepped closer and stroked the mare's back.

"Of course she likes it. You two get acquainted while I get Jupiter." He disappeared into the barn. Minutes later, he led out his big gray gelding.

Casey kept a prudent distance from the animal. "You've seen Jupiter before." Matt said.

"I know. But we've never been formally introduced."

"I'll do it now," he offered.

"No, thanks. I think I'll keep our acquaintance to a nodding one."

Matt laughed. "Let me help you up." He checked the length of the stirrups and, satisfied, gave her a boost up onto Tess's back. He mounted Jupiter, whispering to him in a conspiratorial manner.

She could've sworn the big gray nodded in agreement.

Matt kept the pace slow, allowing her to adjust to the horse's motion.

A flock of Canada geese flew over them, their V-shaped formation resembling dark feather stitches embroidered across the pale blue sky. Prairie grass, bleached white by the sun, rustled under the mild breeze. She shielded her eyes against the brightness of the sun to stare into the distance, seeing the craggy peaks of the Rockies, already capped with snow.

"I can see why people never want to leave here," Casey said. "I wish I'd brought my sketch pad."

"Spoken like a true artist."

She thought she heard a strange bitterness behind the words and wondered at it. But before she could question him, he asked her about her work. "Do you do landscapes?"

"Not normally. I was a commercial artist before... before my husband died. I'd like to illustrate children's books someday."

"Why don't you?"

"It takes time to work up samples. But with Robbie in school full-time now, I plan to start updating my portfolio."

"You're good. More than good," Matt said. "Don't let your talent go to waste."

"Why do you care?" she asked before she could stop herself.

"I just do," he said roughly. "Even when I shouldn't." He didn't give her a chance to ask him what he meant, for he spurred Jupiter into a gallop.

More confident now, Casey tapped Tess lightly with her heels. The mare quickened her pace, but she was no match for Jupiter, who gave every appearance of being able to run forever. Casey gave a relieved sigh when she saw Matt pull Jupiter to a halt.

"Trying to get rid of us?" she asked when she caught up to him.

He pushed his hat back and swiped at his face with a kerchief. "Sorry."

"Did I say something wrong?"

"I had something on my mind."

His tone warned her off. The brightness of the day seeped away as she observed the grim lines bracketing his mouth, lines that hadn't been there earlier. Jupiter whinnied impatiently. Suddenly Matt smiled. "Jupiter's reminding me he doesn't like to be kept waiting."

The heaviness around her heart lifted at his smile, and she returned it. Matt seemed to have forgotten whatever had been troubling him.

As they rode, he told her stories about the area, some touching, others hilarious. He wove local legends into them, delighting her with his knowledge and love of the land. He painted pictures with his words so that she was actually seeing the brave men and women who had tamed the land and built new lives here.

She questioned him eagerly, especially interested in the pioneer women. He indulged her, recounting incidents of the strong women who worked, fought and died alongside their men.

Sometime later, they rode into a grove of cottonwoods that shaded a small lake.

"It's beautiful," Casey said. "Are we stopping here?"

"I thought you might like to." Matt dismounted, then helped her down. "Sore?" he asked, a wicked glean turning his blue eyes gray.

She rubbed her backside experimentally. "Not too."

Matt grinned. "Let me know if you want a rubdown. I give great massages."

She ignored that.

He took a blanket out of his saddlebag and spread it on the ground, then unpacked the picnic basket. Fried chicken, potato salad, fresh peaches and thick wedges of chocolate cake appeared on the blanket.

Casey pretended to groan in dismay. "How many people were you planning to feed?"

"Just you and me. I know what a big appetite you have," he teased. "Of course, if you eat *too* much, you'll be too heavy for Tess to carry. So be careful."

She jabbed his arm, hard. He clutched it, moaning that she'd broken it.

Companionably, they munched on chicken, fighting good-naturedly over who got the last drumstick.

"I can see you as a pioneer wife," Matt said, returning to their earlier conversation.

"Why?"

"You have the spirit, the fire and the will to survive, all the things it must have taken in those times." His eyes were warm as they rested on her. "You remind me of my grandmother. She was a remarkable woman. Small like you, but with a fierce independence that drove my grandfather to distraction."

"I'd like to have known her," Casey said, pleased at the comparison.

"She'd have liked you. 'Give me spunk,' she used to say. 'Anything else is mere window dressing.'"

"Tell me more about her and your grandfather."

A reminiscent smile softened the normally hard lines of Matt's face. "They practically raised Lisa and me. We lived with them when my parents got divorced. My grandfather loved this." He waved his hand to indicate the expanse of prairie. "He'd say, 'Take care of the land and it'll take care of you.'" Matt's voice grew husky. "I've tried to build something he'd be proud of."

She pressed his hand. "I'm sure he would. You obviously loved your grandparents very much."

"We were closer than most kids and their parents are."

"Were they happy? Your grandparents?"

"They were the happiest couple I've ever known. And so much in love it almost hurt to see them together. Grandma said she and Grandpa were making 'memory days.' She told me that when I found someone special to build memory days with her."

Touched by the emotion in his voice, Casey felt the threat of tears in her eyes. "Not many have a chance to love and be loved like that. Having known love like that, it would be hard to settle for anything else."

"Yes, it does make anything else seem pretty second-rate," he agreed. "Did you and your husband have that?"

She didn't resent the question as she might once have. Somehow it seemed right that she should share that part of her life with Matt. "Yes. Only it wasn't long enough," she said quietly, remembering the all too short years she'd had with Dave.

"Do you want to talk about it?"

She did. "Dave and I were college sweethearts. We got married right after graduation, had Robbie a year later. Everything was going well—even his business had started to pick up. I was going to give up my job and try my hand at free-lancing. Then he started getting headaches." Her eyes closed as she remembered how their lives had been ripped apart.

"What was wrong?" Matt asked gently.

"He had a brain tumor. The doctors said it was inoperable. When he...died, I was glad. Glad he didn't have to suffer anymore."

"I'm sorry."

Matt drew her into his arms, and she went willingly. She stayed there, needing comfort. But her feelings of comfort soon changed to something more, something less easily defined, something that caused her to pull away.

"How about you?" she asked, wanting to turn the conversation away from herself. "Isn't there someone special in your life?"

Matt didn't answer but lowered his head and brushed his lips against hers. Slowly he traced her lips with his tongue.

Casey knew a quiet joy at the pleasure his kiss evoked. She wanted to throw herself into his arms and bury her face against his neck, to breathe in the scent that was uniquely his. Suddenly aware of what she was doing, she pushed against his chest. Matt took the hint and dropped his hands. She noticed his breathing was not quite steady as he picked up an apple.

Her own breath came in ragged gasps. Desperately she searched for an answer to her behavior. Her husband had died two years ago. She was lonely. She would have responded to any attractive man.

But the rapid beating of her heart against her ribs made a lie of the explanation. It was not loneliness she was feeling. Far from it.

"Tell me about your parents," she said, determined to keep him talking. For when he was, he couldn't be doing other things. Things like kissing her, things like turning her inside out with needs she hardly remembered she had.

Until now.

Matt gave her a look that left little doubt that he saw through her ploy. "There's not much to tell. My mother's an artist. She had a showing at a gallery in Denver, had a bit of success and left to study in New York."

"Your mother's still alive?" She'd assumed both of his parents were dead.

He nodded. "She's working in Paris. At least she was the last time we heard from her."

"She never returned?"

"No." Matt's eyes took on a hard look. "She hates the ranch. Says it stifled her."

"When did she leave?"

"Twenty years ago."

She did some quick calculations. "You would have been fourteen then." What kind of woman left her children and never returned?

"Almost fifteen."

"And your dad?"

"Dad was a rancher, born and bred. The ranch was his life until he started letting it go downhill. He began drinking heavily, and it wasn't long before the booze killed him.

When he died, my grandfather ran the ranch until I was old enough to take over."

"When was that?"

"When I graduated from college. I was twenty-one. My grandparents died shortly after that."

He lifted his head to stare at the wide sweep of prairie.

She looked at him with new understanding. "You took care of Lisa and the ranch."

"She was pretty independent by then. Look, it was no big deal. I did what had to be done. Anyone would have done the same thing."

"Not anyone," she contradicted softly. Bits and pieces began to come together. Matt's passionate defense of the land, his desire to unite the two pieces of family property. He'd had to grow up fast. Too fast.

"We'd better head back," he said abruptly. He began packing up the remains of their lunch.

She studied this complex man. Successful, dynamic, forceful, yet vulnerable enough to still hurt at his mother's desertion. Twenty years hadn't erased the pain. The dichotomy intrigued her, fascinated her, and scared her more than a little.

Silently she shook crumbs from the blanket and folded it before handing it to him. Just as silently, he tucked it into his saddlebag. He gave her a leg up onto Tess.

"Thanks," she said, and swung into the saddle.

The ride home held none of the morning's easy camaraderie. Casey was beginning to feel quite sore, and she held herself stiffly erect on Tess. The horse's motion, which had earlier felt like a gentle swaying, now became a jarring ride as Matt pushed them faster.

She was thankful when at last they arrived at the barn. She started to dismount, then hesitated, wondering how she was going to manage it. She looked uncertainly at the ground, which suddenly seemed awfully far away.

"Having trouble?" Matt asked. Before she could answer, he grasped her around the waist and swung her off the saddle and onto the ground.

She turned, acutely aware of his hands still resting on her waist, of the amusement in his eyes.

"Sore?"

If he laughs, I'll kill him. "A little."

"I've got some horse liniment in the barn. Works great on sore muscles."

"If you happen to be a horse. I think I'll pass." She smiled faintly, and the tension between them eased fractionally. Trying not to wobble, she led Tess toward the barn. Matt followed her and unsaddled first Jupiter and then Tess. He took a towel and began rubbing down the gelding. Tentatively, Casey copied his movements with Tess.

When they'd finished and returned the horses to their stalls, she said, "I ought to be going. Robbie will be home from school soon."

Matt didn't answer. Instead, he brushed his knuckles along her cheek. The simple gesture stirred her, and she fought to keep from swaying toward him.

When the kiss came, she was prepared. What she wasn't prepared for was the effect it had on her.

There was nothing tentative about this kiss, nothing tentative about Matt as he pulled her to him. With his hand cupping her neck and the other fitted against the small of her back, he held her still, his mouth roaming over hers, hungrily, possessively. Gently he lowered her to the earth floor of the barn.

Casey responded. She had little choice, with his body pressing against her own, his lips never breaking their contact. A soft moan escaped her lips. The hot heavy air of the barn, coupled with the pungent odor of horse and hay, only added to the tension building between them.

How long they stayed there, she couldn't have said.

When at last he released her, she rolled away from him, needing the distance between them. Her breath came in shallow gasps as she tried to understand what had happened.

Matt, too, looked stunned.

"We shouldn't have done that," she said.

He helped her up. "I won't apologize for kissing you. Given the same circumstances, I'd do it again."

She looked up at him. Was there regret in his eyes? Unspoken questions hung in the air.

He brushed a bit of hay from her hair.

She put her hands to her cheeks and felt their heat. Self-consciously, she picked the straw from her hair and then finger-combed it, wondering if he'd try to repeat the kiss. When he didn't, she didn't know if she was relieved or disappointed.

After she'd driven home, she tried to put what had happened into perspective. It was a kiss. A kiss between two adults who were attracted to each other. It was as simple as that.

Except she knew there was nothing simple about it.

Six

Water spurted from the shower faucet like a geyser. Convinced she'd lost her mind, Casey turned the faucet off, then on. Again, the water gushed out.

"Hey, Mom, you're all wet!" Robbie exclaimed.

"I know, isn't it wonderful?" She laughed and turned the water off.

"How come it works now?"

"I don't know, sweetheart. I'm only glad it does." For the rest of the day, she puzzled over the increased water pressure. Not one to complain about sudden good fortune, she accepted it, but still couldn't help wondering...

It wasn't until evening that she found the work order tucked behind, rather than inside, the trash can. A work order with Matt Reilly's signature on it.

Her anger grew as the truth sank in. Matt had arranged it. Because he'd felt sorry for her. The horseback ride had simply been a way to get her out of the house while he did his good deed for the day.

The next morning, after Robbie left for school, she drove to Matt's house. She'd worked herself into a fine temper by then. Who did he think he was, anyway? He had no business meddling in her affairs. She found him in his den and slapped the work order down on his desk.

He folded his arms and tipped his chair back. "Okay. So you know."

"Why?"

"Because I couldn't stand seeing you in that ramshackle house with no water to speak of coming through the pipes. Did you even have enough water to shower, to wash the dishes, to do anything?"

"We had enough."

"When? Every other day? Every two days?"

Her chin lifted. "We were doing all right."

"Maybe I went about it the wrong way, but I did it because I wanted to help you."

She searched his face and, reading the sincerity there, felt instantly contrite. "I know. Only I don't want your charity. Can't you understand?"

"I'm sorry if I offended you, Casey. I never intended that. I guess I was out of line."

"You were. I'll pay you back as soon as I can. If I can sell some of my work—"

"I don't want your money. I want... Oh, forget it." He was already hunched back over his desk.

She stood there for a moment, then turned and left.

Conflicting feelings struggled for dominance as she drove home. She knew Matt had acted out of charity but, dammit, she didn't want charity. She wanted . . . What did she want? For him to look at her like a woman, not as someone to be pitied. What did someone like Matt Reilly know about struggling to make ends meet when the paycheck didn't stretch far enough to put food on the table and pay the rent? About the pride-killing experience of selling everything you had just to pay the bills? About the helplessness of watching someone you love die slowly, bit by agonizing bit?

She shook her head slowly. No, he wouldn't—couldn't—understand, no matter how hard he might try.

It was foolish, this wrenching feeling of closing a door on something special. For nothing had ever really existed between her and Matt. She still wasn't sure if he even liked her. He was physically attracted to her, nothing more. If she'd grown to care for him during these past weeks, she had no one to blame but herself. She'd known the risks involved. Now she must pay the penalty.

Casey sniffed, determined to put her feelings into perspective. Of course, she wasn't in love with him, she told herself. If nothing else, this should convince her they were light-years apart. She knew he meant well. But that didn't erase her sense of humiliation.

Two hours later, she pushed her chair back from the desk and glared at the drawing she'd been working on, acknowledging that her fit of temper wasn't helping any. The figures were stiff, their actions stilted. She wadded the paper up, adding it to the growing pile of trash on the floor. A knock at the door was a welcome distraction.

Matt stood there, the embarrassed expression on his face at odds with his usual self-assurance. "Can I come in?"

She hesitated, then shrugged. "Sure. Why not?"

He grimaced but followed her inside, closing the door behind him. "I came to apologize again."

"Oh?"

"You're not making this any easier."

"I didn't know I was supposed to."

"I'm sorry," he said.

The simplicity of his words touched her more than could any elaborate apology. "It's all right."

"No, it's not. I offended you. I could kick myself."

"I know." Strangely she did. Her anger faded as she realized how difficult this must be for him.

Clutching his hat awkwardly, he appeared more than a little uncomfortable.

"I suppose it's hard for someone like you to know what it's like," she said, wanting to put him at ease.

His mouth hardened, and she backed up. "What do you mean, 'someone like me?' " he demanded.

Aware that she'd blundered, she rushed on, "You know, someone who has everything . . ."

"You've got it all figured out, haven't you?" He jammed his hat on his head and turned on his heel.

Casey grabbed his arm. "I'm sorry. I didn't mean it that way."

He peeled her fingers from his arm. "How would you know what I have or haven't experienced?"

She shrank back at his tone. "I only meant—"

"I know what you meant. You think I was born with a silver spoon in my mouth." His lips twisted into a mirthless smile at the guilty expression in her eyes.

"You weren't?"

"Hardly. Mine has always been a working ranch. What I have, I worked for. And worked hard. Nothing was handed to me."

"I didn't mean that."

Matt took her hand and led her to the front porch. "See that?"

Not sure to what he referred, she shook her head. All she saw was the sun-washed prairie with its backdrop of mountains.

"The land. It can be a man's best friend or his worst enemy. If there's a drought two years in a row, a prairie fire or the price of beef goes down, it can cripple a working ranch. Most places around here are mortgaged to the hilt. I ought to know," he muttered more to himself than to her.

"Your ranch is mortgaged?"

"Not anymore. But when my grandfather took over, we were practically bankrupt."

"But your father—"

"After my mother left, my father drank and gambled away half the land. The rest he let go to waste. It took my grandfather six years just to pay off the bank loan. It took me another ten to buy back most of what my father had lost."

The land he'd tried to buy from her—was that part of what he'd lost? "I didn't know."

"Of course not. You're so hell-bent on making sure your pride isn't being trampled on you've got no time to listen. Maybe if you had, you'd know that around here we help each other. That's all I was trying to do. There's not a man or woman in these parts who wouldn't do the same."

"I didn't understand," she whispered.

He brushed the hair off her cheek. "Quit being such a hard case, and let me help you. Pride won't score you any points, not around here, anyway."

Ashamed, Casey looked down at her scuffed boots. "I'm sorry."

"Hey, it's all right." He fitted a finger under her chin and lifted it till her gaze met his. The warmth she found there unsettled her more than ever.

"Want to prove that I'm forgiven?"

She looked at him warily, and after a moment's hesitation, said, "Sure."

To her surprise he gestured at her desk. "Show me what you've been working on. I'd like to see it."

"Oh. All I've accomplished today is rubbish." She gestured at the pile of trash on the floor.

"Any luck in interesting a publisher?"

"A nibble from one, nothing definite. That's who I'm doing these for. So far I haven't been able to send him much." She bit her lip, not wanting Matt to guess *why* she hadn't sent other samples.

"Why not?"

She sighed, knowing there was no way she could avoid answering him. "Paper, paint. Unfortunately they cost a lot of money."

He frowned. "Why didn't you say something?"

She gave him a level look.

Matt held up his hands. "Okay. I get the message." He chucked her gently under the chin. "And next time, if you need help, call. That's what we do here, okay?"

"Okay."

"So I'd still like to see some of your work," he said. "Don't you have a portfolio?"

"An out-of-date one. The last couple of years...it hasn't been easy to work."

"Can I see what you're working on?"

"They're just sketches for children's books. I don't think you'd be interested."

"Try me." She disappeared into the kitchen, returning in a few minutes with her arms laden with sheaves of paper. Thumbing through them, she picked out the best. "I'm still working on them."

She watched as Matt studied the sketches. He paused over one of her favorites, a watercolor of a small boy fishing at a stream. The boy's eyes were closed, his fishing pole dangling from his hands.

"You're good. Really good. The publisher ought to beg you for more."

Her lips curved into a smile. "You're good for the ego."

He touched a finger to her lips. "I'd better be off, Casey. I just wanted to...clear the air between us." And with that he turned and left the house.

Through the window, Casey watched him mount his horse. As if aware of her gaze, he tipped his hat in her direction. She blushed a furious red and drew the curtains together.

"Mrs. Allen, I warned you. I warned Matt. Now it's gone and happened. I hope you're satisfied."

Casey stared at Sam Meacham in bewilderment. The rancher, astride a quarter horse, loomed over her menacingly. "What happened, Mr. Meacham?"

"Sheilah's broken her leg."

"I'm so sorry. How is she? Can I help? Is she in the hospital? Do you need someone to help with the children?"

He snorted rudely. "Hospital? Why'd she be in a hospital? She's in the barn, of course." He dismounted and stalked toward her, wiping his face with a sweat-stained bandanna.

Alarmed, she took a step backward and stared at him. "You put your wife in the barn?"

"My wife? Lady, you gone plumb crazy? Sheilah's my best mare. And a damn fine racer, too."

She sighed in relief. "Sheilah's just a horse. I'm so glad."

Meacham's face purpled, and a vein throbbed alarmingly in his neck. "Just a horse? Now I know you're crazy. My best horse's broken her leg and you're glad? You're some kind of vicious mean woman, all right, ain't you?"

"Mr. Meacham, I don't understand. You tell me Sheilah's broken her leg. I'm sorry about that, but I don't see what it has to do with me."

"It's those damn varmints you let run wild on your property. Well, they done broke down the ground so that a decent horse can't run on it without breaking its leg."

She gasped. Matt had warned her what might happen, but she'd been too stubborn to listen. Still, she didn't think she was solely at fault. "But if she was on your property, I don't see—"

"She weren't on my property. She knocked over one of *your* flimsy fences and got herself hurt on *your* property." He shot her a look of such righteous indignation she flinched.

"Mr. Meacham, I'm terribly sorry. If I can do anything—"

"You're darn right you can. You can pay the vet's bill. And if Sheilah doesn't recover, I'm suing you for everything you got. I'd planned on racing her, then breeding her. She won't be worth a plug nickel now."

"But it wasn't my fault..."

Meacham was already stomping away. "You heard me, ma'am," he called back over his shoulder. He climbed on his horse and glowered down at her. "You're as bad as old Zach. Worse. At least Zach was one of us. He belonged here. You got no business being here. No business at all."

Casey watched him ride away. "He won't go through with it," she told herself. "He can't hold me responsible." But even as she said the words, she knew she was lying to herself. Matt had warned her, and she'd refused to listen. *If Sheilah doesn't recover*... She shook her head, unable to complete the thought.

Shoulders drooping, she followed the path from the garden to the edge of the field. The prairie-dog town was alive with chirping rodents. One fat animal stood sentinel, posted at the crest of his small mound. A short whistle and back flip from him sent all his friends and relatives scurrying into their burrows.

How could such endearing creatures create so much havoc? She stood there for long minutes, trying to decide what to do. The burning rays of the late-afternoon sun persuaded her to head back to the cabin. She turned to retrace her steps, only to be confronted by the sight of another rider. The familiar figure dismounted and strode toward her.

Matt. She hadn't seen him for three days, not since he'd come over to 'clear the air.' She knew a cowardly impulse to run. The set of his shoulders, the grim lines bracketing his mouth, boded trouble. Instead, she stood her ground.

They measured each other, neither giving way.

She took the initiative. "Guess you heard about Mr. Meacham's horse."

"The whole county's heard by now." Matt pushed a hand through his hair. "I was afraid this would happen. Why didn't you listen?"

Stung at his tone and lack of understanding, Casey lashed out, her anger cutting through the apology she'd been about to make. "Because I couldn't let hundreds of animals be destroyed, that's why!"

"So, instead, you let another *valuable* animal be maimed? Do you know what usually happens to a horse with a broken leg?"

This time, she refused to meet his eyes.

"It's put down. Shot."

Her anger turned to horror. "But legs can mend. I read about a Kentucky Derby winner with a broken leg that healed."

"That was an exception. Sheilah has less than a fifty-fifty chance."

"I told Mr. Meacham I was sorry. I don't know what else to do." Her anger spent, she bowed her head. "I never meant to hurt anyone, let alone an innocent animal." She scuffed the toe of her boot at the tufts of prairie grass that dotted the ground.

"Look, Casey, I know you didn't mean for it to happen. I'm on my way over to Sam's now to see what I can do." His probing gaze didn't allow her to look away this time. "What I don't understand is why. Why do you keep defending these animals when you know the damage they do? It's not like they're an endangered species or anything."

For an answer she motioned him to follow her inside. She walked to the mantel and opened the brass box where she'd put Zach's letter. She handed it to him. Matt unfolded the paper and scanned its contents. He gave a low whistle. "So it was Zach's doing. I should have guessed. But you're not bound by this—legally or morally. You must know that."

"I don't want to see the prairie dogs killed any more than Zach did, but I'm beginning to see the other side of the problem, too. I just don't know what to do about it."

"I'll try to smooth things over with Sam. He's not a vindictive man. I think I can get him to see reason."

All at once Casey was weary. She didn't need another problem. And she didn't need—or want—charity from Matt or Sam Meacham, either. "Don't bother on my account," she snapped. "It's my problem and I'll handle it."

"Like you've already done." He reached out a conciliatory hand toward her, but she ignored it. "I'll talk to Sam, see if I can calm him down," he repeated. When she didn't answer, he muttered, "Be seeing you."

Casey stared after him, wanting to call him back and tell him she was sorry. He'd only come over to help, and she'd thrown it back in his face. All for the sake of pride.

Robbie would be home soon. In the meantime, she had to think.

Seven

Casey hadn't meant to eavesdrop at the hardware store several days later. She'd only stopped in to buy a few supplies, but she couldn't ignore the loud voices that filled the small space.

"Did you hear Sam Meacham's organizing a prairie-dog hunt? Seems he got real mad when his Sheilah took a fall in one of the holes. He's going all out—advertising, the works."

She stole a peek to see who was talking. A paunchy bald man in jeans and boots leaned against a counter talking to the clerk, Kyle Bridges.

"I hear he's thinking of advertising a reward for the man who shoots the most prairie dogs," Kyle put in.

"It'll sure help all us ranchers." The man gave Kyle a sly look. "Won't hurt you none, either. All those hunters in town shopping for supplies. Not to mention the tourists."

"You can bet I'm laying in a stock of ammunition."

The bald man shook his head admiringly. "You've got to hand it to Sam and Matt. I think they're really on to something."

"What's Matt got to do with it?"

"You kidding? Matt's as anxious to get rid of those varmints as the rest of us. They've given him plenty of grief, too."

Casey stood still, afraid if she moved she'd give herself away.

There must be some mistake! she thought. *As much as he dislikes the prairie dogs, Matt wouldn't be involved in anything like that.*

"You sure?" Kyle asked. "That doesn't sound like Matt."

I knew it!

The rancher pushed back his hat and glared at the clerk. "Sure I'm sure. Got it straight from Sam."

Pain welled up in Casey's throat, leaving a bitter taste in her mouth. She waited until the men's backs were turned before slipping out the door, her errand forgotten.

At home, she tried to summon some enthusiasm for varnishing the cabinets. Lisa would be here in a little while to help her. Chagrined, she remembered what she'd gone to the hardware store for—extra paint and brushes.

"You went to the store and forgot the brushes?" Lisa shook her head in mock disgust when she arrived a few minutes later. "They say the mind is the first thing to go."

"What? Oh, yeah." Casey smiled faintly. "Do you just want to forget it for today?"

"No way. We'll make do with the old brushes." Lisa began wiping down the cabinets with a clean cloth. After a while she gave Casey a stern look. "What is this? A one-woman operation?"

Casey flushed. "Sorry." She grabbed a rag and absently dragged it across the cabinet Lisa had just finished.

Lisa took the cloth from Casey and gently pushed her down in a chair. "Okay. What gives?"

"Nothing. I was just . . . Oh, it's nothing."

"Must be an awfully big nothing."

At Casey's silence, Lisa shook her head and said no more.

They worked silently, applying varnish, wiping away the excess. The repetitive motion suited Casey's mood.

Lisa looked critically at the newly gleaming wood. She pointed to the top edge of one cabinet. "I think you missed a spot. Up there. Don't bother," she said, as Casey started to drag a chair over. "I'll get it." Standing on tiptoe, she reached the unvarnished spot. "That's one advantage of being tall."

"Thanks, Lisa. I'd never have finished this by myself."

"That's what friends are for." Lisa stood back to admire their work. "If I do say so myself, I think we did one heck of a good job."

Forcing herself to match her friend's enthusiasm, Casey agreed. "The cabinets look great." Wearily she sank onto a chair, then realized she'd sat on something. "Yuck." She pulled the sticky brush away from her jeans, and to her horror her eyes filled with tears.

Noticing them, Lisa came over and touched her shoulder. "Come on, Casey, what's wrong? And don't tell me it's because you just sat on your paintbrush."

"Nothing's wrong. I just—"

Lisa planted her hands on her hips. "You've been dragging around like you just lost a winning lottery ticket." She gave a lopsided smile. "I've got a good shoulder to cry on."

Casey took a deep breath. "Have you heard anything about a prairie-dog shoot?" she asked, hoping it was all a mistake.

"Heard anything? It's all over town."

"I hear Sam Meacham is behind it."

"That's right. I heard Matt talking about it." Lisa paused as she swished the brushes in turpentine. "That's it, isn't it? You're upset about the hunt."

"Yeah, I am."

"But there's more, isn't there?" Lisa persisted. "I think it has to do with Matt, right? Not just the hunt."

Casey considered lying and knew she couldn't carry it off. "What else? Listen, could we talk about this later?"

"Sure." Lisa dried off the brushes. "Matt's my brother, but I know he can be an awful pain sometimes. My offer of a shoulder still stands."

"I'll remember." Much as she liked Lisa, Casey wanted to be alone and try to figure out what she was going to do. "Thanks again for your help."

Lisa grinned. "I can take a hint."

Casey tried to smile and failed miserably. "I'm sorry."

"It's all right. That's why we're friends."

Casey watched Lisa leave and knew a sudden desire to cry.

Two days later, she drove back to Little Falls. Another visit to the hardware store brought her face-to-face with the last person she wanted to see.

"Casey, we have to talk," Matt said, taking her arm.

"What about?"

Matt glanced about the crowded store, where curious eyes took in their every move. "I'd rather not do it here. Have lunch with me?"

She owed him that much. A tiny hope flickered in her heart. Maybe it was all a mistake. She would ask him about the prairie-dog hunt. He'd deny having a part in it, and...

She let him steer her to a nearby restaurant. When they were seated at a secluded booth in the back, Matt ordered. Neither of them spoke until after the waiter had reappeared and placed huge plates of steaming ribs before them.

Matt took her hand in his, ignoring her attempts to pull it away. "Look, I know you're upset about the prairie-dog hunt. That's what I want to talk to you about."

Please, say you had nothing to do with it, she silently begged.

"I think we can—"

"Did you talk with Sam Meacham about organizing this hunt?" she interrupted.

"I went to see Sam about Sheilah," Matt said, his tone cautious, his eyes wary. "I told you that."

That was no answer. "Did you discuss shooting the prairie dogs and selling tickets to it?"

"We talked about a lot of things."

"Did you or did you not talk about killing the prairie dogs?"

"Yes, we did," he said evenly, "but it wasn't the way you think."

So it was true. Her breath deserted her in a whoosh.

"I don't need to hear anything else you've got to say. I knew we didn't see things exactly the same way, but..." She swiped angrily at the tears that gathered in her eyes. "I didn't believe it. Not even when I heard it the fifth time. Everyone's so excited you'd think it was the Fourth of July, instead of mass murder."

"It's hardly murder."

"Oh. What would you call it? A bunch of hunters with their high-powered rifles shooting at defenseless animals?"

"You're not trying to understand the other side," Matt said, beginning to get riled. "This could mean a lot of money to businesses that might otherwise go under."

"And that's what counts, isn't it?" she asked contemptuously. "Money."

"You bet it counts. Businesses close up, people go hungry without it. You, of all people, ought to understand that."

Casey stood, her plate of ribs almost untouched.

Matt grabbed her hand, pulling her back down. "If you'll give me a chance to explain..."

His nearness threatened to shatter her composure. A day's growth of beard shadowed his face. The masculine scent of him tantalized her nostrils, further sidetracking her from her purpose.

She knew he was right and that she was being unfair. Still, she couldn't condone what he and Sam were planning.

"I don't want to fight with you about this," Matt said. "But neither can I turn my back on people who've been my friends for years. They think this could be good for the town, as well as making the land safe for our stock. I can't completely disagree with them. There might be another way, but don't—"

"I'm sorry, Matt. I know you have to do what you think is right. But so do I." She stood once more. This time he didn't try to stop her.

Casey walked out of the café, her head high. No one looking at her would know of the pain that wrapped itself around her heart.

At home, she flipped through the newspaper listlessly, trying to decide what she should do. An item on the editorial page caught her attention. Readers were invited to write their feelings about the proposed prairie-dog hunt. Two hours later, she looked over the paper she had just pulled from the typewriter. It was good, she decided. Before she could change her mind, she folded the letter into thirds, sealed it in an envelope and dropped it into the mailbox.

Two days later, Casey opened the newspaper to the editorial page with a mixture of anticipation and dread. Her letter was there. The paper had printed the entire thing. She drew a sharp breath as she read it. It sounded so much more vehement now than it had when she'd written it. A tremor of fear skittered down her spine. What would Matt think of it?

She found out soon enough.

The peremptory knock at the door could belong to no one else but Matt. Casey thought of ignoring it and decided she couldn't put it off. When she opened the door, he looked so grim and forbidding she involuntarily took a step backward.

He didn't wait for an invitation and walked inside, slamming the door behind him.

"Why? Why did you do it, Casey?" He waved the paper, folded open at the page of her editorial, at her. "It makes us sound like a bunch of bloodthirsty sadists."

"I'm sorry you see it that way. I only wrote what was happening. If you and your friends don't like it—"

"Don't like it? Every animal-protection agency in the state will pounce on this."

"I'm sorry," she repeated. "But I can't stand by and watch you and Sam Meacham stage a slaughter without trying to do something about it."

"If you'd only given me some time..."

"To do what?"

"To find a way out of this. Now you've gotten Sam and the others so mad they'll never back down."

"What makes you think they'd back down, anyway?"

"There's a chance. There *was* a chance," he corrected. "Do you think I want this? Do you?" His hands cupped her shoulders, and he shook her slightly.

Surprised by his intensity, she looked at him. "I don't know, Matt. I thought I did. One time. But now... I just don't know."

His anger spent, Matt dropped his hands. "I didn't want this contest, and not just because of you. I've never hunted. Never wanted to. This..." He waved his hands, then dropped them in defeat. "If you'd only waited. I was working on something that might have... Oh, what's the use?"

Exhaustion had deepened the fine lines that fanned outward from his eyes and furrowed grooves around his mouth.

Her gaze softened. "Why didn't you tell me you felt this way?"

"If you'll recall, I tried to,"

She recalled a lot more than that. She recalled the kisses they'd shared, the passion that erupted even when they fought. Most of all, she recalled the way he made her feel when he held her.

Matt gathered her to him, his arms closing around her. His mouth sought hers.

Casey moaned as she adapted to the hard demanding planes of his body. It was so simple, when they were like this.

After a few moments Matt drew back, and she felt bereft. "I'm sorry," she whispered. "I wish things could be different."

"So do I, sweetheart," he murmured, pulling her close once more. He rested his chin on the top of her head. "So do I." He sighed heavily. "I have to go. Maybe I can still do something about this mess." He turned and walked out of the house.

Bemused, she stood staring at the door, seeing not it but the tall, infinitely disturbing man who held her heart. She wanted to call him back, to promise anything if only he would stay.

When the letter from a local law firm arrived announcing Sam Meacham's suit against her, she wasn't surprised. The rancher hadn't left her in much doubt about his plans. Now she had to decide what to do about it.

She read further and blanched. Where was she supposed to come up with $100,000? She was still gnawing over the problem the following day while trying to fix another fence. When Sam Meacham drove up in a battered blue pickup, she resisted the urge to hide and made herself walk toward him.

He took one look at the fence she was repairing and muttered something about "a damn fool woman." Taking off his battered Stetson, he said, "I come to tell you something, ma'am."

"If it's about the lawsuit..."

"Sheilah's gonna be all right. That lawsuit was just me being ornery. Matt made me see it weren't right—suing you and all. That ain't why I'm here."

Relief mingled with a healthy dose of indignation. When was Matt going to learn that she could handle her own problems? "Why are you here then?"

"About the prairie-dog shoot..." He paused, shuffling from one foot to the other. "We called it off."

She hardly dared believe her ears. "You called it off. Why?"

He rubbed his hand across a whiskered jaw. "Well, it's like this. Matt and me got to talking about it. He said as how we'd have all those city folk breathing down our necks if we went through with it. We don't need a bunch of outsiders telling us how to run our town. And he promised..." He let his words trail off.

"What?" Casey prompted.

"Never you mind. Matt said he'd take care of things, and he will. The only thing you gotta know is there won't be no hunt." Sam gave her a fierce glare. "But that don't mean I like those vermin destroying the land."

"I know, Mr. Meacham. I'm trying to repair all the fences. It's just taking more time than I thought."

"Well, me and the boys are fixing to do something about that. Day after tomorrow. And, ma'am?"

"Yes?" she asked, still reeling from what he'd said.

"Don't you go messing with the fence anymore. You're a right pretty gal, but you can't string fence. And that's a fact."

Once she'd have taken offense at the criticism, but no longer. He was right. She couldn't string fence. "Thank you, Mr. Meacham. You're a nice man."

Bright color suffused his face as he glanced furtively around. "Don't go saying things like that. Someone might hear."

Automatically she lowered her voice. "It'll be our secret." She held out her hand and tried, unsuccessfully, to suppress a smile.

Reluctantly he took her hand and pressed it in his own callused one. Then he pushed his hat back on his head and headed toward his pickup.

"Mr. Meacham?" she called.

He turned impatiently. "Yes, ma'am?"

"Why didn't Matt tell me himself about the prairie-dog hunt being called off?"

Sam scratched behind his ear, looking suddenly uneasy. "Matt don't hold with a lot of jawin'." He slammed the door and started the engine. The pickup spit out dust as he drove away.

Casey watched him, her smile slowly fading. Once again, Matt had stepped in to solve her problems, first with persuading Sam to drop the suit and then seeing that the prairie-dog hunt was called off. Why couldn't he understand she didn't need someone to take care of her?

She just needed *him*.

She tried to focus on what was important. Both the lawsuit and the hunt had been canceled. She should have been happy. And she was, she assured herself. If only Matt had told her himself. If only he'd trusted her enough to believe she could take care of herself.

Eight

When the envelope appeared in the mail late one afternoon a week later, Casey held her breath. Recognizing the return address of the book publisher to whom she'd sent her work, she opened it with trembling fingers.

She read the letter, and with growing elation, read it a second time.

"They want me!" she shouted. "They want me!"

Ten minutes later, she was bundling Robbie into the car, intent on sharing her news with Matt. "But why do we have to go right now?" Robbie demanded. "I want—"

"Because." *Because I want to tell Matt and maybe, just maybe, he'll realize I don't need a caretaker. Only* him.

"Because why?"

"Because I'm excited and I want to share it with our friends. Okay?"

Her old car bounced over the rutted road, echoing the uneven rhythm of her heart as she thought about seeing Matt again.

At the house, Casey knocked, then waited impatiently.

"He's in the study," the housekeeper said. "Go right on in. Robbie and I can visit in the kitchen. I've got something for him."

Robbie's eyes widened in anticipation. Casey hesitated before tapping on the door, suddenly unsure of herself.

When Matt opened the door, his smile eased her nervousness.

"Matt, I heard from the publisher! He liked what I sent him for the book. He's talking about a multibook contract. Maybe." She paused for breath.

He grinned widely. "Sounds like you've got it made."

"He wants to meet me. In person." The words tumbled out. "Can you believe it?"

"Where *is* the publisher?"

"New York. Isn't that great? I've always wanted to go there. That's where most of the publishing houses are."

"Yeah. Great. When will you be leaving?" he asked tonelessly.

"As soon as possible." She gave him an impulsive hug. "I owe it all to you."

"I didn't have anything to do with it," he said, gently disentangling her arms. "You're the one with the talent."

"You encouraged me to try. Without that, I might never have had the courage to send in my work."

"Whatever you earn is because you have talent, Casey. Don't sell yourself short."

She fixed her gaze on him, puzzled. "Aren't you happy for me, Matt?"

He kissed her lightly. "Of course I am. Have you told Lisa?"

"Not yet."

"Why don't you go tell her now? She's in the barn. I'm sure she'll want to know."

"Okay." Casey backed away slowly. "Aren't you coming with me?"

"I'll be along in a few minutes. I have some things to finish up here."

Much of her excitement had dimmed, but she kept her smile in place. "Sure."

"Isn't it great, Matt?" Lisa demanded when he joined them in the barn fifteen minutes later.

"The greatest."

His smile didn't reach his eyes, Casey noticed uneasily.

"I've volunteered to keep Robbie while Casey's in New York," Lisa said. "Now, all we have to do is to get her some drop-dead clothes, and she's all set."

Casey waited expectantly for Matt to say something.

"It sounds as if you're all set," he said.

She saw Lisa throw Matt a curious look. "I'd better get going," Casey said. "It's late and I have to go home and make supper."

"Why don't you and Robbie stay here for supper?" Lisa protested. "We have to celebrate."

"Thanks, but I'd better not. Robbie needs an early night. And so do I. Thanks for listening to my big news."

She collected Robbie from the house, hoping as she did that there'd be some word from Matt. She quelled the impulse to go up to him and ask him what the matter was.

The ride home held none of her earlier exuberance. She listened to Robbie's chatter about all the things he was going to do with Lisa, but only added an occasional "hmm" in comment.

Later that evening, she wondered at Matt's reaction. She'd have sworn he was genuinely happy for her at first, but his mood had darkened with her announcement that she would be going to New York to meet with the publisher. Just over a week ago, he'd kissed her in a way that still left her reeling whenever she thought about it. Yet today...today he'd treated her like a stranger.

Perhaps she'd imagined it. She shook her head. No, for whatever reason, Matt hadn't been pleased. She hadn't realized how much she'd counted on his approval until now. His indifference cast a gray shadow over her happiness.

The following day, after Robbie left for school, she drove to Matt's home. She found him in the barn brushing down Jupiter.

She waited until he looked up from his task. "Hi," she said softly.

His lips slanted into a half smile. "Hi, yourself. What's up?"

She hesitated. "I wanted to thank you for getting Sam Meacham to call off the lawsuit. And the prairie-dog hunt."

"Don't thank me. It was Sam's idea. I just pointed out a few things to him."

"I wish you'd have let me handle it on my own, but," she rushed on when he would have objected, "I understand why you did it. And I'm grateful."

"Are you? I wonder." He turned his attention back to Jupiter.

She willed him to look at her, but he kept on with his task. "About yesterday... I wondered if I'd offended you or something..." Her voice trailed off uncertainly as she watched him.

He gave Jupiter an affectionate slap on the rump. "Why would you think that?"

"No reason, I guess. Only you seemed so distant." There, she'd said it. It was up to him now.

"Distant?"

She nodded unhappily.

"I've had a lot on my mind lately," he said.

"Then you're happy about my going to New York and everything? You don't mind?"

"Sure, I'm happy. Why wouldn't I be?"

Was he going to answer every question with a question? "I just wondered. That's all." *How lame can you get, Casey?*

"You're happy, aren't you?" He looked at her keenly. "A chance to illustrate children's books. A dream come true."

"Yes, but maybe I shouldn't go. Not yet, anyway. I plan to leave in five days, but Robbie's just getting settled and—"

"Not go? And give up this chance?" He covered the few feet separating them. Framing her face with his hands, he said, "Of course, you should go. I'll be rooting for you. We all will."

Her smile trembled around the edges, but she managed to keep it in place. "Thanks."

He dropped his hands. "Look, you'd better run along now. I know you must have a lot to do."

She paled at the brusqueness of his voice.

"And I've got a lot of work, too." He gestured at the leather soap and pile of tack.

"Will I see you tomorrow?" she asked.

"Probably not. I've got to go out of town. I won't be back for a few days."

"Oh. Well, I'll see you before I go, won't I?"

Already bent over the tack, he shook his head. "I'm going to be pretty busy. Have a good trip."

"Sure." She backed out of the barn, hoping he'd look up and say something. Anything.

Somehow, she managed to get out of the house and into her car before humiliating herself further. She wouldn't waste another tear on him, she vowed.

The lone tear that trailed down her cheek didn't count.

She'd promised to meet Lisa in town to do some shopping. Any other time, she'd have been thrilled at the chance to buy new clothes. But now, she could barely rouse the energy to try on the dresses Lisa handed her.

She sensed Lisa's puzzlement but didn't try to excuse her lack of enthusiasm. How could she explain to Lisa what she didn't understand herself?

Trying to muster some excitement for the trip to New York, Casey spent the rest of the afternoon in her bedroom, putting away the new clothes she and Lisa had bought, but the colors blurred before her eyes. A silky peach dress slipped through her fingers. Would Matt like it?

Angrily she snatched the dress from where it'd fallen to the floor and crammed it into the closet. If Matt didn't care, well, that was just too bad. The opportunity to show a publisher more of her work was a chance in a million. It was everything she'd been working toward. If she didn't grab it, she might not get another chance. She had to take it.

So why did she feel like crying? She didn't have to look far for the answer.

Matt had made it clear he wasn't interested. She'd given him every chance to tell her he cared. A sob caught in her throat as she remembered his indifference this morning.

Suddenly she had a change of plans. She'd take Robbie with her to New York. They wouldn't come back. Even the uncertainty of finding a place there and starting all over again couldn't sway her from her decision. She couldn't bear to be that close to Matt, knowing he didn't return her love.

Reluctantly she told Lisa of her plans when Matt's sister came over the next day.

"I didn't mean it to happen," she said, trying to explain her feelings for Matt. "When I realized what was happening, I even tried to dislike him. But it didn't work."

Lisa looked at Casey with compassionate eyes. "We can't always love to order. Are you sure about Matt? About how he feels, I mean?"

Casey nodded miserably. "He made it pretty clear."

Lisa swore under her breath. "That brother of mine needs a swift kick."

"Will you help me settle things here?"

"Leave everything to me. You're sure you want to sell the house?"

Casey nodded.

"All right," Lisa said. "I guess Matt'll be pleased. He's wanted this property for a long time."

"Lisa," said Casey, "I don't want him to know I'm selling. At least not yet. Not until Robbie and I are good and gone. Okay?"

Lisa nodded and said reluctantly, "Okay, but—"

"No buts," said Casey. "It's better that way." She paused. "There's one thing, though." She paused. "The prairie dogs..."

"Sam Meacham dropped his suit, didn't he?" Lisa asked.

"Yeah. Once Sheilah recovered. He also told me he'd decided not to go through with the shoot and even offered to repair my fences."

"What's the problem, then?"

"I still feel responsible for the animals on Zach's land."

"I won't let them be destroyed," Lisa promised. "I don't know how, but I'll figure out something."

Impulsively Casey hugged her. "I'll never have a better friend than you." Then a frown pleated her brow. "I hate having to ask you to deceive Matt but it won't be for long. He'll be pleased in the end, finally getting his land."

"Yeah, guess so." Lisa didn't sound convinced. "He's away this weekend, so this'll be your chance. Can you and Robbie be ready to leave in two days?"

"I'll be ready," Casey said. "Oh, Lisa, I don't want to go."

"Stay, then," Lisa urged. "Maybe things will work out between you and Matt if you give it more time."

Casey's expression stiffened with resolve. "No. I'd only be kidding myself. You've been a terrific friend, Lisa. I'll never forget you. Or be able to repay you."

Lisa sniffed and wiped her eyes. "If you don't stop, you'll have me bawling like a baby."

"Mom, can we say goodbye to Ralph?" Robbie asked as Lisa helped them load their suitcases into the car Saturday morning.

Casey checked her watch, impatient to be on their way. One look at Robbie's face convinced her a few minutes wouldn't matter.

"Sure we can."

They tramped through the pocked field. While Robbie scampered off to find Ralph, she looked at the rugged landscape, now gilded a burnished brown under the autumn sun. Though some wouldn't find it beautiful, it was to her.

Would they find another place they could call home?

Nine

Casey caught sight of a highway-patrol car in the rearview mirror. Its driver seemed to be motioning her to pull over. Puzzled, she did as directed.

"Ma'am, I have orders to detain you," the boyish-looking officer said.

Fumbling for her license and registration, she missed the hint of a smile in his eyes.

"I don't understand, officer. Have I done something wrong?"

"If you'll just follow me," he said pleasantly.

Feeling she had no choice, Casey nodded. Robbie, who despite the constraints of his seat belt had managed to doze off, looked up and sleepily rubbed his eyes.

"Mom, why are we stopped?"

"We need to follow that policeman." She pointed to the uniformed man and started the car.

Excited at the prospect of meeting a real policeman, Robbie seemed to forget his sadness about leaving. "Are we being arrested? Were you speeding? Will we go to jail? Will they take our fingerprints?"

"I don't know!" she said, frustrated at the delay and concerned about what it might mean. Robbie's questions died away at her abrupt reply. He looked down at his hands. "I'm sorry," he said in a small voice.

Contritely she placed her hand on his. "No, Robbie. I'm the one who's sorry. I shouldn't have snapped at you like that. I guess I'm a little nervous."

"It's all right, Mom. I'll take care of you."

She smiled at that, touched by the seriousness of his reply. "I know you will, honey."

Up ahead, she could see the substation of the highway patrol. She pulled in alongside the patrol car.

The boyish officer held the door open, motioning for her and Robbie to go inside. Robbie clung to her hand, whether in reassurance or fear, she wasn't sure. Indicating chairs for them, the officer then held a whispered consultation with his sergeant, making frequent gestures toward herself.

Casey's anxiety mounted steadily; her grip on Robbie's hand tightened until he tugged it away.

"Mom, you're hurting me," he complained.

"I'm sorry, Robbie," she apologized in a low voice. "I can't imagine what they want with us."

Finally the sergeant approached them, smiling broadly. "Mrs. Allen, please come with me." Casey didn't immediately stand up. She glanced at Robbie.

Interpreting her hesitation correctly, the sergeant reassured her. "There's no cause for alarm. And this young man here—" he smiled at Robbie "—can stay with Officer McBride." He pointed at the young officer who had escorted them there.

The sergeant ushered her into an office marked Private. To her surprise, he didn't remain but backed quickly out, closing the door behind him.

No one sat at the room's solitary desk and at first it appeared empty. A movement at the far corner caught her attention.

"No," she whispered.

Looking exceedingly grim, Matt walked toward her. With nowhere to run and unable to take her eyes from him, Casey remained still.

He stopped several feet short of her. His eyes were bloodshot, his skin gray, and his clothes looked as if he'd slept in them. And she wanted nothing more than to hurl herself into his arms and feel his lips on hers.

Instead, she asked in what she hoped was a calm voice, "You had me brought here?" She didn't wait for him to answer. "Why? And how?"

"The sergeant's an old friend," Matt explained. "He put out your description and license number in a one-hundred-mile radius."

"That's illegal to track me down that way."

"A little," he admitted.

"You're not supposed to be here," she said. "You're on a business trip."

"Obviously I'm not. I got as far as the airport and found I couldn't leave. I came back to try..." He closed the remaining distance between them, and she found herself in his arms, his lips pressed against her own.

"Where were you going, anyway?" she asked when he lifted his mouth.

"Salt Lake City."

"I didn't know you had any business there."

"I don't. It's in Provo."

"Provo?"

"I've been corresponding with a Dr. Jeffers at Brigham Young University. He's an expert on the transplantation of wild animals."

Understanding wreathed her face in smiles. "The prairie dogs. We can relocate their towns."

He nodded. "I've been investigating a way to save them and at the same time make the land safe for the cattle and horses. I found a professor at BYU who's done research on the subject of transplanting prairie dogs. It can be done. It takes time and money, but it works."

"That's where you went two weeks ago?" she guessed. "Why didn't you tell me?"

"I wanted to."

"But why didn't you?"

"A couple of reasons. One, I wasn't sure if you'd like it."

Her brow scrunched into a frown. "Why wouldn't I like it?"

"You're familiar with the concept of balance of nature?"

"You mean, where the animal population takes care of itself?"

He nodded, watching her expression. "The prairie dogs will become part of that balance, along with the other animals that occupy the land."

She swallowed, knowing they would become the prey of hawks, coyotes and snakes. "It sounds like a good plan."

"Even when it means all the prairie dogs won't survive?"

She managed a shaky nod. "What was the second reason you couldn't tell me about this?"

He smiled slightly. "If you remember, you didn't listen much. I wanted to be sure before I talked to you. And I didn't want your gratitude."

"Why not?"

"Because I wanted something much more important."

"What?" she asked, hardly daring to hope.

He barely hesitated. "Your love."

"You have that. You've always had that."

"I couldn't be sure..." His thumb massaged the nape of her neck, destroying any power of thought she might possess. "Why did you leave, Casey?"

She tried to pull away from him, but he only tightened his hold on her. "I'm going to New York, remember?"

"You were taking everything with you. Including Robbie. That doesn't sound like a short trip. I want the truth."

"I was leaving."

"For good?"

She nodded.

"Why?"

She pretended an interest in the calendar on the wall. "I decided it was too good of an opportunity to pass up. Robbie will get to see New York, I'll have time to meet other publishers, and we can do some sight-seeing. If things work out, we might even settle there permanently."

"What about us?" he demanded, tilting her chin so that their eyes met.

"What about us?" she echoed.

"You were leaving without saying goodbye."

"We said our goodbyes, remember?"

"I remember acting like a fool. I also remember wanting to do this." He kissed her again. "And this." He undid the top button of her blouse to place a kiss on the sensitive hollow of her throat.

"I thought you didn't care," she said when talking became possible again. "I couldn't bear to be that close to you and know you didn't..."

"Didn't what?"

"Didn't love me," she mumbled against his chest. Even as she said the words, they caught in her throat.

"And that matters to you?"

She nodded.

"Look at me," he said. "I love you. Love you so much it scares me. I tried to let you go, but found I couldn't."

"Why? Why did you try to let me go?"

"So you could go to New York and have the career you wanted. You deserve a chance at making your dreams come true."

"Everything I've ever wanted is here. You. Robbie. Nothing else matters."

"What about your work?"

She read the doubt in his eyes and ached for the teenage boy who'd never fully recovered from his mother's rejection.

Matt looked away. "My mother accused my father of wanting to hold her back. She said her career never got off the ground because of her family. She wanted acknowledgment of her work, recognition from the art world."

"She didn't get it?"

His lips twisted. "You could say that. After her first success, she was ignored. She blamed everyone and everything, everything except the fact that she couldn't cut it. Finally she left."

"And you're afraid I'll be the same."

"No. I *know* you're good. So good you're going to make it. I didn't want to stand in your way. I didn't want that for you—for us. I love you too much."

His admission humbled her. "And I love you. Don't you know you're more important than any job? The publisher wants me to illustrate a picture book. Maybe even a whole series of books if things work out right, but none of that matters if it means I'd lose you."

"You won't lose me. But I know how important your work is to you. Could you be happy here? We don't have book publishers or anything else that a city like New York can offer. And we aren't likely to, either."

"Those things don't make a home. It's the people you're with that count." She hesitated. "I still have to go to New York and settle things."

"Not without me, you don't."

"I was hoping you'd say that," she said, a smile hovering on her lips. The smile faded as she realized how close she'd come to losing him. "I can illustrate books anywhere, but without you, it doesn't matter."

"I know." Shivers danced along her spine at the huskiness of his voice. "I feel the same way." He proved his words by kissing her, lightly at first, and then more deeply.

"What made you come after me?" she asked.

He grimaced and rubbed his jaw. "Lisa told me a few home truths. Things I would've figured out for myself if I hadn't been acting like a jackass. I want to make memory days with you, Casey. I want a whole passel of memory days. I've been thinking of turning the back porch into a studio. It's got plenty of light and..."

She kissed him. "I love you. But I wouldn't care if we lived in a shack, as long as we're together."

"Are you asking me to marry you?" he said.

"I was trying to."

He groaned and tightened his hold on her. "You little wretch. You put me through agonies."

"And what about me? Sometimes I felt as if you didn't even like me."

"'Like' has always been too tame a word for what I feel for you." His mouth claimed hers again, effectively silencing her.

Her hands reached up to twine around his neck. "It's all right now. Nothing matters now that we're together." Casey snuggled against him and turned up her face for another kiss.

His lips brushed hers, their touch a promise for today and all the tomorrows that followed.

Suddenly she pulled away and looked up at him. "About Robbie..."

Matt smiled. "I'll start investigating how to go about adopting him, if that's okay with you. He'll be the start of our family. He'll make a good big brother for our other children."

"Our other children?"

"At least one of each. With red curls and brown eyes like their mother."

"No," she contradicted. "They'll have brown hair and blue eyes like their father."

"Are you going to start arguing with me already?"

She shook her head. "I'll wait until after we're married." Her voice caught. "I love you so much it hurts."

"Not half as much as I love you."

A rap at the door interrupted what she'd been about to say. Officer McBride gave them an apologetic look. "Sorry to bother you, ma'am, sir, but this young fellow is feeling a mite lonely."

Robbie bounded into the room, took in the situation and grinned hugely. "Hey, Mom, Matt, I wanna go home!"

Casey and Matt exchanged smiles and drew apart. Matt took Robbie's hand. "I guess we'd better get used to this."

Casey watched them together, the small boy holding the big man's hand. Love had come, unexpectedly, wonderfully, in its own time.

ANNIVERSARY WALTZ

Anne Marie Duquette

Dedicated to Mara Villotti
who had the courage
to begin again.

One

She wasn't married?

The piece of paper in her trembling hand had to be wrong! Megan *knew* she was married!

She stared at the document. "This license must be filed with City Hall for marriage of above couple to become effective," it stated.

Her license, her *marriage* license, hadn't been filed! She was holding the original in her hand! Could it possibly be true? She, Mrs. Reed Kendall, was still Miss Megan McCullough?

She read the bold red-print warning again. Why hadn't the license been filed? Wasn't that the best man's job?

"Dear Lord, no..." Megan moaned.

Jerry Davis, her dearest friend in the world, had been best man at the wedding. But Jerry was not a real best man. He hadn't wanted Megan to marry Reed. He'd wanted Megan to marry *him*.

"I'm telling you, Meggie, this guy isn't for you. It's not too late to change your mind," Jerry had pleaded the night before the wedding. They were at the church for the rehearsal; the two of them had been early and were waiting for everyone else to arrive.

"Jerry, I'm nervous enough as it is!" Megan scowled furiously at him. "And don't use my nickname. You know Reed hates it."

Jerry scowled back. "Your parents and friends have called you Meggie since you were an infant. So what if Reed doesn't approve? This is exactly what I'm talking about. The man has you under his thumb already, and the ring's not even on your finger. I'm warning you, it's only going to get worse!"

"Shh!" Megan looked around to see if anyone had heard, but they were still alone. She wished she was already married. By this time tomorrow she would be, and then—

"What's the matter? Afraid your darling Reed might not approve of your talking to me?"

"It's not that—"

"Of course it is." Jerry paced the floor of the church entryway. "I still can't believe he allowed me to be in the wedding party."

"He's an only child. He doesn't have any brothers."

"He has friends, though, and I'm not one of them. You must have brought out the heavy-duty artillery to even get me an invitation, let alone serve as his best man."

"Reed knows that you and I grew up together. He understands how close we are. He was more than happy to include you," Megan said, wincing at the lie. She *hated* lies.

Jerry gave a hollow laugh. "Oh, he understands, all right. He knows I think you're making the biggest mistake of your life. Which you are."

"Jerry, please!" Megan was nearly in tears. "Tomorrow is my wedding day!"

Jerry's jaw set in an ugly line. "Don't you think I know that? I know you'll never marry me. I know you love me like a brother. That part's bad enough. But if I can't make you happy, I at least want you to marry someone who will!"

Megan reached for Jerry's hands. "Reed will."

Jerry shook his head. "He won't. Reed doesn't know the meaning of the word 'compromise.' By this time next year, you'll be miserable. He's an arrogant, conceited, selfish son of a—"

"Jerry! We're in a church!"

Jerry sighed. "He's the kind of man who sets women's rights back fifty years. First he'll make you give up your friends, starting with me. Then he'll make you give up your job. Then it will be your family, and who *knows* what's next. Meggie, don't you see? The man doesn't share. What's his is his, and you're about to become another possession. You can't live that kind of life. You'll wither and die! I know you!"

"You're wrong." Megan looked straight into the eyes of her friend. "And even if you weren't, I'd marry him anyway. I love him, Jerry. I love him so much it hurts."

Jerry exhaled slowly and heavily. "Don't I know it." He closed his eyes, then opened them again. "Well, you're a big girl now. But mark my words. You won't make it to your first anniversary without battle scars. One year and you'll be begging for a divorce."

Megan pushed aside her friend's dire warning. "Reed and I love each other. Everything will be fine. You wait and see." But her words sounded forced, even to her. Oh, where *was* everyone?

"You and Reed—you're both too different! Twelve months, Meggie. That's all I give you."

The two old friends had stared at one another in silence until suddenly there was a commotion just outside the door, and they'd both turned to see her future husband walk in. His eyes narrowed as he noted how close Jerry was standing to Megan.

"If you ever need me, I'm here for you," Jerry had whispered to her. "You call, and I'll come running."

She'd nodded and squeezed his hand, hating the pain she was causing him. Then she turned away from her lifelong companion and friend. She even managed a smile as Reed, his manner proprietary, even haughty, tucked his arm in hers. Then Megan McCullough turned her back on Jerry's warnings, got through the rehearsal, survived her sleepless night, and the next day became Mrs. Reed Kendall.

That was more than ten months ago. Megan moaned as she remembered her wedding day. She put down the unfiled marriage license and buried her face in her hands. As the tears fell, she realized that everything Jerry had prophesied had come true....

First her friends, then her job, then her family had fallen away, all casualties of her love for Reed. They hadn't been deliberate requests on Reed's part or conscious actions on Megan's, but somehow she had ended up with no one in her life but him. And she was still in love with Reed—knew she'd always love him—but how much more would she lose proving it?

Damn Jerry for being right! No, damn Reed for always having the upper hand. Reed might be happy, but Megan wasn't. The dreary existence she now led was slowly draining her. She wanted her life back.

Megan picked up the couriered envelope in which the license had been delivered. Looking inside, she saw a key and two sheets of paper with writing on them. She picked up the first one.

"Dear Meggie," it read, "surprise, surprise! I know it's a shock, but as you can see, I never filed your marriage license. This is kind of hard to explain, but here goes."

Agitated, Megan pushed back a long strand of hair and kept reading.

"I got pretty drunk at the wedding reception, remember?"

Oh, yes, he certainly had. Megan also remembered that Reed's dark disapproval had taken some of the joy out of the day.

"Every time I saw Reed I had another drink," Jerry continued. "I ended up not filing the license out of sheer spite. After I sobered up, I decided to call my lawyer. According to him, you have one year to file a marriage license before it becomes invalid. In addition, until it is filed, you're not legally married."

Good Lord, she wasn't married, after all!

"I know it was a crazy thing to do, but I decided to save you from a fate worse than death—marriage to Reed Kendall. After seeing how miserable he's made you, I'm glad I did."

The word "glad" was underlined three times.

"Reed will never give you a divorce, Megan. We both know that. So I'm sending you your ticket to freedom. Burn this license, and you're home free. Keep it, file it with City Hall, and you'll end up an unhappy, bitter woman—if you aren't already."

She wasn't bitter, she told herself. She wasn't. But she *was* unhappy, desperately so.

"Your anniversary is in six weeks. You have that long to decide. It's your choice. I love you. Jerry."

Megan put the letter down and unfolded the other sheet of paper with trembling hands. "I just had an idea, Meggie. I've decided to leave you the key to my safe-deposit box. If I know my cautious Meggie, you won't burn the license right away. So lock it away for safekeeping until you decide for certain. I'm upstate on business, but will call you tonight."

Megan breathed a sigh of relief on learning that Jerry was out of harm's way. She might have the fiery Irish ancestors, but Reed's temper was the volatile one. She feared for Jerry's safety when Reed found out.

When? She meant *if*. Megan shook her head. Was she actually contemplating telling Reed?

She picked up the license and looked from it to the second note and back again, feeling more than a touch of hysteria. Finally she dropped them both, along with the safe-deposit key, into her bag. Her heart was racing.

To start over again! The idea was so tempting. Maybe *too* tempting! Her marriage must really be on shaky ground for her even to consider going through with Jerry's suggestion. Reed loved her, and she loved him. No matter what their problems, that was never in doubt. Suddenly Megan needed the reassurance of her husband's voice.

She dialed his private office number but reached his secretary, instead.

"Good afternoon. Kendall Diamond Brokerage. Barbara speaking."

"This is..." Megan Kendall? Megan McCullough? Who was she? "Megan," she finally said. "May I speak to Reed, please?"

"Oh, good afternoon, Mrs. Kendall. Your husband's not in the office right now."

Megan's face fell with disappointment. "Can you tell me when he will be?"

"He just left for the airport. He's flying out of town to meet a customer about some African gem purchases. He won't be back until tomorrow." There was an awkward pause. "Didn't he tell you?"

"No. No, he didn't."

"Would you like me to have him call you? I can still reach him in the limo, if you wish."

"I..." Megan struggled for control, hating the sound of pity in the older woman's voice. This wasn't the first time Megan had been embarrassed by Reed's lack of thoughtfulness. "Never mind. I'll talk to him later. Goodbye."

She replaced the receiver with uncharacteristic viciousness, then picked up the unfiled marriage license. She had to get away from this house—the house where she'd spent so many lonely nights waiting for Reed to come home. She had to think!

Suddenly she knew what she had to do. She grabbed her bag, checked the name and address of the bank, which Jerry had written on the key's paper tag, then hurried outside to her car. Jerry said she had six weeks to make up her mind. She was going to use the time, rethink her life. In the meantime, she'd lock the license safely away from Reed.

Megan's hands were shaking so badly it took her three tries to get the car key into the ignition.

They were still shaking when she reached the bank. Even the bank clerk noticed.

"Are you all right, ma'am?" he asked. "Can I get you a glass of water or something?"

"No, no, nothing. I just want to get to Jerry's—to my safe-deposit box."

"I didn't know Mr. Davis had a wife," the clerk said. "I hope he's as good a husband as he is a customer here."

"He's not my husband!" Megan's voice was so loud a few customers glanced her way. How could they know that, as of today, she didn't even *have* a husband?

The clerk apologized profusely, but Megan was too upset to wonder what conclusions he was drawing about her and Jerry's relationship.

"Please follow me. I'll explain the procedure to you, since you haven't been here before. You see, the box can only be opened with a bank key and your key." He led Megan into the vault. "If you were to lose yours, we'd have to conduct an investigation before we could issue you another. That could take months, so guard it carefully."

Megan thought of Reed and nodded vigorously.

"Here we are. Hand me your key, and I'll open your box."

He did so, leaving Megan to gaze into the empty drawer. Why was she here? She must be crazy! She should be downtown at City Hall in the clerk's office, filing her marriage certificate.

Megan thought of being in bed with Reed. How her heart filled with joy every time he brought her body to that sweet fever pitch! How he loved to kiss her and hold her and talk with her—on the rare occasions he was home. She'd fallen in love with Reed the first time she'd laid eyes on him. She loved him still—his face, his laugh, the way he stretched and immediately reached for her when he awoke in the morning.

Could she really give that up without tearing her heart in two?

"Ma'am? I'll leave if you want privacy."

Megan thought of all the lonely nights when Reed was away. She remembered his broken promises to spend more time with her if she'd quit her job.

"Our schedules are just too busy, Megan," he had gently chided. "And you know I can't work around *my* hours."

She remembered all the phone calls from friends begging her to get back into circulation. She remembered not wanting to go without Reed, who was always working. And so she never went at all until little by little the invitations stopped.

Megan hardened her heart. "You can wait here," she told the clerk. "This will only take a second." She reached into her purse and removed the license. With just the slightest hesitation, she put it into the cold steel box and locked it away.

"I'm done."

As Megan walked toward the exit, she heard the clerk say, "Remember, take care of that key."

"I will." She had to. Her happiness—and Reed's—depended on it.

Once outside, Megan tore off the key's identifying paper tag and threw it into the bank's garbage can. Back in the car, she put the bank key on her key chain. There was no way Reed could go after the license now. And once—*if*—he found out, he *would* go after it. Megan was absolutely certain.

Whatever his faults, Reed loved her with a strength that was almost frightening. He believed in loyalty until "death do us part." He would never let her go, especially with Jerry waiting in the wings. The fact that Jerry had never married had always been a sore spot with Reed.

Well, she just wouldn't tell him, Megan decided. She had six weeks to decide—six weeks to see if she and Reed could work out their problems. In the meantime, she might as well go home and wait for Jerry's call. Jerry had wreaked enough havoc in her life for one day. She had to make certain he'd leave well enough—that being Reed—alone. Her nerves were already stretched to the breaking point; she didn't want to deal with Reed's temper, too.

As usual, Los Angeles rush-hour traffic was a mess, and Megan found herself moving nowhere. The events of the day suddenly overwhelmed her, and she rested her forehead against the steering wheel.

"What have I done? Oh, Reed, what's happened to us?" she whispered.

The ringing of the car phone startled her. Megan never got calls. She remembered when Reed first bought her the expensive sports car and loaded it with every possible option. They'd still been newlyweds, and Reed still the smitten groom.

"Reed, you shouldn't spend so much money on me. I'll never use a car phone," she had said, laughing.

"I can afford it. You deserve the best." He'd grinned. "Besides, what better way for us to keep in touch?"

But he'd always been too busy to keep in touch with anyone who wasn't business-related. Wives, it seemed, were low on the totem pole. Or rather, she corrected herself wryly, the telephone pole.

The phone rang again just as Megan lifted her head and reached for the receiver. Maybe it was Jerry calling, telling her this was all a bad joke.

"Hello, Mrs. Kendall? This is Barbara, again, and I have a message from your husband."

Megan fought her embarrassment. "Yes, Barbara?"

"I called Mr. Kendall after you and I talked. He was quite upset at forgetting to inform you of his plans. He said to tell you he's canceled his flight."

"Canceled?"

"That's right. He'll be home for dinner, after all."

Megan felt cold fear course through her veins. The first page of Jerry's letter was still on the coffee table! And she was miles from home and stuck in traffic.

"Tell him I'm not at home! Tell him to wait for me at the office," she said frantically.

"I'm sorry, Mrs. Kendall," Barbara murmured. "Mr. Kendall left the airport an hour ago."

Megan's breath caught in her throat.

"He should be home already."

Two

Megan sat in shock, oblivious to the traffic now inching forward. Several angry horns blew at her from behind. With a start, she hung up the phone and took her foot off the brake. Another horn blared at her slow response, and suddenly Megan was remembering. A blaring horn was how she and Reed had met....

It was two years ago. She'd stepped off a bush plane in the middle of nowhere with one small suitcase in hand and a new ID card in her pants pocket. Her name, Megan McCullough, was emblazoned under the Kendall Diamond Mines logo.

The air was hot and humid, the plane smelled of gasoline and other unpleasant cargo, and a dismayed Megan saw no one waiting to greet her.

"End of the line," the pilot yelled. "Someone will meet you sooner or later."

"But—"

"Your ticket was one way, luv. Get off the strip!"

Megan did. She watched with apprehension as the plane took off, leaving her alone, somewhere in Africa's diamond country.

She had ten minutes by herself, just enough time to wonder what she was doing there. Why in the world had she left her safe job back home to work in a foreign clinic? How could she have left Jerry behind? Had she finally bitten off more than she could chew?

Then a horn sounded, and one look at the man in the Jeep chased away all those fears. The first thing Megan noticed was his vitality. He hit the horn again, waved his arm and gave her a welcoming smile that made her feel all was right with the world. She exhaled a sigh of relief, and waited for his approach.

The breeze blew glossy strands of black hair over the driver's tanned forehead. And as the Jeep came even closer and pulled to a stop, Megan saw the intelligence in his eyes.

"Need a lift, stranger?" he asked in a deep voice.

His partially buttoned khaki shirt revealed a muscled chest and broad shoulders, but there was no masculine preening evident in his person. Megan instinctively knew that this was a man supremely confident with who and what he was.

"If you're from Kendall, I do."

"And if I'm not?"

Megan glanced around at the jungle desolation. "I'll take my chances." She threw her suitcase into the back of the Jeep and climbed in, missing his look of admiration.

"Aren't you going to ask for my identification?" he asked.

Megan shook her head and fastened her seat belt. "It wouldn't make any difference if you were a saint or an ax murderer. My plane is gone and I'm alone in a jungle—for the very first time, I might add—so either way I'm at your mercy. Whoever you are, I'm pleased to meet you. Meggie McCullough."

She held out her hand for him to shake, and this time she did see the admiration in his gaze as he took in her green eyes and lustrous red-gold hair. He took her hand, but instead of shaking it, gently held it.

"Reed Kendall, at your service."

Megan blinked in surprise, then frowned. "Look, I've had a long flight, and I'm in no mood for practical jokes. I'm sure Mr. Kendall has better things to do with his time than play chauffeur."

His eyes were merry. "I probably do, but I decided to take the day off. I needed a reason to get away, and you, Miss McCullough, provided a delightful one." His brown eyes twinkled as he released her hand to shift the Jeep into gear.

Megan found herself blushing at the compliment.

"Still worried I'm an ax murderer?" Reed asked as the vehicle picked up speed and he shifted again into higher gear.

Megan refused to be baited. "Or an imposter. Either way, you're quite charming for a criminal."

Reed gave a totally masculine grin. He reached into the breast pocket of his safari shirt. "Here, read this. Such bravery deserves a reward."

Megan took the plastic-laminated photo ID from his hand, and read it aloud. "Reed Kendall. Kendall Diamond Mines."

She knew he was waiting for a response, but she refused to act the cowering employee. She gazed at the photo and then back at him. "I'm pleased to meet you, Mr. Kendall. But why are *you* here?"

Reed took his eyes off the road to give her a quick glance. "As opposed to another member of my staff?"

"Yes. You must admit it's strange to have the big boss himself pick up new employees at the airstrip."

"Not if he wants to meet each new employee and evaluate him—or her—in person." Megan must have looked unconvinced, because he added, "If I were just out to impress people, I'd put my logo and title on the Jeep."

He wouldn't even need to do that, Megan thought to herself. Reed Kendall was a handsome man, but there was something more than just his looks that appealed to her. She was trying to get a handle on exactly what that was when he said, "We have a long drive ahead of us. Tell me about yourself, Megan McCullough."

"Well, I prefer Meggie to Megan, for starters. I graduated from college in Philadelphia. I have a degree in nursing, and—"

"I want more than just what's on your job application," he interrupted. Suddenly the cheerful voice of the stranger was replaced with the authoritative command of a supervisor. "I've read that."

"Then what would you like to know?"

"Start with your family. How many, how close are you all, and why did they let you come to Africa?"

As Megan tied back her hair to keep it from whipping across her face, she related her family history. "Well, I'm the oldest of six children, and one of four girls. My parents are both first-generation Americans. The family's originally from Ireland. Dad's worked the Pennsylvania steel mills all his life, and Mom's stayed home and raised the family. My parents have been happily married for more than thirty years."

"A rarity," Reed said with a strange expression.

"Thirty years?"

"That, and the happy part. My parents aren't, although they pretend quite well. Go on, Megan."

Megan would much rather have questioned him about *his* parents, but he was her employer. He had the right to call her by her legal first name, instead of her nickname, and ask personal questions. She didn't.

"You asked why they let me come to Africa," she said slowly. "It wasn't a question of getting their permission. I'm twenty-seven years old, hardly a child. I love my family, of course, but I never intended to spend my whole life in my hometown. Since graduation, I've worked in the hospital there, but I decided it was time for a change, and here I am."

"Hmm." Reed didn't sound quite satisfied with her answer. "Most women nowadays want to be lawyers or stockbrokers or high-powered executives. The nursing profession seems almost old-fashioned in these times. I should know. We hardly had anyone respond to our advertisement for a clinic nurse. Why nursing, Megan? How did I end up with you?"

"I..." Megan hesitated, then decided to tell the truth. "I grew up in a hospital."

Reed gave her a sharp look, then turned back toward the road. "You spent a lot of time there?"

"No, I mean I grew up there. I entered one when I was nine and was discharged when I was seventeen. I ate, drank, slept, played and went to school there."

There was silence. Then, "I'm surprised you could even bear to be around the medical profession after an experience like that."

Megan sat up straight with surprise. She'd expected the usual sympathy and the lame platitudes she'd heard a hundred times before. Instead, she was awed by his insight.

"I couldn't, not at first. I hated hospitals, doctors and nurses with a passion. I despised being there and was angry with my parents for abandoning me."

"What changed your mind?"

She thought about that. "More than anything, I wanted to be normal."

"What was wrong with you?"

Megan appreciated Reed's bluntness. "I was born with congenital birth defects of my right hip and leg. Oh, I'm all right now," she said at his concerned look. "My passing your company's medical exam is proof of that. But as a child, I was never able to walk. My brothers and sisters would run and play, and I—" Megan smiled at the memory "—I sat in a wheelchair and cried. I was quite pathetic, really."

"That's understandable, considering," Reed said compassionately. "What happened?"

"Dad's medical insurance wouldn't cover all the treatment I needed, or all the time I'd be in the hospital. Mom sent in an application to Shriners Hospital for Children. They pay for everything if you're admitted."

"You were one of the lucky ones?"

"Yes. Mom packed me a suitcase and I left home." Megan shook her head. "I had no idea it would be for so long."

"But you were cured. Surely it was worth it."

"There was a price, though. When I left home, I lost my family. I grew up alone. My brothers and sisters grew up without me. Oh, I saw them during visiting hours from time to time, but it wasn't the same. Dad was working, and Mom was busy with the other children." Megan's eyes were sad. "When I was finally released, they were strangers to me—and I to them. I suppose in a way they still are."

Reed was silent. The only sound was the Jeep's engine.

After a moment she continued, "The nurses and the other children in my situation became my surrogate family. There were a few special ones, especially among the patients."

Like Jerry Davis. He had been another patient with orthopedic birth defects. The two of them were admitted to the hospital on the same day. As they were the same age, they went to school together. Jerry became the surrogate brother, the surrogate kin, replacing the family Megan had lost. They shared the same doctors, therapists and teachers; they also shared childish confidences and very real physical pain. They even shared a love for medicine. Jerry had gone on to medical school when Megan entered nursing.

"And they inspired you to join the profession?"

Megan nodded, inexplicably comfortable confiding in this stranger. "Who better to take care of patients than someone like me? I understand their needs more than anyone."

"I imagine you do. But why here, Megan? Why a clinic at a diamond mine in Africa? We don't have the kind of patients—or injuries—you've probably worked with."

Megan remembered her initial interview at the employment agency. She'd be caring for those injured while blasting and mining for diamonds—the casualties of a risky profession.

She also remembered Jerry Davis begging her not to leave, reminding her of all the years they were patients at the hospital together. And knowing she could never love him the way he wanted.

"We're so much alike, Meggie," he'd said. "We've shared so much already. Don't go, sweetheart. Stay here and marry me."

But she couldn't, and that was why she was in Africa. Megan had requested an extended leave of absence at the hospital where she'd first been admitted and then employed, the same place Jerry had come back to work as a surgeon specializing in pediatrics. She'd wanted a temporary job that would take her far away.

She couldn't stand to keep refusing him. Like Megan, Jerry had suffered enough hurt in his life. She could only pray that during her absence his emotional wounds would heal.

She turned toward Reed Kendall and gave him a noncommittal answer. "I needed a change of scenery."

"As good a reason as any."

Megan was relieved when the personal questions stopped. She couldn't know that the pain in her eyes was visible for him to see. She only knew that it was far easier to listen to Reed talk about her new job.

"Mining is hard on the machinery and even harder on the human body. I've implemented the most up-to-date safety procedures available, but accidents do occur. That's where you come in. You'll be at the aid station right at the mine."

"I won't be at your clinic?"

"The clinic is away from the mine and all the adjacent blast sites. I need someone on the scene who can handle the day-to-day cuts and scrapes we get. More importantly, I want any serious injuries triaged and treated. I don't want anyone dying en route to the clinic if I can help it."

Megan stared at him with amazement and a growing respect. Diamond mining was an expensive, speculative business. Yet Reed seemed to spare no expense when it came to protecting his employees.

She was later to discover that the man was full of surprises. The initial attraction she felt for him increased into something deeper as the weeks, then months, passed. And wonder of wonders, her feelings were returned. She and Reed gradually spent more and more time with each other, until even the employees knew that something special was happening.

She remembered, oh, so clearly, the night they had first made love. She'd been at his bungalow, watching him strip off a grimy, sweat-stained shirt in front of the kitchen sink. "You really graduated from Harvard?" Megan was asking.

"Summa cum laude, with a master's degree in business and finance. Courtesy of my parents and old money."

He turned on the taps full bore and sluiced his hands and face with water and soap. Megan watched the play of muscles across his back and waited until he was finished.

"Surely you don't need to work so hard for a living, then, Reed. Why did you give up easy street for this?" she asked as he dried himself.

Reed came over and kissed her nose. "Because, my sweet, I had no wish to live my life as the only son and heir of Mr. and Mrs. Kendall." He sank into the kitchen chair opposite her and gave his wet hair a careless swipe with the towel. "My mother never wanted children, but my father held the purse strings. No son, no pocket money, he told Mother, and so I was reluctantly conceived."

"Reed, that sounds so..." Megan's voice trailed off uncertainly.

"Cold-blooded? It was. But Mother considers herself lucky. I wasn't a daughter, so she only had to go through the ordeal—her words, not mine—of being pregnant once. Father had his heir—someone who would take over the Kendall tradition of dabbling in assorted stocks and equally assorted women."

Megan watched in dismay as Reed tossed the towel over the sink, then picked up the drink Megan had fixed for him.

"You needn't look so shocked. It's all quite civilized. Mother is allowed her playmates, too. However, I decided that wasn't for me. I didn't want to be a playboy living off Father's money."

Megan couldn't believe the turn the conversation had taken, for Reed had never talked about his family. She was afraid any comments from her might put a sudden end to it, so she remained silent.

"Unknown to my parents, I worked all through college. Did you know construction pays remarkably well?" Reed lifted an eyebrow as Megan shook her head. "Well, it does. And because of that, I was able to play the stock market. But I didn't do it for fun, like Father had taught me. I played for keeps. After graduation, I took what money I'd earned and made more." He gave her an understated look of triumph. "And more."

"Your parents must have been proud of you," Megan ventured.

"Hardly," Reed drawled. "Father hated me because he couldn't hold his money over my head and make me jump through hoops. And Mother hated me for the same reason. Misery does love company, you know."

Megan didn't like the expression in Reed's eyes. It was more than unpleasant, it was downright frightening. Reed pushed away his drink, his gaze unfocused as he remembered the past.

"So, I paid Father back for my fancy expensive education. With interest, of course. Then I left home for good to try my hand at something new."

He looked back at Megan, and tenderness replaced the dreadful bleakness in his eyes.

"I like taking risks, but I also like excitement. The stock market was useful, but it wasn't what I wanted as a career. One thing led to another, and here I am, grateful for the best thing that's ever come my way."

"The diamond mine?" Megan ventured.

"No." Reed rose from his chair and gently pulled her into his arms. "You."

It was as if a long-standing barrier had fallen. Reed opened himself up to her both physically and emotionally. There was no more holding back.

And when Reed gathered her close and made them as one, Megan felt herself reborn in the beauty of their joining. The years of loneliness in the hospital fell away. The years of having no real family of her own disappeared, and there was only Megan, and Reed, and their love for each other.

The feeling remained in the days that followed. Megan found herself swept into the life of a man who now was everything to her.

"I love you, Megan McCullough," Reed said to her for the very first time one night. He didn't whisper it into her ear or accompany his declaration with sweet murmurs. He spoke the words clearly, so that she could hear every syllable. "I've waited all my life for a woman like you."

A feeling of joy spread through her, rendering her momentarily speechless. She nestled against his bare chest as he held her even tighter.

"I love you, too, Reed." She kissed him, feeling at home and content in his arms. That contentment was replaced by pure happiness at his next words.

"Be my wife, Megan. Marry me."

Megan sat up in his arms, eyes shining. Her reply was on her lips, but Reed laid a finger across them, silencing her.

"Wait. Before you give me your answer, there's something I want you to know. As your husband, I'll do everything within my power to make you happy. But in return, I want you to be faithful to me. Utterly loyal. No lies. I won't marry you without that promise, Megan."

His eyes were dark with emotion. Megan remembered what he'd said about his parents, and the mockery they'd made of their marriage. It was a wonder their son still believed in the institution.

"I promise, Reed."

He wasn't satisfied. "I mean for life, Megan," he warned. "Until death do us part. If that's too much to ask, then I'm not the man for you."

"You *are,* Reed. Pledging myself to you is no sacrifice. It's what I want." And she sealed her promise with a kiss.

His arms tightened around her and his lips seared hers with a passion that soon had her trembling with urgent need. Their lovemaking that night was different for both of them. Reed revealed a power and intensity he'd formerly restrained. Megan couldn't help recognizing the difference any more than she could prevent what had happened.

And from then on, she was his....

Three

Megan pulled into the private road that led to their beachfront home. Usually the rolling green breakers of the Pacific soothed her spirits, but she was in no state to enjoy the summer sunset this evening.

Where had all the joy between her and Reed gone? They had left Africa to settle near Reed's California offices with newly wedded bliss and high hopes. Those had quickly disappeared as Reed became more and more caught up in his business.

If it hadn't been for Jerry Davis's sudden decision to leave Pennsylvania and practice medicine in Los Angeles, Megan would have been lost. Both she and Reed knew the move was prompted by Jerry's feelings for Megan. Megan herself had advised Jerry against it, but Jerry had been firm.

"With Reed for a husband, you'll need a friend, Meggie."

Megan frowned at the memory. Some friend Jerry had turned out to be. Look at the mess she was in now.

She saw Reed's car in the driveway and steeled herself for the task ahead.

Megan walked inside. The cheery "Reed, I'm home" she'd planned died on her lips. Reed was standing in front of the fireplace. His expensive jacket and tie were tossed on the hardwood floor with uncharacteristic abandon.

"No wonder Barbara thought you were upset." Reed held up Jerry's letter, then crumpled it viciously, tossing it with a savage motion to the floor. "It seems you've had quite a day."

Megan placed her purse on the coffee table. "That, Reed, has to be the understatement of the year." She sank onto the couch and closed her eyes, trying to collect her thoughts.

After a moment, she felt his weight beside her, then felt his fingers tenderly stroking her hair. "This fiasco doesn't make us any less married, Megan." He placed a gentle kiss on her hair. "We'll file the damn thing first thing tomorrow, if you haven't already, and that will be the end of it."

Megan opened her eyes. "Will it, Reed?" Her voice sounded like that of a stranger, and Reed froze.

"What's that supposed to mean?" he asked.

She shook her head and didn't answer.

"Megan?" Reed's voice was harsh with urgency. "Answer me!"

"I didn't file the license," she finally said.

"But you're going to, right?"

Megan looked away. Reed's hands flew to her shoulders.

"Where's the license?" he asked hoarsely. "Megan, look at me!"

She did, her eyes full of pain.

"Tell me what you did with the license."

She felt sick inside, not wanting to hurt him but knowing he deserved an answer. "I locked it up."

"You . . ." He couldn't finish.

Her next words came out so softly he had to strain to hear them. "I don't know if I want to be married to you anymore."

There was silence in the room. Then Reed angrily rose to his feet. He walked to the huge bay window overlooking the beach and took a deep breath. Megan watched him carefully. She wasn't fooled into thinking he would remain calm. His clenched fists and next words confirmed it.

"Damn Jerry Davis to hell! If he were here now, I'd wring his neck!"

"Jerry has nothing to do with this!"

Reed whirled around at that. "I see. Our wedding license should have filed itself," he said sarcastically. "Wake up, Megan. The man is still in love with you! This latest stunt proves it. He's never accepted our marriage. He never will."

"He's never accepted the fact that I'm unhappy."

Reed's angry tirade stopped abruptly. "You're unhappy?" he repeated in a shocked voice. "I make you unhappy, Megan?"

"Yes." The single syllable escaped her lips before she could prevent it. At Reed's stricken expression, she held out her hand to him. "Reed, come sit down. Let me try to explain."

He did, and Megan studied him with love in her heart. His eyes were dark with confusion and hurt. The self-assured air that was so much a part of him was badly shaken. They held too much power over each other, she suddenly realized.

She must have spoken aloud, for Reed echoed her words.

"Too much power? Megan, I don't understand. We love each other! The one thing I've always been sure of is that."

"Sometimes we love each other too much, Reed." Megan reached for his hands. "You take me for granted, and I let you. We're both at fault."

Reed gently traced her palms with his thumbs. "This is about today, isn't it? Because I forgot to tell you I was going out of town. Megan, I'm sorry."

"It's more than just that!" Megan snatched her hands away in irritation. "I have no life of my own anymore. I have no job, no friends, and I never get back to see my family. I've put my life on hold to try and spend more time with you, but it hasn't worked. You're never here, and I'm miserable."

"I'll try to clear up my schedule some, and—"

"I've heard that story before!" Megan said sharply, getting to her feet. "I'm tired of waiting. I'm tired of your promises. You're a wealthy man, yet you'd rather spend all your time making more money, instead of spending time with your wife. I'm tired of that, too!"

Reed stood with her, capturing her arm when she would have strode away. "My God, Megan, is that how you see things?"

"What am I supposed to think?" she asked bitterly. "You're *never* here. And I'm not a part of your life anymore, like I was in Africa. I'm just a convenience. And sometimes, it feels like I'm not even that." To her horror, tears started falling from her eyes. She, who never cried in front of others, not even during all those years in the hospital.

"Megan, don't," Reed said, holding her face in his hands. "I'll do better by you, I swear." He kissed the corner of her eye, then her cheek, then started a butterfly-light trail down her neck.

"I love you, Megan. You know I do."

She nodded. That was all the signal Reed needed. His mouth came down hard on hers and he pulled her to him. In his arms she was his willing prisoner. Under his touch she came alive as she never did with anyone else.

Then they were in bed, their clothes on the floor, their bodies close.

"Reed, why can't it be like this all the time?" Megan whispered as his hands set her pulses racing with desire. It had been weeks since they'd made love, because Reed had been staying late at the office. "Is your work so important?"

"It's nothing compared to you, my love. Nothing." Then his mouth covered hers, and his body covered hers, and there was no more talking. There was only Reed and Megan, and the magic they had together.

"I must be the world's biggest idiot," Reed said later. They lay entwined in each other's arms, spent with passion. "Sending you to bed alone night after night."

Megan propped her head on her hand and studied him. "Then why do you, Reed?"

He shrugged. "I get so caught up in my work. Believe it or not, Megan, I enjoy what I do. I could never be like my father. He had money in the bank, so his conscience was clear when he let life pass him by."

But life was passing her by, too, Megan thought. Her honesty compelled her to say, "That's me, Reed. I'm just like him."

He smiled, unwilling to take her seriously. "Don't be silly, Megan. You're not at all like him." He gave her one last kiss on the nose. "Now go to sleep. I want you at the city clerk's office first thing tomorrow morning."

But Megan couldn't sleep. Long after Reed had dropped off, she lay awake, her mind in turmoil. Reed was very generous. He considered everything that was his, hers, and Megan had more money than she knew what to do with. Then, suddenly, she felt ashamed, for Reed's wealth had allowed her to sit home and do nothing.

But Reed wasn't the only guilty party to her unhappiness. She had caused much of it herself.

Reed stirred in his sleep, and Megan studied him with hope in her heart. At least they were finally being honest with each other. Perhaps now things would get better between them.

She made up her mind. She would file her marriage license tomorrow morning, just as Reed suggested. In fact, they could both do it. It had been ages since they'd spent a day together. Maybe they could look in on some of the friends they'd neglected for so long.

Megan sighed with contentment. She placed one arm around Reed's sleeping form and was just about to close her eyes when the phone rang.

She grabbed the phone on the bedside stand before it could ring a second time.

"Hi, Meggie. It's me."

"Jerry!" Megan turned in alarm toward Reed, but he slept on.

"At your service. So, enjoy your day?"

"No, I didn't, thanks to you," she hissed. "I thought you were my friend, Jerry! I trusted you! I didn't appreciate your little surprise, and neither did Reed."

"You actually went and told him?" Jerry gave a slow whistle. "Meggie, you're braver than I thought."

"It was an accident. I left your letter on the coffee table when I went to the bank. Reed found it when he came home."

"So you didn't go to City Hall, after all," Jerry said with real pleasure. "I didn't think you would. And Reed actually came home for a change. I wish I could have seen his face when he heard the news."

"No, you don't, Jerry. He said he wanted to break your neck!" Reed stirred at her vehemence. Megan watched anxiously as he settled down again, then lowered her voice. "And if you were here, I might have let him. You had no right to interfere in my marriage."

Jerry laughed sarcastically. "What marriage, Miss McCullough?"

"Jerry, I'm warning you..."

"All right, I'll behave." Jerry suddenly grew serious again. "Meggie, I just want you to be happy. If it's Reed you really want, then make him appreciate you! Use that license as a weapon. I guarantee you it's a powerful one."

"I don't play those kinds of games with Reed, and you know it."

"And that's why he's walked all over you. I love you dearly, Meggie mine, but that doormat complex of yours has got to go. Or else your marriage will pay the price."

Megan cringed at his words. "We did talk, Jerry. Everything's okay now."

"Oh, Meggie...you are so naive. You and Reed have a real problem. I'd bet my last cent all you got from him was a kiss and a promise, and an empty one at that. You can't just expect everything to be better in the morning. If I know Reed, he isn't going to change overnight."

Megan felt a vague sense of unease. They hadn't talked much, it was true. Reed had been hurt, she'd been upset, then somehow they'd ended up in bed together. Just as Jerry had guessed.

"Don't do anything rash, Meggie. Guard that license with your life. If Reed wants you, let him fight for you! Don't make things easy for him anymore."

"He said he'd try harder, Jerry," Megan insisted. "He really did."

"You're a fool, Megan McCullough. A damned fool!"

"If I am, that's my business. Mine and Reed's. Not yours."

There was silence on the other end of the line. Then, "I suppose I deserved that. I'll stand aside—for now. But I'm warning you, Meggie, nothing's going to change. And if Reed doesn't want you anymore, then I do."

Jerry hung up. Megan replaced the receiver with trembling fingers. If it wasn't so tragic, it would be almost funny. The man she wanted most in the world was rarely there for her, while the man she could never love always was.

Megan lay down again and forced herself to close her eyes. Jerry was wrong. Everything between her and Reed would be fine.

Sometime during the night Megan finally fell asleep. When she awoke, Reed was in front of the dresser mirror, knotting his tie.

"Reed?"

"Good morning, sweetheart."

Megan raised her head to check the alarm clock. "It's only five-thirty. Where are you going?"

"To work, of course." He finished with the tie. "But I'll be home early, I promise." He reached for his jacket on the back of the chair.

Megan sat up, clutching the sheet to her chest. "But...I thought we could spend the day together. It's been ages since you took any time off."

"I took time off yesterday, Megan. That's why I have to go in today. I'm running behind." He slid his wallet into his pocket. "I'll try to call you at lunch. Don't forget to file the license with the city clerk."

He gave her a quick kiss on the cheek, then picked up his car keys. "I'm going to be late. Have a good day now."

"But, Reed!"

"I'll try to call you."

"When?"

There was no answer. He was already gone. Megan was alone again, with nothing to look forward to except a phone call that might or might not come. Suddenly she saw herself years from now, still alone, still waiting for the phone to ring.

An icy chill ran through her veins. Megan felt more than just alone. She felt lifeless.

Something had to change. She stood up with determination and headed for the shower. Her linen skirt and silk blouse would be just the thing for job-hunting. She'd be at the door of the employment office at her old L.A. workplace the minute they opened.

They were always looking for good nurses, she knew. She wasn't coming home until she'd received a bona fide offer of employment. And then . . .

Megan turned on the shower and reached for the shampoo. Then she was going to hunt up her old address book and call or write every single one of her friends and family. It might take a few weeks, even longer, to rekindle her personal life, but her mind was made up.

Mrs. Kendall was gone. Reed or no Reed, Meggie McCullough was back.

Four

"Where the hell have you been?" Reed said the minute Megan walked in the house. "It's almost midnight!"

Megan looked at her watch. Goodness, but it *was* late! For the first time in months, she'd actually had a day where time didn't hang heavily on her hands. She smiled with real satisfaction.

"I'm glad you find this amusing." Reed took her jacket and purse from her, his movements revealing a barely controlled anger. "I've been worried sick!"

But Reed's ill temper couldn't spoil Megan's mood. "Why? You've come home much later than this, and I'm not allowed to complain."

Reed slammed her purse down on the mantel with a roughness that didn't bode well for its contents. "Have you ever heard of a phone?"

"I didn't want to risk waking you," she replied, echoing Reed's often-used excuse. She kicked off her high heels and padded into the kitchen. It'd been ages since she'd had an appetite like this.

Reed was right behind her. "You're actually enjoying this, aren't you? First you're late, then no phone call, then you throw my words back in my face. All right, I get the message."

"Message?" Megan turned away from the refrigerator she was peering into. "What message?"

"What's good for the goose is good for the gander. Isn't that the point you're trying to get across?"

"Reed, you know me better than that. I never try to score points. I was busy. It's as simple as that." Megan turned back toward the refrigerator. Lord, she was so hungry she could eat the proverbial horse. She pulled out the fixings for a sandwich and brought them to the table.

"Busy doing what?" Reed asked. He set a place for her, but his attention wasn't on his task. A piece of silverware dropped to the floor. Reed swore and substituted a fresh piece.

"Trying to get my old job back," she said calmly. She laid a generous supply of deli meat on her bread, then added lettuce and tomatoes.

"Trying to get your old job back?"

Megan scooped up a dollop of mustard with her knife. "Reed, would you stop repeating everything I say?" she requested. "I went back to the hospital to see about getting back my job on the children's ward."

"And?"

"Unfortunately they didn't have any openings."

Reed relaxed and sat down at the table. "Why didn't you say so in the first place?"

Megan didn't like seeing Reed's obvious relief. "I settled for another job, instead," she announced. "I'll be working the swing shift. In fact, I was able to start my training today. That's why I'm so late."

Megan remembered her interview at the personnel office. The woman in charge, Lynn Peerson, was an old friend of Megan's.

"Meggie, you know I hated to see you leave us," she'd said. "And you know I'd love to have you back. But there just aren't any openings in pediatrics right now."

"I'll take anything," Megan had said with desperation. "Anything."

Lynn flipped through her paperwork. "Well, we do have one opening," she said slowly, "but I don't know if you'd be interested. It's a trauma job, and it's only temporary."

"I've been trained in trauma nursing," Megan eagerly replied. "I had to be certified before I took that job in Africa, remember?"

Lynn nodded. "That's right, you did. But this job is the swing shift—three to eleven," Lynn warned. "I know your husband works days."

"That's no problem," Megan said in a determined voice.

"There's more. It's with the hospital's med-evac helicopter."

"Life Flight?" The Life Flight program had only been in the planning stages when Megan had resigned her earlier position.

"Yes. I don't know how you feel about flying with a trauma team. It's hard grueling work. There's a lot of action and a lot of stress."

"Did the last nurse suffer burnout?"

"No, she's in her final trimester of pregnancy. It was getting too hard for her to load and unload patients into the helicopter. She had to take maternity leave but should be back in about six weeks. That's why the position is open in the meantime."

Megan couldn't hide her excitement. Hard work was just what she needed. "I'm definitely interested, Lynn."

"Hmm." Lynn considered only a moment. "You'd need a training period to familiarize yourself with the helicopter's medical equipment. When can you start?"

Megan's eyes had gleamed with excitement. "Right now."

Reed's insistent voice brought Megan back to the present.

"I thought we decided you weren't going to work. You said we never have enough time together."

Megan poured herself a glass of milk, then rummaged in the cupboards for the potato chips. "And *you* said we'd spend more time together if I quit. Which we haven't. I'm tired of being home by myself."

She finally sat down and took a big bite of her sandwich.

"If you're working the swing shift I'll never see you!"

"You never see me now," Megan said between bites. How lovely to have an appetite again. "You're always gone."

"What would you have me do? Stay home all day? Become an aging playboy like my father? I despise that way of life."

Megan heard the anger in his voice. "I know that, Reed. And perhaps that's part of the reason you're so bored with me. I stay home all day and play the part of the useless wealthy wife. Like your mother."

Reed's face blanched. "You aren't useless, Megan. You and my mother are poles apart."

"Are we really? I wonder." Megan took a sip of milk, ignoring the hurt deep inside. The time for tears was past. It was time to face reality. "Perhaps a divorce is what you've wanted all along. Perhaps cutting me out of your life is your way of easing me into that possibility. Maybe you've even found yourself another woman."

"Megan, of course not!"

"I wish to God you had!" she flung back. "At least if there was another woman, I could understand why you avoid me."

Reed stood up, his hands tightly holding the edge of the table. "I've never heard you talk this way before, Megan. Never."

"That's because you're used to Megan the doormat. Megan, the adoring wife. Megan, the world's biggest fool." She picked up the second half of her sandwich. "She's gone, Reed. They're all gone. Meggie Mc-Cullough is back."

Reed straightened his chair back with awkward jerky motions. "You didn't file our marriage certificate, did you." It was a statement, not a question.

"No." She turned away from the pain in his eyes. She loved him, but she couldn't give in now. Megan knew one thing for certain. Even as a child, Reed had valued only what he'd earned with his own sweat. She had to make him value her the same way.

Her throat was tight with emotion. She reached for her milk, but Reed dashed it away with one savage swipe of his hand. The glass hurtled through the air, then exploded against the tile floor. Megan stared with wide eyes at the white splatters all over the cabinet doors.

"Jerry Davis is a dead man." His voice was terrible to hear. "If it takes every cent I have, I'll ruin him."

"Reed, you're such a fool!" Megan cried. She pushed herself to her feet and leaned over the table. "You don't understand! This isn't about you and Jerry. It's about you and me! *Me!* Just once can't you consider *my* feelings?"

Reed looked at her with disbelief. Then abruptly he turned and left the room, the sound of glass crunching under his shoes.

Megan forced herself to sit back down. She'd given up too many meals on account of Reed. This was one meal she intended to finish, and finish it she did.

Later she made her way to the bedroom, leaving the glass and spilled milk on the floor. Reed had made the mess. Reed could clean it up. But Reed was nowhere to be found. He wasn't in their bedroom, and after Megan had showered and climbed under the covers he still hadn't shown up.

She sighed heavily and turned out the light. The old Megan would have checked to see if his car was in the garage. The new Megan didn't. But either way, one thing remained unchanged. Megan was in bed alone, with only an aching heart to keep her company.

The next morning she was awake early. She didn't have to be at her training session until three, but she did have to buy a couple of new uniforms. The white dresses and slip-on nurses' shoes she wore on the pediatric wards were impractical for helicopter work. Lynn had given Megan the address of the local uniform shop that sold the one-piece jumpsuits and laced shoes Life Flight required its crew to wear.

Megan also planned to stop at the stylist's for a haircut. She's always worn her hair in a shoulder-length, easy-to-care-for pageboy until she'd stopped working. Then Reed had asked her to grow it long. She'd have no time for elaborate hairdos or her long manicured nails now. Both would have to go, and good riddance, Megan thought.

They were part of her old, useless life-style. Reed was right about one thing. She *wasn't* like his mother. The wealthy's privilege of staying home and doing nothing wasn't for her.

She climbed out of bed and slipped a robe over her naked body. She'd have a quick breakfast before getting dressed.

The kitchen floor and table were spotless, Megan saw. Reed must have cleaned up the mess sometime during the night. There was even a freshly brewed pot of coffee. Megan sniffed with appreciation and poured herself a cup.

"I'll have one, too, if you don't mind."

Megan whirled around in surprise. "Reed! I thought you'd be at work by now." She looked at his bare feet and chest, and his jeans. His hair was tousled, and he hadn't shaved. "Where have you been?"

"Down at the beach, walking."

Megan felt a pang in her heart. She and Reed always used to walk together. They both loved the ocean; that was why Reed had bought shoreline property in Malibu. But somehow those walks had dwindled in number, then finally disappeared altogether.

"I decided to take the day off," Reed said. He took the coffee she offered him and sat down.

"I hope you didn't on my account," Megan said worriedly.

"And if I did?"

"I hate to disappoint you, but I have to shop for new uniforms, get my hair done and run a few other errands."

"I could come with you," Reed offered.

"I'd like that." Megan smiled, then the smile faded. "But I'm meeting an old friend of mine for lunch."

"Jerry?" Reed asked with contained fury.

"No, Donna. She's a nurse. She and her husband, Bill, were always asking the two of us over." Megan put sugar in her coffee and slowly stirred it. "You never did get around to meeting her."

The accusation hung in the air.

"Anyway," she continued after a moment, "I'm getting back in touch with all my old friends. My plans are already made for the day, and I'm not going to break them. So if you want to go into work, go get changed," she said firmly.

Reed remained where he was. "It's been a long time since you and I had breakfast together."

"Yes, it has."

Megan popped two pieces of bread into the toaster. Reed stood up and moved behind her, his arms around her waist.

"It's been a long time since we've had a morning all to ourselves." His lips gently brushed against her neck, and Megan felt herself weakening.

"Reed, shouldn't you be getting in the shower?"

"Only if you come with me." Reed reached around and untied the belt of her robe. The sides parted, exposing her bare skin to his touch.

"I showered last night." Megan shivered as he pulled the robe down off her shoulders. His right hand gently caressed her breast, while the other traveled up and down a trim hip. "Reed, I know what you're trying to do, and it won't work."

He spun her around in his arms. Megan moaned at the contact of his naked chest with hers. His eyes glittered with triumph.

"Won't it, my love?"

Then he kissed her, hard and long and sweet. The kiss was Megan's undoing. They didn't make it to the bedroom. They didn't even make it to the living-room couch. Instead, their bodies came together on the plush rug before the cold fireplace, Megan urging him on with a passionate want that had them both trembling.

And despite the intensity of that wild, frantic joining, they both cried out—not words of desire, but words of love. Megan clung to him with a desperation that frightened her, afraid to let go, but knowing she must. Reed held her close, letting her choose her own time to pull free.

It almost seemed as if they could have remained that way forever....

It was finally Megan who sat up, pushing at her hair. Reed grabbed her arm and pulled her back to him.

"No, Megan, stay."

She shook her head. "I've got to go."

"I can make you stay. I can have you begging me to love you again." The expression on his face was fierce. His hands tightened on her arms, imprisoning her. "You know I can."

Megan looked into the intimidating depths of his eyes and wasn't afraid. "You've always had my body. I've never wanted any man except you to touch me."

Reed's face lit up with victory. Megan knew he thought he'd won until she turned away from his kiss.

"But you don't have my heart, Reed—not anymore. If you want any chance of winning it back, you'll let me go."

Reed's hands instantly released her. The look on his face was one of total astonishment. For the very first time in their marriage, Megan had the upper hand.

She'd never thought it would hurt so much.

Five

"I can't believe what I'm seeing. Meggie McCullough, back at work."

The familiar voice startled Megan. She was out on the helipad, restocking the helicopter with medical supplies.

"I wish you wouldn't sneak up on me like that, Jerry," Megan said through the open window, but her warm smile took the sting from her words. Jerry was leaning on the perimeter fence. "What are you doing in this neck of the woods?"

"Hoping to take you to dinner. Your boss told me you eat at six-thirty, and it's almost that now."

Megan nodded. "Well, your timing is perfect. I'm done here. Just let me lock up." She reached into her jumpsuit for her keys, secured the medical supplies and drugs, and closed the helicopter's door. Then she opened the gate to the fence and gave Jerry a hug.

"I love your new look." Jerry took in the name tag, the digital pager that hung from her beige jumpsuit and the much shorter hair. "And I even get a hug, to boot. The old Meggie would have looked over her shoulder first to see if Reed was watching."

"You needn't sound so pleased with yourself," Megan replied tartly as Jerry took her arm. "This was all my doing, not yours."

"Yes, but I was the one who gave you the kick in the pants," he said smugly. "I deserve a reward."

"Or a jail sentence. I haven't made up my mind," Megan said, but she was still smiling. "Come on, the hospital cafeteria is in the basement. Believe it or not, they make a mean cheeseburger."

Once they were seated with their meals, Jerry studied her and said, "You look good, Meggie. You really do."

"I feel good—about myself, anyway. I'm working, and my life has a purpose again. It isn't pediatrics, but I like it. And it beats sitting at home waiting for Reed."

"How's Reed taking all this?" Jerry asked.

Megan dunked a french fry in catsup, considering. "I'm not sure. At first he was furious. Then he was positive he could change my mind. Now he's taking me seriously, at least for now."

"That's good, right?"

"I don't know. So far Reed's behavior has been perfect. Calls me like clockwork, keeps regular hours, waits on me hand and foot when I get home from work. And he hasn't mentioned my not filing the marriage license. Not once since the day he found out about it." Megan frowned. "Frankly, I'm waiting for the other shoe to drop."

"I see your point. Still, you can't blame the guy for trying. To be honest, I never thought Reed had it in him."

Megan shook her head. "Reed's been a model husband, but it's not the real Reed. I don't want him acting this way just because I'm threatening to leave him.

I want him to act this way because he thinks our marriage is important.''

''In other words, you don't want to be married to a phony.''

Megan winced at the words, but had to acknowledge their truth. ''Something like that. I don't want Reed making a token effort. I have the sneaking suspicion that once that license is filed, he'll be right back to his old ways.''

Jerry stabbed a french fry with a vengeance. ''And making you miserable again.''

''He doesn't mean to,'' Megan insisted. ''And he has been awfully good to me these past couple of weeks.''

''Perhaps, but I wouldn't be surprised if the true Reed Kendall shows up sooner or later. This performance of his can't last forever, and we both know it. You'll be right back where you started, trapped in a rotten marriage.''

''I don't want that.''

Jerry hesitated just a moment. ''Then, Meggie, you may have to face the fact that your marriage is over.''

''I can't!'' Megan cried out in a voice so filled with pain it made a few heads swivel her way.

Jerry pushed aside his plate and reached for her hand. ''Sweetheart, I'm sorry. You know I wouldn't hurt you for the world.''

Megan pulled her hand away. ''You're part of the reason I'm in this mess, Jerry. I wish I'd never invited you to my wedding!''

''I wish you hadn't, either. Watching the woman I love marry a man totally wrong for her...'' Jerry's voice broke. He cleared his throat and started again. ''Look, Meggie, there's a way to find out if Reed's serious about your marriage.''

She lifted her head, her eyes wary.

"Tell Reed you've filed the license. Don't actually do it," he said. "Just *tell* him you have."

"You mean lie?" Megan said incredulously. "In all the time I've been married to Reed, I've never lied to him."

"I say now's a good time to start. It's an easy way to make the real Reed Kendall emerge," Jerry urged. "If he's a changed man, fine. If not, you can leave him with a minimum of fuss."

Megan cringed at the painful words, but continued listening.

"You know Reed will never give you a divorce. You can't afford all the smart lawyers he can. So save yourself a lot of heartache. Tell him you're now husband and wife, then sit back and watch his behavior. Who knows, maybe he'll continue being that model husband. If I had you for a wife, I know I would."

Megan felt her spirits rise. "Maybe you're right."

"I can't predict what Reed will do, Meggie," Jerry warned. "But at least this way you'll know for certain where you really stand."

Megan's expression was pensive. "I know where I stand. Reed loves me."

Jerry picked up his fork and reached for his pie. "Then, Meggie, you have nothing to fear."

Megan thought about Jerry's words during the drive home. She'd never lied to Reed before, and now she was going to. She couldn't deny feeling guilty and nervous, and yes, fearful. The moral implications of what she was about to do went against everything she believed in. Deceiving the man she loved was a contradiction of that very love.

But Jerry was correct about one thing. Reed would never agree to a divorce. And as much as it would hurt, Megan couldn't go back to the life she'd led before. If she stayed with Reed, she wouldn't have the strength to resist him. She knew herself too well. Leaving him would be the only chance for her to save Meggie McCullough from dying a slow lonely death.

She broke out in a sweat, and she rolled down the car window. The salty sea air wafted across her face, but tonight it didn't offer its familiar comfort. She checked her watch. It was after midnight. Reed would be waiting for her. He'd waited up every night since she'd started working again. She wondered how long that would last once he assumed they were married.

She shivered—but not from the night air.

Sure enough, the lights were on as Megan pulled into the driveway. Reed's voice greeted her as she stepped inside the door.

"Hi, sweetheart. Long day?" He took her purse and the bag with her soiled uniform, and handed her a drink.

"Thanks, Reed." She gave him a kiss on the cheek and took a grateful sip of the limeade. "Sorry I'm late, but we had a bad wreck on the interstate. We didn't get back to the hospital until after eleven."

"Was everything all right?" Reed asked as they both sat down on the couch.

Megan smiled at his concern. She remembered how interested he was in her work while in Africa. She'd often thought he would make an excellent nurse himself. He had a compassion and concern for the helpless that came straight from the heart.

"Yes. It was pretty hairy there for a while, but it looks as if our patient's going to be all right. We got to him in time."

"That makes all the difference," Reed said. "Perhaps I should look into getting a medical helicopter for the mine."

Megan shook her head. "No, it wouldn't be practical for you or your workers. The upkeep and medical staff would be wasted on all but the most serious traumatic injuries. And thanks to your safety policies, there aren't many of those. The aid station you have on the mine site and your clinic are more than adequate. I should know."

Reed nodded. "I'm glad. I'd hate to think I was neglecting my employees. Mining is a dangerous occupation. They deserve the best." He gave her a lopsided grin that had her heart doing somersaults. "However, so do you. I should know better than to bombard you with shoptalk the moment you walk in the door. That's probably the last thing you want to hear."

"Oh, no. I love talking to you about anything, anytime. I always have."

Reed edged a little closer and put his arm around her shoulders. "Do you still feel like talking?" he asked with a slight smile. "Or do you have any other... inclinations?"

Megan smiled back. She knew exactly what he had in mind. "I have those, too, Reed, but right now I'd like to go for a walk. I'm all keyed up from that last flight. It was touch and go for a while there with the patient, and I'm still too pumped up with adrenaline to sleep."

Reed kissed her gently on the lips, then lifted the glass out of her hand and placed it on the coffee table. "We can wait until later," he promised in a husky voice.

A few minutes later they were walking barefoot on the sand. The foam from the breakers hissed and splashed the bottoms of their jeans, while the breeze blew cool air over their bare arms.

"Cold?" Reed asked, his hand in hers.

"No, it feels good." Megan sighed with contentment, then turned toward Reed. The soft light from the full moon shone on his strong jaw and high cheekbones.

"You're a beautiful woman, Megan," Reed said as they continued their walk. "Even more beautiful when you're happy."

Megan let her smile speak for her. She was always happy when she was with Reed.

"I should never have neglected you," he said softly. "I guess I haven't been a very good husband."

Megan let go of his hand and put her arm around his waist. "Your parents' marriage didn't give you much of a role model," she said. "I had none at all growing up in a hospital. Neither one of us got much training for being married."

"Which we're not." Reed's voice held quiet reproach. "Are we, Megan?"

"I've always thought of you as my husband," Megan replied. "Whether the license is filed or not, that will never change."

Reed said nothing. They walked awhile in companionable silence, their arms tenderly locked around each other's waists. Megan wished it could always be like this, just the two of them. They were a good distance from the house before Reed spoke again.

"Shall we turn around?"

"Yes. I'm ready to go back."

"Perhaps tomorrow will be a little calmer for you at work."

"You never know. Some days we get as many as three or four calls and lots of emergencies. Other days we just sit around and do nothing. I hate that."

Reed looked at her with new understanding. "I imagine you do. You've had enough of that this past year, haven't you?"

"It's my own fault," Megan replied, not wanting to spoil the peace between them. "And my new job helps. I'm on the waiting list at work to get back into pediatric nursing. It might take me a year or so, but eventually I'll get there."

"You always did love children. I remember in Africa how they used to flock around you."

Megan laughed. "Only because I carried around pockets of candy, Reed, not because I was Earth Mother extraordinaire."

Reed shook his head. "It was more than just the candy those children loved. I realize that, even if you don't." A pause, then, "You've never talked about having your own children, Megan. Why?"

She hesitated and Reed instantly picked up on it.

"It's because of me, isn't it?"

"I know you'd make a good father, Reed," she said in a soft voice. "I keep waiting for your work schedule to clear up."

"In other words, you don't want to become a single parent," he said bluntly.

"I didn't say that."

"Don't deny it, Megan. We both know I'm never home."

Megan stopped walking and looped her arms around his neck. ''You've been home lately. And your business hasn't fallen into the ground.''

''No, it hasn't. I must admit the change has done us both good.''

Megan rested her head on his chest. ''Worlds of good,'' she echoed. She felt Reed's cheek rest atop her hair and let his love enclose her in a warm safe haven.

''So what are you doing tomorrow morning?'' Reed asked, still holding her tight. ''Do you think you'll have time for breakfast with your husband? Or lunch?''

''Oh, Reed, I can't,'' Megan moaned. She lifted her head, her eyes filled with disappointment. ''I have to be at UCLA at eight.''

''The university? Whatever for?''

''I have an appointment with a counselor to see about getting licensed as a nurse practitioner. I was finished with the required classes and only had to take the board certification exam...'' Her voice drifted off. When she'd married Reed, her testing, along with everything else, was put on hold. It was a shame, considering she had everything she needed to be qualified. ''I thought about taking some refresher classes first.''

''You're going back to school?''

''Yes. I didn't get a chance to tell you. I'm sorry.''

Reed put her slightly away from him. His actions were gentle, but Megan felt the tenseness in his body. ''So when will you be attending classes?''

''In the mornings, with a practicum from noon till two.''

''So you'll be gone all day at school, then working all evening?''

Megan heard the disapproval in his voice, but was unwilling to back down. ''Since I was locked into the swing shift, it seemed like the perfect opportunity to register. I've always wanted to be a certified nurse practitioner. I could do so much more. I wish I'd been certified when I was in Africa. There never seemed to be enough doctors to go around. I want to be prepared in case that opportunity to help ever comes up again."

Again silence fell between them. The waves continued to crash onto the shore while Megan waited for Reed to speak. Would he order her to give up her dreams again? Would she have to finally make a stand against the only man she'd ever loved?

"I guess you'll be pretty busy with both work and school. Let me know if there's anything I can do to help out," he replied.

Megan felt her knees buckle with relief. She discovered she was holding her breath and let it out on a long sigh.

"I'll be just fine," she managed to say. "But thank you."

"Well, we'd better get back to the house. You're going to need your sleep."

But later in bed, Megan didn't sleep. She and Reed lay together in the most intimate of embraces. The pleasure and exquisite tenderness of his lovemaking had brought her to tears. Even now, after their passion was long spent, she was reluctant to close her eyes.

"Go to sleep, sweet Megan," Reed murmured, kissing her neck, "or you'll never get up in the morning."

"I hate to leave you, even to sleep."

Reed cupped her face in his hands. "Have I neglected you so much?" he said, and Megan heard the self-condemnation in his tone. "Close your eyes. I'll be here when you wake up in the morning."

She gazed at him in mild disbelief.

Reed smiled. "Don't look at me like that. I promise. Now kiss me good-night. You have a lot to do tomorrow."

Megan took a deep breath. "I'll make sure I go to City Hall, too. I have some unfinished business to take care of."

"Oh, Megan, I do love you."

The look of joy and gratitude that Reed gave her took Megan's breath away. Then his lips and touch chased away fears. And for a second time that night, Megan postponed her rest.

Not that it mattered. Because long after Reed lay peacefully sleeping at her side, Megan was wide awake.

She'd never known how hard it was to sleep with a guilty conscience. . . .

Six

Her feelings of guilt continued into the following week, for Reed was more attentive, more loving, than ever. He even took time off when the Life Flight helicopter was grounded with mechanical problems, and Megan found herself with an unexpected three days off.

"What are you going to do, Megan? Anything in particular?"

"Not really." She stretched luxuriously in bed. "Today's Friday. I don't have classes, and the hospital says we won't get the helicopter back until Monday."

Reed reached for her waist and pulled her closer to him. "I hate your working weekends. But since you're not going to work, I'm not, either. I have a surprise for you."

He sat up, the sheet falling from his bare chest, and reached toward the nightstand.

"Here."

Megan took the envelope he offered. "What's this?" she asked, puzzled. "Plane tickets?"

"I thought you might like to fly back East this weekend and see your family."

"Reed! Are you serious?" Megan flipped through the itinerary with excitement. "But we have to be at the airport in two hours. We'll never make it!"

"Calm down." Reed caught her as she would have jumped out of bed. "I packed for both of us last night while you were at work. All we have to do is throw on some clothes. The airport limo will pick us up in an hour."

"An hour?" Megan relaxed. "I can change in a fraction of that time." She wound her arms around his neck and said with a wicked grin. "What will I do in the meantime?"

Reed's eyes twinkled. "You could thank me for the tickets."

Megan was only too happy to oblige.

Her good mood continued throughout the plane ride. "I can't believe we're actually going home," she said. "It's been a long time. I haven't seen anyone since our..."

She faltered on the word, but Reed picked up the slack.

"Since our wedding. Hard to believe we've been married almost a year."

Megan shifted uneasily in her seat and looked out the plane's window, thinking of the license still locked in the bank.

"What shall we do for our anniversary?" he asked. "It's only three weeks away."

Megan put a smile on her face and turned away from the window. "What did you have in mind?"

"A huge bouquet of flowers, wildly extravagant gifts, a romantic dinner, or all of the above. Whatever makes you happy."

Megan considered carefully. "You know what I'd really like to do, Reed? Go back to Africa."

"Africa?" Reed was startled. "Megan, why? The living conditions at the mine aren't the stuff romantic anniversaries are made of."

"Oh, but, Reed, they are! We were so happy there. We worked hard, but we played hard, too. I didn't care that the bungalow was lucky to have running water. I didn't mind the heat, or the dirt, or any of that, because we were together. I have good memories of the time we spent there."

Reed gave her an assessing look. "You actually sound like you miss it."

"I do," Megan said simply. "I don't know why you won't take me with you on your business trips to the mine. I've asked you often enough."

"I thought you were just being polite. Most women wouldn't want to give up a comfortable home for a primitive bungalow in the middle of nowhere."

"I'm not most women, Reed. I really wanted to go," she said, hurt at all the opportunities they'd already missed.

Reed took her hand. His face was filled with regret and bewilderment. "Sometimes, Megan, I wonder if I really know you at all."

She managed a shaky smile. "I wonder the same thing about myself, sometimes. Perhaps we should compare notes."

Reed lovingly traced her cheek with his forefinger. "We'll do that in Africa, on our anniversary. We can have the flowers, gifts and romantic dinner there. Maybe this time you'll let me give you a necklace of Kendall diamonds."

"No, Reed. I have my engagement ring from you." She fingered the flawless stone on her finger. "That's the only thing I ever wanted. That, and you."

Reed shook his head with wonder. He leaned over and kissed her full on the mouth, oblivious of the other passengers. "Lucky man that I am, you've got me," he murmured.

Do I really? Megan wondered. *And for how long?*

But her outward appearance showed none of her anxiety. She maintained a calm and composed air until the plane landed and the taxi took them to her parents' home.

"Meggie, it's so good to see you again!" Mrs. McCullough embraced her daughter on the doorstep while Mr. McCullough shook Reed's hand. "What a surprise! I only wish you'd told us earlier."

"We had very little notice ourselves," Reed said. "Did we come at a bad time?"

"The rest of the family is out of town," Megan's father said. "Your great-great-uncle died, Megan, and everyone went to the funeral except us. We were going, too, but when we heard you were coming, we decided to stay home."

"I'm sorry, Dad. I didn't know."

Reed offered his condolences, but Mrs. McCullough dismissed his apologies for keeping them home.

"Don't apologize, Reed," she said. "Great-uncle Charles was a wise old man. He'd be the first to agree that the living come first. I wouldn't miss seeing you and Meggie for the world. The rest of the family can represent us at the funeral. Come on in. You must be starving."

Reed took Megan's arm, and the four of them walked inside. Despite the family death, dinner was a lighthearted affair.

"Married life must agree with you, Meggie," Mrs. McCullough observed. "You seem to be one of those fortunate women who sail through marriage."

"We've had our share of ups and downs," Reed said. "Most of which, I'm afraid, have been my fault. I haven't been a model husband, but I've turned over a new leaf."

"Don't be ridiculous," Mrs. McCullough scolded. "You must be doing something right. Megan looks so happy. She was such a sad little girl, you know."

"Mom, please," Megan said, but her mother ignored her embarrassment.

"It's true. She was very lonely in the hospital and desperate for attention. She'd do anything to get her father and me to stay a few extra minutes. I really used to worry about her. She was frantic when we'd leave."

"That was a long time ago, Mom. I'm fine now."

Megan concentrated on her meal, aware that all eyes were on her. She never liked to think about all those years alone in the hospital. The loneliness hurt far worse than the physical pain of her treatments. Even Jerry and the staff were a poor substitute for the family she loved.

"And your mother and I are both glad of it, Meggie. Sometimes I wonder if we did the right thing, leaving you all alone. Still, you seemed to get used to it."

I never got used to it. Not with you, not with Reed. But she couldn't ruin the meal by saying that. So she gave them a polite smile and took another mouthful of food. Her parents were fooled, but Reed wasn't.

Later that night in her parents' guest room, Reed brought up the subject again.

"Megan, I never realized how isolated your childhood was."

She stopped in the act of brushing her hair. "Why bring it up now? That's all in the past."

Reed unbuttoned his shirt. "Is it? You were alone so much in your youth. Maybe that's why you hate me working the way I do."

Megan felt a chill of foreboding run down her spine. She slowly replaced the brush on the vanity table and swiveled around to face him. "What are you saying, Reed? That I'm a clinging wife because of my lonely childhood?"

"I never said you were a clinging wife." Reed turned down the covers and sat on the edge of the bed to take off his shoes.

"You implied it."

Reed didn't deny the accusation. "You have to admit you hate being alone."

"What I hate," she said with slow-growing anger, "is your smug, totally erroneous armchair psychology."

"Megan, please—"

"Don't Megan me! You're making excuses for your behavior, as always. Most men work forty hours a week. You work easily twice that on a regular basis, and often more. Any woman would resent that, even one without my background. Yes, you've been around more these past couple of weeks—but how long will *that* last?" She shook her head. "You're not married to me, Reed. You're married to your job! I might as well be single for all I see of you!"

"You knew I had a career when you agreed to marry me," Reed said irritably. "I've told you time and time again I have no intention of becoming like my father."

"I am sick to death of you using your father as an excuse!" Megan retorted. "But since you brought him up, let me say that you're more like him than you know.''

Reed rose to his feet, his fists clenched. ''The hell I am!''

Megan's eyes narrowed. ''You are! You give me money, instead of your time, like him. You give me gifts, instead of giving me yourself, like him. You live in your own little world that holds no room for a wife. You even have your own mistress like your father, only you prefer an office to warm flesh. You don't know how to be a good husband any more than he did. As far as I'm concerned, you're a regular chip off the old block!''

Reed sprang forward. He grabbed her arms and jerked her to her feet. ''How dare you? I love you, Megan! My father never loved anyone except himself. He never took care of his wife.''

Megan met his gaze head on. ''Neither have you! You've put me on a pedestal and left me there! I don't want to be loved from afar, Reed! I'm a flesh-and-blood woman. I want my husband's arms around me. I want children at my feet. Lord knows I've prayed for them often enough.''

Her lips twisted bitterly. ''I'll be lucky if I ever conceive. On the rare occasions you do bother to make love to me, you usually have ulterior motives, like wanting me to quit work, or to file our marriage license. My God, Reed, how do you think that makes me feel?''

It took Reed a moment to answer. When he did, his voice was bitter. ''Considering your low opinion of me, Megan, I'm surprised you even bothered to file that license.''

Megan yanked her arms free. ''I didn't!''

Reed's face blanched. They both stood frozen for seemingly endless minutes. Megan wished herself dead a hundred times over for putting that awful look on his face.

It was a while before he was able to say, ''You lied?'' The words were choked and strangled. ''You lied to me, Megan?''

''Yes,'' Megan whispered. ''Like you lied to me. You promised until death do us part.'' She shook her head, tears filling her eyes. ''But you left me a long, long time ago.''

Megan sank into the chair and buried her face in her hands. She couldn't bear to look at Reed any longer. She closed her eyes and fought her tears. Reed hated to see her cry. She wouldn't make things any worse for him than she already had.

It didn't matter. When she looked up, Reed was gone.

Seven

He left a note of apology for her parents, saying he was flying to New York on business. As Kendall Diamonds had another branch there, Megan's parents were understanding. Megan was all too painfully aware that no note was left for her.

Now she was desperate to get back home. She planned to cut her weekend short, but that was not to be. The rest of her family returned from the funeral and weren't about to let her leave. As it was, Megan barely made her scheduled flight. Everyone kept pressing her to stay.

Only the fact that she had to be back at work convinced them to let her go.

"Don't be such a stranger," her mother said when kissing her goodbye. "You and Reed come again real soon."

Megan nearly broke down and wept. She didn't even know where Reed was.

Once at the airport, she immediately checked with the ticket agent. When she heard Reed had cashed in his ticket for an earlier flight home, she felt a little better. Megan desperately wanted to see him and apologize. Not for what she'd said about their marriage—for those words had been too long unspoken—but for breaking her promise.

I want you to be faithful. Utterly loyal. No lies. I won't marry you without that promise, Reed had said when he'd proposed to her.

Megan had given him her solemn vow. Yet she'd broken it by listening to Jerry Davis and lying to Reed. That was a grave error, and one she intended to rectify. She could hardly wait for the plane to touch down at Los Angeles International. The cab ride home seemed to take forever, and Megan's nerves were practically in shreds by the time they finally reached the house.

She hurriedly paid the driver and raced inside.

"Reed?" she called. "Reed, are you home?"

Only silence greeted her. Megan dropped purse and suitcase on the floor and hurried through the house. There was no sign of him. A check of the garage revealed that his car was gone. His suitcase wasn't in the storage room, either.

Megan slumped with disappointment. It was late Sunday night. Why wasn't he home?

On a sudden impulse she called his office. The answering service picked up.

"No, Mrs. Kendall. Your husband isn't working today. He's not expected back until tomorrow."

"Thank you." Megan hung up numbly. She busied herself with unpacking and getting her things ready for the morning. She'd have a full day with both class and work.

She could only hope she'd be well rested. She didn't think she'd get much sleep wondering where Reed was. No matter how much practice she had going to bed alone, she never got used to it.

Never.

Three days later Reed still hadn't appeared or called, neither at home nor at the office. She had a hard time concentrating in class and had to force herself to stay alert at work. Finally in desperation she called Jerry.

"No, I haven't heard from Reed. He's left you?" Jerry asked with barely controlled anger.

"I... I don't know," Megan said miserably. "That's what I'm trying to find out."

"Stay put, Meggie. I'm on my way over."

Megan counted the minutes until Jerry arrived. She was at the door waiting to let him in the moment he pulled into the driveway.

"Oh, Jerry, thanks for coming. I'm sorry to bother you so late at night, but I had to talk to somebody."

"I'm not worried about me. I'm worried about you. Meggie, what's going on? Where's Reed?"

Megan sat down on the couch, her face the picture of despair. "I wish I knew."

"Tell me what happened." Jerry sat down next to her. "I thought you said Reed was on his best behavior."

"He was. We even flew to my parents' home on Friday."

"Talk about once in a blue moon." Jerry was incredulous. "Reed actually took you to see your family?"

"Yes. Things were going so well. Reed arranged everything. We were supposed to spend the whole weekend there, but—" Megan broke off abruptly.

Jerry took her hands in his. "But what, Meggie?"

"He accused me of being a clinging wife...."

"That'd be quite a trick, since he's never home to cling to," Jerry said angrily. "Go on."

"I got really angry and said some things I shouldn't have."

"Like?"

"I told him I'd lied about filing the marriage license. He got up and left. He didn't stay one night at my parents'. He didn't even say goodbye." Her voice broke. "I haven't seen him since."

"Oh, Meggie, I'm sorry. I wish there was something I could do."

Jerry put his arms around her and held her tight. Megan rested her head on the shoulder of her dearest friend, taking the comfort he offered, but wishing more than anything that it was Reed's arms around her, Reed's voice whispering in her ear.

She sat quietly for a long time until a familiar voice reached her ears.

"Well, isn't this a touching scene."

Megan jerked her head up, her pulse quickening with excitement.

"I should have known it wouldn't take you long to show up on my doorstep, Davis." Reed's voice was diamond-hard. "But then, you have a nasty habit of showing up when you're least wanted. Starting with my wedding."

Jerry flushed an angry red. "I was invited. Just like I was invited here."

"Not by me, you weren't." Reed's eyes glittered with anger. "You've been a thorn in my side since the day Megan chose me over you. I've put up with it because you're Megan's friend, but I'll be damned if I will any longer."

He grabbed Jerry's arm and yanked him to his feet. "Get away from my wife! And get out of my house before I throw you out!"

"And leave Megan with you? Not that it would be very long, considering your track record. How could you abandon her?"

Jerry shook himself free and tried to get back to Megan. Reed immediately stepped in front of her, effectively blocking Jerry's way.

"Stop it, you two! I won't have you fighting!" She placed a soothing hand on Reed's shoulder, but he refused to be calmed.

"I walk into my own home and find my wife in the arms of another man. What do you expect me to do, Megan? Offer to fix him a drink?"

"Please don't be angry, Reed. I was frantic for news about you. Jerry knew I was upset."

"So naturally he had to race over here and comfort you. What did you have planned next, Jerry? As if I couldn't guess."

"Reed! You know Jerry and I aren't...wouldn't..." Her words trailed off.

"Only because you won't allow it. Jerry would have you in bed in a second if it were up to him. It wouldn't even matter to him that you're married. Isn't that right, Jerry?"

Jerry's face grew even redder. "But thanks to me, Meggie's *not,* is she?" he retorted.

Reed's fists clenched, and Megan threw her arms around him, trapping his arms at his sides.

"Jerry, please go," she begged. "This is our business—mine and Reed's."

"Not anymore," Jerry spat out. "You made it my business when you used my safe-deposit box to store your wedding license."

Reed pushed Megan's hands away and turned toward her in furious shock.

"You made it my business when you agreed to my plan," Jerry continued.

"Plan?" Reed's voice was hoarse. "What plan, Megan?"

"*My* plan," Jerry announced. "Meggie was going to file your license, but she didn't trust you. So I advised her to keep it locked up, pretend she'd filed it, and then wait and see." His expression was smug. "She didn't have to wait long, did she? You walked out on her without even so much as a goodbye."

Reed's expression was terrible to see. "Lying to me was his idea, Megan? Not yours?"

"Yes." Her answer was a bare whisper. "Reed, I'm sorry."

"Sorry? You involved him in our marriage, you let him influence you, and you're sorry? Megan, couldn't you even keep this between the two of us? Do you trust me so little?"

Megan dropped her eyes in shame, unable to meet his gaze. "Please," she begged. "I did what I thought was right."

"You did what *Jerry* thought was right—right for him. Not for us."

Reed looked at her as though she was a stranger. "I'm going out," he said in a tight voice. "When I get back, I want him gone. See to it."

"Reed, wait. Don't go! Reed, come back!" She made to go after him, but Jerry got to her before she could reach the door.

"Let me go, Jerry!" Megan frantically tried to escape his embrace. "I have to go after him."

"He doesn't want you, Meggie! Don't you see that? But I do, damn it. I do!"

Megan tried to turn away from Jerry's kiss, but he wouldn't let her. His lips met hers with all the hunger Reed's did, but there was one big difference. Megan always responded to Reed. Jerry's kiss did nothing for her. After a moment, Jerry realized what Megan had always known.

"It's not there between us, is it?"

Megan wiped at her mouth with a trembling hand. "There was never an 'us.' All we had was our friendship. And if I've lost Reed because of you, we won't even have that."

"Meggie, you don't mean it!"

"I'm serious, Jerry. I was never more serious in my life. Now I want you to leave. Please don't come here again."

"Don't say that," he pleaded.

Megan backed away from him when he would have taken her in his arms once more. "Go home, Jerry."

Jerry's face turned an angry red. "I'll go—for now. But I'll be back. Because your sad excuse for a marriage isn't *my* fault. It's Reed's."

Megan watched Jerry leave. As the door closed behind him, she said sadly, "And mine, Jerry. And mine."

She was sitting quietly on the couch when Reed returned. He looked at her, but said nothing. Instead, he went to the bar and poured himself a drink.

"Where were you?" she asked.

"Out on the beach, taking a walk." His lips twisted in irony. "I seem to be doing a lot of walking lately."

"No, I mean over the weekend. Did you really go to New York?"

"Yes." He sat down on the bar stool, leaving the drink untouched. "I figured I might as well salvage something of the weekend. I took care of some things in my New York office, then flew home immediately after."

"Always business. Even in the midst of all this." Megan sighed.

"Not just business, Megan. I did some thinking, too." He stared out into the distance at the waves breaking beyond the huge bay window, his expression unreadable. "You're right about one thing. We don't have much of a marriage. Maybe we should call it quits."

Megan felt her heart contract and her veins turn to ice. "You can't mean that!"

"We make each other miserable, Megan. Tonight's just another example."

"That was my fault," Megan said. She hurried to Reed's side. "I should never have lied to you."

"It's not just the lie, Megan. It's not even the license being unfiled. It's much worse than that. I never set out to make you unhappy. Believe it or not, I thought we had a good marriage. We might not have been together much, but I always knew you were there for me." He gave her a bittersweet smile. "At least, I thought you were. I was happy, and I foolishly thought you were, too."

"Reed—"

"It appears I've been living under a delusion." He finally lifted his glass. "Here's to reality."

"We'll just try harder." Megan reached for him, but he deliberately avoided her touch.

"At what? A marriage that doesn't exist, either on paper or in actuality? No."

His answer was stark and unyielding, and Megan felt fear grip her heart.

"It's time to face facts. License or not, our marriage is over."

"It isn't! Reed, you have to believe me—this isn't what I wanted when I didn't file our license!"

"What *did* you want, Megan?"

She fought hard for control. "I wanted to wake you up. I wanted you to see how things really were."

"You did that, Megan. You did that."

A terrible silence descended. Reed stared at his drink while Megan damned herself for not filing the license the day Jerry mailed it to her. She'd only hurt herself, and worst of all, she'd hurt Reed. It was a long time before she could bring herself to speak again.

"What now, Reed? What do we do now?"

"What most unhappy couples do. You go your way and I'll go mine."

"You mean split up?" Megan said in an anguished voice.

Reed nodded once, as if not trusting himself to speak.

Megan picked up her purse. She withdrew her checkbook and savings-account passbook with trembling hands, then walked over to the bar and laid them down in front of Reed. Then she removed her house key from her key ring and placed that before him, too.

He looked up, confused. "What's this?"

"I'm the one who should leave. Everything here belongs to you." She hesitated. "I hope you'll let me keep my car. I know you paid for it, but I need some way to get to work." She bravely pushed the pile toward him.

Reed covered her hand with his. "No, Megan. What's mine has always been yours. Besides, this house has been your home more than it's ever been mine. I'll go."

Megan felt hope at his touch. "Reed, you don't have to. I don't *want* you to," she said desperately. "I love you."

He gently pulled his hand away from hers. "And I love you. But it seems, Megan, that isn't enough."

He rose to his feet, leaving his unfinished drink on the bar. "I'll be at the office if you need me for anything. I don't want you to worry about money. I'll take care of things, as always."

"Damn it, Reed, I never worried about money or *things.* All I ever wanted you to take care of was *me!*"

"Then give Jerry Davis a call. I'm sure he'll be willing to oblige."

His words wounded deeply, and Megan was filled with sorrow, knowing that was his intention.

"Goodbye, Megan. I hope you find what you're looking for."

Megan's cry, "But I already have!," went unheeded. She was alone.

Eight

Megan never knew how she survived that awful night when Reed packed his bags and left. She never knew how she made it through those terrible days afterward, realizing he wasn't coming back.

Thank goodness for her job and her classes. She threw herself into work with a vengeance, hoping to wear herself out so she wouldn't lie awake at night. She accomplished the former, but not the latter. Megan couldn't sleep in the big empty bed she'd shared with Reed. Memories of the past and futile wishes for the future tormented her.

Finally in desperation she started sleeping on the couch. At least there she could snatch a few hours of rest to get her through the day.

From Reed, she heard nothing. Money was automatically deposited in her bank account, and the household bills were paid through Reed's office. The few times Reed needed to communicate with her, it was done through Barbara. When Megan tried to reach Reed, Barbara insisted she leave a message.

"I'm sorry, Mrs. Kendall," Barbara apologized. "But I have my orders. He isn't to be disturbed."

"By anyone, or just by me?"

There was an embarrassed silence on the other end of the line, and Megan knew she had her answer. She defiantly drove to Reed's building in downtown Los Angeles. The security guards were apologetic, but refused her entrance.

"I'm sorry, Mrs. Kendall. We have our orders."

Megan had proudly held back the tears and left. What she'd always feared had finally happened. Reed had cut her out of his life completely.

She didn't try to contact him again.

"Megan, you have to accept the fact that Reed doesn't want you," Jerry told her one afternoon as they walked along the beach. Despite her wishes, he had started stopping by on a regular basis, and Megan was too lonely to send him away. "You don't eat, you don't sleep. You've got to get your mind off him."

She couldn't deny his words. There were dark circles under her eyes, and her appetite had all but disappeared.

"If you're not careful, you're going to make yourself sick."

"I'm not." She lifted her chin with pride. "I'm doing quite well, thank you. I have class and my job, and I keep busy."

"Too busy, if you ask me." Jerry reached for her arm and stopped her progress across the sand. "Doesn't your replacement at the hospital come back in a few weeks?"

Megan frowned at the thought. "Yes."

"What will you do then?"

"I don't know. There still aren't any openings in pediatrics. I checked."

"Perhaps that's a good thing. You need some time to get over this. You should take a nice long rest."

Megan pulled her arm away and stared out over the water. "I don't want to rest," she said with irritation. "I've had enough of that to last me a lifetime."

"Meggie, don't be angry. I shouldn't have said rest. I should have said honeymoon."

Megan stared at him in amazement. "With whom? Reed?"

"No, damn it! With me!"

"You?"

"Yes! I can give you everything you want from a man. Love, companionship, children. We can even work together. I have a good practice in pediatrics. The two of us could make it even better."

Megan was unable to take in his words. "You can't be serious."

"I'm more serious than I've ever been about anything in my life. Just think, Meggie, the two of us together again. Happy again, like before you met Reed."

"Jerry, haven't you listened to anything I've said these past few weeks? We had some good times. But I don't love you. Not like that."

"Meggie, we've loved each other since we were children. We've shared so much! First the hospital where we grew up, and now our profession. We have so much in common to build on. Let's not throw that away."

Megan shook her head. "I love Reed. I'll always love Reed," she said simply.

"After the way he treated you?" Jerry's voice rose in frustration. "After all the mistakes he's made?"

"I've made some, too," Megan replied slowly. "And the biggest one I made in our marriage was listening to you. The only thing Reed ever asked from me was loyalty. I let him down."

She watched the water foam white over her feet, then recede again. "I can never forgive myself for that."

"He doesn't love you like I do!"

Megan met her friend's tortured gaze and gave him a sad smile. "Even if that was true, it doesn't matter. I want Reed. I can't—I won't—settle for anyone else."

"Even if it means spending the rest of your life alone?" Jerry asked hoarsely.

Megan's eyes took in the waves as they broke onto the shoreline. "When I was in the hospital all those years, I thought being alone—being without anyone's physical presence—was the worst thing in the world. I was wrong. The worst thing is knowing the people you love don't care."

"Meggie—"

"As long as I knew Reed loved me, I was never really alone. Only I was too stupid to realize it." Megan's voice broke and she closed her eyes.

Jerry tried to put his arms around her for comfort, but Megan shook her head. Her grief was too personal to share with anyone—except the one man she'd driven away.

Jerry stood by awkwardly. Megan wished he would leave.

"What will you do, Meggie?"

She took a long shuddering breath. "I don't know. Pray for a miracle, I guess."

Jerry awkwardly patted her shoulder. "I'm sorry. I never meant to make you unhappy."

She managed to give him a tiny smile before she turned and headed for the house. "It's not your fault, Jerry. It never was."

Much to her relief, he didn't follow her. She watched as he drove away. Megan had the place to herself, along with the familiar pangs of loneliness. She stared at the phone, willing it to ring and be Reed. Suddenly she couldn't stand it any longer. She had to get away from the house before she went crazy.

She grabbed her car keys and purse and headed for the front door. Her life wasn't over, she told herself. And her marriage wasn't over yet, either. She still had almost two weeks before her anniversary—plenty of time in which to legally become Mrs. Reed Kendall.

Megan traveled the route that would take her to the bank. She'd leave the safe-deposit key with a clerk for Jerry to collect and file the marriage license today. If Reed really didn't want to be married to her, he'd have a court fight on his hands. She wasn't going to make things easy for him.

Megan smiled to herself as she retrieved the license. Reed had fallen in love with her once. If she asked for his forgiveness, he might fall in love with her again, given the chance. And in the meantime, Megan would show him that she could wait—alone—as long as necessary.

"My goodness, but isn't this a bit late to be presented for filing?" The elderly clerk at City Hall peered at the date on the license, then removed his bifocals. "What in the world took you so long?"

Megan decided nothing but the truth would suffice. "An old friend was best man at my wedding. He took it upon himself to hide this because he thought I'd picked the wrong man."

The clerk gave Megan a look of confusion. "Did you?"

"No," Megan said fiercely. "That's why I'm here. Would you please file this and give me a copy for my records?"

The clerk put his glasses back on, then nodded. "I expect your husband was pretty upset when he heard."

Megan felt the familiar pain stab at her heart but offered the clerk a brave smile. "I'm trying to set things straight," she managed.

The clerk returned her smile. "You wait here, ma'am. This may take a little longer than usual, but I'll have you proper and legal yet."

A half hour later Megan left City Hall with a validated marriage license in her purse. There was a sense of rightness about being Reed's wife, a sense of contentment. Her next stop was the hospital's personnel office.

"Megan, what are you doing here?" Lynn asked. "Isn't today your day off?"

"Yes, it is. I wanted to see when my last day of work is with Life Flight."

"I don't even need to check my files for that. You have just two more weeks left, Megan, if you want it."

"If I want it?"

Lynn nodded. "The woman you replaced is ready to come back from maternity leave sooner than she expected. But I told her you probably wanted to finish out the original assignment, as we haven't had any other openings come up for you."

"I need to talk to you about that," Megan said. "I want you to take me off the waiting list."

"Off the waiting list? Are you going back to school full-time? Or have you found other employment?" Lynn asked with dismay.

"Neither. I've finished my classes. I'm going back to Africa."

"To work for your husband's company again?"

"Actually, I hadn't considered that, though it's a definite possibility," Megan said thoughtfully. "Our anniversary is in two weeks, and I—we—wanted to spend it where we first met. If my replacement is eager to come back to work, I'm willing to step aside."

"Let me call her. I can let you know right now," Lynn said, picking up the phone.

A few minutes later it was official. Megan was free to leave.

"How long are you going to be gone?" Lynn asked. "I'm sure an opening will come up here sooner or later. We can always use good nurses like you."

"So can my husband's clinic," Megan said firmly. "Thanks, Lynn, but I think I'm going to get my old job back."

Lynn smiled at Megan's enthusiasm. "That shouldn't be too hard. You *are* the boss's wife."

Megan rose from her chair and nodded. Yes, she was the boss's wife. And she intended to take full advantage of that....

Back home, she dialed the long-distance operator and soon had her husband's African clinic on the line.

"We could certainly use you back here, Mrs. Kendall," the clinic director said. "We've had a terrible flu epidemic, and we're shorthanded. Both the miners and my staff have been hit hard."

"I'm on my way," Megan said. "Have personnel put me back on the clinic staff. I'll let you know my travel arrangements so someone can pick me up."

"Very good, Mrs. Kendall." To Megan's relief, he didn't question her authority at all. "Shall we expect Mr. Kendall, too?"

"No, he'll be tied up with business here in Los Angeles for quite some time," Megan replied, not actually knowing, but guessing it was the truth. "It'll be just me on the plane."

"We'll look forward to seeing you, then. Goodbye."

She hung up. It was all too easy, really. She'd just have to pack a few things, forward her mail, buy herself a plane ticket—and wait for Reed.

She knew he would come. He regularly kept tabs on the mine and his business. Megan was positive she'd seen him more at the clinic than she ever had here in town. She would win him back then. She knew it.

She reached for her bag and withdrew her marriage license. She debated sending it to Reed in the mail, then changed her mind. If Reed wasn't taking her phone calls, who knows what he might have instructed Barbara to do with any mail from her.

There weren't any pushy secretaries or apologetic security guards at the clinic. Reed couldn't avoid her there when he went to check on his men. The license would go with her, Megan decided. She would give it to Reed in person. She owed him that.

Besides, Megan had another reason for wanting to see Reed face-to-face.

She was pregnant.

Nine

The fans in the Kendall Diamond Mines clinic whirled at full speed, but they only moved the hot night air around. Nothing could dissipate the heat.

"How many more patients do we have waiting outside?" Megan asked, wiping a sweaty brow with the back of one hand. The flu epidemic was still in full force, and everyone had been working overtime.

"None for you," the head doctor said firmly. "You've been here since sunrise, and it's dark now. Go home, Mrs. Kendall. Get some rest."

"I don't mind staying," she argued.

"And I don't want your husband breathing down my neck if you get sick yourself. Please, for my peace of mind, go to your bungalow."

Megan frowned but did as she was told. Ordinarily she hated getting special treatment because she was the boss's wife. However, if truth be told, the thought of a meal and getting off her feet held a lot of appeal. The only negative aspect of her pregnancy had been a nagging fatigue. As she knew that was perfectly normal and rest was the only cure, she didn't argue further.

"I'll see you all tomorrow," she called out.

Already the staff was busy with the next patient. So much for being indispensable, Megan thought. Still, she was satisfied with her day's work. The gratitude of the patients was touching. It made her feel as though she'd accomplished something, even if her feet did ache and her once-pristine uniform was soiled.

She'd take a long cool shower before eating, she decided. Then she'd fix herself dinner. Despite missing Reed, she was hungry these days. She was careful to take good care of herself. She'd wanted children for so long she was determined to give Reed's child a good start in life.

That's odd, Megan thought. *I didn't leave any lights on in the bungalow.* She hurried to her door and stepped inside.

"Reed!" Megan cried out with joy. She'd hoped and prayed for him so long it was hard to believe he was actually here. And when his arms wrapped around her, she thought she was in paradise. It wasn't until she heard his angry voice that she came back to reality.

"Megan, where have you been? I've been worried sick."

"I..." She looked at her uniform, then back up at him. "I'm working at the clinic."

"All this time?"

"I know it's late, but—"

"I mean the past two weeks, Megan! Have you been here for the past two weeks?"

"Yes. Didn't you know?"

"Of course not! I thought you were in Los Angeles." Reed ran a hand through his hair with agitation. "I've been looking for you all this time. I still have people looking for you back home."

Megan's disappointment was acute. ''You didn't come out here because of me?''

''How the hell was I supposed to know you were in Africa? For all I know you could have been kidnapped. Even Jerry didn't know where you were.''

''You checked with Jerry?''

''Of course I did! I was concerned, Megan! You could have told me!''

''How?'' Megan returned his accusation with one of her own. ''You wouldn't take my calls, and your guards wouldn't let me in the building. What did you expect me to do, Reed? Hire a skywriter?''

Reed flushed at her sarcasm.

''I'm sorry, Megan. I was angry. I never thought you'd actually leave town.''

''No, you wouldn't. Even at our worst, you always expect me to be quietly waiting for you.'' Megan took the opportunity to pull away from his embrace. She sank onto the room's tiny couch with none of her customary grace. ''My job with Life Flight was only temporary, and there weren't any openings at the hospital. I needed something new, so I put myself back on the payroll out here.''

''You put yourself back on the payroll?'' he echoed.

''It wasn't hard. I am the boss's wife, after all, and no one thought to question me. Or you, it appears. I'm sorry you were worried, Reed. You didn't have to search any farther for me than your latest personnel records. You used to take it upon yourself to personally meet each new employee, remember?''

There was silence, and Megan knew Reed was recalling the first time they'd met.

"Besides needing a job," she went on, "I needed to get away from Jerry. Coming here took care of that, too."

Reed continued to stand. Megan studied him carefully, suddenly aware of the dark shadows under his eyes, the tautness of the skin over his cheekbones and the stubble of beard on his chin.

"Jerry was frantic when I told him you were missing," he said. "Both of us thought the worst. Why didn't you at least let *him* know you were coming here?"

Megan took off her shoes and tucked her bare feet under her. "I didn't want him following me. Jerry's wreaked enough havoc with my life. Two years ago I came to Africa to get away from him. I should have stayed away," she said emphatically.

"Because he loves you? Or because—" Reed's voice grew hoarse "—you love him?"

"No, because I *don't* love him, and I can't convince him of that. No matter what happens between us, Jerry's going to have to let me go. I only have room for one man in my heart." She looked up at Reed, her eyes filled with love. "Jerry Davis isn't that man. He wants more from me than I'm willing to give. He always has. And when I give him a little, it costs me dear." Megan swallowed hard, unable to go on.

Reed came and sat down next to her. "Like what happened to us?" he quietly asked.

She nodded, her eyes closed with pain.

Reed took her hands in his. "I once asked you for your loyalty, Megan. Your actions may not have shown it lately, but deep down I know you've always been true."

She opened her eyes with surprise—and with the first faint glimmering of hope.

"I came back to the house—back to you—only to find you gone. Megan, I went crazy. I went tearing over to the hospital and then the university. No one knew where you were," he said in a tortured voice. "Not even Jerry."

"But Reed, I told Lynn—"

"Lynn who?"

"Lynn Peerson. She works in personnel at the hospital. She knew I was coming back here. I didn't keep it a secret."

"Damn! She wasn't in the office when I was. I talked to a man who said you'd left, and your name had been taken off the waiting list for any other jobs. He couldn't give me any more information. I didn't know what to think, what to do."

Megan tentatively laid a hand on his shoulder, hoping she wouldn't be rebuffed. "I'm sorry you were worried, Reed. You know I'm a sensible woman—well, most of the time," she corrected.

"All of the time," Reed said. He gathered her close, much to her delight. "Megan, I've been so foolish. You were right."

"About what?"

"About me giving you everything except myself." His eyes were dark, haunted. "My father never shared anything without a price tag. I thought being a good husband meant giving you whatever you wanted, no strings attached."

"But, Reed, all I ever wanted was you! I didn't want your money and what it could buy."

"I've had a lot of time to think lately, and I finally figured that out. But when I went to you, you'd gone. Oh, Megan, I thought it was too late for us."

She felt a shudder run through his body and held him close. "So you hired people to find me?"

"Yes. And I came here."

She was puzzled. "On business?"

"*Personal* business. Tomorrow is our anniversary. You said you wanted to spend it in Africa. I was desperately hoping you'd show up."

Joy flooded her heart. "And I was hoping *you'd* show up. I wanted that more than anything in the world."

She kissed him with all the love and devotion in her soul. And when Reed kissed her back, again and again, it wasn't his usual kiss of all-consuming passion. It held a new, deeper intimacy that welcomed her back and promised a future for both of them.

"Reed, I've made so many mistakes. Can you ever forgive me?"

"Forgive you? I've been the guilty party here."

Megan shook her head. "Not the only one. I've been a clinging wife, just like you said. I realized it after you left. When I was a child in the hospital, I was denied my family's presence—their physical presence. I felt abandoned and unloved."

"And when I was gone so much you felt those same old fears?" Reed said with compassion.

"Yes. I never realized until lately that when someone loves you, you're never alone. I've been so stupid." She laid her head on his shoulder, smiling when he kissed her hair.

"I think we've both been a little short on sense, Meggie."

Megan sat bolt upright. "Reed! You called me Meggie!"

"Yes. Do you mind?"

Megan thought about that. The way Reed said her name had always made her feel special. "My family calls me Meggie, and so do my friends. You're the only one who calls me Megan." She gave him a loving look. "I think I'd like to keep it that way."

"As long as you decide to keep *me,*" Reed said fiercely.

"Just you try to have it any other way." Megan nestled against him.

They sat entwined together in silence, aware of each other in the most acute sense, yet comfortable enough to stay still.

A whistle blew outside, signaling the end of the shift.

"It's eleven o'clock," Reed said with obvious surprise.

Megan nodded. "Do you realize that in another hour it's our anniversary? Oh, yes," she said when Reed would have spoken. "It's official. I filed our license with City Hall before I came here, and I have the copy to prove it. To quote the old clerk who waited on me, we're 'proper and legal' now."

The look on Reed's face, then his tight embrace, took Megan's breath away.

"Reed, let go! I can't breathe."

He relaxed his hold but didn't release her. "I was planning on jumping through hoops to get you to marry me again, my love. I want you for my wife. I want you as the mother of my children. I never dreamed . . ."

Reed's kiss this time left Megan trembling with desire.

"Reed," she said in a shaky voice, "let's go to bed. Now."

He stroked her face gently. "Let's wait until it's officially our anniversary. You need a shower and, I suspect, a good meal. Why don't you clean up while I fix us something to eat?"

Megan sighed, then asked hesitantly, "Reed? Did you mean what you said?"

"About what, my love?"

"About children. Do you really want them? Will you make time for them?"

"Them, *and* you," he solemnly assured her. "I swear it, Megan."

She smiled and rose to her feet. "There's a casserole in the refrigerator. Just heat it up. I'll be back before dinner's ready," she promised, giving him a kiss on the forehead.

"Take your time." Reed grinned. "We have all night."

Megan nodded, her heart finally at rest. As she stepped into the shower, she ran her hand over the slight swell of her stomach. She wondered if Reed would be able to guess she was pregnant. Probably not, she thought. She wasn't very far along. She'd have to tell him later.

But not on their anniversary, she decided. Not tonight. Tonight was just for her and Reed. She shivered with joyous anticipation. If only she didn't have to bother with eating. She hoped Reed wasn't making a big fuss in the kitchen.

He wasn't. The casserole was heating quickly on top of the stove. He kept a watchful eye on it while waiting for his overseas call to go through. Finally it did.

"Hello?"

"It's Kendall," Reed said bluntly. "She's here."

Jerry Davis exhaled on a slow breath of air. "Thank God. Is she okay?"

"Yes. Megan came to Africa to celebrate our anniversary, just like we planned. She filed our marriage certificate, Davis."

There was a moment's silence on the other end. Then, "She's really all right?"

"Yes. We both are."

"I appreciate your calling me," Jerry said. "I know you didn't have to."

"You're Megan's friend. And except for that damn license, Davis, you've played fair. I'll grant you that."

"I won't next time," Jerry said fervently. "If you make Meggie unhappy again, I'll be back."

"There won't be a next time." The conviction in Reed's voice rang true. "Ever."

When Jerry spoke again, even Reed winced at the pain in the other man's voice. "Send Meggie my best."

"I will." A pause. Then, "Davis?"

"Yeah?"

Reed hesitated just a moment. "Thanks." With that, he hung up. For a long time he stood motionless, his fingers still around the receiver. It wasn't until the casserole started to bubble and steam that he regained his composure.

When Megan emerged from her shower, Reed was stirring their dinner with easy strokes.

Megan sniffed appreciatively over his shoulder. "Almost ready?" she asked.

Reed ignored the question. "I love you, Megan." He reached for her and tucked her under his chin. He held her tight with one arm and continued to stir with the other. "I'm the luckiest man alive."

Megan's pulse quickened at the look in his eyes.

"Forget the dinner." She took the spoon from his hand and tossed it into the sink. Her eyes were bright and shining as she turned to face her husband. "Everything's really going to be all right, isn't it."

It was a statement, not a question. Reed smiled, guided her lips to his and answered her, anyway.

"It is, my love." He kissed her once, kissed her twice, then kissed her again. "Happy anniversary, Megan."

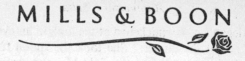

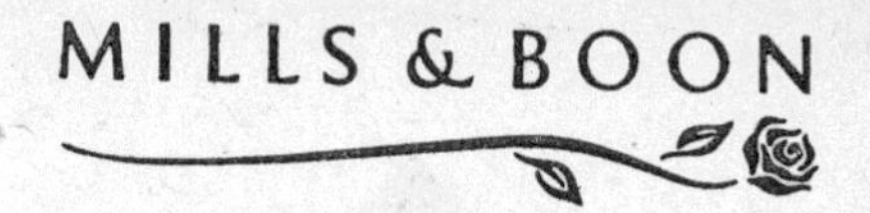

MEDICAL ROMANCE

LOVE ON CALL

April's Titles:

BUSH DOCTOR'S BRIDE
Marion Lennox

FORGOTTEN PAIN
Josie Metcalfe

COUNTRY DOCTORS
Gill Sanderson

COURTING DR GROVES
Meredith Webber

Available from W.H. Smith, John Menzies, Volume One, Forbuoys, Martins, Woolworths, Tesco, Asda, Safeway and other paperback stockists.

Readers in South Africa - write to:
IBS, Private Bag X3010, Randburg 2125.

April's irresistible novels from

Temptation

STRANGER IN MY ARMS by Madeline Harper

Secret Fantasies

Do you have a secret fantasy? Kasey Halliday does. She's always wanted to be swept off her feet by a dark, handsome stranger. Will Eastman, Kasey's enigmatic new neighbour, fits the bill perfectly. But when mysterious accidents start to occur, Kasey realizes more than just her heart is in danger…

THE TEXAN by Janice Kaiser

The 500th Temptation

Brady Coleman vowed to bring his sister's killer to justice. But the rough-and-tumble Texan desperately needed the help of beautiful Jane Stewart. And when her vulnerable heart longed for Brady, how could she refuse?

JILT TRIP by Heather MacAllister

Grooms on the Run

Carter Belden was *not* having a good day. He was supposed to be getting married, but his best man was late, his pager wouldn't stop bleeping and then he was kidnapped before the ceremony—by his ex-wife!

THREE GROOMS AND A WEDDING by JoAnn Ross

Bachelor Arms

Ever since Blythe Fielding had hired private investigator Gage Remington to solve a decades-old mystery, she had had second thoughts about walking down the aisle with her fiancé. Gage was sexy, dangerous and compelling. How could Blythe resist the unknown passion his eyes promised her?

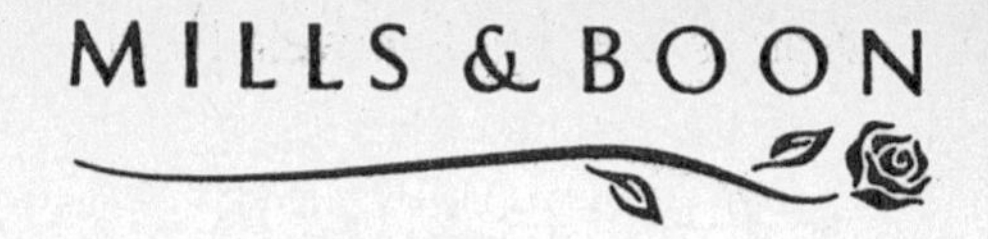

May's Romances

Each month you can choose from a wide variety of romance with Mills & Boon. Below are the new titles for May '96.

LAST STOP MARRIAGE	Emma Darcy
RELATIVE SINS	Anne Mather
HUSBAND MATERIAL	Emma Goldrick
A FAULKNER POSSESSION	Margaret Way
UNTAMED LOVER	Sharon Kendrick
A SIMPLE TEXAS WEDDING	Ruth Jean Dale
THE COLORADO COUNTESS	Stephanie Howard
A NIGHT TO REMEMBER	Anne Weale
TO TAME A PROUD HEART	Cathy Williams
SEDUCED BY THE ENEMY	Kathryn Ross
PERFECT CHANCE	Amanda Carpenter
CONFLICT OF HEARTS	Liz Fielding
A PAST TO DENY	Kate Proctor
NO OBJECTIONS	Kate Denton
HEADING FOR TROUBLE!	Linda Miles
WHITE MIDNIGHT	Kathleen O'Brien

Available from WH Smith, John Menzies, Volume One, Forbuoys, Martins, Woolworths, Tesco, Asda, Safeway and other paperback stockists.

May's irresistible novels from

Temptation

THE LAST HERO by Alyssa Dean

Rebels & Rogues

For Commander Wade Brillings, duty came first. So when he suspected that beautiful Cassandra Lloyd was part of a smuggling ring, he had to stick close to her. *Really close.* Experience told Wade to keep his hands off her, but his heart said something else...

THE TEMPTING by Lisa Harris

Secret Fantasies

Do you have a secret fantasy? Carol Glendower does. She wants her husband back—alive and well. A mysterious turn of events means Carol now has a chance to find Evan again. Are her dreams taunting her? Or is there a chance that this could be for real?

NOT THIS GUY! by Glenda Sanders

Grooms on the Run

Single-mum Angelina Winters couldn't believe her luck when she met charming Mike Calder. For a while, she thought she and Mike had a good thing going, but then she saw his list of what he wanted in a woman and realized she scored a perfect zero!

LOVERS AND STRANGERS by Candace Schuler

Bachelor Arms

Cynical reporter Jack Shannon hoped that by moving back to Bachelor Arms, he could lay old ghosts to rest. Sexy Faith McCray had a few ghosts of her own. She wanted to give Jack all the love he'd ever need—but was he brave enough to accept it?

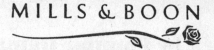

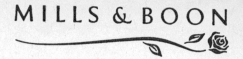

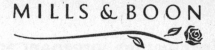

June's irresistible novels from

Temptation

THE TRAILBLAZER by Vicki Lewis Thompson

Urban Cowboys

Businessman Ry McGuinnes was determined to find adventure in the West, but he didn't expect his greatest challenge to be Freddy Singleton, the sexy fore*woman* of the ranch he owned. Independent and resourceful, her biggest concern was persuading Ry to pack his bags and hightail it back to the city!

MAKE-BELIEVE HONEYMOON by Kristine Rolofson

Jilted Kate Stewart decided there was no reason why she shouldn't go on the trip to London that was supposed to have been her honeymoon. Kate soon realized that she wasn't all *that* heartbroken, especially when she met sexy, dark and brooding William Landry. But how would Kate react when she discovered his real reasons for seducing her?

KISS OF THE BEAST by Mallory Rush

Secret Fantasies

Eva Campbell has a secret fantasy. Smart but vulnerable, she wants the perfect man—a man *programmed* to fulfil her every desire. She could never have bargained for a man like Urich. Sexy, mysterious and compelling, he is everything she could have asked for. Only she was supposed to be in control, and that's the last thing she feels with Urich…

SEDUCED AND BETRAYED by Candace Schuler

Bachelor Arms

Hollywood bad boy Zeke Blackstone is back at the Bachelor Arms to help arrange his daughter's wedding. And that means he must come face-to-face with his ex-wife, gorgeous Ariel Cameron. Ariel's belief that Zeke betrayed her tore apart their marriage. Could this wedding reunite them?